Wi

ENLIGHTENMENT

ENLIGHTENMENT

MAUREEN FREELY

THE OVERLOOK PRESS
WOODSTOCK & NEW YORK

This edition first published in the United States in 2008 by
The Overlook Press, Peter Mayer Publishers, Inc.
Woodstock & New York

WOODSTOCK:
One Overlook Drive
Woodstock, NY 12498
www.overlookpress.com
[for individual orders, bulk and special sales, contact our Woodstock office]

NEW YORK:
141 Wooster Street
New York, NY 10012

First published in Great Britain in 2007 by Marion Boyars Publishers Ltd.

"A Journey" from the collection *Beyond The Wall: Selected Poems* by Nâzım Hikmet,
translated by Ruth Christie, Richard McKane and Talat Sait Halman
(Anvil Press with Yapi Kredi Yayinlari 2002) © Ruth Christie.

Cataloging-in-Publication Data is available from the Library of Congress

Book design and type formatting by Bernard Schleifer
Manufactured in the United States of America
ISBN 978-1-59020-074-2
10 9 8 7 6 5 4 3 2 1

To Frank

"The first task of any intelligence organization is to establish where the danger is." Thomas Powers in the *New York Review of Books*, September 26, 2002

"The second task of any intelligence organization, after identifying where the danger lies, is to protect its secrets." Thomas Powers in the *New York Review of Books*, October 10, 2002

I
In Answer
to Your
Question

I AM WRITING THIS for you, Mary Ann. The others are faceless, so it helps, when I look into this screen, to imagine you as my first reader. Let me begin, then, by addressing the points you raised in your last message. You asked if I was certain of this woman's innocence. My answer is an unqualified yes. She is a committed pacifist and has been all her life. If that bulky jacket did indeed conceal explosives, you can be sure it was someone else who put them there. Either that or the picture you sent me has been digitally enhanced.

You also asked if I could give you some idea of my whereabouts. I regret to say that (for now, at least) I am unable to do so. Nor would it be wise, at this point, to tell you why. But I am happy to tell you about my passports. As my records will show (and please do feel free to check these for yourself) I am a US citizen by birth, though I do also have an Irish passport. I have never been a citizen of Turkey, nor do I plan to become one. But in some sense it will always be my home.

In answer to your final question — and I will go into some detail here, as I cannot expect you or your colleagues to accept me at face value unless I explain who I am, how I came to be that person, and the circuitous route by which I wandered into this murky intrigue — I was eight years old when my family moved to Istanbul. This was in 1960, which means (among other things) that we made the trip across the

Atlantic in a prop plane. Crossing Europe, we were low enough to see the cars on the roads. But – and I expect the same was true for Jeannie Wakefield ten years later – I was not at all frightened. My thoughts were on our golden destination, which I knew, and assumed to know intimately, from an old issue of the National Geographic. All summer long, I'd been gazing into its lush and perfectly composed illustrations, imagining myself inside them.

There are no words to describe my first impression of the real thing. It hit me like a hand, ripping the pictures out of my head and tearing them to shreds. I can recall a thousand swirling details of that first drive in from the airport, but I have no sense of the whole. There was the yellow haze rising from the Sea of Marmara but not the sea itself; the flock of tankers and fishing boats but not the horizon on which they sat; the red and crumbling fragments of the old city walls but no history to explain them. I could barely breathe from the stench of burning flesh I could not yet trace to the tanning factories, the injured violins that I could not yet accept as music, the belching chaos of jeeps, trucks, horses, carts and Chevrolets. Tiny gypsies weaved amongst us with flowers no one wanted, and crooked old men with sofas strapped to their backs. Pressed against the sky was a forest of minarets and domes. The Golden Horn, which wasn't golden. The Bosphorus, so blue it stung my eyes.

The city thinned as we crawled along the European shore, winding our way from bay to promontory, and promontory to bay, through narrow streets that opened without warning into coastal roads, coming so close to Asia at some points that we could see the windows of the houses and at other times veering so far back into Europe that we could see no windows whatsoever, but I had no idea where we were by then, no idea at all. Until that day, I had never seen a landscape that wasn't planned or protected, or a street that wasn't zoned.

After an hour that seemed like a day, our bus turned up a steep and narrow cobblestone lane. We crawled up past a cemetery in which the tombstones wore turbans. Skirting a dark and crenellated tower, we climbed higher still, to pass through a stone gate covered with ivy. Beyond was a cool green hush and a leafy campus that consoled me because it looked so much like the one we'd left behind in Boston. There was a path. I followed it around a corner. I stepped out onto a terrace, and there it was: my golden destination. My picture from the

National Geographic. The castle on its wooded hillside; the Bosphorus with its endless parade of tankers, ferries and fishing boats. Lining its Asian shore, the villas and palaces that seemed close enough to touch, and behind them, the brown rolling hills that must, I thought, stretch as far as China.

The terrace on which I was standing belonged to Robert College, where my father was to teach physics. Founded by American Protestants in the 19th century to educate the city's Westernizing elites, it would later be nationalized and renamed. When we arrived in 1960, it was still a private university, run by a board based in New York. Most of its faculty came from the US, and most, like my father, came on three-year contracts.

But by 1963, my parents had fallen in love with the city and couldn't bear the thought of leaving. Imagine looking out of the window in the morning, they said, and not seeing the Bosphorus. So my father signed another contract, and then another. They managed to hang on until 1970, the year I turned eighteen.

Robert College was no longer a peaceful or secluded place by then – the political turmoil sweeping across Turkey had swept us up, too. The only sensible thing was to move back to Boston. This was where they were, Mary Ann, when your sister and I were classmates. She may remember the beautiful home they made for themselves there. But they never stopped pining for the Bosphorus (and all that it implied). So in the mid-80s, when Turkey seemed to be returning to its former peaceful self, they moved back to Istanbul. They've been here ever since. Their house is only a few hundred yards from the one where I grew up.

Had things worked out differently, I might have settled here, too. And this is my connection to the story you've asked me to tell you. I am sure I never spoke of it with your sister, because at the time we knew each other, I spoke of it to no one. There was a boy, you see. And it was serious, very serious.

By the time I left Istanbul, in June 1970, we were engaged. But we kept it secret. Because he suspected his parents were reading his mail, we did not even mention it in our letters. As soon as I got to Boston, I found myself a waitressing job, working long hours all summer and neglecting my studies that autumn until I'd saved enough money to buy us two weeks together in a country where no one knew us. In mid-

December, I went to Paris to meet him. But he never turned up. For three days, I sat in our room at the Hotel des Grandes Écoles, waiting for the message that never came.

His letter was waiting for me when I got back to Boston. He'd met someone else – someone, he said, who was quite like me "except that she's more innocent." I wrote him back. A three-word postcard: "ROT IN HELL." Early the next summer, I opened an envelope with no return address to find a garish clipping from a Turkish newspaper to see that my wish had been granted.

The only way I could fend off the wordless horror that swept over me at that moment – and continued to sweep over me, for years to come, every time I put my head on a pillow – was to sever all connections with the place from which it came. But I was, I now see, only buying myself time. The twists and turns of life have brought me back, and now here I am, strangled by my own principles, forced, through wicked circumstance, to defend my usurper.

I met her for the first time late last summer. Though it would be more accurate to say that it was arranged that we should meet. I was back in Istanbul for one of my flying visits, to keep my mother company while my father was in hospital having a hip replaced. So let me set the scene for you: it was early evening, and we were on the balcony, having drinks. My mother was bringing me up to date on the latest gossip about people I knew only by name, and as she spoke, I gazed out at the branches I felt I knew leaf by leaf, though the trees themselves were twice as tall as they'd been when I was a child. There was something about the light – or something behind it. The sun had already set behind the hills on our side of the Bosphorus, but filtering through the blue-green foliage in my mother's garden I could almost see the reflected gold from the hills of Asia.

No hint of the sea between us – just the low hum of a passing tanker, the putter of a fishing boat, a car backfiring on the road leading down to the shore. Below us, in the Burç Club, a man was testing a microphone. Filing down the White Walk were the first guests for what my mother told me was the third alumni wedding to be held at the club since Wednesday. As a woman in a filmy dress picked her way past a family of lazily growling dogs, she faltered on her stilettos but was righted by the man next to her. He glanced sternly into our garden, whereupon, following his gaze, I, too, saw the most curious scene: a thin and anxious woman in a bellydancing outfit, posing on what I assumed to be a log. Crouched next to the wall was a photographer casting furtive looks in our direction.

"Do you know this man?" I asked my mother. "Does he have permission to be here?"

She shrugged her shoulders. "It's not for me to say."

I offered to call someone in Buildings and Grounds. She shook her head. "Why bother? Anyway, the joke's on them." She launched into a story that seemed at first to have nothing to do with the photographer and his model: one morning last summer, when my mother had been sitting in this same chair, drinking her coffee and minding her own business, a posse of workmen had "just barged" into the garden with no warning and started digging holes. "It turned out they were from the city sewers project. They brought in one more pipe than they had room for, so that's what the bellydancer down there is sitting on. Not very photogenic if you ask me!"

She swang around in her chair, bronzed, leggy and devil-may-care. Pointing at the cheese sticks on the copper tray between us, she said, "Eat!" As I topped up her martini, she told me about a Dodge Ruthwen, who had taught engineering here between 1960 and 1963, but who also played stride piano. "And oh – his voice!" His son ("He was a year behind you at the community school, darling, but now he's at the Smithsonian") had stopped by last week to say hello. "He's staying with the Winchalls – you do remember them, don't you? She was the head of USIS and he was a historian. They were here in the late 60s, and again in the late 80s. Now they've bought a house out on the Princes Islands . . ." Name after name I didn't remember, wave after wave of fun-lovers, swishing in for their three year contracts, and leaving to be replaced by others just like them. Did they ever pause to ask themselves why there were here?

Airily, I repeated something I'd heard the poet Derek Walcott say at a reading a few years back: though the United States was an empire, it was invisible to most of its citizens.

"So?" my mother said.

"So we're all part of an empire we don't even know exists."

My mother flared her nostrils. "The problem with you, Miss M – "

"Can you please stop calling me that?"

"The problem with you, Miss M, is that you're so busy designing umbrellas, you lose sight of the people underneath."

She lifted up her glass, to stare at the ice cubes. "Which reminds me. That old flame of yours."

"Which one?" I said.

"That film-maker. The one who let you down so badly, and then got into all that trouble. His name escapes me. His film name, I mean."

"It's Yankı," I said.

"Yankee?"

"There's no 'ee' at the end, just 'uh.' Yankı. With an undotted 'i'."

"Yes, dear. But why?"

"It means 'echo' in Turkish. You did know that, didn't you?" My mother nodded, somewhat uneasily, I thought. "And he's Turkish," I continued, trying to keep my voice light, "but not just Turkish. He's an echo of something else. He was born in the US, remember?"

"It still sounds too much like Yankee."

"That's the point."

"Why?"

"It's a play on words."

"Is it? Really? It sounds rather forced to me. But never mind. It's the films that count. Though I have to say. They're rather obtuse. The one I saw, anyway. *My Cold War*. It won that big prize."

"So I heard," I said.

"Did you see it?"

I shook my head.

"Someone told me it was about that terrible thing he was involved in, you know, in 1971. So of course, I was curious. But as you probably know . . ."

I nodded.

". . . it turned out to be about his childhood. He had so much to say about his childhood that he ran out of film by 1970. All we're left with is a whole screen of dangling questions, which he promises to answer in a future Part Two. Fat chance of that happening now, though."

"Why?"

"He's been arrested."

"Where?"

"In America."

"What for?"

Tapping her cigarette against the ashtray, she said, "The jury's out on that, I'm afraid. All I know is that he was flying into JFK – this was some time last week. He was on some sort of tour. He's big with the students there, I hear. Someone we know at NYU went out to meet him. Well, he waited and waited, but there was no sign of anyone remotely resembling an obtuse documentary-maker. So finally he went over to this officious-looking Brownshirt – I just can't believe they have the nerve to dress these people in brown, can you? Do they have any idea of the historical ironies? Apparently not. Because when our friend went over to this hulking Homeland Security *Übermensch*, and mentioned who he was waiting for, all hell broke loose, and he was arrested, too."

"For what?" I asked.

"If you can believe it – for terrorism. They didn't hold him for long, but it looks as if that old flame of yours – they nabbed him at passport control – did I mention that? Well, anyway, it looks as if he might be in for the long haul. The rumor is that they've sent him to Guadalajara."

"*Guadalajara?*"

"I meant Guantanamo, as you well know. But honestly. If he's a terrorist, then we're all terrorists. Which is no joking matter, because that is what it seems to be coming to." She lit up a new cigarette. "But here's the worst part. When your old flame was arrested . . ."

"Why do you have to keep calling him that?"

"When this old flame of yours was arrested, he was with his five-year-old son. Really, his wife should have been with them, too, but there was some sort of complication with her passport. She's a US citizen, too, you know, but have you heard what they're doing now? Anyone who applies for a new passport from abroad has to wait two weeks, because the consulate has to send the forms back to Washington to be processed. *And* we have to pay through the nose for the privilege. And believe you me – the diplomatic pouch does not come cheap. Anyway – you must remember this wife of his. Jeannie Wakefield?"

I shook my head. My mother took a drag from her cigarette.

"That's funny," she said. "Because she wants to see you."

2

E MET ON the terrace of the Hotel Bebek, early the next evening. Curiosity having proven more powerful than dread. A year or two earlier, I had seen a picture of her in the paper – the Turner Prize in London, or the Something Else in New York or was it Paris (and what a rude shock it had been to scan the caption and see her name – Jeannie Wakefield, of all the people for him to marry, after all he had done, it made no sense!) so I recognized her right away. But it was immediately clear that Jeannie Wakefield knew nothing about me, except that I was my parents' daughter and a journalist. So I felt I had to say something.

"You were?" she said. I could see, from her puzzled frown, that this was news to her. "I mean," she continued. "I hope you don't mind my asking, because it's none of my business. But – what sort of friend?" Before I could answer, the waiter came with our drinks, or a ship went by, or perhaps it was yet another acquaintance waving from the other end of the crowded terrace. Whatever the interruption, it was enough to stop the thought.

How she looked that day: not as beautiful as I'd once imagined, and with her jeans and her T-shirt and her flyaway hair, not the svelte blonde of her photographs. But younger than her age, with solemn blue eyes, an intense gaze and a lop-sided smile that made me regret, if only briefly, any ill will I'd felt towards her. She leaned forward when she spoke, as if we were already best friends. And when I spoke – you'd think I was an oracle. She'd tilt her head and look straight into my eyes, nodding gravely, weighing my every word.

Until I asked after her son, rather too abruptly. Her eyes fell to her hands, as if in shame. As she studied her nails, and the boats in the bay, and the sprig of mint in her gin and tonic, and the napkin she had wound around her finger, I thought how odd it felt, how disturbing and how utterly unsatisfying, to see her suffer.

"I'm sorry," I found the grace to say.

She waved my words away. "No, no, please, there's no need. In fact, this was what I wanted to talk to you about."

Her little boy's name was Emre, and she did not know where he was. When they'd arrested his father at JFK, they'd taken Emre into care. Now he was living with some sort of foster family ("so he's safe – I don't know where he is, but thank God, he's safe. He's a healthy boy, you know. As old as I was when I had him. Which is not to say I didn't think it was a miracle. It was nerve-wracking, I can tell you. I knew he was my last chance."). There was some hope they might release the boy to a relative. But they were insisting on a US resident, and the only relative who met that requirement was her eighty-year-old aunt. Jeannie was sure she'd find a way around this when she got to the US. It wasn't as if she didn't know the ropes. She was a lawyer – a human rights lawyer, no less. But she could do nothing without her US passport, which she had sent in for renewal two months earlier, on the assurance it would take no more than two weeks to be processed. Of course, she'd made enquiries, so now she knew why it was that her application for renewal had gone awry. She was on some kind of list – "the same one, I presume, that my husband's on. So if I go back, with a valid passport or without it, I've been led to understand that they'll arrest me, too."

Here the waiter interrupted us to ask if there was anything we needed. She looked up at him as if he were offering her a diamond ring on a cushion. How this man must look forward to her visits here (I could not help but think). How obsequious she must look to the fine ladies watching so unsmilingly from the next table. After she had thanked the waiter seven or eight times for the drinks he had yet to bring us, she turned to me with her lopsided smile and said, "It's so very kind of you to see me when your parents must want to spend every second with you, but I can"t tell you how grateful I am. You see, I really do need your help."

What she wanted, it now emerged (was I surprised? I can't have been, this happened all the time) was for me to publicize her plight. "Children's rights – that's one of your areas, isn't it? That's why I thought of you. We need someone who understands the issues." If I could alert the world to the case, highlighting in particular the outrage they'd perpetrated on a five-year-old boy, and by implication, his parents, she was sure there would be an outcry, and this could only help to expedite her son's return.

"As for the rest of it – the charges against my husband are, of course ridiculous. But if you agree to take this on, we'd want you to feel free to conduct your own investigations, and what's more we'd want to help you. We can open up our office. You can read any document, go through our files, see any film – finished or otherwise. Go through our address books. Speak to our friends. Our enemies, even. We have nothing to hide," she said, though I sensed a note of uncertainty in her indignance.

"Of course," she continued, "we've done some filming near the border with Iraq, and in cities like Diyarbakır. So it's perfectly possible that some of our subjects had political affiliations we didn't know about. But if you've seen any of our films, you'll know they don't engage with politics directly. They're about people, and the worlds they make. What we try to capture is the interface – what ideas do to people and people to ideas."

She went on to elaborate – though I have, to my regret, no recollection of what she said. I was too annoyed by her pronouns. "We" she kept saying. Did she have no thoughts of her own? His films were "our" films, and he didn't have a name. If she referred to Sinan as a separate entity, it was as "my husband." But even at the time, I didn't think she was doing this on purpose. She didn't have a clue who I was. She genuinely liked me, and she genuinely believed I liked her back. If there is such a thing as a tragic flaw, Jeannie Wakefield's would be her reluctance to believe that anyone she liked or trusted might be less than entirely straight with her.

She told me it didn't matter where I placed this article she hoped I'd write. It could be in the U.S. or it could be in England. "That's where you're based right now, isn't it?" She looked at me hopefully, and my annoyance grew. There is no pleasant way of telling someone why their story might not be of interest to the general public, but in this case – even if she didn't know who I was – she must, I thought, have some inkling as to what the problem was.

Or did she not know what her husband got up to all those years ago, in the spring of 1971?

"Look," I said, still struggling for a polite way out. "I know it sounds terrible, but what you're asking me to do is, essentially, a human interest story. You want me to write it in such a way that people feel angry on your behalf and want to campaign for you. For that to happen, they have to believe that you and everyone else involved in this case have led blameless lives since they left their cradles. Which means I have to simplify and sentimentalize, pull every heartstring I can find, and since 9/11 and all that, they're in very short supply. Especially when the story's set in a predominantly Muslim country." I paused, to choose my words. "Especially if those involved have pasts that can be used against them."

"But . . ."

"To be absolutely brutal – you can't have a record."

"But we don't!" she said.

I think I just stared at her. What sort of a marriage was it, if this was what Sinan had led her to believe? What sort of lawyer could she be, if she was blind even to the legal facts? A vengeful thought flashed through my mind. If I set her straight, it would serve him right. But there was something in her eyes – the trust, the blind, stubborn trust – that made me want to be a better person.

So I backpeddled. 'Look,' I said. 'There might be some way of placing a story in England. But in the U.S., which is where you really need the media attention, it won"t be so easy. Turkey is just too far away from them, and too close to Afghanistan and Iraq. There's zero interest unless it answers one of two questions. 'Is the shopping good?' 'Does Turkey harbor terrorists?'"

"There you are then! That's your peg!"

She did not seem to see me flinch. Or she read nothing into it. Gazing out at the bay, she said, "I do understand what you're saying, you know. They think we're terrorists, and as long as they do, they'll also think we're getting what we deserve. So yes, it's a challenge. But tell me

– isn't it the sort of challenge that makes your job worthwhile? Cutting through the prejudice . . . changing readers' minds . . . forcing them to look at their blind spots . . . making the invisible visible . . ." That last remark came back to haunt me, after Jeannie Wakefield disappeared.

Right then, all I wanted was some air. So I glanced at my watch, and exclaimed when I saw the time. So desperate was I to rush off that I promised to make some phone calls, just in case – try and drum up some interest, or at least flag the story, with a view to trying again later. I offered to drop by her house in the morning, to let her know how I had got on. "Just tell me where you live," I said.

"For the moment," she said, "I'm still at the Pasha's Library."

In the end we walked up the hill together. I have no recollection of what we said along the way, or why I agreed to go to back with her to the Pasha's Library right then, or how I managed to breathe after I did. The Pasha's Library! Of all the places in the city I did not want to revisit, this was the one I was most desperate to avoid. I think I truly hated Sinan at that moment – on her behalf as well as mine. That he would marry this woman and not just not tell her the truth about what he'd done, but move her into *that house* . . . But of course – as she reminded me when we reached the green iron gate at Hisar Meydan – she had her own attachments to this place. It was where she'd spent her first year in Istanbul. "In '70–'71. I guess we never met because you'd left by then?" I managed a nod. "You know the house, though," she said.

"Oh, yes, I know the house," I said.

"And my father?"

"Of course."

She pushed open the gate and we walked in.

3

T HE PASHA'S LIBRARY (for those of you who have never visited Istanbul) is a 19th century kiosk that hangs like a birdcage over the village of Rumeli Hisar. It is high enough so that you can see the undulations of the Bosphorus almost to the point where they open up to the Black Sea. It was built by a pasha who, after a lifetime of forging links between East and West and squandering his family's fortune on Parisian women, arrived at a moment when he wanted to escape from the world without losing sight of it. But the view has the opposite effect on most people. They see it through the cypress trees the moment they walk through the garden gate and from that moment on it is as if a rope is pulling them. They stop at the ledge but their eyes keep travelling. They forget why they are there, or what they think about the people they have come to see. When they get around to speaking, it is as if they have just woken up and cannot quite remember their dream.

In May of 1970, I spent seven secret nights here with Sinan. William Wakefield, Jeannie's father, was away on some kind of business, and Sinan had got the key from my – our – friend Chloe, whose mother was supposed to be watering the plants. When, as the eighth night fell, we'd said our last farewells – in this very garden, on the marble bench next to the ledge – the moon was just sliding up from behind the darkened hills of Asia, and the waters of the Bosphorus looked like molten lava.

Tonight, thirty-four years later, the Bosphorus and the hills of Asia were little more than shadows behind the great glittering arcs of the new suspension bridge. The nightingales had given way to the steady hum of traffic. The great glass porch that surrounded the old library on three sides was ablaze with light, and so, too, were the windows in the raised roof that so affronted me, if only because it did not figure in my memory. But when we went inside, every carpet, every table, every chair seemed the same. We walked through the library, and onto the glass porch. The sky beyond was the same intense blue, until I got too close to the glass, and all I could see was my face.

I turned around. There, on the chaise longue where I'd lost my virginity, was Jeannie's father. He stood up to greet me. But even as we shook hands, I could feel him reading my mind.

He looked much as I remembered him – tanned, beefy and balding. Relaxed and affable, with bright, beady eyes. "Can I fix you a drink?" he said. "You look like you need one. What will you have?"

"Whatever you're having."

"I don't think so," he said. "I had to give up years ago." As he moved towards the drinks cabinet – Sinan and I had made good use of that, too, as I recalled – he filled in the blanks. "No, I haven't been here all along, in case you wanted to ask. I went back to the States not long after you did – well, a year after you did, if you want to be precise. In June 1971. Of course, bearing in mind what was happening at the time, I never expected to come back. Then in 2000, I did, but only to see little Emre. Never quite managed to leave, though. Come to my place in Bebek and you'll see why. The view's not quite as good as this one here, but . . ."

He handed me a bourbon and water. "That's your poison, isn't it?"

"Is it?"

"If my memory serves me, it certainly was once. Anyway, it's good to see you. Of course I feel as if we've been in touch all along. I read that book of yours. Congratulations. And of course I see your by-line. Though I haven't seen as much of you lately. Did you get tired of freelancing? I suppose that university job of yours keeps you pretty busy."

This was the William Wakefield I remembered. He couldn't go for two minutes without letting you know how much he knew.

"Listen, I hope you can help us," he now said. "God knows we need all the help we can get. You must be asking yourself why. I mean considering I've turned myself into some sort of pundit. You've seen me, I assume?"

"I've heard you," I said. This would have been a year or two earlier, on Radio 4 or the World Service, either just before the invasion of Iraq or just afterwards. "In fact, I was quite surprised to hear you being so critical of US policy."

"Good. That's what I wanted. As the big guys know, I know whereof I speak. Though of course, I speak only for myself. I'm retired. Retired years ago, in fact. But I'll be damned if I'm going to be their apologist."

"That's fine by me," I said.

"You grew up abroad. You can see things from the outside. Those rubes in Washington can't see their own johnsons. If people like me don't set them straight . . . So I've made myself a few enemies in the upper reaches, as they say. But for crying out loud, where are their hearts? We"re talking about a five-year-old boy here! An innocent five-year-old boy! They're holding him as insurance. That much is clear."

"But Dad, it really isn't!" said Jeannie, clasping her hands. "We can't say anything for sure yet. It's early days."

Her father paused, to gaze at her with sad affection. "Jeannie's right," he said, turning back to me. "For the moment, let's just call it a hunch. But it's pretty clear that the big guys don't want to touch this story. Someone's called them off the scent."

"But Dad, that makes no sense," Jeannie protested.

Her father sighed. "One thing I've learned during my long and checkered career. If the play makes no sense, check out the action backstage." He leaned way forward, tapping on his water glass. "Or more to the point, look at the history. This is not Chapter One. Just look at the cast of characters!" He paused, ostensibly to smile, but his eyes fixed on mine in a way that made me wonder if he really meant what he had just said, or if he was just testing.

"Yes," he said. "It's a fishy business – I'll give you that much! It goes way back. We've been set up. To put it more succinctly, I've been set up. But believe you me . . ."

Before he could elaborate, a woman called down from upstairs. I recognized her voice at once, though it took me some time to place it. I always have a hard time placing voices and faces when they're not where I expect them to be, and never in a million years would I have expected to find this woman in this company.

William Wakefield – Jeannie's father – came to Istanbul in 1966. He worked at the US Consulate. Officially, he was the agricultural attaché, though that didn't fool anybody. His Turkish was too good, and so were his binoculars. We all knew he was a spy. A rather unusual spy, if truth be told. Or perhaps just an ordinary spy gone native. When he first arrived, he had a wife, who had a daughter by an earlier marriage, and for a while, this girl and I were friends. Whenever I came over to the Pasha's Library to visit, William Wakefield would be out on this porch, nursing a bourbon and counseling a troubled youth.

Some were Turkish boys whose wealthy parents controlled their every move but spent no time with them. Most were lost Americans – ex-army or ex-peace corps, or kids who'd dropped out of college and set out for India, got as far as Turkey and run out of money. More often than not, William knew the parents. But he did things for them that their parents were never to know about. He'd helped one friend of mine get an abortion. When another friend bought a lump of hash from a police informer, he'd been able to secure her prompt release on the quiet. As fervently as William believed in freedom, he believed himself to be its watchdog. And he was always watching. And what he didn't know, he guessed.

But by the time I left, in 1970, he was beginning to slip. He was drinking heavily, and stepping out with my soon to be ex-best friend Chloe's recently divorced mother, and, I suspect, already getting up people's noses in Washington. They weren't heeding his advice back then, either. And it can't have been a good time to be an American spy in Turkey. Though the Turkish state had been (and would continue to be) America's staunchest Cold War ally, by the end of the 60s, the Turkish people were overwhelmingly against us – because of Cyprus, because of Vietnam, because the 17,000 US troops stationed here, ostensibly to protect them from the Soviet threat, had begun to feel like an occupying army. It was widely believed that the military, the prime minister, and everyone beneath him were US puppets. In the popular imagination, it was CIA pulling their strings.

What William Wakefield's job actually entailed I do not know. But he made no effort to hide his interest in Robert College. By the late 60s, my parents and most of their colleagues were preoccupied by the same issues that were tearing up college campuses in the US – civil rights, the assassinations, Vietnam, Cambodia. Many had, like my parents, left the US to escape the McCarthy Era. Because they leaned to the left politically and led vaguely bohemian lives, the people at the US Consulate took a dim view of them. We were a hotbed of Communism, they often said. The Soviets must have overheard. Certainly, I remember a string of very friendly men from the Soviet Consulate coming uninvited to my parents' parties. The only people they befriended were the drunks who saw them as a source of Russian vodka. But William Wakefield, who was a regular at these parties, too, would never fail to take my friends and me aside and warn us not to speak to these men or accept their gifts.

My closest friends at that point were mostly American – and mostly children of my father's colleagues. But by the late 60s, I had left the international community school and was studying at the American College for Girls, where tuition was in English and all but two of my classmates were Turkish. The boys we knew were mostly from Robert Academy, the boys' *lycée* that was our brother school. Or they had already graduated and moved on to Robert College, where the students had themselves drifted steadily leftwards during the 60s, in much the same way as students in Europe and the US, aided and abetted by the handful of young Americans who shared their sentiments. My own political education began with one such teacher – a Miss Broome, from Mount Holyoke, who taught us English. Sinan was a protégé of her lover, a Dutch Harding, who taught mathematics at Robert Academy. His degree was from Columbia, and he was, we were told, a veteran of its famous 1968 strike.

That, in any event, was what Sinan told me during our brief time together.

When I stepped back into the Pasha's Library late last summer, all I knew about the Trunk Murder was what I'd read in that lurid newspaper clipping that an anonymous ill-wisher had sent to me all those years ago. Which is not as strange as it might sound. In the early 70s, links between Turkey and the outside world were severely limited. The economy was closed to all but essential imports. Foreign travel was unusual for Turkish citizens and difficult to arrange. The phone lines were unreliable, and there was no direct dialing abroad. Letters from America could take up to a month to arrive or longer. All the television and radio stations were owned by the state and expressed its views.

By June 1971, when that lurid clipping reached me, newspapers were subject to censorship just as severe. Because by then the military had stepped in, to clamp down on the leftwing students whose ever more violent riots, pitched battles, bombs and kidnappings had, they said, taken the country to the brink of anarchy. A large part of the intelligentsia (including many friends of my parents) and thousands of students (including many of my father's former students) were behind bars. This had not, however, stopped the bombs and the kidnappings. From ex-students living in the US, my father heard it rumored that these incidents were provocations orchestrated by MİT, Turkey's notorious intelligence service – with the CIA offering a helping hand.

Whatever the truth of the matter, such rumors showed that there was still some public sympathy for the students. This changed abruptly in the first week of June 1971, when a cell led by a student named Mahir Çayan kidnapped the Israeli consul and killed him. It was later rumored that the cell-member who orchestrated this event was a colonel in the Turkish army – an *agent provocateur* – though the newspapers of the time made no mention of him. He had, it was alleged, already fled the country when his comrades barricaded themselves into an apartment building on the Asian side of the city, keeping an army officer's twelve-year-old daughter hostage until the police stormed the apartment, shooting to kill. This was one of two scandals that turned the public against the student left. The other, which came less than a week later, was the so-called Trunk Murder.

The story as I had it from the lurid newspaper cutting went like this: a Maoist cell consisting of the sons and daughters of some of Turkey's leading diplomats and industrialists had befriended one Jeannie Wakefield, the daughter of a US consular official, poisoning her mind and drawing her, perhaps unknowingly, into a plot against her father. All members of the cell were taken into custody after a bomb planted in the consular car left only his Turkish chauffeur in critical condition. However, they were later released. (It was implied that this was due to parental pressure.)

The following day, the cell decamped to the *garçonniere* in the village of Rumeli Hisar that doubled as their secret hideaway. Shaken by the discovery that the authorities were fully acquainted with every aspect of their illegal activities, they became convinced that one of their number must be an informer. Having subjected the accused to a kangaroo trial and found him guilty, they had killed him, chopped him up, and put him into a trunk.

The victim was their teacher and political mentor, Dutch Harding.

The boys in the group had vanished after the murder, leaving it to the girls to dispose of the body. But while they were dragging the trunk from a taxi onto a private yacht that belonged to one of their parents, the driver noticed a trail of blood, and duly informed the authorities. The girls were then taken in for questioning. One had fallen out of a fourth floor window and nearly died.

Running across the top of the lurid newspaper article were the culprits' *lycée* graduation photographs. With their black robes and mortarboards, they looked at first to be members of the same studious family. Or perhaps it was shock that had kept me from recognizing them right away.

Because the boys were Sinan and his best friend Haluk. The girls were my ex-best friend, Chloe Cabot, and two Turkish classmates of ours from the Girls' College, also former friends about whom I had very mixed feelings. Their names were Lüset and Suna. Suna was the one who had fallen out of the fourth floor window during interrogation. It was Suna I had heard calling down the stairs.

Perhaps everyone carries around a story like this – an unimaginable horror, visited upon a childhood friend, or the boy next door, or the girl you haven't seen since she sat between you and the window in second grade. When you knew them, they were ordinary in every way. As deeply as you bore into your memory, as mercilessly as you dredge it, you can find no sign that marked them for their fate. But you need to find it – it must be there – it must have happened for a reason, because it if didn't, it could also have happened to you. So if you can't find the answer in the past, then you must at least try and conjure up the scene of the crime, make some sense of it – understand, at the very least, how A led to B.

For years, I'd tried. Lost years of sleep, struggling to force the facts I had – the facts I thought I had – into a shape that made sense. But I never got very far. I could imagine Sinan with another girl, a girl like me, but more innocent. I could see them arm in arm at the Pasha's Library, breaking my heart as they watched the moon rise over the Bosphorus, on the marble bench at the edge of the secret garden. I could see Jeannie's father, standing on the glass porch, affably clocking them. And if I gazed over the ledge into the village of Rumeli Hisar, I could see the *garçonniere*: the glasses piled up in the sink, and the shoes and socks strewn across the floor, and the never-washed sheets. I could imagine my lost friends at the table, reading coffee grounds, pretending to believe the outrageous fortunes they found in them, but laughing all the while. I could imagine Suna tapping Sinan's coffee cup and saying, 'So this spy who's betrayed us. What are we to do with him?' But no matter how hard I tried, I could not imagine what Sinan might have said in reply. A curtain descended, and my mind went black.

From time to time, a scene would drift in from the shadows. Always the same cast of characters, and always in the *garçonniere* – but arranged into a new formation. Sometimes Suna had the gun, sometimes it was Chloe or the cipher who had replaced me. Sometimes Jeannie Wakefield was an innocent bystander, and sometimes she was the accuser. Sometimes she was facing an armchair whose occupant I couldn't see, and sometimes she was standing over the body lying face down on the floor. Sometimes it was Sinan standing over the mentor who had betrayed him, and sometimes it was Haluk. Sometimes it wasn't a gun in his hand, but the hatchet I could never bring myself to believe he'd used to chop Dutch Harding's body into pieces. No matter how I arranged the scene, it refused to stay in place. There were too many variables, and too few facts. There had been a murder. I seemed to know almost everyone implicated in it. But I did not know which one was the killer. And neither could I understand what might have driven him or her to kill the softspoken, bookish, arrogantly inert Dutch Harding.

I just couldn't see him as an *agent provocateur*.

But I could see the girls, abandoned, and left to clear away the evidence, lugging the trunk down the stairwell, across the cobblestones to the waiting taxi. Their hearts stopping when the taxi driver threw it into the trunk and cried, "What do you have in there, a body?" Their hearts stopping again as they paid him off in front of Lüset's father's yacht, and as they dragged the trunk up over the curb, and looked behind to see a trail of blood.

Suna, in the interrogation room. On the window ledge, dangling her legs. In the shadows behind her, the shape of a man. In the street below, Sinan, saying nothing, but pleading with his eyes. What did he want her to do? Go back into the room or jump?

Things he'd said during our seven-night tryst came floating back to me. Things that, under other circumstances, would have meant nothing. I'd be sitting in a lecture hall at Wellesley, jotting down notes about Savanarola – or in the dining hall, at the salad bar – and I'd see him on the chaise longue, smiling his sulky smile, stroking my arm, bringing my hand to his lips, to kiss each finger, one by one.

"You're bad. As bad as I am, aren't you?"

"You're like me, you don't know when to stop."

"How far are you willing to go with me? No – how far will you follow?"

"You want to know what I did last night? I learned how to make a Molotov Cocktail . . . You don't believe me? Fine, it's settled. Next time you're coming too . . ."

"What? I don't think so. You are coming because I say you're coming!"

"I'm a bloodthirsty Turk, after all. Can't you see the knife between my lips?"

If I'd stayed – if he'd kept his promise – if we'd kept to our plan – would he have pulled me into this cell of his, and this murder? Had he tried, would I have the sense to pull away from him, or would I have melted at the sight of him, as I had done a thousand times over, each and every one of the seven secret nights we'd spent together? If there was such a thing as a point of no return, would I have recognized it – or sailed along regardless like the rest of them? I needed to believe that I was made of different stuff than they were. But I knew I wasn't. It could have been me in that room, if I'd stayed, if he'd kept his promise. I'd been spared only because he'd fallen out of love with me – if he'd ever been in love with me – and chosen someone else. Did that mean I had no part in it? For I had wished them to hell. And my dream had come true.

Six months after the murder, in December 1971 when I was a sophomore at Wellesley, I ran into Chloe Cabot, my ex-best friend, in Harvard Square. (And yes – you may have guessed this already. Our final disagreement had been about Sinan. Though they'd been only friends, they'd been close friends. Though she'd had no real reason to feel jealous, she'd acted as if I'd stolen him away.) This chance meeting in Harvard Square was the first I knew Chloe was not languishing in a jail in Turkey. For someone who'd been involved in a murder, she was disturbingly offhand.

She had just started at Radcliffe, she told me. She hated it, of course. She didn't think she'd last. Our short and stilted conversation tapered into a silence: this would, I knew, be my only chance to ask her what had really happened. But as I searched for the right words, a wave of terror passed through me. I was afraid, I suppose, that she might tell me the truth.

Later that winter, in a burst of belated courage, I did make an effort to track her down, only to be told that she had taken a leave of absence.

The following summer – this would have been June, 1972 – I was helping a friend paint a room in a house on Cape Cod when my eyes happened to fall on the sheet of newsprint we were using for our brushes. It was a front page from one of Boston's underground papers, and at the bottom was a little black box in which it was stated that on June the whatever the paper had run a story about a murder, allegedly involving a CIA operative then stationed in Istanbul, Turkey. Because the author, Jeannie Wakefield, was personally acquainted with all involved, the editors had been less than diligent in checking her facts. As it had since emerged that her story was false in just about every particular, the editors, along with the author, wished to offer their most sincere apologies, and their most sincere thanks to the Turkish Ambassador, who had kindly offered to furnish the full facts of the case in a later issue. I forgot to keep my surprise to myself – of all the places to see this story, and this name! It was my friend who, eager to know more about this murky tale, got straight on the phone to the underground newspaper. But for the obvious legal reasons, and to my huge relief, they refused to send her the issue with Jeannie's original article. So once again, it was out of my hands. From time to time, late at night, when I couldn't sleep, I would regret having made no second effort. But never for long.

I had the sense, at least, to recognize that the real problem was in my mind, that, strictly speaking, the Trunk Murder had nothing to do with me, that any new facts I gleaned were unlikely to explain to me why I felt as if it did. Slowly, I weaned myself off it. If my thoughts returned regardless, I learned not to play along. No more rearrangements of the cast at the scene of the crime, no more long nights lolling on the window ledge, staring into the abyss. Though the scenes still came back to me, they were less and less frequent. Slowly the life drained out of them, until no one spoke, and no one moved, and nothing in the shadows or the street below disturbed or even interested me.

Much later, when my parents were back in Istanbul, I did hear passing references from time to time – enough to know that Sinan (who had spent many years in Denmark) worked in films, that his old friend Haluk (who had spent many years in England and was now back in the bosom of his industrialist family) was rumored to be Sinan's chief backer, that Suna (who, like her friend Lüset, had been released from prison in the mid-70s) was now in the sociology department at the University, and that Chloe, (who had returned to Istanbul in the late 80s) had been blissfully married to a plastic surgeon until he died of leukemia. I felt no urge, and made no effort, to get back into touch.

4

BUT NOW HERE they were, in the Pasha's Library, the entire cast minus Sinan. Bustling about the great new loft that they'd turned into some sort of incident room. At first they didn't see me. And, in a sense, neither could I see them. I am wondering if it's even possible to explain how I felt at that moment – what thoughts crossed my mind as I stood there, contemplating the path not taken.

I noticed first of all how gracefully they occupied it. Four shapes, huddled around a desk, a screen, a pool of lamplight. Heads and shoulders rising and falling to the rhythm of their whispers. Their every gesture speaking of the years I had not shared with them.

They were reading some sort of massive document. From the limpness of the paper, I guessed it was a fax. It was Chloe I could see most clearly, though at first I knew her only from the way she licked her finger as she leafed through the papers on her lap. And her feet – even after all these years, she still turned them in. But there was no other sign of the awkward teenager I had once known. The bulges and blemishes had been airbrushed away. Now she was all angles and gold bracelets and linen cut on the bias. No sign of a curl, even, in her sleek and backcombed copper hair. She had the "careless poise" I remembered our discussing in the abstract with some passion at restaurant tables all over the Mediterranean, as our parents drank and we designed outfits and *accoutrements* for the ideal woman.

I remembered in particular an argument we'd had about engagement rings when I was twelve and she was eleven. Chloe's was to be the "second largest emerald in the world." When I asked what she'd do if the love of her life turned up with a diamond, she'd said, "Well, obviously. I'd have to say no." As her hand flitted to her lips, a flash of green told me she had not been disappointed.

The gentle, bearlike creature sitting next to her – could it really be Haluk, the Playboy of the Eastern World? This man seemed too comfortable inside his skin to have been the restive boy I could still see smiling so blandly as his foot tapped the accelerator. Only when he turned to comfort the woman sitting next to him did I catch a glimpse of . . .

Lüset! She had not changed at all. She was the same porcelain doll. She was kissing Haluk on the cheek – how strange! But there was no time to consider why. For now here was Suna. The same. Only more so. As her blazing blue eyes cut through me, I could hear her last words to me: "*I repudiate you. I repudiate you. And once more. I repudiate you. I have said it three times now. And still you stand before me?*"

What had I said in reply? I remembered only her retort. "*So stay there! Stand there like a candle for all eternity. It changes nothing! For me – for all true patriots of Turkey – you have ceased to exist.*" Was she still holding to her promise, or had she failed to recognize me? I did not have time to ask, because now Jeannie had run to Suna's side. "Is this it, finally?" she asked.

Suna nodded gravely. "But it's not good news."

"Is this the top page?" Jeannie asked. She plopped down on a stool and began to read. Her fists were clenched and soon she began to sob. Chloe gestured at Lüset, who answered with a silent nod.

After she had spirited Jeannie away, the others exchanged dark looks and darker murmurs. It was bad, very bad. There was something Suna had found on the Internet that she wanted the others to see. As they huddled around her laptop, I found myself a chair in the corner, where, to keep myself occupied, I surveyed the room. In the center were two small sofas – one red, one blue – sitting on a carpet of the same color scheme. Between them was a glass coffee table piled high with glossy magazines and newspapers, a slender brass floor lamp, and a yellow box of Duplo, tipped on its side. As I looked across the vast parquet floor, I could see assorted *Star Wars* action figures, a large Transformer, and an overturned train.

Next to the stairs was a large glass tank. Inside it was a large snake coiled around a tree branch. In spite of myself, I smiled. Another cobra! After all these years! Windows ran along all four walls – from where I sat I could see the full span of the new suspension bridge, and below its glittering arcs, the slow parade of night buses rolling into Anatolia. Running below the windows along three walls was a custom-made desk, long enough to accommodate five workstations. On the wall behind me was a collection of framed posters – most from Sinan's films, and one from his beautiful mother's brief singing career. Running above the windows were the framed photographs that told the story I could have done without: Sinan arm-in-arm with Jeannie. Sinan cradling his infant son. Emre learning to crawl, Emre taking his first step, Emre staring at the three candles on his birthday cake. Sinan holding up a silver cup, and, over the bookshelf on which someone – his adoring wife? – had arranged his trophies, a photograph of Sinan standing on a windswept hilltop, looking into the distance, smiling like a man. His frame was wider than I remembered. As was his face. But his eyes were the same – dark, sulky, and idly seeking trouble. For a moment I remembered how it had felt, to sit with him on that chaise longue, to see him lie back on the headrest, hands behind his head, smiling and archly patient, never doubting that if he looked into my eyes long enough, my resistance would crumble.

Quickly, I looked away. Chloe was sitting on the chair in front of a laptop; Suna and Haluk were reading over her shoulders. From time to time, one of them would cry out in disbelief. And Chloe would look up gravely and say, "Should we even be reading this garbage?" Or: "Are you ready for me to scroll down?" When they reached the end, Haluk straightened himself out, put his fingers through his thinning hair, and gazed out the window. "Where did you find this, Suna?" He was speaking in English, but when Suna replied, and Chloe interrupted, they had slipped into Turkish. I only caught a phrase here and there, but this in itself was familiar, and oddly reassuring. What Turkish I'd learned, all those years ago, I'd learned from boyfriends and classmates: I'd sat there for hours, days, and months on end, struggling to fit together the words that made sense. But I could always read their emotions. Even if I did not know what they said, I knew how they felt. As I watched my three former friends whispering in their huddle, throwing their heads back from time to time to revert to English – "Why would the State Department release such a thing?" "How can we be sure this is a genuine article?" "There is, of course, only one question we must ask, and that is, Cui bono?" – I remembered, for the first time in thirty-five years, why I'd once liked them.

Cui bono. In the old days, Suna could not go five minutes without asking "*Cui bono?*" I must have shifted in my chair because now Chloe looked up. When she saw me, her eyes widened into a very familiar stare. "Crumbs!"

Suna subjected me to another of her fierce blue glares. Then she broke into the warm smile I'd arranged to forget. "It's you!" she cried. "It really is you!" She ran across the room to embrace me. "How long have you been here, cowering like a mouse! Why so quiet? You should have said something! No, it is our fault. We should not have been so rude. Sit, sit down, tell me your news. Tell me what I can offer you. Some tea? Something to eat?" She sat me down on the red sofa and sat herself down on the blue one, clearing the glass table between us for the tea that soon arrived. Pausing from time to time to urge me to eat more of the sweet and salty biscuits that had arrived on the same tray, she asked me about my life and work, and I asked her about hers. But whenever the conversation lagged, and she reached across the table to give my arm an affectionate squeeze, the new Suna faded to make way for the old one, calling to me across the cafeteria. "*Sit down. Have some of my cake. Do you like it? How wonderful. How very glad I am. But now, my darling, I have a question. I was wondering if you could explain to me why the running dogs of capitalism are continuing their illegal invasion of North Vietnam . . .*"

"*Elma yanak*," Suna said suddenly. "Apple cheeks. That's what we called you, wasn't it?"

"You know what we called you, don't you?" I said.

"What?"

"Suna the Terrible."

Suna laughed, as if reminded of happier days. "And I was terrible. Wasn't I? But now you've forgiven me. That's good. So I forgive you, too. No matter what your crime." Lighting a cigarette, her lips still curved, she turned to me and asked, "Do you happen to remember what your crime was, by the way?"

"Cultural imperialism," I said.

"Such a broad term. Can't you be more specific?"

"If I'm not mistaken, I was polluting the country by my very presence."

"Hah!" she said, throwing back her head in laughter. "And my crime?"

"I never really worked that out," I said. "Perhaps you could tell me."

I was surprised by my own words, but more surprised to see how little they affected her. Still smiling, she rattled off something in Turkish that made Chloe roll her eyes and Haluk laugh heartily. But when Suna turned back to me, her face was serious again. "You're going to help us. Am I right?"

"I can't make any promises," I said. "But of course I'll try."

"We're very worried." She looked up anxiously at the others and they confirmed her words with dark nods. "It's far worse than Jeannie knows."

"There are some new and virulent rumors circulating," Chloe explained. "We think we know where they're coming from, but we can't be sure."

"But if you ask the most obvious question," said Suna, "in other words, 'Cui bono?', it is clear that the rumormongers' aim is to discredit Sinan, do whatever necessary to make him look like the terrorist they so fear. But now there's a new twist. Our enemies are seeking to weaken Sinan's links with those who love him – make his own wife doubt him! Let me show you." Walking over to the newspapers and picking up the one on the top, she pointed to the loud red advertisement running along the left hand side of the page – a sleek and smiling middle aged man, speaking on a cell phone, smiling in profile at a young girl on another mobile phone who was gazing up at him in abject admiration, and beneath this tableau, a single word: "ŞENLİK." "Does this man's face ring any bells?"

Here Haluk put a hand on Suna's shoulder. He said something in Turkish that sounded like a warning. "You're right," Suna said. Turning back to me, she said, "We'll speak about this later. Tomorrow, perhaps? In the meantime, tell me. You need to begin your research, and we need to help you."

"Jeannie had some papers she thought I should see."

"Did she mention anything in particular?"

"It was something of an open invitation," I said. "I think she wants to make it clear that she has nothing to hide."

"Ah! Yes! We forget at our peril that we ourselves are under suspicion."

"That's not what I meant," I said.

"Oh really? Then what did you mean? Let me think. Ah. Now I see it. To prove to the world that we're not terrorists, you must first pretend you wish to prove it to yourself . . ."

"Crudely speaking, yes."

"And to prove it to yourself, you must go way, way, back – if not to our prehistory, like this rumormonger who has come back to re-infest our lives, then to those other rumors. I take it you know which ones."

She turned to the window, puffing ominously on her cigarette, and as I watched her, I felt the sour pit of fear in my stomach. I had forgotten what it was like with her – how a friendly exchange could slide into a war of words from which there was no escape.

"I'm not sure I know what rumors you're talking about," I said carefully.

"You don't? Oh, please. My friend! Are you as wide-eyed as all that? But never mind. I have lived with this for a long time. And am used to seeing it in people's eyes, as I can see it in yours . . . So please. Dear friend. Come with me. As it happens, we do not have to go too far." Taking my hand, she led me to the window and pointed down at the glittering houses and apartments spilling down the hill beneath us. "Do you see that window, the third floor up, in the building just down there? It has red curtains, and behind them a chandelier is burning. Do you know what happened in that very room – how long has it been – thirty-three years ago last June? No, of course you don't. But of course – you've heard so many things. Such horrors! Guns and kidnappings and kangaroo trials and informers and cold-blooded murders and bleeding trunks – but tell me, did anyone ever . . ."

"Suna! *Allah aşkına.*"

This was Lüset, who had come upstairs to join us at the window. Had she done nothing in her life, other than rush into rooms to plead with her reckless friend? She took my hand. "Welcome back," she said. After a pause, she said, "It is a very difficult time, so I hope you can be patient with us."

"I never . . ."

She raised a hand to silence me. "The past is the past. But that's why we need you. We need someone who understands our situation, but who also has a voice abroad. I'm afraid that our own journalists, who do not have the high standards of other countries, have only made matters worse. They do nothing but circulate old and discredited rumors. They still can't mention us without also mentioning this murder that never happened."

I turned around, and looked at each of them in turn.

I must have gasped. "The Trunk Murder never happened?"

"You didn't know?" Chloe said.

"Do you mean to say that..."

"No – wait a minute," said Chloe. "I need to get this straight. Are you saying no one ever told you? That all this time, you've thought . . . ?"

I turned to Suna. "So what actually happened?"

"Nothing happened." This was William Wakefield, who was standing at the top of the stairs. "Nothing at all!" But there was something about the way he stood there, grinning at me with his arms akimbo, that told me he was lying.

I did keep my promise and dropped by Suna's office at the university the next day. But she was on the phone and late for a faculty meeting so I found myself sitting there across the desk, trying to compose myself, and the questions swirling about my mind. Of all the things I needed her to explain to me, the first was this: even assuming that this murder had never happened, how could it be that a person of her political complexion could be on such friendly, such intimate, terms with a man she knew to have been a spy? As I watched her bent over her phone, her arms going back and forth – was she doodling? Underlining? Taking notes? – it suddenly hit me. She was erasing the past.

In the end she didn't have time for the promised chat. She had, however, gathered up some papers for me. I went back to London laden down with documents and DVDs and a huge folder of photographs and news cuttings.

I laid them out on my study floor as soon as I got home and for many weeks, that was where they stayed. Every time I mustered up enough resolve to look at them, a wave of nausea came over me. I felt sorry for

Jeannie, and my conscience told me I should help her find her son. But my heart clouded over when I thought about the others, and our strange reunion at the Pasha's Library, and my shameful response to it.

You'd think I'd be glad to hear that a murder involving so many people I knew so well had never happened. That even if I still had doubts, I'd want to lose them – hope, at least, that these people were telling me the truth. Instead I felt bereft, as if they had robbed me of my own past.

What did it mean to say nothing had happened? Where did the erasure begin and where did it end? How much of my past was fiction not fact? These were the questions that ate into me, every time I tried to do the right thing. And I did try, if only in half-hearted spurts. I left a few messages with editors, though I didn't chase them up. I answered Jeannie's many falsely cheerful and desperately undemanding emails with falsely worded excuses. I wrote to Sinan's lawyers, asking for information they did not forward to me. I kept track of the case through the website set up on his behalf by a student organization somewhere in New York State, but only to confirm that there had been no progress. I unpacked the DVDs. Resolved, every night for many weeks running, to watch at least one of his films. But the only one I saw was the one I saw by accident – a documentary on BBC2 about a neighborhood in the hills above my parents' house.

I tuned in just at the end: four men, unmistakably Turkish, watching a traffic altercation from a coffeehouse. An uppity lady in a Mercedes shaking her fist at the man unloading the lorry that was blocking the road as her chauffeur called him the son of a donkey. The men from the coffeehouse listening impassively, the camera slipping down the street, down the hill, to the Bosphorus.

In the credits rolling over it, I saw his name, and though I knew I had no cause, I still felt duped.

The last email I received from Jeannie was an apology. She was writing to ask if I would mind putting a hold on the story until we had a chance to speak. New information had come to light, she said. She would be truly grateful if I could help her 'process the ramifications.' But since there were leads to follow before she could honestly say she had the whole picture, it could wait until I was next in Istanbul. In the meantime, had I had a chance to see Sinan's films? There was one in particular – *My Cold War* – that "might be good to review."

I bounced back an evasive reply, giving her the dates of my next visit.

A few days later, I sat down on my study floor and went through my DVDs until I had found the one marked *My Cold War*. It was, as my mother had said, only half the story, but it was not, strictly speaking, the story of his childhood. Although it was told in an artful, playful way, interspersing its talking heads with footage from home movies, and news reels, old photographs, and ironic clips from old Turkish films, it had a menacing momentum that left me feeling as if I was trapped in the passenger seat of a car speeding towards a cliff. It began with Sinan's birth in Washington DC in 1950, and his early childhood in an assortment of embassies around the world – the "innocent years," when he had believed Turkey "to be a great world power, as great as the United States and the Soviet Union put together," and his father to be "the hero who had stood between these two towering giants, and kept the Cold War cold." He then moved on to his troubled teenage years in Istanbul, by which time he had, in his words, "discovered where Turkey was in the scheme of things," and that his father, "far from being a hero, was a lackey, pleased to do whatever his American masters commanded." His disillusionment was compounded, he said, by the fact that he himself was "being prepared for the same fate." He went on to describe his years at Robert Academy, when he was "told to be a Turk at home, and an American in the classroom, until all I wanted was to blow the whole place up, and me with it." He went on to imply that, without the steadying hand of a trusted mentor – he did not mention Dutch Harding by name – he might well have done so.

Cut to the student protests of the late 60s – the demonstrations, the riots, the bombs, the pitched battles, the day the workers marched on the city – and Suna, analyzing the anti-American mood. "Of course, there were political elements. There was Korea, Cyprus, Vietnam. But for us, all children of the rich, the privileged, the carefully educated, the ruling elite – the beneficiaries of the best our American allies had to offer – there was a more personal problem. Our fathers were the collaborators. The Turks who made sure Turkey did as it was told."

As pictures from our yearbooks filled the screen, Suna added, "Perversely, this only added to the glamor of the Americans who presided over us. Even as we ridiculed the shortness of their trousers, we envied their confidence, their freedom, their loose-limbed children. They were the untouchables!"

My heart froze when I heard those words, as I anticipated the cold slap of my own name. But the face that now flashed on the screen was not mine. It was Jeannie's.

"And of all the lovely American girls who passed through this boy's hands," Suna's cruel voice continued, "the most untouchable would be the daughter of the spy who watched over us."

As Jeannie faded from view, questions flashed across the screen:

"What happened next?
Who was the true mastermind?
Where is he now?
What does he have to say about himself?
Who are his new paymasters?
Cui bono?"

5

I T WAS LESS THAN a week later that I ran into a colleague of mine named Jordan Frick. I say "colleague" in the looser sense of the word. He was a feared and respected war reporter, while I wrote on and off in the same paper about mothers and babies. But we'd known each other for decades.

We had, in fact, first met in Istanbul, in 1970. And if you're beginning to wonder how there can be so many people wandering around the edges of my life who share a connection to Istanbul – let me just say that there are a lot of us, and that we seem to favor work that keeps us wandering. Jordan had first gone to Turkey with the Peace Corps, and had stayed on, supporting himself as a stringer for various papers in the US. But when our paths first crossed in June 1970 – at a party, at the house Dutch Harding shared with my mentor, the saintly Miss Broome – Jordan Frick was on his way back to the US: to make his parents happy, he had agreed to a Master's at Harvard. When I told him I would be attending college in the area, he gave me his number. The following winter, after Sinan dropped me, I called him. He took me out to the Café Pamplona, where I had cried for two hours, and he had listened, and understood. Not once did he tell me I was better off without the bastard, or that I'd meet someone else tomorrow, or that these things happened to everyone, or that time would ease the pain.

He just said he was sorry to hear what I'd been through, as I didn't deserve it, and sorry that he would not be there to help me through the next part, as he had decided to stop trying to please his parents. So he was curtailing his studies and flying out to Mexico City that weekend to follow a story. I must have said I hoped to live like that one day, because he said, "Then good. Our paths will cross again."

And they had, many times. In October 2005 it was at the Frontline Club. The event that evening was a panel discussion of "Extraordinary Rendition" – though there were rumors circulating about spy planes transporting suspects to countries where torture was legal, the story had yet to break. But the will was there, most especially in the Frontline Club that evening, so I was not surprised to look across the room and see Jordan, who in recent months had been filing a great deal from Uzbekistan.

How he looked that day: not as ragged as he sometimes did when he came in from the wild, but, with his lion's mane of windblown hair, his scorched tan, and his faded clothes, still dressed for the mountains. He was leaning on the bar at the back, his craggy face impassive, his eyes fixed on the man in the back row who had just stood up to ask the panel a question. When this man identified himself as a spokesman from the Uzbeki Embassy, and a ripple of disapproval went through the audience, Jordan showed no reaction whatsoever. When the guests on the panel faltered in their answers, Jordan lifted his hand and was immediately noticed. The entire audience turned around to watch, in fact. But as he rattled out the questions that the panel might consider directing to the man from the embassy, "not to mention the government it purports to serve," he looked right over their heads. Not for the first time, I was unsettled by his weary calm; though he spoke with principled purpose, there was no outrage. It was as if he were here to make reparations for a crime only he remembered, and only he could expiate – as if he had been sentenced to speak for the dead, and walk the earth in their shoes.

"I thought I'd find you here," he said, when I tapped him on the shoulder in the clubroom. "In fact, we need to talk." He bought me a drink and led me through the smoky crowd, smiling warmly at anyone who tried to pull him into a conversation and saying, "Let's catch up later." When we'd sat down at the round table in the corner, he told me he was just back from Turkey, which was in a "very strange mood." I asked for specifics and he waved his hand. "Oh you know. This kerfuffle about the Armenians. This branding of their most famous author as a traitor for starting it. You have never seen so many flags. But put all that to one side for a moment." He looked me in the eye, and as he did so, his eyebrows shot up, almost of their own accord. "Jeannie Wakefield."

"You know her, too?"

He nodded.

"From way back when?"

He nodded again, "I'm not sure I ever told you this part," he said. "But all those years ago – in 1970 or was in 1971, when I dropped out of graduate school, and decided to do journalism for real . . ."

"When you went off to Mexico City, to follow that story . . ."

He tilted his head to one side, as if in search of a lost memory. "Yes, well. That fizzled out pretty fast, as it happens. I mean I had to get out of town. The upshot is that I ended up back in Istanbul, more or less by default, because I knew I could pick up work there. I had contacts. I don't know if anyone ever told you, but one of them was Jeannie's father."

"How did that happen?"

"When I first went out to Turkey – you know, with the Peace Corps – we started with a summer course at Robert College, and William Wakefield was floating around the edges, in some sort of advisory role. Anyway, that was how I met him. When things turned sour – that's another story – he went out of his way to help me. Our man at the consulate, in every way. I was aware of the drawbacks, so I can't say I let my guard down. But he seemed to need me more than I needed him. Anyway, he fed me things. Things that a stringer fresh out of college can only pray for. You could say I have him to thank for kickstarting my career." Here he paused. "I hear you saw him last time you were in Istanbul."

"Do I take that to mean you two are still friends?" I asked.

A long silence. "If I were you," he said, "I would look for another word."

Another long silence. "When's the last time you and Jeannie spoke?"

I told him about her last email, and how I had replied to it.

"So are you going?" he asked.

"Yes, later this month," I said. "My parents . . ."

"If I were you," he said. "I'd bring that trip forward. Or do you not want to help her?" He had never spoken to me so angrily, and it threw me.

"Perhaps you could explain what's going on," I said.

"I think I'll let her do that."

"Why?"

"Let's put it like this – I owe it to her. You owe it to her, too, by the way. You made her a promise. She's counting on you to write this story."

"If it's so important," I shot back, more sharply than I'd ever done with him, "then why aren't *you* doing it?" He looked up in surprise. Emboldened, I said, "After all, you'd never have the trouble placing it that I will. You're a name. You can choose your own stories."

His lips thinned. "I think you've been in this business long enough to know that stories choose you, and not the other way around. But I'll tell you one thing. I'd give anything to be in your shoes. I'd love nothing more than to put it all down in black and white – everything I know, everything I've been carrying around with me. Maybe one day I will. But not now. Most definitely, not now."

"Why not?" I asked.

"I know too much."

"Could I trouble you to be more specific?"

"No," he said. "But if you get back out there in time – and I mean, as soon as is humanly possible – you might just be able to help her puzzle this out."

"This new information, you mean."

He nodded, slowly.

"You've discussed it with her yourself?"

He stood up to leave. "Listen," he said. "I'm sorry. I'm heading out on a plane at the crack of dawn. Baku first but then who knows, and I'm not sure how the reception will be. Anyway, here's my mobile number. Leave me a message when you get back and I'll do what I can." He turned away, and then he turned back again. "Listen. She trusts you, and I don't want to spoil that. She trusts you, and at this precise moment, she very definitely does not trust me."

The next morning I made my first serious attempt to place the article. The editor – and it was Jordan who had suggested I try him first – was so keen on the idea that he stopped me halfway through my description of Sinan's career. "I know his films, of course. And I've known for some time about these ridiculous charges. But until Jordan told me, I had no idea he had married into the CIA. This is hot stuff!"

Within the hour, I had my e-ticket. By lunchtime, I was on my way out to Heathrow. By ten that evening, I was landing at Istanbul airport, and by eleven, I was dragging my suitcase up the dark stairs to my parents' apartment.

"We're all so glad you're here," my mother told me at breakfast the next morning. "Finally! Someone's prepared to listen! And who better than you? Jeannie's so relieved I can't tell you. She called last night, by the way, and left you a message. She's waiting for you at home. She can give you the whole day."

It is never a good sign when people say that. No one in their right mind should give a journalist the whole day. As I set off down the white walk, I counted the rules I had broken by taking this on. Never write a story about a friend. Never write a story about someone with whom you have a history. Never let anyone, even someone you admire, push you into a story you know you shouldn't do.

I prepared my speech. "So Jeannie. Before we go any further, it would be best for both of us if we lay down the ground rules. You say you have nothing to hide. But you must understand that once I get going, I may find out things you'd rather not know. If I do, I reserve the right to . . ."

Even before I turned the corner, I could hear the machines.

A white van and a black sedan were parked in front of the Pasha's Library, and the green metal gate was propped open. Inside the garden was a team of workmen, digging up a hole. I assumed this was just more sewer work, so I proceeded down the path to the front door. It was unlocked, so I went straight in. The kitchen was empty, as was the old library and the porch. Hearing footsteps over my head, I bounded up to the office. There, sitting on the red sofa, was a man I did not recall ever having met before, though there was something about his sleek, smooth smile that struck me as familiar.

He stood up and offered me his hand. "İsmet Şen," he said. Though his manner was Turkish, he had a strong American accent. 'And you must be . . ."

"Where's Jeannie?"

"Ah. So you haven't heard," he said. He had an air of regret.

Sitting down again, and clasping his hands, he said, "Had you managed to arrive yesterday . . . I know she was eager to see you! But who knows, perhaps she's just stepped out for a few hours. With luck, she'll be back by lunchtime, or supper. More likely, supper. You can hold the fort, can't you?" He furrowed his brow. "Something must have frightened her. The poor creature has been extremely edgy lately, and who can blame her?"

"Has anyone called her father? If anyone knows where she is, it'll be him."

"Ah. So you haven't heard about her father,' said İsmet Şen. "I'm so sorry. I assumed Jordan Frick would have mentioned it . . ."

"You've been speaking to Jordan Frick?"

"He is known to us, of course. Naturally, we cannot hope to keep him away from this story forever. But until that moment comes, we are, of course, trying to do as much as we can behind the scenes. Jeannie's father was, after all, someone I counted as a valued colleague. Even a friend."

"But now he's . . . what?"

İsmet sighed, regretfully. His shoulders sagged to match his expression. I asked for the details. William Wakefield had been shot, in the back, in his apartment in Bebek. He declined to give me a date. "For this tragedy, too, is still under wraps. As for the weapon, as far as we can ascertain, it was the gun sitting on the table between us."

I looked down at the table between us. Between the newspapers and the *Cornucopia* magazines, there was indeed a gun.

İsmet Şen picked it up. Passing it playfully between his two hands, he said, "Yes, this was the gun. Of this at least we are certain. But if you are asking who pulled the trigger – this remains an open question. But . . ." Another smooth, sleek smile. "Perhaps not for much longer, now you are here to help us."

Slowly, he put the gun down again. Slowly, he stood up. At the stairs, he turned around to smile at me. "You have been offered the run of the office. So you do not need me to tell you how to proceed. Suffice it to say, that we, too . . ."

"We. Who are 'we'?"

"Oh, I'm sorry. I should have explained. It's force of habit, I'm afraid. I, too, had to retire many, many years ago, of course! But I still try to be help-ful. Especially with tragedies such as this one. Mishandled, it could cause problems between my country and yours, and at such a sensitive moment! So think of me as a go-between. And of course – this is my house."

"How so?"

"I am, quite simply, the owner. Or rather, the owner's silent partner. The long and the short of it – in case you were thinking of asking – is that I have every right to be here. As much as Jeannie, if she walked through the door right now, might find that surprising. Though in fact, they'd overrun their lease. Which reminds me. I am being a bad host! What can I offer you?"

"Nothing," I said. This seemed to be the answer he expected. "I'll leave you to it, then," he said. Halfway down the stairs he paused and came upstairs again. Striding over to the coffee table, and picking up the gun, he said, "I'd better keep that with me. All things considered, it's best to be prepared. I'll be downstairs if you need me. But take your time! And please, by all means, use the phone!"

Though I'd never been the sort to court danger, there had, over the years, been a number of occasions when I'd gone to do a routine inter-view and found myself in a room from which my exit was barred, more often than not by a man who had given every indication of being trust-worthy until turning the lock. No one can ever know how they will respond to such a situation until they've had to face it. We each have our own chemistry. Mine gives me arrogance. I feel no fear. I don't ask ques-tions. Above all, I don't react. So this is how you want to play it, I thought as I watched my jailer disappear down the stairs. So fine. We'll see who wins.

But I wasn't going to rush – that was for sure. I swivelled my chair, surveyed the room as I waited for my mind to clear. The Duplo was gone, as were the trains. The cobra was gone, too, and only one of the laptops was running.

When I tried to connect the laptop to the Internet, I was informed there was no dial tone. No dial tone, either, on the landline. I had just dialed my mother's number on my cell phone – but forgotten to do the country code – when I heard İsmet coming up the stairs. Quickly, I put my phone down on the desk. Smoothly, he asked me what I'd like for lunch.

"As it turns out, our hostess has left us a full refrigerator."

I thanked him but said I wasn't hungry. "Well, let me know the moment you are," he said. Then he reached out for my cell phone and slipped it into his pocket. "I'll hold on to this, too, if you don't mind."

"What – am I under house arrest now?" I asked.

"Madam!" he cried. "I am simply trying to protect you. There is no one – no one – more eager to get to the bottom of this sorry affair than yours truly. Did I not say I am, among so many other things, Sinan's uncle? By marriage only, of course. But these things still matter. I've known him since he was this high. Long enough to feature in that film of his! Look, come here." He walked over to the poster on the wall where the cobra tank had been. Under the banner – *My Cold War* in a child's scrawl, over a flag that was half stars and stripes, and half hammer and sickle – was a collage of family photographs. Pointing at one of them – Sinan with his beautiful mother, flanked by three men – he said, "There, that's me in white. The man holding Sinan's hand is his father. And the one in the Hawaiian shirt – that's Jeannie's father! A happy time. Who could have known? What can I say, except that I am ready to answer any question you wish to ask? Though perhaps this won't be necessary. Perhaps, just by seeing our happy photograph, you can imagine the rest? Isn't that your *modus operandi*? Blurring the line between the real and the imagined, to plumb the truths of the heart?"

"How much do you know about me?"

"A lot more than Jeannie Wakefield. On that note, I'll leave you to it."

After he left, I closed my eyes, and for five minutes, I let nothing into my mind but the sensation of my own breathing. Then I opened my eyes and I could hear the diggers outside again. I opened the filing cabinet under the long desk. It did not look as if it had been disturbed, or even discreetly searched. But on the shelf where I remembered seeing Sinan's trophies was a collection of black and red hardbacked notebooks. These turned out to be an incomplete selection of Jeannie's diaries. They were not in chronological order. The first, written in a neat, small hand, was dated 1981. The next was dated 1970, and the handwriting was so childish I thought for a moment that it was someone else's. The last was dated 2005, and the script was so full of hooks and jabs that I could barely read it. When I tried to put it back on the shelf, an envelope fell out. When I opened the envelope, I found three ziplock bags, two containing locks of golden hair — her son's? — and one containing a tangle that looked like it was from a hairbrush.

Next to the laptop I had failed to connect to the Internet was a half drunk cup of coffee, a pen, a used tissue, an open diary, and a pair of glasses. Running my eyes along the bottom of the screen, I saw a bar indicating the document Jeannie must have minimized, just before she fled the house. Microsoft Word — LET. I clicked on the tab and the following words flashed before me:

"I saw the truth last night. My friend — there is no other way to put it. I walked away from the screen and looked up at the sky and there it was, scrawled across the stars — the story he never told me. I can see it all now. I can see the shape of my life as clearly as if I were standing outside it.

And I have to ask. Did Suna know all along, or did she guess? She was the one who lured me here, after all, and I am marveling now at the lightness of her tone.

Oh, and by the way, she said. There was a new site I might like to visit. I could get there by going to the US State Department and following the links. Quite a cache: tens of thousands of declassified documents, all in their original form. Anything I'd ever want to know about Chile in 1973 and Guatemala circa 1976. She didn't mention Turkey and neither did the site, but there was something in her choice of words that gave me pause, and that must be why I started typing in my father's name.

I had no idea where I was going, but it was only a matter of time before I would arrive at this terrible place I see before me. I can no longer remember how I got here: I clicked on search, the screen went dark for a minute, and there it was.

At first I could hardly believe what my eyes were telling me. I could barely breathe. Bed was out of the question. So I went out to the porch, watched the cars and buses rolling across the bridge, the dark tankers sliding under it. And in no particular order I thought of all the clues I'd disregarded, all the signs winking along the track. There was a moment when they almost got the better of me. But now the light is coming back into the sky and my strength is returning and I know at last what I've been put here to do. And how, dear friend, you can help me."

I looked up at the bar at the top of the screen: Microsoft Word: LETTER TO M 31.10.05. I was the dear friend. I glanced at my watch – she'd written those lines on the same day she'd sent me that last email. I looked down at the bottom of the screen to see how many pages there were in the document. Fifty-three. If İsmet Şen had not been sitting downstairs – if my pride had not dictated that he was never to know how much I dreaded the fifty-two pages still awaiting me – I would, I'm sure, have fled right then. Instead I calmed myself. I would find out the truth. And then I would do what I – not he – wanted with it. Having steadied my breathing, I sat down and read on. I do not know how long this took, and neither can I recall what was going through my head as I scrolled down and down the endless page. When I was done, I felt cold, and light-headed. But I still knew where I had to go – to the shelf, to the diaries.

I did not read them in order – could not have borne reading them in order – though if I had, it would not have mattered. Because there were gaps, so many gaps! I skipped from book to book, catching phrases that caught my curiosity and reading until I could no longer catch my breath. It was late afternoon when I came across the passage that confirmed what I must have feared all along, even as I told myself that strictly speaking, this had nothing to do with me. Well it did now.

I walked to the window, and there it was: the landscape that had once cradled us. The castle, the wooded slope, the rooftops of Rumeli Hisar, the Bosphorus, the parade of tankers, ferries, fishing boats. Lining the Asian shore, the villas and palaces that seemed close enough to touch, and behind them, the rolling hills that I once thought must stretch as far as China. A moving postcard, a world unto itself. I'd never seen it – seen it properly – from this exalted angle, and though it was the most beautiful thing I'd ever seen, it froze my heart.

My eyes moved along the Asian shore – Kandilli, Anadolu Hisar, and under the bridge to Kanlıca – until I'd found the *yalı* I had just been reading about. The sun was setting somewhere in the hills behind me, and the *yalı*'s windows burned yellow in the fading light.

Was it just another rumor, or was there some truth in it? In no particular order, I thought of all the things it might explain.

Then I thought of a few other things.

As a cloud of dread descended over me – as my heart twisted and turned – I reminded myself that I had been led to this window. That I had spent my afternoon on a meticulously furnished stage.

Why, I wondered?

As I reviewed the possible answers, I felt a ghost passing its cold fingers across the nape of my neck.

I stood still, very still, until I had regained my composure.

Then I turned back to the room, made a quick (and, as it turned out, inadequate) inventory of the things I knew Jeannie would be praying for me to keep safe from prying and destroying eyes.

I headed for the stairs, my handbag clamped under my arm. But there was no sign of İsmet Şen downstairs. On the table next to the chaise longue I found my cell phone and, slipped underneath it, İsmet's business card, and – bizarrely, grotesquely – a special offer from Şenlik, his telecommunications company.

The diggers had left, and the hole they had been digging had been filled back in. There was no van in front of the gate, and no black sedan, either. I walked towards my parents' house, my heart racing, my knees almost giving way. But there was no point in running. I had escaped the house, but not the truth. When I reached the white walk, I looked up towards the flight of stairs at the far end and saw a dishevelled woman racing towards me with arms outstretched. It was Suna. She was crying, "Oh thank God! Thank God you are here!" Before I knew it, she had locked me into a tearful embrace that almost stopped me breathing. As I stood there, patting her back, I at last saw the shape of the trap closing in on me. And what I believed, in my innocence, to be the only way out.

6

A S SOME OF YOU will already know, they gave me the front of the *Review* section that Sunday, plus the better part of page two. This was at least four times the space to which I was accustomed, but it still felt as if I had been asked to fit this story on a postage stamp. I wrote it on the third day of my stay in Istanbul, which meant that I had no time to check facts or pursue the strong suspicion that had kept me awake most of the night. There was also the matter of Jordan Frick, for as he himself had warned me, Jeannie's view of him was radically different from my own, and (to me) deeply troubling. But I remembered, too, what Jordan had said to me. Jeannie was in trouble, and my first job was to help her through it.

"The best way to make a lie come true," (I wrote) "is to repeat it ad infinitum; if we have come in recent years to believe in a 'war between the civilizations,' it is because we are ruled by liars who tell us it is so. In fact, there is no neat dividing line between East and West: in Europe alone, there are fifteen million Muslims. In Turkey, so often described as the 'gateway to the Islamic world,' there has been a secular, westward-looking state since 1923. But so great is our desire to divide the world into warring halves that we refuse to consider any fact, or indeed any historical reality, that threatens to blur the picture.

At the same time, we are fascinated by the lonely few whose very existence defies our reductive impulses. The Turkish filmmaker Yankı is one such enigma. This is an alias — his real name is Sinan Sinanoğlu. But his pseudonym reflects his hybrid roots and mixed allegiances. For in Turkish, 'Yankı' means 'echo.' while also echoing another word more familiar to us. Born in 1950 in Washington DC to Turkish diplomat parents, Sinan Sinanoğlu is a dual national. He was educated in both his countries, and while in Turkey, he attended an American-owned lycée that has been educating Istanbul's elites since 1863. The very existence of this school ought to be enough to demonstrate that the links between Turkey and the US are long and old and very tangled. But to accept such a claim you must have a map on which to place it. You must have some sense, at least, of how the US has conducted its many and varied adventures outside its borders across two centuries. The sad fact is that even those of us who were brought up and caught up in this saga have only the sketchiest acquaintance with it. We know about the World Wars and the Cold War, Vietnam and Iraq. We know of the millions of Americans who served in these wars, but we know next to nothing of the peace-time armies of teachers, missionaries, entrepreneurs, engineers, diplomats, community organizers and agricultural consultants whose contributions, be they laudable or suspect, had a far deeper effect on the countries that invited them in.

But as Sinan himself might say, art feeds on the shadows. If there is a single wish behind the thirteen films he has made over the past decade, it is his determination to bring this hidden world into the light. It is, perhaps, a testament to the power of his art that he now finds himself wasting away in a US prison, falsely accused of terrorist links.

This, then, is the story of a witch hunt — a witch hunt so peculiarly 'now,' and so tied up with the paranoias of our times, that one is tempted to see it as emblematic. If the Committee on UnAmerican Activities continues to cast its long shadow over our memories of the 1950s, we can be certain that Homeland Security will do the same in the dark chapter we are living through today. Once again, we're obsessed with the enemy within. Once again, we mistrust anyone and anything that fails to conform to pure types. Once again, it is the hybrid who arouses our most sinister suspicions.

So perhaps this is the moment to present my own hybrid credentials. I am the daughter of an American physicist who came to Istanbul in 1960, to teach at the same university where Sinan was later a student. I am personally acquainted with everyone in this story. As a teenager, I briefly counted myself as one of Sinan's friends. I also knew William Wakefield, the father of his present wife. Although she and I did not overlap, we moved in the same circles at the girls' lycée we both attended. We met for the first time late last summer. Until she disappeared, I was helping (or rather, failing to help her) with her husband's case.

The facts of this case are as follows: when Sinan Sinanoğlu flew into JFK with his five-year-old-son late last summer, he was expecting a short delay at

passport control – but he'd been through this ordeal so many times since 9/11
that he was not unduly worried. It was just a question of answering a few ques-
tions honestly, and staying polite . . ."

Here followed an account of Sinan's arrest, and his son's disappearance into the system, and a heavily doctored version of my efforts over
the previous two months to help Jeannie defend Sinan's innocence and
secure Emre's return. I made sure to mention that she, too, was now
missing. Though I did not say why, I did find a way to work the words
"extraordinary" and "rendered" into the sentence.

I made passing references to Turkey's troubled human rights record,
to its curbs on free expression, and of course to the famous author who
was to stand trial later that year for insulting the state. But I did not mention Jordan Frick, and neither did I mention my own troubled histories
with any of the others. Instead I did what was expected of me, seizing
every opportunity to narrow the emotional gap between my subjects and
my readers. Inevitably this involved some air-brushing. When the time
came for me to explain why it was that Sinan had been arrested, and why
his wife had gone missing, I was sorely tempted to name names, to trace
this vicious, senseless vendetta back to what I now believed to be its ori-
gin. But I knew this would be unwise. And (bearing in mind that I had
no proof) unethical. My job today was not to complicate or prevaricate,
but to write clearly and urgently from the heart. There would be plenty
of time for the contradictions and inconsistencies later, when we'd found
Jeannie, when we'd got Sinan out of jail.

So I chose my words carefully, until I thought my head would burst.
My caution made me slow, and I was still a thousand words short when
the newspaper made its first call to ask why I hadn't filed yet. The light
had gone out of the sky by then; my mother had settled herself in her
armchair with her evening cocktail and was tapping her foot in a way
that others might find entirely unremarkable but that I knew was her
way of telling me she was running out of patience. The clock struck
seven and she asked how much longer I'd be. Just to answer her made my
head spin. I could feel great strings of thoughts flying out of it. As I struggled to right myself, an accusing shadow came flying at me through the
fog, and I knew then that I had no choice but to say this one thing. If I
left all my other furies unvoiced, I would have at least set this one free:

"It is tempting to see this as a story of the here and now, as a sinister footnote in the war against terror, an insight, perhaps, into the dirty wars it has spawned throughout the region. An intrepid film-maker who is travelling around the southeast of Turkey, possibly very close to the border with Northern Iraq, happens to stray into an arena that certain powerful parties do not wish to be photographed. An arena, perhaps, that would make Abu Ghraib look like a nativity play. This could well be so, and if so, could soon be proven. Sinan's loyal associates have already unearthed incriminating footage, and as their hunt continues, they are sure to find more.

But to see what I have related here as the first chapter in a yet to unfold story — to ignore the history — is to miss the point. Above all, it is to misunderstand what it means to live in a country ruled by never-named outside interests, where thought is still a crime, where truth-telling has long been a prisonable — and life-threatening — offense. Where the most dangerous thing that any journalist can ever do is to suggest out loud what all Turks acknowledge in whispers — that this is a democracy in name only. That it is ruled by a network of faceless entities known as the 'deep state.'

The thing to know about Sinan Sinanoğlu — and the same holds for most of his friends, and indeed, his entire generation — is that he has never controlled his own destiny. All his life, he has been fought over, manipulated, lied about, jealously guarded, framed. All his life, he has been feared — for the very thing that has landed him in prison. He is feared because of the very power he's never been allowed to exercise — the power that comes from being conversant with more than one system of thought, from being able to travel between and draw from cultures that pretend to be in opposition to each other. To those who have seen fit to incarcerate him, Sinan Sinanoğlu bears all the tell-tale signs of a double agent. Such a pity, then, that no one's thought to look more closely at the three or four men most likely to have had a hand in his entrapment.

At least two of them were, by their own admission, working for intelligence networks in Turkey in 1971, when parties unknown had Sinan and several others framed for a murder that was later established never to have happened. By the time the truth came out, two of those falsely accused young innocents had spent a decade each in hiding and three had served time in prison. One nearly died after jumping out of a fourth floor window during what has been euphemistically described as an 'interrogation.' Though all were fortunate enough to return to fruitful and reasonably peaceful lives, all have done so more quietly than they might have done had they not endured those years of torture and terror.

All, that is, except for Sinan Sinanoğlu, who with each new film has asked bolder questions. And never has he been so bold as in My Cold War, when he turned his camera on his own childhood.

As his case continues, we should, of course, devote our first efforts to his prompt release. But we should also be looking at the would-be fathers who have always hovered over him. Why is his silence so important to them? As Cicero might have put it, cui bono?"

I filed these words on a Friday evening. They came out in England that Sunday, at which point anyone who might have wanted to read them in Turkey (or anywhere else in the world, for that matter) could have done so on the net. That Monday, my piece appeared in translation in three Turkish newspapers. It appeared in three more on Tuesday, and on the same day there was quite rabid coverage of the case and my take on it in various columns. Some went so far as to denounce Sinan as a traitor and Jeannie as a missionary who had come to Turkey to "complete the dream first hatched in the Treaty of Sèvres, namely to destroy the Turkish nation and parcel it out to the powers of the West." I was denounced as a fifth columnist, a meddling human rights campaigner, and an *agent provocateur*. And how dare I suggest there was such a thing as a deep state? None of this particularly concerned me, nor did it seem to concern Suna when we met to discuss them (though she told me I'd been an idiot to mention the deep state), and any colleague familiar with the Turkish press will back me up on this, I'm sure. It's routine for Turkish papers to cover stories about Turkey in the Western press, and when they do, the lesser papers routinely twist the original words to suit whatever the editor's agenda happens to be that day. The misleading headlines are not, however, always as ominous as they look. It is understood, even by relatively unsophisticated readers, that the newspapers tell lies: the only way to see through those lies is to divine their authors' "true intentions."

One or two columnists mentioned my father's name, and his place of residence, and this, I think, is what paved the way for the death threats. My father took the first two calls, but because the voices were unfamiliar and the Turkish garbled, he assumed them to be wrong numbers. I took the third call, and I understood every word. But the first time something of this order happens to you, it's hard to know what to do.

How do you hide from someone you can't see? Who can protect you? As we sat around the supper table, these questions were as abstract as they were unanswerable. As my mother said, it was all too preposterous to believe. But in the same breath she said, 'You know, I was expecting something like this.' She did not accuse me directly but she didn't need to. I knew I had been reckless. But it had never occurred to me that I'd be putting anyone at risk but myself. I was sick with horror at my stupidity.

I was due to leave for London the following morning, and now I felt I couldn't do so unless I took my parents with me. This they refused to do. "Our lives are here." When I offered to put off my departure, they gave each other furtive looks that I had no trouble reading. It was my presence that was putting them in danger. "I'm sure it will blow over," my mother said. "So long as you keep quiet. And why shouldn't you? You can rest with an easy conscience. You've done your bit, after all." It was late in the evening by then, but I knew I could not leave it like this, so I rang Suna, who came right over. She made light of the death threats – "Welcome to the club!" she told my father, smiling broadly. "I don't mind telling you, the company is excellent! I myself received no less than four such phone calls, only yesterday! As for a certain colleague of yours . . ." She mentioned a name, and then another. They all laughed, as if it were all a harmless sport. But as she headed for the balcony to smoke a cigarette, she pulled me out with her. "I didn't fool *you*, I hope," she said. I shook my head. As she watched her smoke rise into the chilly night, she said, "I take it your parents are refusing to go with you to London?" I told her she had guessed correctly and she said, "This is a shame. But leave it with me, darling. I shall keep them safe. In Turkey, as you know, we never forget our teachers."

"In the meantime, should my parents call the authorities?" I asked.

"Ah!" she cried in horrified disdain. "Which authorities did you happen to have in mind?"

"The police?"

"The police. Hah. That is very precious."

"Or perhaps the US Consulate. They must keep track of such things. They might have some good advice."

"Yes, and they might also have something to say to you about your article last Sunday. Do you think they were pleased? No," she said. "Leave it to me. Leave it to *us*. We love your parents, probably more than you do. We'll take good care of them." She paused, and then she added, "We're grateful to you, too, you know! In spite of certain slurs . . . but we discussed all this during our long and delicious argument yesterday, so there is no need to fret further. So all I need to add is something by way of a warning. It is clear, from these responses, that you have managed a direct hit. You may just have been guessing, but you were closer to the truth than we could have known. This is good! But be careful. You are sure to be approached. If not on the journey home, then soon afterwards. Watch what you say. Watch your back too. Keep in touch, but be careful, too, about how you say it. Assume there are others listening to our phone calls, and others reading our emails. Anything you say to me, you are saying to everyone. This is my first golden rule for you. And the second is: carry on as normal. Don't let them scare you, and above all, don't let them see you scared."

"I wouldn't dream of it," I said.

"One more thing, then. The most important. Don't forget who your friends are."

"Why would I want to do that?"

"A final request, then. Don't rewrite the past."

7

ON MY FLIGHT HOME I was seated next to a Turk in his thirties who had once played for Arsenal but had to give up soccer due to injury and now ran a dry cleaning business in North London. He had been in Istanbul for his mother's funeral, and he had no special message for me. Neither, it seemed, did anyone else. As I went about London during the week that followed, there were people here and there who mentioned they'd "seen the great piece," but they had nothing else to say about it. By the end of the week, we had already moved to the next stage: "I saw your byline the other day, but I can't for the life of me remember what paper it was, or what you were on about." Which was fine by me.

Because by now I'd worked out why it was that I'd been spirited into the Pasha's Library, and what I'd been meant to make of it.

Or to put it differently, instead of looking where they wanted me to look, I'd glanced over my shoulder.

I'm still not sure how the news of my enlightenment got out.

I'd been home for a week when I got the first email message. The name of the sender was not familiar to me, but the domain was a university in New York State, so I opened it, expecting that it would be a friend of a friend as per usual, or a student needing a favor.

It was only one sentence.

"What do you want from me?"

I paid it no attention. But the next day, I received another.

"You fucking bitch. If you're going to ruin my life, and destroy my family, too, you can at least do me the courtesy of saying what you want from me."

This I tried to ignore, too, though the words stayed with me. I was worried enough to ring my old friend Jordan Frick, who was back from Uzbekistan, and who was worried enough to come over to see the emails for himself. When we checked my messages, there was a third email. This was a very long one, and I shall not quote it here. Suffice it to say that it contained information that only two people in the world know, myself being one of them. Impossible as that may seem. And yes, I am aware that, technically speaking, it is impossible for a man charged with terrorism to gain access to the Internet. But I am assuming that even the Patriot Act makes some space for legal counsel. So perhaps this was the conduit. During the week we were communicating, the gaps between my answers and his replies would indicate that we were being aided and abetted by a messenger.

I am assuming there is no need to reproduce the full correspondence here, Mary Ann, as you've already seen it. Again, let me thank you for seeing the threats as serious. This is a very nasty business, especially now, and I can't tell you how dispiriting it is when your life is in danger and no one in officialdom will take you seriously. You were the first person to do so, and for that I can never thank you enough. The same goes for everyone else at the Center for Democratic Change.

I know we are still of two minds about Jeannie Wakefield – and I can understand why anyone seeing her likeness in that doctored photograph might jump to conclusions.

But you, at least, are prepared to see her as innocent unless proven guilty. It heartens me to know that even today, even in Washington, there are still organizations like the CDC that insist on due process. If we all band together, we can and will see justice done. In the meantime, I would ask for your patience. To say what I have to say, I need time. And a few other luxuries as well.

Which brings me to the email I received a few moments ago from the correspondent who might or might not be Sinan:

"How much do you know?"

My answer: not as much as I'd like. But rest assured: what I don't know, I can imagine.

II
Everyday Life in the Days of the Cold War

8

SHE WAS BORN in Havana, of all places. I'm not sure what her father was up to in Cuba, or what the sign on his door pretended. Whatever it was, Jeannie's mother didn't like it. Within months of the birth, she and the baby were back in Northampton, Massachusetts. Before much longer, Jeannie's father had moved on, too. His next posting was in Caracas. Then he jumped continents and landed in Ankara. After that it was Delhi, Manila and Colombo. Somewhere along the line, he married a second wife and divorced her. The wife he brought with him to Istanbul in 1966 was his third. By 1970, she, too, had moved on – to Washington, DC, to pursue a law degree. The story on the grapevine (and I remember people being quite shocked by this at the time) was that William Wakefield was paying her tuition.

So he wasn't your standard chauvinist. He had his own ideas about what a man should do, and what a father should aim for. I know he regretted not knowing his daughter because once, at a party at my parents', after he'd had far too much to drink, he'd told me so, in what seemed to me then to be excruciating detail. Though he was sure Jeannie's mother was giving her "the finest of American upbringings" – there was 'a world out there' and it pained him to think that his daughter had never had a chance to see it.

But one day . . . This was the message, implied or explicit, in every postcard he wrote to her. Would he have been surprised to know she'd pinned 971 of them to her bedroom walls? Hyderabad, Luxor and Petra. Montevideo, Anchorage, and Hong Kong. Harbors, mountains and sky-lines. Statues, mausoleums and ships. Each of them a testament to the bigger, better world her father was waiting to show her. The idea to spend a year with him in Istanbul had been hers, not his.

Her mother had of course balked at the idea. Istanbul was too far away, and far too dangerous – though a bachelor pad anywhere else in the world would have been just as bad. Her main fear (well-founded, as it turned out) was that Jeannie would be left to fend for herself. This was a man who let "nothing and no one come between him and his job." However, she seems not to have known what his job really was. Had she so much as guessed the truth, she most certainly would have used it as her trump card.

Instead it was Radcliffe that had the final say. They'd offered her a place, and instead of doing what most people did, and grabbing the chance before it disappeared, Jeannie had written to them to remind them that she was only sixteen, and would she not derive greater riches from her college career if she deferred for a year? She told them about her father, and her longing to see the world that had been kept from her for so long. She wrote about reading Gibbon, and the real Richard Burton. Gertrude Bell, Rose Macaulay and Freya Stark. There was not a waking hour, she said, when she did not ask herself how long it would be before she saw the enigmas of Near Eastern Culture at first hand. In so saying, she established herself as just the sort of student Radcliffe dreamed of serving. They wrote straight back to Jeannie saying that they were more than happy to back her plan. Their only stipulation was that (while she was in Istanbul, at least, and in addition to the journal she had already promised) she committed herself to some sort of formal study.

Six weeks later, she said goodbye to her distraught mother at JFK Airport and boarded the PamAm flight for Istanbul. She began her jour-nal in what only an adolescent could call a spirit of forgiveness ("it is easy to be charitable to one's mother when one is looking down on her from a distance of 30,000 feet.").

Her next entry, dated June 16th, begins in the same lofty tones:

"I am glad now I had to wait so long. Glad I had a chance to read the history, and absorb it – make it real, at least in my head. For when we turned up that narrow, cobblestone lane that would take us along the great walls of Rumeli Hisar, and I set eyes on that first crenalated tower, I felt myself inside Gibbon's prose. I know this sounds ridiculous, but I could see the Ottoman armies pouring over those walls, I could hear their battlecries as they thundered off to take the flower of the Eastern Roman Empire from the Greeks, its previous owners. I was so in the thick of it that I was literally beginning to hyperventilate. And then, when Father took me into the garden of his house to show me his view – when I stood here on this great glass porch, gazing with wild surmise at the distant and inscrutable twists and turns of the Bosphorus, I felt History itself rolling over me. I understood, for the first time, the meaning of the word "awe" . . ."

Here she stopped, knowing every gushing word to be a lie.

9

WHO AM I WRITING FOR? This is what she later recalled asking herself. Though she knew the answer: she was writing for the seasoned and urbane woman she hoped to become. In truth it was even worse than that. Even more twisted and duplicitous. She was putting down the story of her first fortnight in Istanbul as she wanted to remember it. As she wished she had lived it. As she would pretend she had, forever more.

Looking up from her narrow desk to gaze at her lying reflection in the window, set against the iron grilles, she examined The Nose, and then The Left Nostril: it had grown. She shut her notebook, which stared back at her importantly. As if to say, a notebook of my caliber – or have you forgotten I am made of the finest leather? – should be treated with respect. She was ready to surrender to its superior wisdom – give up, go downstairs, call a friend, perhaps, or watch television – but of course, she couldn't; she was not in Northampton but half a world away, locked away in a tower, with only her faltering imagination to keep her company – or that's how it felt in the dark of night, when all she could hear was the trembling of a passing ship and the howls of the dogs in the hills.

A noise downstairs. A cross between a screech and a crash. A chair. He must have knocked it over. Her chest tightened, as she listened to her father swear. And now a hard, sharp knock, which took her longer to decipher – her father hitting the ice tray against the counter? Then silence, and footsteps, stopping at the foot of the stairs. She held her breath, but then there was the creak of the door into the library. She let herself exhale.

She opened to the first page: "The Journal of Jeannie Wakefield On Her First Venture into the Near East, June 1970 – ." Such poppycock! Such pretension! You'd think, from her verbiage, that she'd already come and gone. But she'd only been here for a fortnight, and already she wanted to leave. If she were to write the truth, it would go like this:

"It was my idea to come here – my idea, even if it's true what Mother said, even if it was Father who planted it and fed it with every postcard he ever sent me. It was my idea, and I had to fight long and hard to make it happen. But now here I am, standing at the end of the longest limb in the world, in a house that smells like oatmeal. And last night . . ."

But she couldn't bear to think of last night. Her heart churned at the very prospect. She opened the notebook, returned to her task, and as she described the great monuments she'd visited since her arrival, and the splendid vistas on which her eyes had feasted, she was again grateful for the calm and the courage this pretense brought her.

Soon she had mentioned every mosque, cistern and bridge. Rereading her account so far, she saw it for what it was – a droning catalogue of inanimate objects. She rushed to correct the oversight:

"But enough about us. My next task is to give some sense of the city as a living, breathing entity. You'd think I hadn't met a soul, when actually, I've been doing a fair amount of mixing! We had a lovely evening on the Hiawatha (the consular yacht) on Wednesday, with a group of Dad's colleagues, and the night after that we went up the road to meet Dad's girlfriend, which is a strange word to use for a woman in her forties. But she is, in fact, a lovely person. She did everything in her power to make me feel at home.

Chloe, her daughter, was somewhat less forthcoming, though we seemed to have forged an alliance of sorts. Because yesterday . . ."

Ye Gods! Just to write that word sapped the last of her courage. But she could not give up now. She had started; she'd persevere to the end, and perhaps, when she got there, she would have succeeded in making some sense of this.

> *"…yesterday, Chloe introduced me to two boys she's friendly with. We ended up spending the whole day together – and a pretty big chunk of the night, too. It was, for me at least, an emotional rollercoaster. We didn't just have a car at our disposal, but a speedboat! Most of the time, I literally had no idea where I was, and I think I must be the sort of person who needs to know this. But all in all, I am glad to have had the chance to explore the strange world these boys inhabit; if nothing else, it offered a fascinating insight into the lives and mores of Turkish youth. Though I have to admit say that the process of getting to know an alien culture is a lot less straightforward than I originally assumed. I am loath to add to my already burgeoning list of questions . . ."*

And she mustn't. Mustn't! The burgeoning list at the back of her note-book was for important questions. Questions about History and Monuments. Things she'd need to know for college. While the questions she was loath to add to her burgeoning list were petty, and personal, and sometimes even unkind. Like: why did Turkish teenagers think it was so amazing to own a six-year-old Mustang? And why, once they owned them, did they drive them like maniacs? Why, when they'd just almost killed you, did they turn around and wink? Why did they laugh when it really wasn't funny, and why, when they'd said something that she had to hope was a joke, did they not even crack a smile? And why, when they'd given you every indication that . . .

> *". . . enough of this nonsense. There can be no substitute for the simple facts, which are as follows. Yesterday morning . . ."*

Yesterday morning, she had gone downstairs to find her father sit-ting in the library with two strangers. One was a sharp dresser with bland, attentive eyes, whom her father introduced as "İsmet, my oppo-site number." The other was a lank American who, she guessed, was not long out of college. He had a chiseled face punctuated by eyes set too deep for her to see their color. His close-cropped hair ended a good inch before his tan began, and gave him the air of a shorn sheep. He was hunched over her father's radio, fiddling with the knobs, but when he saw her, his eyebrows shot up, almost of their own accord.

"What's with the protocol?" he asked. "Don't I get introduced, too?"

"Now that I think of it, no," her father said.

"Have it yor way," said the young American. He stuck out his hand. "Pleased to meet you. Call me No Name. And your name is?"

"Don't give him an inch," said her father.

"Thanks," said No Name.

"My pleasure," said her father, and Jeannie could tell that he meant it. Annoyed (because she did not need such protection), but also ashamed of feeling annoyed, she went off to the kitchen. Her father followed her in to apologize for "springing those goons on you." Something urgent had come up, he explained. "And as usual, yours truly has to deal with it. Typical! You'd think they had something better to do. Don't they ever go to the beach?" By "they" she now knew he did not mean his colleagues at the consulate but Communist insurgents.

"I'm sorry I have to leave you in the lurch like this," he said as he ruffled her hair. Which was, she was sure, a perfectly reasonable thing for a father to do, though there was something not right about it, something cold. It left her wondering if a father was only really a father if you grew up in the same house.

Knowing this to be something he wondered about, too, she gave him her best attempt at a smile, though if she were to be honest, the real thing she was smiling about was the prospect of a morning to herself. "You won't be alone all day, I've made sure of that," her father said, responding with his usual (but still alarming) alacrity to the thought she had not voiced. "My friend Amy is sending that wonderful daughter of hers over to take you out for the afternoon. If she can't show you a good time, then no one can."

"I didn't have high hopes, though. We'd already met and failed to click. She took about five minutes to file me away as 'tedious' and to me, she was a moody, ill-mannered girl with sultry eyes and a fondness for words that should never be allowed out of a dictionary. Which was why, when she turned up after lunch wearing a tiny tie-dye dress and huge round sunglasses and a killer pout, I just said, 'Listen, we don't have to do this.'

'Okay then,' she said. 'That's sort of how I feel, too.' But then she said, 'I love this view.' Then she lost herself inside it, as people do. When she came back to herself, she lit up a Marlboro in a stiff, ceremonial way that betrayed her newness to the ritual. Then she laid out the options.

There was the Covered Bazaar. But it would be a hot and dusty trip and 'deadly dull, because my mother wouldn't give me any money.' There were the Prince's Islands, 'but the trip out there will be long and agonizing and even if you wear those jeans you'll get harassed.' The third option was a beach on the Black Sea, but there was a strong undertow and the lifeguards were hopeless. 'Or I could take you to meet some boys I know.' Her pout faltered at that point, so I said, 'Tell me more about these boys.'

'They're just boys.' Then she added, 'They're fun.'

'Turkish?'

'Yes,' she said. 'But their English is better than yours. Well sort of, I mean one of them. And even the other one has read Chaucer in the original and you probably haven't.' "

That, for some reason, had decided it. A quarter of an hour later, they were at Robert College, on the terrace with the postcard view of the Bosphorus. The wall was lined with students sitting with their backs to it, and facing the student dormitory, which was festooned with the same anti-American banners she'd seen in so many other parts of the city, and that her father had been more than happy (too happy?) to translate. But this afternoon, it was too hot to wonder why. The trees gave some shade but the only movement of air came from the tablecloths a group of waiters were shaking as they set up tables for a reception next to the statue of the man she now knew to be Atatürk, the nation's founding father.

She turned her attention to the two boys in the tennis court.

"If I'm going to be absolutely honest, the one I noticed the first was the one everyone must notice first, because he looked like he had walked off the cover of Sports Illustrated. Bronze-limbed and golden-curled – an Apollo in his tennis whites! He had an easy smile and no inclination to hurry and if he missed a shot, he just burst out laughing.

His friend was thinner and darker and more intense. He'd made no concessions to the tennis god. He was wearing a black Grateful Dead T-shirt and paint-splashed cut-off jeans, and he moved like a cat. "

He had short, black hair that was just beginning to curl its way out of a regulation haircut, and large, dark eyes, and a sunny smile that had a note of defiance in it. When a ball went over the fence, and he came out to hunt in the bushes, Jeannie noticed a bead of water rolling down his face. When he saw Jeannie noticing him, he stopped short and, for a few moments, stared back. Sulkily, expectantly – as if they had history. Was he waiting for her to smile and wave? Before she could decide, he stood up and walked away.

"I'm still not sure what game he was playing at that point. Or Chloe. Or Apollo, whose name turned out to be Haluk. Only that there was a great deal of hemming and hawing, with everyone wandering around pretending they didn't recognize anyone, until suddenly they were throwing their tennis rackets into the back of a not very new Mustang (though apparently it is quite a coup to be the owner of a not very new Mustang in this inscrutable country) and before I knew it, we were in the Mustang, too, myself in the backseat next to the dark boy who introduced himself as "John Reed, the author of The Shot That Was Heard around the World*" and had the nerve to expect me to believe him. What does he take me for, an ignoramus?*

His real name is Sinan."

10

THIS HE'D REVEALED some time later, after several brushes with death, when they were illegally parked in front of the Bebek police station, overlooked by a soldier who was cradling a rusty submachine gun in his arms. (No one else had found this at all alarming, or even strange.) Haluk and Chloe (who seemed to be an item, though their conspiratorial manner suggested this was somehow controversial) had gone off on some undisclosed errand, and Jeannie had taken advantage of the lull to ask this sulky cat-boy a few key questions. To which Sinan's answers were: no, they hadn't ever met before, though he'd heard a lot about her from her father. And yes, her father knew his father, who was currently the Ambassador to Pakistan. What's more, her father knew his mother, who was currently trying to revive her singing career in Paris. "And while we're on the subject, my name isn't really John Reed."

"Actually, I sort of worked that out already," Jeannie said. "So Sinan," she added, when he had told her his real name. "It sounds like you're all alone here."

That was how it had all started. Though (as seemed to be the custom in the baiting game) he'd begun with the truth. "Alone? You are sadly, very sadly mistaken. There is the maid, always the maid breathing over me. And my father's sister. And about a million other relatives. Right now,

I'm mostly at Haluk's. I don't know if Chloe mentioned this, but we're cousins."

"It all sounds very cozy," Jeannie said.

Sinan snorted. "Cozy. That's good."

"Why?" she asked.

"You want the truth? Okay, then. I'll tell you. Haluk's father – my uncle – is a gangster."

"Seriously?"

"Seriously. Strictly speaking, he's an arms dealer, and let me tell you. You don't want an arms dealer making sure you do your home-work." Sighing for effect, he'd added, "We can't do anything with-out his knowing. Not even if he's out of the country, like he is today. Let me put it this way. In the vast prison that is Turkey, his reach is infinite."

"That's quite an indictment," Jeannie had said, but in a way that made it clear she was not buying it.

His eyes darkened. "We try to make the best of it, of course. But right now we're under house arrest, and I mean literally. You see, we failed an exam – the same exam – and so summer was cancelled. We're supposed to be studying. Haluk's grandparents are supposed to be our jailers. They let us out because they feel sorry for us, but if Haluk's father finds out, he'll kill them. And he will. He has spies everywhere. We can't even have an ice cream without him hearing about it."

Losing her patience now, she'd asked, "Why are you telling me all this?"

"Because it's true," he'd insisted. "And everyone knows it."

"But that doesn't mean he'd want you blabbing about it, does it?"

"In a country like this, it makes no difference one way or the other."

"Why not?"

"It's accepted. It's just how things are."

"That," Jeannie said, "is what people say when they bow to defeatism." The faintest glitter in his eyes this time. "So you think I am defeatist."

"Not just a defeatist, but a liar."

"You want me to prove it? Okay, then. I will."

So their next stop had been a swimming club called the Lido, where it was immediately clear that there were indeed a lot of people watching their every move. Mothers, anyway. One by one they ambled past to say hello to the two boys, to ask after their parents, to inquire after "these delightful girls," and from time to time, to ask after another girl called Suna. Though the name meant nothing to Jeannie, it did to Chloe, who flicked her head at the very mention of it. When Jeannie asked who Suna was, Sinan explained that she was someone who thought she was going out with Haluk. "Well is she?" Jeannie had then asked. She wasn't. "Then why does she think so?" The answer: "This is Turkey."

Before she could ask for a fuller explanation, they were joined by a dark-haired woman Jeannie guessed to be in her forties. Though she had no sense of her face, just gold and red nail varnish, sunglasses and flashing white teeth, she'd found her gaze unnerving. She could not, of course, understand the tense exchange that ensued – only that she was its object.

Then without warning this woman threw back her head in raucous laughter. Offering her hand to Jeannie, she said, "How rude I've been. Allow me to introduce myself." She turned out to be "Suna's mother."

"I hear you have only just arrived in this country and have yet to acquaint yourself with our strange ways."

So Jeannie had told her, with a sincerity that this woman seemed to find very amusing, that she was doing her best.

"Ah, yes. I'm sure you will continue to do so, too. But I hear from these boys that you refuse to believe a thing they say."

To which Jeannie had replied that they'd been telling her some pretty preposterous things.

"Ah – for example – that Haluk's father is a gangster?"

Yes, that was one thing. "Though I find it hard to believe."

"Why?" asked Suna's mother, leaning forward with a smile.

"Because in America, no one ever admits to that sort of thing. They'd have to lie about it. You know, hide behind a front."

"Where did you find this girl? What a treasure! So innocent! So sweet!"

"I can't say I warmed to the Lido, though I should perhaps describe it. Strictly speaking, it is a swimming club about halfway into the city proper. It has a large saltwater pool that gives the impression of spilling over into the Bosphorus, and

its clientele, I'm told, is very select. However, the ivy-covered hotel overlooking the pool is, I'm told, an infamous rendezvous hotel where businessmen enter-tain their floozies. (Though not, I hope, the ones whose wives belong to the pool.) To add to the bizarre mix, Simon and Garfunkel were on the intercom, extolling 'parsley, sage, rosemary and thyme.' I can't say I was impressed by the Lido's fixtures. The tables and deckchairs were clunky and would not have looked out of place in a bus terminal. But the waiters sparkled white, and the women sparkled gold, and though I couldn't see the eyes behind the dark glasses, I still felt a growing chill.

So I was not at all sorry when we suddenly had to return at breakneck speed to Haluk's house, which is one of those big modern villas on the water, just outside Bebek. It has wall-to-wall picture windows on the side facing the water, and highly polished parquet floors dotted here and there with glass-topped tables and black naugahyde sofas. We went straight out to the seaside terrace; an expanse of white marble ending in a pier where a speedboat named Kitten II bobbed in the waves.

We had only just settled into our deckchairs when the phone rang and Haluk dashed back inside. Sinan explained it was Haluk's father, calling to make sure he was at home studying.

They were still conversing when an owlish couple shuffled into the room. Haluk's grandparents. They were wearing matching grey slippers, and there was fear in their eyes until Haluk told them who I was. It turns out they know my father. Is there anyone here who doesn't?

At this point a maid appeared with a dish of baklava. Although she offered it to everyone, I was the only one to accept. Haluk's grandmother lavished me with praise as I ate her first serving, speaking also of the despair she felt about the others. The problem with the young, she said, was that they were all too thin. It made them ill, and it was illness, she thought, that propelled them into tom-foolery. 'But you, you are different. I can tell from your appetite and the puri-ty of your face.'

She kept pressing more baklava on me, and I ended up eating four por-tions. No one else ate a thing. I was also the only one who made any effort to keep the conversation going."

In the fifty-three page letter she left for me on her computer at the Pasha's Library, Jeannie describes how she stopped at this point, "to steel myself, to prepare to stab myself with the truth. But somehow, when my pen returned to paper it refused to bend to my will, skipping instead to the next section," she said. This, then, is what she'd skipped over: after she had described her plans for the year, and her great and growing interest in Near East Culture, and run out of anything interesting to say, Jeannie had remarked on what a beautiful house this was. To which the grandmother replied, "You are very kind. Yes, we are fortunate. The Bosphorus breathes life into our souls." She'd then asked if she and her husband lived there alone. "Or does your son – Haluk's father, I mean – live here, too?"

"It depends on his travels and responsibilities," the grandmother had replied.

To which Jeannie had said, "I hear he's a gangster." At which the grandfather stopped chewing. The grandmother let out a tiny cry. Chloe let out the faintest of guffaws and the boys stayed hunched over their plates. "Sinan!" the grandfather cried in a great rumbling voice. There followed a furious interrogation. By the end of it, Sinan's tan had turned deep red. And then it was Haluk's turn. Then the grandmother turned back to Jeannie and said, "Oh, what is to become of us? Oh, this dreadful malnutrition!"

"The hunger has gone to their heads!" she cried. "This is why they have fed you such lies about Haluk's father!" And that was not all. For according to Haluk's grandmother, it was hunger that had made "our boys" fail their Turkish History exam. It was hunger that had made Haluk answer a question about the founding of the Republic in "nonsensical verse." Sinan had been even hungrier, she said: he had answered in Chinese ideograms, copied, as Sinan himself later confessed, from a book "penned by none other than that nonsensical ingrate, Chairman Mao. This is clearly a case of sugar deficiency," she told Jeannie. It also explained why, when his Turkish History teacher had called on him to recite the passage they'd been instructed to learn by heart, Sinan had "made a mockery of the motherland" by choosing instead to recite a passage from the Koran.

To which Sinan said, "Actually, I was making a mockery of rote learning."

At which the grandmother turned to Jeannie and said, "Have you learned what is the Turkish word is for youth? It is "*delikanlı*," and the true translation is "crazy blood." I fear that the blood of these two boys is very crazy."

With that, she and her husband shuffled off to take a nap. After a few moments of silence, Sinan put his hands on his head and let out such a wail you'd think someone had died. But no, he was laughing. Both he and Haluk were laughing so hard they were in pain. They got up and threw their arms around each other. They staggered apart and held their stomachs and doubled over and embraced each other again, and then, with tears in his eyes, Sinan came over, took Jeannie's head in his hands and kissed her forehead. "Thank you, thank you."

"Thank you for what?" she said. This sent them back into hysterics. "What?" I said. "Everyone knows he's a gangster except for his own parents?"

"For God's sake," said Chloe. "Don't you get it? They set you up."

"I'm sorry, I'm so sorry," said Sinan.

"So am I!" Jeannie said, fighting tears. "You shouldn't do that, you know!"

At which Chloe told the boys they'd "both been asinine."

"Asinine?" said Haluk. "Please, madame, can you define your fine words?"

"I'd rather eat my hat," Chloe said. Turning to Jeannie, she added, "Listen, if you've had enough of this, we can go home."

But the boys fell to their knees and apologized, promised to stop playing stupid games, promised the girls that if they stayed, they'd take them out for the evening on Kitten II. "I thought you were under house arrest," Jeannie said.

"Yes, but if we work hard . . ."

"You're *not* working hard, though. You're goofing off."

They liked this expression and repeated it and laughed.

"Why's it called Kitten II, anyway?"

"If I told you," said Sinan, "you wouldn't believe me."

They told her anyway, and she did.

But how could she have done otherwise? Everything here seemed equally strange, so equally plausible. Was it not plausible that a speedboat named Kitten II might be a descendant of another speedboat named Kitten I? You couldn't just disbelieve every word someone uttered. Why would anyone who didn't have an older brother want to pretend, just for the sake of it, that he had?

What they'd told her (taking care to do so out of Chloe's hearing) was that Haluk's older brother had been out gallivanting in Bebek Bay one afternoon when he'd seen a group of men in dark glasses board the powerboat that the CIA kept in Bebek Bay to follow and photograph any interesting Soviet ship that happened to pass by. Upon seeing him, the boys had claimed (their eyes narrowing as they spoke), the spy boat had given chase, and in his panic Haluk's brother had steered into the path of the Soviet vessel, and "crashed to his death." Chloe had seen it happen, Sinan and Haluk told Jeannie in whispers. She still had nightmares about it, which is why they never mentioned it in her presence. Haluk, meanwhile, was being groomed to take his lost brother's place and join the gangsterhood. In Jeannie's fifty-three-page letter to me, she recalled feeling "obliged" to believe them "though of course Sinan did have to take me down to the jetty by the mosque to prove to me that there was indeed a powerboat moored there that met with his description. Once I'd seen it, it seemed very important to share his sorrow. Once I'd done that, I was halfway to what I would now call falling in love."

By six that afternoon, the boys had abandoned their books for a game of ping-pong. It could hardly be called a game, as their balls landed in the sea more often than on the table. Every time one of them lost a ball, the other would turn to him and say, "You shouldn't do that, you know!" – imitating Jeannie's voice. But she could only admire them for laughing at all, for they'd stared death in the face. The only time Jeannie had ever stared death in the face was when she had buried her pet goldfish. She watched Haluk daydreaming at the water's edge and all she could think was, no; he really doesn't have the makings of a gangster, does he? She watched Sinan laugh as he dispatched his last ping-pong ball to the sea, and how she marvelled at his spirit. To stand and laugh, in the very place where he had seen his doomed cousin speed off to his death…she'd never have that strength, and now, as she watched Sinan put his fingers through the damp curls clinging to the base of his neck, she again shared his sorrow. The tragedy had left no mark. But she could see it now, lurking under every surface.

Perhaps (she thought later, as she sat in her lonely bedroom, staring at the reflection of the Left Nostril) perhaps she had seen the tragedy lurking under every surface because she'd wanted to see it. Perhaps because *she had reached the point where she had no idea how to judge anything she saw.* But there was something else going on here. If she were to be totally honest, she'd stayed on because when her eyes met Sinan's, she'd thought . . . She'd seen – what? A promise, or a mirage?

She didn't know her own mind any more. That's what it had come to. But perhaps, if she retraced the road to her final humiliation, she'd find her way back. But she had to be vigilant. She had to guard against the strategic omission of details that didn't fit into the picture she so desperately desired.

So the facts were these: she'd had a happy afternoon, sitting there, fooled and foolish in her lounge chair, waiting for her future to unfold.

"I was bewitched, I'm sure, by the slow unfurling splendor of the evening, as the harsh heat of the afternoon dissolved into a golden light, and the sea turned from turquoise to azure to pink and silver. The ferries hissed as they slipped past the pier, the glass windows vibrated with every passing tanker, and the speedboat rocked back and forth, back and forth in the waves every ship and boat, large and small, left in its wake. A breeze started up, bringing with it the smell of fish and roasting corn and chestnuts. The windows of the houses on the Asian shore turned gold with the setting sun.

As the sun disappeared behind the house, and the grandparents returned to the terrace, their stilted ceremonial English soon gave way to the mellifluous Turkish of the boys.

In the middle of all this, the phone rang again. 'Ah, and not a moment too soon,' said the grandmother, as Haluk rushed inside. His grandfather soon followed. 'Well, my boy' he said when they came out again. 'It seems you have won.' Minutes later, we were waving the grandparents goodbye as we sped off on Kitten II."

And if she were to tell the truth, she'd have to admit she'd suffered not one moment of hesitation. It was only now she had to ask herself why these overprotective grandparents had no qualms about their speeding off in the exact replica of a boat that had killed Haluk's brother – or why she hadn't either. Though she didn't dare say the word. Speak of love and be struck dead, for all to laugh around her grave!

Where had they gone? Later, when her father had asked her, she'd had to admit she had no idea. The first discotheque was almost certainly on the Asian side, and the next had definitely been in Europe, on the

Marmara, somewhere near the airport. Both were the brainchildren of the same deranged decorator. Lots of plastic garden furniture and shrubs decorated with fairy lights. Light fixtures that looked like toadstools, dance floors the size of serving trays. Tom Jones and Creedence Clearwater Revival. Jose Feliciano and Petula Clark and Adamo. Jane Birkin singing "Je T'Aime" with Serge Gainsbourg. Serge Gainsbourg and Brigitte Bardot singing "Bonny and Clyde." In the first club, they were the only ones there who weren't waiters. In the second, Jeannie was the only one in jeans. All the Turkish women were wearing things that suggested pricetags in the thousands, with elaborate hairstyles and jewelry to match.

When Haluk led Chloe off to dance, and Sinan asked Jeannie if she'd like to dance, too, she said, "Listen, if you don't mind, I'll hide here in the shadows."

"Don't be so self-conscious," he said, "There's no point, anyway. They've already seen you. And now they're talking about you, too."

"Because I'm wearing jeans?"

"Yes, this is terrible," he said, propping his elbows on the table and leaning forward to stare into her eyes. Darkly. Dangerously. What could he be thinking? "I've promised myself not to tease you any more, because if you fall for one more joke you'll break my heart. So I'll tell you the truth. I hate this place. I hate the way they look at you. Do you know why they look at you like that? It's not just because you're tall, and blonde, and American." His eyes were shimmering like two black wells now. His voice was beginning to race. "It's because you're with me. This is very interesting to them because they all know who I am and how bad. And worst of all, they can see I've fallen in love."

She could feel his sigh, piercing right into her. "You have?"

"Of course I have," he said. There was a trace of impatience in his voice, as if she'd asked, are you wearing shoes? "Of course I'm madly in love with you. I'd be stupid not to be." Reaching across the table, taking her hand, he looked straight into her eyes again. She couldn't hold his gaze.

"I'm sorry," she'd said. Squeaked. "No one's ever said anything like this to me before." She had not added that no boy she knew would ever dare be so forward. The closest she'd ever got was, "Your hands are warm . . ." during the last slow dance and (at the senior prom), "Your hair is your crowning glory."

When she found the courage to look up again, she caught the tail end of a smile. "Is this another one of your jokes?"

He shook his head. He bit his lip, squeezed her hand, and if she were to tell the truth, she caved in a little more. "Don't you like me at all?" he asked. "Not even a tiny bit?"

She thought she did, but she wasn't sure (*wasn't sure!*) it was a good idea to say so. He squeezed her hand again, and then, after glancing quickly over his shoulder, he winced. "Here we go," he said.

"We'd been sitting at this discotheque for some time, not dancing, just chatting at a table in the corner, when I saw two girls crossing the dance floor. When they arrived at our table, at first they just stood there.

But then the taller of the two prodded Sinan on the back. He jumped to his feet. 'What a surprise!' he said breathlessly. 'I had no idea you were here! Jeannie, this is Lüset,' he said, gesturing at the smaller of the two, a neat, slender creature with long brown hair, large black eyes and china-white skin. 'Lüset, this is Jeannie. And Jeannie, this is . . .' His voice trailed away.

The taller girl had smouldering blue eyes and a fine aquiline nose with distended nostrils; her hair was pulled back, leaving two long black ringlets that shook as she settled herself into a chair.

Sinan cleared his throat. 'Jeannie, this is Suna.'

'So pleased to make your acquaintance,' Suna said. She jerked her chair over the gravel. 'Yes, my name is Suna, and I am so, so, very, very pleased to make the acquaintance of yet another half-witted stewardess.'

In an even voice, Sinan corrected her. 'Actually, she's not a stewardess.'

'Oh?' said Suna, as she removed a cigarette from her beaded purse. Sinan reached over to light it. She gazed into the night as she inhaled. As she exhaled, she flashed me a poisonous smile and asked, 'So, then. What is it that you are intending to do in our country? Work as a go-go girl? I was hearing of just such a vacancy at Hidromel.'

'As it happens,' said Sinan evenly, 'Jeannie is here only to study. And to visit to her father. He works at the US Consulate.'

'The US Consulate. Hah! How fitting!' Suna knocked her cigarette sharply against the ashtray. 'In all honesty, I cannot for the life of me understand why I didn't guess this ironic travesty in the first place.'

Lüset put her hand on Suna's arm and said something supplicating in Turkish. Suna waved her away. 'So!' she said, turning back to me. 'Let us become acquainted. How old are you? Where do you live? What are your plans and aspirations? I want to know all this and so much more. But first things first. My dear boy, can you give me the whereabouts of Haluk, our fair-weather friend?'

Sinan waved his arm in the direction of the dance floor.

'Yes, you are right, I see him now. And who is that on his arm?' Suna asked, leaning forward. 'Ah!' she said. Inhaling furiously.

I decided to take matters into my own hands. 'I take it you and Chloe know each other?'

'We attend the same school,' Suna said.

'And is Haluk really your boyfriend?'

'Haluk is my friend, yes, but he can do as he likes. As indeed I can. If I like, I can throw him into the sea. The fact of the matter is that neither of us believes that love can be discussed in terms of private property. What we have between us exists on a higher plane.'

This provoked a groan from Lüset. There followed an altercation in Turkish. Sinan joined in, and after a lot of shouting and gesticulating, Suna rearranged herself into a pose of calmness. Turning back to me, she said, 'I am sorry for my temper. I hope you will permit me to move on to more civilized subjects. Allow me now to pull a rabbit out of the hat. Yes, tell me. Tell me first and foremost how you justify your country. Let us begin with the hegemonic rationalizations of the army that is as we are speaking invading the virgin soils of North Vietnam.'

'I wouldn't dream of justifying them,' I said. 'I happen to think the war is wrong!'

'You think the war is wrong,' she said, sucking in the smoke so hard I thought she might swallow the cigarette. 'Well, that is very interesting. What an exceptional mind you must have, to grow up in the fountainhead of imperialist ideology and still to know this war is wrong!'

'I'm hardly the only one. I'm one of millions!'

'Then it is all the more reprehensible that you have been content to toler-ate a list of war crimes that is, quite frankly, growing every day. How do you justify a moral failure of this magnitude?' I said something about Kent State.

'Ah Kent State. Yes, how tragic. Tell me, were you there?'

'Of course I wasn't. I'm not even in college yet.'

'My point exactly. When push has come to shove, you have done absolutely nothing. You continue as before, waving your flag as you plunder our coffers and corrupt our youth.'

'But that's just ridiculous! I haven't plundered anything. How could I?'

'Then let us move on to a more promising subject. Yes, let us speak of the CIA stoolpigeon making unlawful interventions in the internal workings of my country and who is also, as I hardly need to tell you, your father.'

'Suna!' Sinan and Lüset shouted together.

Suna put her hand up. 'Please,' she said. 'Do not attempt to speak for our friend. Let us hear what she has to say.'

But what she expected me to say, I cannot begin to imagine. I have never heard such a preposterous suggestion. They might as well tell me my father is Clark Kent. All I could think was, why are these people so negative? So that's what I said."

11

INUTES LATER, a furious Sinan was piling her into a taxi. "I've had enough of that girl. She's my friend but she never knows where to stop." He'd seethed, silent, straight-backed, all the way back to Rumeli Hisar. This leg of the journey had proved as strange as the others: they'd had to go through several army checkpoints. Jeannie now knew that these were in place in anticipation of the great trade union march that would begin only a few hours later. But from Sinan's impassive response to the soldiers who peered in at each checkpoint, waving their submachine guns, you'd have thought it was something that happened every day.

When they got to Hisar Meydan, Jeannie invited him inside, but Sinan refused. They ended up in Chloe's house, for which he mysteriously had a key.

They'd been sitting silently in the swinging chair on the porch, sharing a joint that seemed to bring him no pleasure, when he'd uttered – not to her so much as to the night sky – the words she'd so fatally understood.

"How much has your father explained to you?" was his opening sally. When she'd asked the obvious, "About what?" he'd seemed both exasperated and perplexed. "Has he at least not warned you?"

To which she'd again had to ask, "About what?"

"About the rumors people circulate. About anyone who happens to live here, if they happen to have a US passport. Which, by the way, includes me." He paused expectantly, as if Jeannie had no choice but to make the connections now he'd laid it all out for her. When she failed to do so, he sighed tragically and took her hand. "These rumors about spies."

"Don't worry," she'd said. "I don't take them seriously."

"That's right! You shouldn't! But at the same time, don't underestimate the damage these rumors can do to you. To all of us! There are people who wish you ill. Wish me ill, too. If you don't know this – if you don't take their ill intentions seriously – you're leaving yourself exposed. Dangerously exposed. But don't worry. I'm making you a promise now. I'm promising to look after you. It's the least I can do."

"Are you sure?" Jeannie said stupidly. He looked into her eyes, in disbelief. Then burst out laughing. "Yes, I promise. Despite everything you've seen so far."

Pressing her hands between his, he said, "So you have to promise me. Promise me you'll let me know whenever someone gives you a hard time."

He'd gone on to apologize for "all the stupid games" they'd played with her, promising never to play them again. For he knew now that she was that rare thing, a true innocent. Hearing that, she had let her head take its fatal fall against Sinan's warm shoulder.

But how quickly, how efficiently he had lifted it up and restored it to its former pillow! His words still rang in her head: "Listen," he said. "I really mean it. I was teasing you before, making up so many lies, just to see how you'd react. It was cruel of me. Immature. But that's over now. Now I want to be friends. True friends. Am I making myself clear? But nothing more. You see, my heart is taken. You don't mind, do you? It's better like this, anyway. For all sorts of reasons. What you need from me is protection. What you need is a true friend. If we let something else happen . . ."

"Like what?" she'd asked.

"If we let something else happen, sooner or later, I would betray you."

Oh the horror of it! To assume love – only to be repulsed with pitying kindness! She would never be able to look him in the eye again.

Why she had not mustered what was left of her dignity and left then and there she cannot say. What a fool of herself she had made instead. Oh, how she had cried. How she had lied! The things she had said! She had told him how scared she was, how unnerving it was not to understand anything that people said to her, to walk into trap after trap, how she didn't know how she was going to face any of them, ever again. How coming here had been a big mistake, how it was too late now to start having a father, how the time had come to accept herself as she really was, a girl who couldn't cope with anything larger than Northampton. And he had stayed to console her, like the good, cold friend he'd become. She must have fallen asleep on his shoulder – had she been hoping against hope, even then? But no, when she awoke, it was to the gruesome sight of Chloe's pimply younger brother. And it was morning. And her head was pounding. The next time she'd looked up, it was Amy, Chloe's mother. She was fully made up, and the only word for her bright blonde hair was "coiffed." Her lips were pursed and her brow was furrowed. But her voice was matter-of-fact. "Your father's downstairs. And I have to say, he's a little concerned."

Oh, the shame, when she went downstairs to Amy's kitchen and met her father's wounded, worried eyes.

"Nice time?" he'd asked.

She'd nodded, carefully.

"Well, I'm glad to hear it. Or not, as the case may be."

But after they had returned to the Pasha's Library, after he told her about the nature of the crisis that had called him away (that workers' march on the city) and what would happen next (tanks, raised bridges, rubber bullets and mass arrests), and why it meant that he was going to have to go back to work flat out and just hope that maybe, by the end of the summer, enough of "these rats" would have gone to the beach so that they could, too, he turned to her and said, "I don't want you to misunderstand me, though. I'm not upset. In fact, this is beyond my wildest dreams."

When she'd asked him what he meant, he'd shrugged his shoulders "Well – all of it. You being here. Wanting to spend a year with me. Knowing we'll be doing all these things together, but also not having to worry when I have to be somewhere else, because you have friends. Knowing that you like it over there –" he gestured in the direction of Amy's house. "It's all too good to be true. I suppose the fly in the ointment is Talat's boy, what's his name, Haluk. He's trouble. I hope you didn't let him take advantage of you."

"I wouldn't dream of it."

He looked relieved. "So it's Sinan, is it?"

"Not really," she squeaked, and the horror sank in. *They all thought she'd spent the night with Sinan. They all thought she was involved with a boy who in actual shaming fact was interested in her only as a friend.*

"You know him, too, I take it?" she eventually managed.

"Yes, of course, I do. I even know his father. We used to be golfing buddies. Starting in Caracas of all places. But mostly in Washington. Way back when. You know, before you were born. Did he tell you his mother was a singer?"

"All he said was she was trying to be."

That made him laugh. "He would, wouldn't he? I don't know about now, but she was pretty damned good. There was even a time when . . ." His voice died away. "So I couldn't be happier, Jeannie. Give or take a fly or two in that ointment. I don't think much of that cousin of his, and the two of them together have a nose for trouble but . . " He paused as his eyes travelled northwards. "I'm just happy you'll be spending time with someone I trust."

And what was *that* supposed to mean? But there it was. She'd been paired up by her own father. Paired up and humiliated. If she were a serious person, she would have told him so. Asked him a few other questions while she was at it. Like, what exactly are you doing here, anyway? And if you are, why am I here, too? By the time she fell asleep, she had drafted the conversation she would have with her father at breakfast. A new understanding, she'd call it, based on truthful sharing. She would tell her father that Sinan was just a friend, and that she was happy with it that way. Very happy indeed! She would ask him, very casually, if he happened to know who this mysterious girl was with the prior claim to Sinan's heart. She would leave it at that. They would then move on to discuss his work. She'd approach this subject in neutral and pragmatic tones, assuring her father first that whatever he did, she was sure it was serious and socially responsible and essentially patriotic, and probably no more than simple desk work, a simple and straightforward compiling of the sort of facts every government must have at its fingertips if it is to make wise decisions.

She would then outline her plans for the year. No romance. No attachment. Just serious scholarship. Learning about a new world would be joy enough. There was no need to muddy the water with love, or longing, or the cold comforts of friendship.

Until the next morning, when, halfway through breakfast, the phone rang.

12

"I wonder what it will be like when I leave this place and no longer wake up to ships. There's an endless procession passing beneath us, in darkness and in light. They're all shapes and sizes — from tankers, oceanliners and warships glistening with radar, to rowboats and ferries and wooden fishing boats that bounce along the water's surface like crescent moons. The little ones are as brightly painted as children's paintings, the ferries were built in Glasgow eighty years ago and look like artworks from a more innocent age. The Turkish Maritime Liners are white with orange anchors on their funnels, the cargo ships tend to be grey or black or rusting red, but there are no rules here and that's what's so exhilarating. You never know what's coming at you around the corner.

The ships look so stately from up here but Sinan says that the Russian pilots are often drunk and sometimes run aground. He's pointed out a few places — gruesome empty lots where once stood beautiful Ottoman waterside villas. No one can do anything about it, apparently. This is an international waterway and ships come and go as they please.

Some are high in the sea and others so low you can imagine them sinking under a single wave. They all have flags and I've taken to using Dad's binoculars to find out where they're registered. Most are Turkish, but it's the ominous Soviet vessels that linger in the mind. I have yet to master the Cyrillic alphabet so I can't decipher all their names, though obviously I have no trouble figuring out which are from the Bulgarian port of BAPNA.

Yesterday, when Chloe and I were walking into Bebek, we saw nine peo-

ple jumping off a ship from BAPNA. Defectors, we assume. Chloe says I should think of the Bosphorus as Berlin-on-the-Sea. She also claims that she saw the missiles on their way to Cuba in 1962, and then on their way back again after the crisis was over. Dad says the Bosphorus is a lot more important than Berlin. It's our outermost outpost – not just where the free world ends, but where the free world has the best view of the other side. Where else can you watch the Soviet might pass before your eyes as you eat your breakfast?"

June 25th 1970

"The hardest part of living in a foreign country must be getting used to what they eat for breakfast.

What they eat here is toast (not so strange in itself, I know, but the bread is a different consistency, springy with hard, thick crusts, and never comes sliced). They eat the toast with butter, jam, cucumbers, tomatoes, green peppers, a thick slice of white cheese, and milkless sugary tea they serve in tiny curved glasses rimmed with gold.

They drink tea in these glasses all day long. If you go to the Covered Bazaar to buy a carpet, a boy rushes out and brings the teas back on a swinging copper tray, and no one can take a car ferry across the Bosphorus without their glass of tea, although there is often more sugar in it than water. I never put in more than one or two cubes, but Sinan likes six. Six!

Dad says most of his colleagues eat the same breakfast ("the same crap") as they did when they were in the States. He says it took him a while to "go native" but now he can't imagine life without his Turkish breakfast. The maid comes in at seven most days so she's the one who usually makes it, and I'm sure that's part of the charm."

June 29th 1970

"That's something else that's taking some getting used to – every house seems to have a maid. Some are Armenian and Chloe's is Greek but most are recent arrivals from Anatolia. Ours is called Meliha, or Meliha Hanım to be polite. Her hometown (which she calls her "memleket," which means "country") is near Rize on the Black Sea, but actually she lives in the shantytown just above Robert College. (Her house is a gecekondu, which means "built overnight." Her husband is a janitor at the college.)

Meliha's food is excellent – soups, lamb stews, pilaf, stuffed tomatoes, peppers and zucchini, salads in which everything is chopped up very fine, with mountains of mint – and I think it's a shame when we eat out instead and it goes to waste. She doesn't drink alcohol, and sometimes I worry about what she makes of all those bourbon bottles. She washes our clothes by hand. She polishes the floor every day, on her hands and knees, and the copperware once a *week. She's highly tolerant of my pathetic attempts to fashion my twenty-three words of Turkish into a conversation.*

I asked Dad what we paid her and was not impressed.

We also have a driver. A driver! His name is Korkmaz, which means fearless. He has worked for the Consulate for twenty years, and every time he takes me anywhere, he tells me how much he loves Americans. (He may well be the only one.)"

June 29th 1970

"That's something else I've been trying to get to grips with – how much they hate us here. It used to be the other extreme. Apparently it changed overnight in 1964 when Greece and Turkey nearly went to war over Cyprus. But President Johnson pulled the plug. He said neither side could use NATO weapons. Both countries were left feeling humiliated – that's Dad's word for it. The word I hear from Sinan and Haluk is 'occupied.'"

June 30th 1970

"I've been trying to define the way they talk. Not Sinan – he went to too many American schools during his travels. But the others have this singsong tone and they never use the word you'd expect. It's not that they make mistakes – they have huge and terrifying vocabularies – it's just that they never use a simple word where a weightier one will do – they really have read Chaucer in the original, too. And the complete works of Strindberg. They did calculus in their cradles, where they also picked up several other European languages. It's nothing to be bilingual here. You can't show your face unless you can boast four or five. They don't just quote philosophers I've barely heard of – they quote them ironically.

But they discuss their minds and hearts as if they were perfume sets. As in, "In one corner of my mind I sense a lingering anguish. But linked with this corner is another in which there remains a nuance of joy." And in spite of all the other nuances I fail to catch – the insinuations, the playful airs that should have told me that A's and B's kind words were insincere and the true meanings lurking behind their façades of friendship – they are perfectly happy to admit to strong emotions at the drop of a hat. Sinan included. If he's in a mood.

As in, 'How are you today, Sinan?'

'I am in despair at the falseness of the world. My future looms before me like a guillotine. I am suffocating. Here . . .' and now he'll take my hand and press it against his chest, 'Even my heart longs to escape.'

All this in his easy American accent, which makes it all sound even stranger."

July 2nd 1970

"Another adjustment: the sidewalks. I have yet to find a single stretch that goes for more than eight yards without some gaping hole or an iron prong rising out of the concrete like some sort of demented tree. No one except me is ever fazed by this. I've never seen anyone but me trip or fall. The same goes for the traffic. There is, as far as I've been able to ascertain, only one set of traffic lights in the city and when Sinan and I passed them the other day, there was a policeman standing next to it, begging us to stop.

Elsewhere it's what Chloe calls the "foot first, nose first rule." Cars will stop for you if your foot reaches a piece of the road before the nose of their car does. How pedestrians negotiate this rule is never quite clear. No one except for me ever bothers to look before they step into the road. Dad says they must be praying. It seems to work.

The best way to travel around the city is in the shared taxis. (The Turkish word for these is "dolmuş"). These tend to be two-tone 58 Chevrolets. (The same goes for almost all the other cars you see – they must have shipped them in en masse and then stopped abruptly, because now it's almost impossible to import a car, and even if you're a foreigner they stamp it on your passport and you can't leave the country without spending four days in offices drinking tea to get permission to put it in a pound). The shared taxis use the bus stops but you can flag them down anywhere along the route and get off anywhere, too. They're cheap, and so infinitely preferable to the buses which are gruesome, packed like sardines.

Sadly, many of the sardines are perverts. Chloe and I took a bus the other day and the man next to us put his hand in my crotch. I was very upset about it, and the thing that stays with me is his face; so detached and faraway, as if he didn't know what his slimy hand was up to."

July 6th 1970

"Unless you count the PX, there are no supermarkets in this city– not what I would call a supermarket, anyway – and no real department stores and nothing even remotely resembling a mall. You buy stockings and shoelaces at the stationery store. The butter comes from one little village near Istanbul that was colonized by Poles in the 19th century. You have to go to the Greek delicatessen near the British Consulate downtown to buy pork. Most people seem to buy their flowers from gypsies and get their milk from a man who comes around with a donkey three times a week. (Then you have to pasteurize it.) There's an ECZANE (pharmacy) and a KUAFÖR (hairdresser) every ten feet or so and just about as many banks. But lots of products you just never see. There's no pet food, for example. Chloe's cat lives on the lungs their maid cooks up for her. They sell lungs whole at the butchers in Bebek.

To buy a meal in Bebek you have to go from shop to shop but it's a poetic experience if you don't mind seeing food in its natural form, id est lamb carcasses dangling from hooks and fish displayed in pleasing patterns on marbles slabs with their gills pulled out so that you can see how fresh they are and their mouths gaping. My favorite shops are the fruit and vegetable sellers – in the place of an outside wall, there is a cascade of the brightest peaches, melons, lettuces, tomatoes and cucumbers I have ever seen.

Everything you buy goes into a string bag, but according to Haluk its days are numbered. Already you are seeing a proliferation of plastic bags and there is a disturbing degree of littering. If they give up the string bag, things will go from bad to worse. But when I said as much to Haluk at the beach yesterday, he said, 'If the Americans can have plastic, why can't we?' He can't appreciate anything unless it's new."

July 6th 1970

"I don't think I've ever seen a place where people spend so much time outside. You drive along and it's an endless string of shops and coffeehouses and restaurants spilling out onto the sidewalk, and next to the door is a chair where a man is sitting fumbling with his worry beads. The store signs are askew and the neon lighting harsh and so many of the shops sell things you can't imagine anyone wanting – grim brown suits and grimmer housecoats, plastic shoes and basins and aluminum spoons so thin you could bend them with your eyes, bright pink satin quilts and bolts of glittering fabric even a belly dancer couldn't wear. There are stray cats everywhere, most of them mangy, and dogs that trot around in packs, and packs of boys with crewcuts kicking balls between the cars. The smell of roasting meat blends in with the exhaust fumes. The idling engines and car horns merge with the click-click of the backgammon pieces coming through the windows of the coffeehouse. The cries of the simit vendors blend in with the muezzin calling the faithful to prayer and the cheers from the empty lot where a boy has just scored a goal, while beyond the silhouettes of men fishing at its edge is a ferry whispering its way across the sea.

I look at this scene and I think of Northampton with its serene and empty lawns."

July 7th 1970

"No one ever wears shoes inside, by the way. Except for us barbarians. I've lost count of the number of times we've gone to visit one of Sinan's bodyguards (and that is one thing he wasn't exaggerating, he really does have a whole army of relatives and 'friends of the family' watching his every move) and I've looked down at my feet to find they still have shoes on them. I don't know why I keep forgetting. The first thing you see when you get inside any of these houses is a double or even triple row shoe park. And then great expanses of glistening marble and parquet floor. The vogue here is for chandeliers so there's no hiding any lapse from the public glare.

You have never seen such beady eyes as I've seen on these aunts of his – I feel as if they can see through to my underwear and have found it lacking.

Sinan tells terrible stories about them. If they're rich, it's because they've swindled someone or entered into some ungodly pact with some crooked politician. If they're not arms dealers themselves, then their brothers are. If they're married, they're having an affair with someone whose spouse conveniently fell off a balcony and died last Tuesday. If they're bankers or developers or something in Ankara, they've just been implicated in a fraud. And yet they can spend entire afternoons sitting on terraces with their deceived and deceiving relatives, smiling fakely, drinking glass after glass of tea. It's not enough to dismiss them – as Sinan does – as hypocrites.

I don't think I've ever been anywhere where they do so much sitting."

July 8th 1970

"I know I've never been anywhere where they play cards this much. It's terrifying! I made the mistake of playing the other day with Sinan and some of his cousins. After I'd lost badly three times in a row, I found that I was the only one who'd not been keeping track of every card. Apparently everyone counts cards here. They start on their mother's knees.

I decided to sit it out after that. But I still couldn't follow Sinan's game. He tried to explain later, but I don't think it could ever be reassuring to have a tortuous Byzantine subterfuge mapped out for you after it's just passed you by completely.

I can only wonder, not for the first time, what else I've been missing."

July 10th 1970

"Summer really was cancelled yesterday, for reasons that are still unclear. Officially, i.e. according to God, i.e. Haluk's father, they're not allowed out at all until they've done this stupid resit. Of course that's not stopping them. But there will be hell to pay if they get caught, so that means snatching an hour here and an hour there, and never going out at night, and that's very sad, when you think the curfew's only just been lifted. I'm not sure what caused the crackdown. It has to do with Haluk and Sinan sneaking out one morning when they were supposed to be studying, but they won't say where or why. Just: 'There was something we had to do.'

Whatever that was, it seems to have something to do with Sinan's mother's apartment, which is where Sinan lives, apparently, when she's not in Paris. To judge from the shrouds covering every piece of furniture, she's been in Paris for some time.

The four of us went there this afternoon, but only for about half an hour, most of which, I regret to report, Haluk and Chloe spent in the master bedroom.

I sat on the balcony, while Sinan darted back and forth furtively. There's something on his mind, but he won't tell me. And when it comes down to it, all things considered — what right do I have to ask?"

July 12th 1970

"Another visit to the House of Shrouds. I'm beginning to feel like Chloe's chaperone. If I am, I'm not a very good one! I really do wonder sometimes if she knows what she's doing. But I also wonder why I end up on the balcony and why Sinan won't let me see his room."

July 13th 1970

"Today, after he'd left me alone on the balcony for some time, I tried to make a joke of it. What had he been doing in his bedroom, stashing guns? He didn't laugh."

July 15th 1970

"I woke up this morning feeling extraordinarily happy, as if someone had given me some enormous present I'd always longed for, but of course no one had. I thought then I must have dreamt it, but when I was sitting on the porch with my tea watching the ships pass, I looked at the date on the paper Dad was reading and then my mood dropped like a stone. It's a month to the day since I met my friend Sinan.

My friend Sinan.

I told myself not to be stupid. That it was better this way, because friends could trust each other, and know each other, in ways that were never possible in affairs of the heart. But later, when I was sitting on that balcony again in the House of Shrouds, I looked down at the street and saw this man pulling a basket out of a parked car, and it was only when he walked into the apartment with the same basket a few minutes later that I realized that man must have been Sinan.

I must have watched him for a whole minute without knowing who he was."

WHAT I KNOW ABOUT HIM:

- *Early life in seven different embassies, but he says they were all the same.*
- *Cared for mostly by servants, a different set in each one.*
- *Four different primary schools, three English and one American.*
- *When he was five he and his chauffeur were caught in crossfire between demonstrators and the police, and at seven he witnessed a* coup d'état.

- At eleven, he met Nasser and Tito.
- His mother really was a singer, which really is unusual for a woman of her class and background, and next to impossible for the wife of a diplomat.
- When he was twelve she ran off with a Brazilian crooner.
- He then ran off with someone else, so after the divorce Sinan and his mother came back to Istanbul, where, after two unhappy years in a Turkish school where he could not bear the discipline, he moved to Robert Academy, where his father decided he should take the Turkish courses as well as the ones taught in English. This was a terrible mistake, because he still could not bear the discipline. He refused to accept it. And this led to open war.
- They are making him take this resit to break his will.
- It won't break his will, but he'll have to pretend, just to get them off his case.
- He's never been close to his father, but now, after this, he hates him.
- His mother is away a lot, but she loves him in her way.
- He's going to study engineering, to please his mother and keep his father off his back, but has no intention of ever being an engineer.
- He has other plans. That's all he'll say about it: other plans.

WHAT I DON'T KNOW:

- What he's thinking.
- How he feels about me.
- How he feel about this girl who took his heart.
- Who she is.
- Why not even Chloe seems to know this.
- Why this girl whoever she is, is so important, when she's not even here.
- What's holding him back.
- Why he always leaves before he has to.
- Where I stand with him.
- What I'll do if the answer is nowhere.
- Why he makes me so happy, just by entering the room.
- Where he goes when he leaves."

July 21st 1970

"Still stuck in the same place."

July 29th 1970

"I did talk about it with Chloe today, and she was sympathetic, though some-what blasé (her favorite word). I think it's easier for her to live with all this *because she's used to it, having grown up here. I mean all this subterfuge, these rumors that you never know are true or not, and the way people will tell you these things about themselves that defy belief but then withhold everything else. When I asked her why they did this, she just shrugged her shoulders and said, 'To keep you guessing?' When I asked why they would want to do that, she said, 'Well, obviously. So you can't control them.'*

She's much better than I am at accepting the world as it is."

August 2nd 1970

"I had a dream this morning, when I was floating in and out of sleep and it sums up how I'm feeling. I'm playing cards, and even though I have mysteriously learned how to count them, I'm still losing. Because the deck keeps changing – one time it is all hearts. The next time there are five queens of spades. Sometimes there are fifty-seven cards in all, and sometimes only fifty-one. So I know someone at the table is cheating. I know something is wrong. But I can't say what until all the cards have been dealt and I've lost again."

August 3rd 1970

"Today we took Kitten II over to Kanlıca and went to one of those yogurt cafés, and Sinan and I took the ferry back. I tried to take advantage of our time alone together to say something, but the words just evaporated."

August 4th 1970

"Today it was very hot and all I did was go over to Chloe's house and make peanut butter cookies. The recipe was from a book called An American Cook in Turkey.*"*

August 5th 1970

"What would I have said, a few months back, if someone had told me I'd spend my summer making cookies from a book called An American Cook in Turkey?"

August 6th 1970

"Today I tried to walk into Bebek along the shore. But there were hundreds of boys sunning themselves on the pavement and they kept throwing themselves in my path and trying to look up my skirt. I tried to cross to the other side, a car slowed down and the driver hissed something ugly and guttural I couldn't understand though of course I didn't need to. I pretended he didn't exist and kept walking towards Bebek and eventually he gave up, but I hated having to keep my head down.

I hate it that I can't go anywhere in this city without a boy.

*PLACES GIRLS AREN'T SUPPOSED TO GO
BY THEM-SELVES IN THIS CITY:*

- *Beerhalls.*
- *Restaurants.*
- *Cafés.*
- *Any street.*
- *Any public place, except perhaps for the breakfast room at the
  Hilton, but after five in the evening, not even there.*

*PLACES GIRLS CAN GO BY THEMSELVES WITHOUT
RUNNING THE RISK OF BEING HARASSED:*

- *Their room."*

August 7th 1970

"Well, I've seen his room now, and it was not what I expected.

I don't know what I was expecting.

*It happened very suddenly. I didn't plan it. I just blurted it out — 'I want
to see your room' — and he just looked at me, and said, 'Why?'*

I said, 'Because it's there.'

'Why now?' he asked.

I said, 'Because I want to see what you have in there.'

*Then there was a long silence, punctuated by distraught sighs. After which,
he said, 'Okay. But I warn you. You'll regret it.'*

*The blinds were drawn. All you could see was this large and glowing emer-
ald of terrarium, lots of ferns around a log. I went over to stare at it, I think
because I couldn't think what else to do. He came over next to me and we sat
there staring at the ferns together. 'It's beautiful, isn't it?' he said. I agreed. 'I
was so sure you'd be scared,' he said, and I said, 'Why would I be scared?' He
said, 'Because most people are.' I must have given him a look, because he added,
'In Turkey, anyway.'*

'This really is a very strange country,' I said.

'No,' he said. 'You're the one who's strange.'

Then he said, 'But I'm glad you're strange.' And kissed me.

*It was only later, much later, that I looked at the terrarium again and saw
the cobra.*

I think, under normal circumstances, I would have been terrified.

*It's not his. He's looking after it for a teacher. It's been very difficult, though.
Especially getting the mice.*

*But apparently he's very indebted to this teacher, who taught him 'how to
see the world.' I don't feel very warm towards this man at the moment, because
apparently he's warned Sinan off me.*

When I asked Sinan why, he said, 'Because of who you are.'
This teacher's American, too, though. His name is Dutch."

August 15th 1970

"Today we took the cobra out to Büyükada, where a woman named Zehra is going to look after it while Sinan is away. (He takes the resit on Tuesday morning and flies out to his father in Pakistan that afternoon.)

On the way to the ferry, we bought the mice, from a man called Rauf. Rauf's shop (he's a tailor, of all things, specializing in men's shirts) is between Tünel and Tepebaşı. On the ground floor is a louche bar where we went to drink tea afterwards. The woman in charge was about sixty, big and blonde and apparently quite something on the accordion – and falling over with warmth and kindness. She knew French, so that is how we conversed. Apparently she is Russian and came here in 1917 in 'a Cossack's pocket.' When I asked what that meant, she said it was a very long story, but that she would be happy to tell me if I had the patience. Then a customer walked in and Sinan came down the stairs with Rauf so I had to leave without it.

We walked down to the bridge because now we had two baskets, and although the lids were both firmly fastened; the mice were making too much noise to take into a taxi. We still caused quite a commotion. We had ten dogs and twenty urchins following us by the time we got to the quay.

The ferry was packed, it being Saturday, but we had a whole bench to ourselves.

Zehra (the snake-sitter) was another strange one – dark and thin and tragic. No smiles for us, but three for the cobra. She had seven dogs in her garden and twice that many cats and after midnight she goes all over the island putting out food for strays. Although she's very poor, she lives in a beautiful if rundown old house that an old man bequeathed to her after an angel came to him in a dream. When Zehra took out one of the mice to stroke it, a tear rolled down her face.

She had an aquarium but it wasn't big enough, so we had to go to the other end of town to borrow one from a man with the most furrowed brow I have ever seen in my life. Apparently, he's a former prison guard who took up painting while he was doing a term himself for killing an inmate who insulted his mother. His paintings are of children playing in gardens and are what you call primitive but Sinan bought one, which struck me as kind.

The ferry back to the city stopped at Heybeli, Burgaz, and Kınalı, and as I watched all those people strolling back and forth along those small and glittering waterfronts, I could almost see their secret stories trailing like comets behind them.

We didn't go straight home because Zehra had given Sinan some medicine to give to her sister in Kumkapı. We had a hard time finding her apartment, even with eleven portly moustachioed men in undershirts helping us. She was too ill to come downstairs, so she lowered a basket from the window. It was after midnight by the time I got home. Dad was waiting up for me. (A little the worse for wear, I'm afraid.) He told me Mom had called. Apparently there was a piece in the New York Times about the cholera in Asia, and she was worried I might become Turkey's first reported victim.

'She's jumping the gun,' he said. 'But I hope you didn't have any mussels today.' I did, though. Lots.

Mom says she wants me to come home if it turns into a full-blown epidemic. She can say what she likes.

Tonight, before I wrote this, I tried to write to her, to explain why I have to stay here. But I couldn't find the words.

I am not the same person who waved her goodbye nine weeks ago.

I have walked with Sinan beyond the boundaries of my old life and what I've seen has changed me, inexorably and forever.

I am sitting on the edge of the world, gazing into the unknown, and every light shimmering in the distance, every shadow behind it, hints at something greater, truer, deeper.

I must venture on.'"

13

JEANNIE'S JOURNAL ENTRIES for the autumn months of 1970 are fragmentary and sporadic, and even now, as I leaf through the pages, I can see her spreading herself too thin. There are no confessional outbursts from here on in, no mad visions, no details about where she and Sinan met or what they did or did not do – no sense of how she felt about him – or herself, or her father. Instead there are sketches – a film crew she saw shooting a lover's quarrel one afternoon at the foot of the Aşıyan, a woman she noticed at the fruit and vegetable shop, examining zucchini as if they were criminals. An article in the paper about a man who went blind when he was knifed in the head only to regain his sight the moment the doctor pulled the knife out. Her thoughts on the Nâzım Hikmet poem that Sinan read to her in Turkish and then tried to translate for her the day before he left to visit his father in Pakistan. (It was about a journey, about never regretting it, even if it led to death.) Folded between the same pages, two poems Sinan wrote on the plane out ("The Tragedy of Innocence" and "The Turbulence in My Heart Knows No Master") along with a postcard of a mosque. On the pages that follow are Jeannie's impressions of Alexandroupolis, Kavala, Thasos and the roads she and her father travelled during the small trip they took together to Northern Greece at the end of August:

"Six months ago — had I been able to peer into the future and see us — Father and me — sitting in the front of that car, rounding a hairpin bend, gazing out at a lonely goat under the only tree on the browned and terraced hillside, I would have wondered only how it would feel to have a dream come true with such precision. I would never, I think, have identified with the goat."

There is a long description of the soldier with the submachine gun who searched their car at the border when they were re-entering Turkey. An even longer description of Nafi Baba's tomb — its fine curved windows, lined with little burnt out candles and knotted ribbons, its desolate beauty, and Jeannie's thoughts as she sits on the empty hillside next to it and looks down at the castle and the blue ribbon of the Bosphorus snaking around it. But no mention of Sinan, who must have brought her here the day he got back. And only a passing mention of the "talk" she and her father had that same evening.

He wanted her to ask Sinan to visit one of these days. Perhaps that same weekend? Perhaps for supper? He knew this was not the local custom, but Sinan was not entirely local, "so he won't think this means I expect him to ask for your hand in marriage." When Jeannie prevaricated ("I still think this is weird") he said, "Look, if you're seeing this much of him, I don't want him skulking around in the shadows outside like he was tonight. He should come inside, say hello, be civil. Act like a grown-up. It's not as if he's a stranger, after all."

"I don't understand what you're driving at," Jeannie insisted.

"Then let me put it this way. Have you ever asked him what it is, exactly, that stops him coming inside?"

She never did, though. She just didn't have the confidence. She thought she might lose him if she asked for the truth. I have no written proof for this. But I'm sure of it. This is the one part of the story when she really does step into my shoes.

On the first Monday of September, 1970, Jeannie Wakefield became a special student at my old school. She was a special student for the same reason I had been: though most classes at the American College for Girls were taught in English, regular students were obliged by law to study certain subjects in Turkish. Anyone who didn't was classified as special. There were only a handful of us. We were all foreign, and we left without diplomas. In my case, that was not a set-back, as I found a good college willing to accept me on the basis of my transcript. In Jeannie's case, it didn't matter either: she had that place waiting for her at Radcliffe.

On my last day in Istanbul – in November 2005, almost a week after Jeannie's disappearance, and two days after my incriminating article came out in the Observer – I went back to see the school again for myself. It was my first visit in thirty-five years. As I walked up the long, steep path to Gould Hall, and gazed up at its great and glaring pillars, I was still late for mathematics class. As I climbed the last steps, my school-books still scraped against my ribs. I pulled open the door, and there was Marble Hall, as cool and white and mausoleum-like as ever. There, in the corner, was a glass door covered in ruffled gauze. There, behind it, was the little room we'd used for the school newspaper, and the Current Affairs Club. From time to time, Miss Broome's reading group had met here, too. Even when we had no express purpose, Chloe and Suna and Lüset and I would come with our midmorning coffees, and just to stand at the threshold was to feel the sting of our arguments.

I opened the door, and there was Suna, blue eyes blazing. I must have gasped – I wasn't expecting this – but she was quick to reassure me. With a faintly mocking smile, she told me that she'd "come in friendship," having tracked me down with the help of my parents. She'd been heading in this direction anyway, for lunch, at the alumni club. Had I not seen it, at the far end of the campus? Never mind, she said, as she let her smile soften. This was "our hour for memories." There, on the table, was a large scrapbook with mementos of our fevered years together.

First, our newspaper. Or rather Suna's newspaper, conveying Suna's views, under a dazzling array of pennames. Salome, Mrs Rosenthal, Emma Goldman, Mata Hari. All shared the same stormy style. Especially when it came to student council meetings. You'd have thought we were in Moscow circa 1917. "More Heads Roll in Bloody Coup." "Yasemin Ağaoğlu Reveals Vanguardist Tendencies." "Masses Go Hungry as VP Merve Akyol Fails to Oppose Cafeteria Price Hikes."

Wedged between these tracts were Lüset's famously cryptic cartoons. One featured a man in a fez next to a man in a top hat. Both were looking at a cow with a woman's head. The caption read, "Do we really want this?"

Another featured a dead girl with her head in an oven. Next to her was a policeman. Behind him, the distraught parents were wringing their hands. The caption read, "But where is the weapon?"

It was surprise, I think, that made me laugh. "I'd forgotten these." Suna gave me a cryptic smile and turned the page. "But this one you cannot have forgotten because it was after your time," she informed me. I looked at the date: October 1970. I was at Wellesley by then, and Jeannie had stepped into my shoes.

On the front page were the usual student council exposés. On page two I found, amid more cryptic cartoons, three painfully earnest pieces by my replacement. One was a short biography of the little White Russian who'd made us coffee. Another was an appreciation of *ayran*, the yogurt drink. The third was an essay entitled "What is Education For?"

Looking more closely at the cartoons running alongside these pieces, I saw that they were not by Lüset, and not at all cryptic. They featured grimacing young women with thought balloons. The thoughts were in Turkish, so most of our teachers wouldn't have understood them. They ranged from "What is this drivel?" to "If the dogs of capitalism can really run, let them run home to where they belong." None of this really surprised me. The Suna I had known in 1970 had fierce views about who belonged where, and she would not have been happy to share her sacred space with anyone, least of all Jeannie; it would only have happened, I guessed, under duress. "So tell me," I asked Suna. "How exactly did she win you over?"

"I hated her – that goes without saying," Suna explained. "Not Jeannie in the flesh, of course, but everything she stood for. And of course Jeannie was going everywhere with Chloe in those days. Bearing in mind that Chloe and I were still competing for that ingrate, Haluk, it was all very painful. And yes, I was terrible. Yes, I lived up to my name. Especially when this Jeannie upstart complained to her father that I was refusing to give her space in my paper. He complained to Chloe's mother! Who complained to our advisor! You remember her, don't you? The saintly Miss Broome. That was why I was forced to make room for Jeannie. But as you can well imagine, I made her pay."

"Yes, it was a very terrible price I extracted from her," Suna recalled with some pride. "When she came to the next meeting, first I dared her to denounce us for expressing ourselves in our native tongue inside the school walls, in direct contravention of school regulations. Of course, she told us very haughtily that she was not a sneak or a spy. She used this very word, spy. She was, she told us, an ordinary student insisting on her 'ordinary' rights.' So of course, when the rest of us went into Turkish, I peppered my sentences with jokes at her expense that soon had everyone except Jeannie herself laughing. However! This did not scare her away. I had no choice but to become less cryptic. I now began to pepper my Turkish with little phrases in English. Phrases like 'human microbe' and 'foreign sirens who suck on the flower of our youth.' Of course I made long critiques of her own offerings, and as you can see, it would not have cost me much effort." Again, Suna smiled.

"But then Jeannie surprised me. She stood up for me!" Suna turned the page. It was the last page of the scrapbook. "You are looking at the final issue of our brave little school newspaper, and the piece that shut it down."

The offending article, by "L.A. Internationale." was headlined: "Miss Markham Linked with Running Dogs of Capitalism." Miss Markham was our old principal. The "'link'" was her brother, a US pilot serving in Vietnam. She had, said L.A. Internationale, brought fresh color to this villain's cheeks by allowing her school to be infiltrated by the daughter of a "well-known CIA operative."

"Our worthy principal hauled us in, of course,'" Suna told me. "Of course Miss Markham instructed me to apologize to Jeannie. But then, to my surprise, Jeannie stepped forward to insist that she was not offended: it was a practical joke! And what was a joke between friends? Miss Markham was not convinced. 'It's a strange friend who slanders your father in the school newspaper.' These were her words. Still Jeannie insisted. She told Miss Markham that I, Suna the Terrible, could never hurt her. She had no fear of me, because we were in all ways equals.

And the moment she said that, I thought, 'Yes, that's the truth.' So we became friends. Though I am sure I do not need to remind you that this word means something different to me than it does to most people."

An understatement if ever there was one. But it made me think. As I made my way down the steep and winding path to the Bosphorus, pausing from time to time to look up at the gnarled and curving branches of the Judas trees, and (in deference to a long lost habit) stopping on the 138th step to catch the first glimpse of the sea, I asked myself: had Suna and I ever been friends? Had I risen to her challenge as Jeannie had – refusing Suna's ill will, appealing to her better nature – might we have resolved our differences, too? On balance, I thought not. Suna had good reasons to mistrust me. But on the most important point she was wrong.

As she well knows. As she would be forced to admit if I had the time, courage and stamina to press the point. My family did not move to Turkey to colonize it. My father came here to teach. He was not an employee of the US government, nor was he here to further its ambitions. He did not report to a desk in Washington. He was not a spy.

So when Suna sat me down next to me all those years ago in the ACG cafeteria, and insisted that my father was a spy, or *in all but name* a spy, or *in some sense, even worse than a spy*, I could indulge in the burning anger that is the preserve of the unjustly accused. I could stamp my feet. Point my finger. Scream!

Jeannie could do none of these things. For her there were only two options. Either she made excuses – for Suna, for Sinan, for herself, her father, everyone – and "ventured on." Or she faced the truth, the whole truth, and let her life unravel, until there was nothing but truth left.

14

BUT NOT YET. Please God, not yet. Does anyone face a choice like that unless it's forced on them? I can read her journal and see her unvoiced anxieties seeping into every sentence. No description is neutral. Even the city is doomed.

By October 1970, cholera had come to Istanbul. Although all reported cases were in the shanty towns on its western edge, there were draconian measures to keep it from spreading. Every restaurant and cafeteria in the city shut down.

"So now the city, with its locked and inward looking shutters, has become my metaphor. For every day, there are fewer places I'm allowed to go. Every day, there is either an anti-American demonstration in Taksim or rumors of an unauthorized march that could turn into a riot. The universities downtown have turned into war zones. Robert College is still relatively peaceful, but there is still boycott after boycott, and, every few days, a noisy forum in Albert Long Hall to argue about the boycotts. It is not unusual to see a pair of students begin to push and shove each other, even kick each other's shins as their friends struggle to pull them off.

But when I reach the terrace, I find Sinan alone, aloof and reading a book. It is never a textbook. This is a point of honor — even when we study in the library. He hates engineering in practice more than he had hated it in theory. He is still attending class, although he finds it hard, in his foot-dragging misery, to concentrate. He finds it harder still to bear the adults

who threaten, chide and cajole him and police our every move. I find
this unconscionable. Sinan shrugs it off – perhaps he can't afford not to.
But there is so much anger in his eyes sometimes, I think they might catch
fire."

The date for that entry is October 23rd 1970. The next entry is dated
January 7th 1971, and it offers only the most cursory references to the
months in between. But in the letter she left me on her computer, just
before she disappeared, Jeannie described them to me in bitter, jagged
detail.

Each detail serves the moral of her self-lacerating story: people who
can't face up to the truth need scapegoats. The best scapegoats were the
ones you never got to know as people. "So inevitably (she wrote) Dutch
Harding was doomed to become mine."

It happened slowly, and in stages. It would be many months before
their orbits intersected. Was this deliberate on Sinan's part? If so, why?
In her letter, she still wasn't sure.

Certainly he made no effort to *hide* him from her, or her from him.
As she wandered about the campus on Sinan's arm that autumn, he
would occasionally point out a long-haired man in a sheepskin coat
dashing into the Robert College library or snaking his way though a
crowd at the opposite end of the playing field and say, "That's Dutch
over there. Can you see him?" Although he was always too far away for
Jeannie to see him properly, she felt she knew him, for she and Sinan
could not have a serious conversation without Dutch coming into it.
"Well, you know what Dutch says about this, don't you?" Sinan would
say. Or "Dutch has an interesting take on this." Or "I used to think that,
too, until Dutch reminded me that . . ." But never once did he say: "It's
about time that you met."

At first, this really bothered her:

"I did not yet understand how important it was for Sinan to have one person
in his life who did not have perfect knowledge of his movements. Nor did I know
how far his elders and betters would go to oversee his studies, his social life and
even his future. All that changed when Sinan's father swooped into town in
mid-November, brandishing that shameful report."

The showdown took place at Süreyya's – then the most expensive restaurant in the city, although it was situated over a BP station. It was the only time Jeannie ever met Sinan's father: she remembered him as a "grey, grim eminence, with grave, appraising eyes." She remembered, too, that Sinan was wearing a navy blue sports jacket she'd never seen and never saw again. He sat as if he had a board up his shirt and peeled an orange with his knife and fork.

Whatever Jeannie said, the father's reply was, "Aha! How fascinating!" He was all smiles, even when the conversation turned to Sinan's studies. Sinan was all deference. "Yes, Father." "Of course, Father." "Certainly, Father." His answers were truthful, if strained and rehearsed. He was attending his classes, keeping up with his work, not enjoying it, but keeping an open mind.

Then his father reached into his pocket, took out an envelope, and passed it across the table. Inside was what looked like a typed letter. After Sinan had read it, he threw it down, folded his arms, and glared through the filmy green curtains at the Bosphorus. "So," said his father. "I await your explanation."

"There is no explanation," said Sinan. "I'll see who I want."

"In a free country, this might be possible. In ours, alas . . ."

"I have a right to my own life," Sinan retorted.

"You are forgetting who you are," his father replied.

"Who am I then?"

"A Turk."

At which Sinan picked up the piece of paper, crumpled it into a ball, and threw it across the table. Startled by his bad manners, Jeannie picked it up and smoothed it out. Though the report was in Turkish, she could see the name Dutch Harding. When she asked Sinan why, he snorted, and said, "My father has been spying on me. Or rather, he has hired a scum to do it for him. You see, he doesn't like the company I keep. He thinks they're leading me astray."

At which Sinan's father put up a protesting hand, and said, "Please! Don't exaggerate! This has nothing to do with you, my dear Miss Wakefield. Nothing at all!" But he said it in such a way that left her wondering.

★　★　★

What did this man have against her? That evening, after supper, after her father had opened the subject ("I hear you met my old golfing buddy"), she tried to find the words to ask. But the words rebelled, forming themselves into another question: "What does this man have against his son?"

"Nothing," her father answered. "As strange as it may seem, he loves his boy to death."

"So why the snooping? Why the intimidation?"

"Ah," said her father. "To answer that, I need to give you some of the history." As he rocked his chair and locked his arms behind his head, he studied her carefully. "Sinan's told you none of this, I take it?"

He went on to explain that there had been a war going on between Sinan's parents since long before the divorce. "You could even say it started before the poor boy was even born." Sinan's father's uncle was a general who had fought alongside Atatürk (and against the Greeks) in the War of Independence. He had gone on to help found a narrowly nationalist political party that later became overtly fascist. Sinan's father had never been a member of that party, but he had stern views about national honor and patriotic duty. No son of his was going to fritter his life away in the arts: so Sinan had three options: the army, the foreign service or engineering.

Sinan's mother, on the other hand, came from a famously bohemian and artistic Ottoman family that had ("like Atatürk himself") been based in Salonica until the end of the Ottoman Empire. They had moved to Istanbul in the 1920s, and though they were enthusiastic supporters of Atatürk's republic, they refused to give up their love of things Greek. They had even sent Sibel and her siblings to one of Istanbul's Greek schools. There was, my father said, no link between this eccentricity and "a later political scandal" that had resulted in one of Sinan's maternal aunts defecting with her husband to the Soviet Union, "though various scandalmongers seem to think otherwise."

"So the two sides of Sinan's family have always fought over him. As families do. But in this case there's a twist." As much as Sinan's mother might have wished her son to follow her into the world of art, she was as fearful of Communism as her ex-husband. "Hence this brouhaha over his friendship with Dutch Harding. Hence this report."

"So you know about it," Jeannie said.

"Not only do I know about it. I've read it," he was proud to say.

"Why?" Jeannie asked. "How?"

Smiling through pursed lips, he said, "It just so happens that I know the guy. The author, I mean. We don't always work in tandem, but it's always better when we keep each other informed. We're on the same side, after all. Though in this case I am of the view that my friends on the Turkish side are over-reacting."

Because (as he now informed his daughter) it was important for youth to make up its mind about things. Treat tomorrow's leaders with respect, and eventually they come round. Come down hard and heavy on them, and they swing the other way. "The more they make a fuss about Dutch Harding, the more they add to his allure. Which is tragic, and laughable, because . . ."

He left the sentence hanging, and he refused to name the author of the report. But later that week, Jeannie met him. Though it would be more accurate to say they renewed their acquaintance.

The Saturday before Thanksgiving, William Wakefield gave a party. It was an annual event, and a sought-after invitation, though possibly this had more to do with the host's famous view than any great affection for the man himself. It was one of the few occasions when the Robert College set mingled with the consular and business people from downtown. William's Turkish "friends" were also there in force.

Sinan came with his mother, who had by now returned from Paris to "watch over" him. She was as glamorous as her pictures – svelte and sculpted, with large, heavily accented almond eyes, thick black hair chopped in the manner of Cleopatra, and a way of holding herself that suggested sorrows borne but never forgotten. Everyone was watching when she strode across the library with open arms to kiss Jeannie's father's cheeks.

"Then it was my turn. There was a warm but thorough examination before the full embrace. I can still feel her hands: there was a warning in them. 'So at last! We meet!'

Sinan stood at her side, looking grim. Why? Because she was beautiful? Because he wanted to protect her? Because she'd cramped his style? She kept taking his hand and pulling him over to meet a 'dear, dear friend' and then she'd notice a speck on his shirt collar and say something despairing as she flicked if off. She'd kiss him on his forehead and ask the dear, dear friend if she had "ever seen a boy so handsome" and then she'd see another dearer friend across the library and sail away."

She didn't stay long. Sinan escorted her to the outside gate, returning very slowly, circling the trees in the garden as he smoked. On rejoining Jeannie, he nodded in the direction of a sharply dressed middle-aged man on the porch.

İsmet smiled, as if he'd been expecting them. He gave Jeannie a crisp handshake and it was then that she recognized him as the man with the policemen's eyes, the man who'd been working with her father that morning back in June. When she told him so, he said, "Good memory!"

Sinan spat something at him in Turkish.

"Whoa, boy. Slow down," said İsmet. "That's a pretty big mouthful."

This prompted another torrent.

"You know?" İsmet replied. "This just isn't fair to our lovely friend here."

Speaking in English, Sinan said, "Don't worry. She knows what I think."

"Oh to be twenty," said İsmet, flashing his teeth. "You know, this boyfriend of yours cuts quite a romantic figure. He's quite a poet, in fact."

"You know nothing about me," Sinan snarled.

"Oh, but I do," said İsmet sharply. "What I choose to disclose – that's another matter entirely." He turned to Jeannie. "How long have you been here now? Three, four months? No, it's almost six, isn't it? The novelty must be wearing off. You must be wondering what you've let yourself in for!"

He paused to light a cigarette. His lighter was large, heavy and gold. "For example, yours truly. You meet me through your father. You hear I am 'his other half.' Then later you discover I am linked also with Sinan. You hear that his father and I did our military service together. Did he not tell you this? Oh dear. That must mean he also neglected to inform you I was married to his aunt."

"Until she died," said Sinan. "Ask him how she died."

This time it was İsmet who spoke in Turkish. And when Sinan responded, also in Turkish, his voice was loud enough to attract their host's notice.

Pressing his hand down on İsmet's shoulder, William Wakefield told his "other half" to lay off. Turning to Sinan, he added, "That means you, too, boy!" And perhaps he got the tone wrong, perhaps the tone he used was only acceptable if you were speaking to your own son.

"I just met your daughter's boyfriend," Jeannie heard a nondescript American woman tell her father some time later. "He's a little mercurial, don't you think?" When William said no, he was just in a bad mood, she said, "Isn't he a little old for her?" Again William said no. His daughter was seventeen and Sinan had only just turned twenty. To which the American woman said, "Three years is a lot at that age. And then there's the culture gap."

William said she shouldn't worry about that too much. "Sinan's lived all over the world." But the woman persisted. "I suppose what concerns me most about Jeannie is that she seems to be doing a lot of care-taking."

"You think so?"

"If I were her mother, I'd be telling her to cool off."

"I wouldn't dare," William replied. "Jeannie has a mind of her own. And she's crazy about this boy. They're inseparable."

"All the more reason to tread carefully," said this woman. "When all is said and done . . ." But Jeannie was never to know what happened when all was said and done, because now Sinan was leading her to the door.

There were fairy lights on the trees so anyone could have looked out and seen them kissing. When Jeannie pointed this out, he only held her tighter. "If I didn't know you, I'd think you were doing this for show," Jeannie said.

And he said, "Why shouldn't I? We're inseparable. Remember?"

The next day he took her to the House of Shrouds to have lunch with his mother. Sibel was politeness itself when Jeannie first walked in – thanking her for the splendid party, asking after her father, asking Jeannie about her "passions and interests," plying her with food, and paying no attention to the son smoldering in the corner. Jeannie was never to know what sparked off the argument, because the first sally, like so many that followed, was in a language she didn't know. She listened in her usual way, fishing for familiar names and words. Though Dutch Harding came up most frequently, Jeannie heard her own name, too. So rashly she interrupted. "What exactly do you have against me, by the way?"

Sibel took her hand. "My darling, you are a delight! It is simply . . ." and she took her hand away. "This boy of ours is young. Do you understand, my sweet? I have no wish to ruin his fun. What is life, if not for fun? But fun is all, yes?"

Failing to secure agreement, she turned to Sinan and, in stern and cutting French, she said, "She does not look so pretty when she's angry. In fact, she looks like a goat." This Jeannie had no trouble understanding.

Sibel seemed to know this. For now she reached out, smiling, and flicked her finger against Jeannie's chin. "There, that's better," she said, in English. "When you don't puff out your lower lip, you are, as I said, simply divine."

Turning back to her son, she launched into what Jeannie now assumed to be Greek. Her voice, at first soft and cajoling, grew steadily louder and more urgent. Sinan kept his answers short and his voice guarded, until she said something that made him slam his fist on the table. She raised her arms, as if to beseech God, "*Ah, mais ça suffit. Vraiment j'en ai assez!*"

After she had slammed her way out of the apartment, Sinan hurled himself into a chair to steam in silence, raising his hand in warning every time Jeannie asked what was wrong. Then he relented. Leading her into his bedroom, he said, "This is what's wrong." Where the terrarium had been, there was a pile of ironed shirts and paired socks. "You remember the books on those shelves? Well, guess what? My mother threw them out. I just came home last night and Dutch's precious books were gone. What am I going to say to him?"

He sat down on his bed. Jeannie sat down next to him but he pushed her comforting hand away. Accustomed now to his flights of temper, she lay down on the bed next to him and waited. Was this care-taking? she wondered. She gazed into the shadows where the terrarium was no longer and thought back to the day she'd first seen it. She thought about the snake, and their trip with the snake to the islands, and the glittering waterfronts they'd passed on the night ferry. She imagined the night ferry changing its mind at the last minute, looping back to return them to the Sea of Marmara and the glittering harbors of Kınalı, Burgaz, Heybeliada and Büyükada . . . slipping across the dark sea to Yalova, Bandırma and the Marmara Islands, to the Dardanelles, and Çanakkale, Gallipoli, Imbros, Samothraki, Alexandroupolis, Kavala . . .

A door slammed. Then another. The overhead light flicked on. There, looming over them, was Sinan's mother. More Greek fury. But Sinan refused to budge. 'You can say whatever you like,' he said in French. 'We're not doing anything. You know why? We can't! We'd have more privacy in a panopticon!'

'Then go to a panopticon, why don't you?'

'You don't even know what a panopticon is.'

'Of course I do! What do you take me for?'

'A follower of Bentham — what else?'

'Ah! And who might this Monsieur Bentham be?'

'The author of one of the books you threw away.'

'One day you'll thank me! And perhaps you'll then explain to me why, with all the girls in the world, you had to choose this one!'

'I "chose" her because the moment I saw her, I knew you'd hate her!'

'Ah! Mais vraiment, c'est insupportable. Vraiment ça suffit!'

Jeannie knew now what she wanted to ask Sinan, but she had no idea how.

"So I got up and turned off the light, lay down again next to him, and resumed my travels. I went back to Büyükada, retracing our lost, happy steps, except that this time, after we'd visited the prison-guard-turned-prison-artist, and waved at the elderly couple speaking Ladino on the porch next door, the couple had waved back, and invited us to stroll around their garden. And over supper, because of course we stayed for supper, they talked of their ancestors, who'd come to Istanbul to escape the Spanish Inquisition. We lost all sense of time, and suddenly there was only just enough time to make the last ferry...but along the way we met a man with an Albanian grandfather, a Circassian grandmother, and an Armenian wife. They all had stories to tell,

and though the stories looped back on themselves, swirled out of orbit, careened around blind corners, the chain never broke. Each story led on to another story, and the last returned us to our starting point. When we reached the waterfront, the night ferry was still waiting, and I was as far from the real world as if I'd been riding on the tail of a comet."

"Jeannie? Are you asleep?"

"No. Just thinking."

"What about?"

"About a trip I wish we'd taken."

"Where to?"

She told him.

"You could go to jail for that, you know," he said.

"For a daydream?"

"You'd be surprised." He propped himself on his pillows. She put her head on his chest. "I'm angry with my mother. But also, I understand her reasons. You've heard about my aunt, yes? I mean Emine. The one who had to defect. One day, perhaps, I'll tell you the story. All I'll say now is that İsmet had his hand in it. And İsmet is not done. He will not be done until he has purified me. So naturally, he suspects my mother. She isn't pure, you see. İsmet believes Turks must be pure. Dutch, on the other hand, says there's no such thing as a *Turk*."

"But that's nonsense," Jeannie said.

"What he meant," Sinan explained, "is that the 'Turk' is not a historical reality but an ideological construct. This construct was designed by our founding father, to legitimize his nationalist project. Do you have any idea what my father would do to me if he heard me say that?"

"Laugh?"

He punched the wall. "They're all such hypocrites! So I read a few books! Do they think a gun is going to jump out from the pages and take up arms against the state? Just because I read a book, it doesn't mean I agree with it! Whatever happened to critical thinking?" His voice was racing. "Dutch says that the entire Western tradition is based on critical thinking. Did you know that? He says you can't get anywhere unless there's part of you standing outside, asking questions."

"Why don't you ever question him, then?"

"Oh, I do! Of course I do! You still don't understand! Dutch has never pretended to be right about everything. In class, when he got something wrong, and we told him, you know what he'd do? He'd just laugh. Do you know how rare that is in Turkey?"

"You still let him dictate your thoughts," Jeannie dared to say.

"Oh you think so, do you? Well, then let me ask you this then. If I let him dictate my thoughts, if I let *anyone* dictate my thoughts, do you think we'd be lying together on this bed?"

15

WHAT EXACTLY DID he mean? She did not dare ask. Just to think of asking made her mind go blank. But she began to notice things. They refused to organize themselves into a picture, and for the same reason, they plagued her.

She noticed, for example, that she and her father didn't really have a relationship. At least, not the sort of relationship that she then thought ought to come naturally to fathers and their daughters. So while he was glad, even proud, to have her living with him, and eager, almost too eager, to sit down with a bourbon and a pile of books to ruminate on what he insisted on calling the burning issues of our time, she could feel no real bond. No — it was worse than that. She felt as if she was more an idea to him than a real person.

"This hurt me. Possibly because he, too, had always been more of an idea to me than a real person. It could hardly have been any other way, seeing as we had, until now, seen so little of each other. The problem was that I could not bear the cracks now forming in the image of Father I had always carried around with me. With every crack, it was harder for me to avoid seeing the man he really was. Or the father he wasn't.

For example: Thanksgiving, which we celebrated at Chloe's. When Sinan turned up two hours late and glowering, I asked if he was okay. But it was my father who took him outside for a chat.

Though Sinan was looking more cheerful when they returned, there was still an edge to his voice as he downed three bourbon sours too quickly. 'That's more like it!' said my father, pouring him a fourth. 'Let the good times roll. Let's party!' I can still hear his reckless laugh. The others laughing with him. I can even see how everyone was sitting, what they were wearing, and whether their glasses were half empty or half full. Which is not so surprising if you think of it. Keep a daughter in the dark, and she has no recourse but to develop a photographic memory.

So here's the scene: it's six in the evening, but due to a dip in the gas supply, the turkey won't be done until nine. Amy is dashing to and fro looking elegant and otherworldly in her mauve velvet bell-sleeved blouse and palazzo trousers. We're playing the truth game. My father has just told three tales against himself and now he wants us to cross-examine him, to decide which one we believe. One involves a hitman, another a stolen baby. The third concerns a foiled assassination attempt, and when Sinan presses him for details, Chloe's brother Neil (the family patriot) tells my father not to answer. 'You'd be endangering national security!'

Then Amy steps in. 'Can't you find something more edifying to talk about, on this day of all days? I've never heard anything so silly.'

My father sighs. 'Women! They always spoil the fun.'

He is joking, of course. But at the same time, he means it.

This is a man who is tiring of his mask, who, in spite of his better judgment, wishes someone would just reach out and tear it off. He is tired of keeping secrets, tired of slaving over reports that no one but his hated superiors will ever see, tired of always knowing better than the misinformed masses, tired of the Suits back home misinforming the higher-ups whenever his information does not suit their political agendas.

He's tired of consulates and diplomatic parties and trips to the Covered Bazaar with this year's batch of new arrivals who've been sent to Turkey even though they are experts on Latin America because that is how the people in Washington make sure their diplomats stay loyal.

He wants out. Forget politics. Make a new life with Amy, put down roots here, really get to grips with the history of the city. Write a book, perhaps. Do a little traveling. Teach a course or two. Have fun. Most of all, he longs to pick up the phone and dial a certain office outside Washington and 'tell them to shove it.'

But for now, it's consolation enough to fret about someone else who is hemmed in on all sides, who deserves a bigger, better life and still has the chance to find it — given the right sort of guidance.

'Come in for a nightcap, why don't you,' my father says to Sinan as we make our way home. He sends me upstairs. 'This won't be long,' he says.

But when I come downstairs at four in the morning, they are still deep in conversation. The air is stale — smoke flavored with bourbon. Sinan is sitting, perched forward in his chair, frowning but also nodding as my father gently chides him for 'avoiding the issue,' for playing into the problem, for 'sneaking around' and 'making dubious friends' instead of standing up to his father 'like a man,' for letting 'fashionable rebels' dictate his thoughts, instead of asking what he has to give to the world, what he has that is special. Sinan's shoulders sag with every new reproach, and then there is the searing shock of recognition.

This is what it looks like.

This is what a good father can do.

This is how my father might have talked to me, if I'd been a boy."

As autumn progressed, so, too, did the arguments about safety. Which had everything to do with Jeannie not being a boy. Though her father trusted her, though his confidence in Jeannie's "innate" common sense was absolute, though he did not want to cramp her style, he couldn't just leave her "to it" as he might have done the son he'd never had. This was a tricky city for young women at the best of times, and now, with things heating up the way they were, he didn't want her to think she could just go anywhere: "I'd hate to see you walk into something ugly," he said. "Even if nothing bad happened, you'd lose your nerve." As the bombs grew more numerous that autumn, and the little scuffles between students and the police in the downtown universities escalated into gunbattles, he kept adding new names to the list of places Jeannie had to promise to avoid.

She'd tell him where she wanted to go and he'd shake his head and say, "Not on a Saturday afternoon, you're not," or "That's no place for a blonde pony-tail." His five categories of danger in descending order were: "absolutely not," "you must be joking," "only if you have no alternative," "that should be okay but I still want you to keep your eyes peeled," and "what a relief."

"Of course I resented this. Of course I had no way of understanding that it was not just a question of physical safety. He wanted to protect me from reality. He knew, perhaps from bitter experience, that too great a dose of reality would force the issue. As indeed it did."

One place she was meant to avoid at all cost was Beyazıt Square, in the Old City. But on the Tuesday after Thanksgiving, something went wrong with the school heating system and they were let out early, and Lüset asked the gang to go down with her to the Covered Bazaar to help her buy a leather coat.

Usually you had to fight your way past milling crowds, staggering porters, and darting boys with trays of tea. But today the main thoroughfare was almost empty – for every customer there were ten anxious shopkeepers trying to charm her into buying their finest necklace, carpet, copper tray. They all used the same gestures, and the same eye tricks. Jeannie could almost hear the beat they all danced to. In the beginning, when Chloe and she were walking in front, there was an effort to guess their nationality. French? Dutch? German? English? American? At the sound of Suna's harsh, admonishing Turkish, their smirks faded into abject murmurs, obsequious nods and bowed heads.

They visited every leather shop in the bazaar: Lüset, for whom shopping was a loathsome chore, couldn't find a single coat she liked. With each new coat that Suna found, Lüset would puff out her lips, confer with her reflection, shake her head. Suna would snort and light up a cigarette. Chloe would pick out the coat of her dreams, the glacé leather monstrosity she'd have bought in a flash had she been rich like Lüset. Suna would take one look at it and say, "But what can you be thinking, my dear girl? This is a disaster. Look at those buttons! Those seams! And the leather! Is it even leather, or plastic for the price of leather?"

When they had worked their fruitless way to the far end of the bazaar, Suna remembered that there was a book she needed for the talk she'd be giving at Current Affairs Club the following afternoon. It was her wish, she said, "to draw a line between last weekend's bombing of the US Officer's Club in Ankara and the forgotten atrocities of the Korean War." Off they went to Sahaflar, the second hand book market, to watch Suna and Lüset browse. The air was chilly and although most stalls had braziers, Jeannie still got the shivers. Was this why they noticed her? From time to time a stallkeeper asked Suna who "these foreigners" were. Without looking up, she would say they were Americans. On hearing this, the other customers – all very serious customers, serious leftwing students with Che Guevara moustaches and army surplus coats – would glare at them.

"I don't know about you," Chloe said to Jeannie. "But I'm

beginning to feel . . . *hmm* . . . What's the word I'm looking for?"

"American?" Jeannie said.

As another customer looked up to glare at them, they began to giggle. "So what do you say?" said Chloe. "Time for the Americans to go home?"

They'd meant to go straight down to the sea and catch a ferry from Eminönü but they dipped into a side street to shake off two men who seemed to be following them, and soon they were lost. The meandering alleyways of that neighbourhood were always teeming in the daytime, but this afternoon they were more crowded and agitated than ever. Turning into a main street, they were almost knocked down by a ragged cluster of men running in the opposite direction. Hearing a roar in the distance – and a muffled chant, a siren, breaking glass – Beyazıt Square, it had to be – they turned around, too. But they made the mistake of running into a cul-de-sac. When they turned around, there were upwards of twenty men blocking the way. One was holding a club.

The men were swarthy, angry, hungry, bewildered. "Let me handle this," said Chloe. She addressed the men in Turkish. But no one moved.

They were so close Jeannie could smell them. One man stepped forward and lifted a lock of Jeannie's hair. There was a murmuring, the same three-syllable word hissing from lip to lip. But just as the man closest to Jeannie pushed closer a second man stepped aside to let the girls pass. Chloe grabbed Jeannie's hand and pulled her around the corner into the street. They hurled themselves downhill, down to the next corner, where they made the mistake of looking over their shoulders. There they all were. Swarthy, angry, hungry, bewildered, and waiting to be told what to do. The man with the club let out a cry and they all came hurtling down the street.

> "We were saved, in the end, by a man who ran a button shop. He'd gone outside to see what the noise was about. When I tripped on a cobblestone, he picked me up and pulled us inside.
>
> I remember peeking around his counter, watching our assailants rush past. And the worried crowd of well-wishers that gathered around us afterwards, the tea they brought us, the sting of the iodine our saviour poured over my knee. The murmured question, repeated with every new arrival. 'Where are they from?' The answer, rippling through the crowded shop and into the street. 'They're American. American. American.'

A swarthy man was staring through the window. Insolent, contemptuous, disgusted. What did he see in my face that made him hate me so? How could he hate me so, when he didn't know a thing about me?

The buttonseller insisted that his boy escort us to the ferry station. We must have been in shock, because when the ferry pulled away from the shore, we both burst out laughing.

We did the same when we walked into Chloe's kitchen. When her mother asked what was so funny, Chloe said, 'Absolutely nothing.'

'Are you sure? You look dishevelled.'

'No, honestly, I'm feeling fine,' Chloe said. 'I would even go so far as to say I feel . . . American?'

Chloe's mother was not amused. She stood in the doorway, her arms akimbo. 'Being American is not a joke, you know. You should be proud of who you are.'

That night I dreamt I was Sisyphus, rolling not one rock up a hill, but two."

But not for much longer. Walking into the little dining room off Marble Hall the following afternoon, Jeannie found Suna laying out papers for the Current Affairs Club. Normally this involved much barking of orders, but today she was so fired up she hardly noticed the others. For at last she had found "the perfect illustration of our problem."

Next to a cursory report on the bombing of the US Officer's Club in Ankara the previous weekend (clipped from the International Herald Tribune, with the words "no casualties" highlighted in yellow magic marker) she had placed a sheet of paper on which she had listed by nationality the number of dead in the Korean War. At the top of the list was Turkey. Above Exhibits A and B was another sheet of paper on which Suna had written: "CONNECT THE DOTS."

"Just the sight of those three words made my blood boil. So I asked her. What exactly was she trying to say? Her answer: 'It's my thought for the day.' My retort: it made no sense."

Oh yes, it did, Suna insisted. But only if her esteemed American friend was brave enough to 'connect the dots'.

"I could tell from her smug smile that she knew what those three words did to me. So I asked her: What did a war that happened almost twenty years ago have to do with a bombing that happened last week?"

"To an American, perhaps nothing," said Suna airily. "But to a Turk, everything. You used us as cannon fodder in Korea, you know. But did you ever apologize?"

To which Jeannie replied: "It wasn't me who used Turks as cannon fodder in Korea."

To which Suna said nothing. Instead she began to hum. So Jeannie said it again. This time she shouted:

"IT WASN'T ME!"

I hate crying (she confessed in her letter). I hate people seeing me cry. I hate it when I have to ask them to pass me a tissue, because I forgot mine at home. I hate blowing my nose in front of them, and running out of tissues again, and seeing the pity in their eyes. I longed to run out of the room, out of the building. I didn't want anyone to see how red my eyes were, most especially Miss Broome. Who was due any minute now. Who would be so concerned, so attentive, and so keen to discuss my distress. Suna seemed to understand all this. After she had brought me my tissues, and conferred in whispers with Chloe and Lüset, she said, 'I think we should go for a walk. But don't worry. No one will see us. We'll leave by the back.'

She didn't even flinch when the alarm went off. 'If you walk normally, no one will notice.' So we walked normally to the far end of the plateau. We sat down on the marble bench and watched the passing ships.

'I am truly sorry about yesterday,' she said then. 'I had no idea. I should have been more sensitive. But I am a very strange person, with very strange moods, and I am always saying things I shouldn't say. I know.'

I told her I liked it that she spoke her mind, but then I caved in again.

'No more tears! It's an order! The general commands you! Here, I brought more tissues. Please. For I have more to say.'

She had a confession to make. So terrible she could hardly bring herself to say it. 'I love having arguments with you. What sort of monster does that make me?'

A human being?

'Don't laugh. I'm serious. I love arguing with you, because you're my equal. I love arguing with you, because you listen. You never say, "Oh Suna," or "Suna, please!" like the others. As if I were some sort of Marxist-Leninist circus clown. No, you listen, and then you ask a good question, a question that makes me wish I were an acrobat. Because we're equals, most of the time we're equals. Except today. Today you were upset.'

It wasn't her fault, I said. That, she said, was neither here nor there. 'I should have noticed.' A little detail — a change in the way I waved my hand, a catch in my breath, just one of the ten thousand things Lüset noticed.

'*Instead I rolled on. Like a steamroller, to quote Lüset. What I said was not just stupid, but untrue. You did not send those Turkish soldiers to Korea, and you were not the one who used them as cannon fodder. But do you know what, my friend? Even if you had, I'd defend you to the death.'*

She took my hand. 'So can we be friends again? Will you forgive me my huzursuzluklar, *and the senseless storms that threaten our future? Oh please say yes, Jeannie. I long to argue with you forever.' "*

How clear the air was when Jeannie set off for home that evening. As she made her way down the steep and winding path to the Bosphorus, pausing from time to time to look up at the gnarled and curving branches of the Judas trees, stopping on the 138th step to catch the first glimpse of the sea, she made her plans. She chose her words, so carefully that she was on and off the bus and halfway up the Aflıyan before she had composed them to her satisfaction. For once it didn't feel too steep. For once she did not trip on a single cobblestone or cower in the shadow of the castle or turbaned tombs that lined the cemetery wall.

"I knew what I had to do, as surely as I knew the wind on my back."

How golden the *meydan* looked in the late afternoon sun. How dusty their green gate. How sharp and damp the evening air as she walked down the path. How dark the churning waters of the Bosphorus. How easy it was to pull up a chair next to her father's great desk and ask the question. As the words hung in the air, he showed no surprise. She might as well have asked what they were having for supper. Tipping back his chair, he said, "So let me guess. Someone's been giving you a hard time?" But how easy it was for her to insist on a proper answer.

This was his answer: "Basically, I'm a desk guy. Mostly, I just sit at that desk of mine and analyse information."

Which was just not good enough. So she kept pressing. He didn't seem to mind. "The short answer is that there is no short answer. It varies. Sometimes we pay for our information, or people owe us a favor. Or they want revenge. Mostly they're lying. And mindbogglingly boring. That's our greatest secret, the one no thriller can divulge . . ."

"What I still don't understand is what you do all day."

"The truth, Jeannie, is that I spend most of my day in meetings."

"What sort of meetings?"

"Meetings with goons."

"And then?"

"I write reports about these meetings for other goons who don't know what the hell I'm talking about, and care even less."

"Then what's the point?" she asked. "Why do you do this to yourself?"

"Well, look at it like this . . ." he began. She cut him off.

"What's the point of being here if they don't like us, Dad?"

'The army likes us. The army loves us!'

'Yes,' she said. 'But what about the people?'

'The people might not like us, but they'd like the Soviet alternative a hell of a lot less, believe you me." Tipping back his chair, he recited his tired mantra. "So that's why we're here, Jeannie. To defend freedom, justice and democracy, the principles that made our country great. Life, liberty and the pursuit of happiness – remember? Not that you've looked very happy lately."

"I'm fine," she said.

"Then what's the problem?"

"There isn't one!"

"I'm wondering if it isn't that Bolshevik classmate of yours who pushed you into this." She shook her head, perhaps a little too vigorously. "Then is it Sinan?" She shook her head again. "In that case, it must be his parents," her father said.

"What makes you say that?"

"Parents are very interfering here. Though not without cause."

"So tell me. What's this cause?"

He waved his hand, as if to swat a fly. "Oh who knows? They could be worried we might spirit Sinan off to the US of A. Which wouldn't be a bad idea! This is just between you and me, by the way. Same goes for the other matter we were discussing. I don't say this lightly. Do you hear?"

"What – you want to turn me into a liar, just like you?"

"I'm telling you to exercise caution. Listen, rumors in and of themselves can't hurt you. They're a dime a dozen, and there's safety in numbers. But if you go around with a sign on your back . . ."

"I don't have to tell anyone. They know already."

"What I mean is, don't let them know you know." He stood up, and as Jeannie did the same, he turned to beam at her.

She didn't know this look. What was it — concerned? Abashed? Solicitous? No, condescending. Patting her on the head, he said, "Poor old Jeannie. All the woes of the world on her back. Is all this getting too much for you? What I meant was…you were so full of life when you got here. So full of curiosity and joy. You'd look into a horizon and dream of what was beyond it. You'd watch people walking along the waterfront and see their stories trailing after them like comets. But now . . ." He fixed her with his beadiest and most regretful gaze.

"I'm fine," she said.

"You're sure, now." It was a question.

"I'm just tired," she said. "I haven't been sleeping."

"Well, maybe this will help."

"That night it did. But the following morning, as I was walking up the long steep path to Gould Hall, lost in the disordered euphoria that can only come from having demanded the truth and received it (I was right, it wasn't just my mind tricking me, I stood up to him! I spoke my mind! But it's not as bad as I feared, it's just a job and someone has to do it, if it's only analysing information, what harm can there be in that?) *the odd thing my father had said at the very end of our conversation floated back into my mind. And that was when it hit me. I had never talked to my father about horizons or waterfronts or stories trailing after people like comets. He knew all this because he'd read my journal."*

III
The Coup

16

ET ME PAUSE HERE, Mary Ann, to answer a question that one of your number raised in a recent email. As the mother of two grown children, I do understand where it comes from. It must be very hard for someone in Washington DC to take on board – especially if that person is sitting in the well-appointed, amply funded and closely guarded offices of the Center for Democratic Change. Here we have a seventeen-year-old girl who'd come close to death or serious injury at the hands of an anti-American rabble in the streets of Istanbul. Why did she not take the first plane home? To quote your colleague – there are two parents involved here. If William Wakefield refused to see the writing on the wall, why did Jeannie's mother also fail to act, once it became clear that the city was fast becoming a no-go zone for US personnel?

In fact, she did, though she was hampered at first by poor information. To illustrate my point, let me backtrack to the first incident your colleague mentions: the bombing of the NCO Club by leftwing students in Ankara in late November 1970. Sadly, it did not make the *New York Times*, so Jeannie's mother never heard of it.

As for the incident in late December – when another group of leftwing students threw firebombs at the Prime Minister's car in downtown Istanbul – the *New York Times* did run a short item on his narrow escape. Solicitous mother that she was, Nancy Wakefield called Istanbul at once to register her concern. But her ex-husband insisted there was nothing to worry about. The bomb, he said, was "a flash in a pan."

In January, there was a lull – though the New York Times ran a long piece in the middle of the month that alluded to dangerous student extremists pushing the country towards civil war. However, the author was confident that the Prime Minister would keep the ship of state on course, and when William Wakefield spoke to his ex-wife, he quoted from this article.

A week later, students barricaded themselves into the faculty buildings of a university in Ankara and fought back the police with gunfire, firebombs, dynamite and stones. Eight people were injured, and forty-five were arrested. There was no report in the *New York Times*, and therefore no phone call from Northampton.

In February 1971 Turkey became "a story." When Demirel, the Prime Minister, introduced legislation that would make it a prisonable offence to "interfere with commercial activity, occupy factories, make bombs, insult or resist officers of the law, interfere with public services or road transport and deface official posters," the *New York Times* devoted the better part of a page to putting his move into context. Again, they described the threat as seen from the Prime Minister's office: the universities were full of dangerous anarchists, subversives and extremists. The most dangerous were their leaders, who were not really students, he said, but *agents provocateurs*. Their demands, he said, had nothing to do with university reform but with "extreme Marxism and Maoism." And yes, this did give Jeannie's mother pause.

So imagine her horror when, four days later, she opened her morning paper to read that a band of extreme leftwing students connected to Revolutionary Youth, Turkey's largest leftwing student association, had kidnapped a US sergeant in Ankara. Though they released him seventeen hours later, the Turkish authorities were now under pressure to take visible and decisive action to end the wave of terrorist attacks on US personnel, so they instigated a series of arms searches in the country's largest universities. They met with heavy resistance. In one raid at Hacettepe Medical University in Ankara, there were twenty people injured and two hundred arrests.

Reporting on the wave of bomb blasts in other parts of the country, the *New York Times* spoke of an "expanded urban guerrilla move-

ment," increasing hatred of "US imperialism," and the growing danger
to which US citizens living in Turkey were now exposed. Reading this,
Nancy Wakefield began her campaign in earnest, but she had made little headway when, in early March, a group calling itself the Turkish
People's Liberation Army, kidnapped four US airmen as they were driving out of an airbase near the capital. The kidnappers sent a letter to a
newspaper to announce that they were "purging the country of all
American and foreign enemies" and to promise that the hostages would
be killed unless they received $400,000 dollars by the following night.

The government responded by sending two thousand policemen
and militiamen out to search the universities, where they reported finding a "huge amount" of explosives, guns and ammunition. Students
occupying one dormitory in Ankara tried to fend them off with gunfire and dynamite. Two died on the scene and twelve were injured. The
next day, reconnaissance planes and jeeps provided by the US for opium
control joined the search for the kidnapped airmen. A day later, the
hostages returned to base unharmed: their kidnappers had panicked and
fled. The search for the kidnappers continued unabated, but a government spokesman said that the job was made more difficult by the fact
that the perpetrators of the crime were almost certainly "university or
graduate students of middle-class background." They were probably, he
said, hiding out "in some plush home."

The story was front-page news for the better part of a week, so
there were daily calls from Northampton. Over and over, William
Wakefield stalled her, and if you are wondering why he felt justified to
do so, it was because only a handful of the 16,000 US personnel in
Turkey had been touched by the violence, and no action whatsoever
had been directed against their thousands of dependent children.

He assured his ex-wife that "things" were happening behind the
scenes: the military was losing its patience and preparing to step in. The
clincher would be the CENTO summit, scheduled to take place in
Ankara at the end of March. There was, he said, no way the authorities
were going to expose the US Secretary of State and twenty-odd other
leading Western statesmen to any risks. He was right: two weeks before
the summit, on March 12th 1971, the commanders of the Turkish army
issued an ultimatum and Demirel stepped down.

But still the violence continued, and on the night of the 14th of

March, there were four bomb attacks against US interests in Istanbul – a Turkish-American trade bank, two newspapers, and the US Consulate. The following morning, two students shot and wounded the American manager of an English language bookshop. Later that same day, Northampton called, in tears this time, demanding Jeannie's immediate return.

Knowing that his ex-wife was genuinely distraught, but determined not to let her have her way, William Wakefield went on the offensive. He told her she was to stop drawing wild conclusions from what she read in a "paper that doesn't even bother to have a bureau here." Yes, the universities in downtown Istanbul were war zones, "and no one can claim I've tried to hide this from you. But Jeannie never goes near those places, nor would she want to. And there are, I assure you, no gunbattles at Robert College." Technically this was true, but there had been several small bombs, a long string of noisy boycotts, and a fierce campaign to nationalize the university. At least half of the student body belonged to Revolutionary Youth. There was no need to go into this: it had not been mentioned in the *New York Times*.

So once again, Jeannie was off the hook. But freedom came at a price – as her father, still nursing a grievance, was only too happy to remind her. She would only be able to stay in Turkey for as long as she let him lie for her.

17

ARCH 15TH 1971
"Dear Mother,
I hope you don't mind me calling you that. It just feels more grown up.
And I hope you're feeling better after your conversation with Dad this morning.
I'm fine – I really am. More than fine! I'm sure that's hard to believe, when
you've been reading such distressing things in the New York Times. But if you
were here with me right now, you'd have a hard time believing any of it.

As I write these words I am sitting with my friends in Nazmi's, a beauti-
ful garden café just outside Bebek, on the shores of the Bosphorus. It's four in
the afternoon and the light . . ."

How to describe the light pouring over them? How to capture the
truth in words before it changed? The frost glowing in each little pane
of glass, the flashes of gold at the edges, the fierce patches of blue
beyond, the heat pumping out of the stove behind her, the scraping
chairs and happy murmurs, the aroma of *böreks* . . .

She looked down the table. Occupying the middle section was a
group of students she had only just met. At the far end were Haluk and
Chloe, holding hands across the table. Between them, at the head of the
table, sat Suna, peering peevishly into an open textbook. Suna was
helping Haluk with his homework; he was having a hard time under-

standing, and an even harder time being seen to struggle. Chloe, meanwhile, was struggling but not quite managing to look as if she was above all this. Lüset had captured the trio perfectly in a surreptitious sketch on a napkin: Haluk's hunched shoulders, Chloe's pout, and the fire in Suna's eyes as she tapped the textbook with her pencil for didactic effect.

> *"We come here often after school. The food is delicious and you can stay for as long as you like even if all you've ordered is a drink and a light snack. We bring our homework with us . . ."*

News flash! Chloe had turned to the boy to her right. The boy with the large green eyes and the indolent laugh. Haluk was not happy about it. Slamming his book shut, he glared at his rival. This prompted a lecture on jealousy.

"But it's human," Haluk said in English.

"Your job is not to be human, but to be enlightened," Suna replied.

He put his hands over his eyes. This provoked a second tirade, but it soon fizzled out, because now the green-eyed boy was telling a long, involved joke.

> *"It's a really nice group of kids I'm here with today, and everyone's in a happy mood, in spite of all the bad news in the papers — which are biased by the way — the government is being really paranoid, and overreacting like crazy, because all the students really want is the freedom to express themselves and read the books of their own choice . . ."*

The windowpanes had steamed up so much by now that they were losing their golden edges. The waiters had just brought them a new platter of *böreks* but hers were still too hot to eat. "Did you burn your mouth?" asked Sinan. Not too badly, she replied. He brushed a strand of hair from her face and, draping his arm around her, turned back to hear the green-eyed boy. Though Jeannie could pick out a fair number of words, the sentences were long, and the suffixes confusing, and they all spoke so fast. Did the girl next to Haluk have a secret crush on him? When she caught Jeannie watching, she fixed her with a glare.

She interrupted the conversation to ask who Jeannie was. Sinan answered sharply — his girlfriend. After a tense silence, the conversation resumed. When Jeannie lost the thread, she turned her attention to the other customers.

At the next table there was a couple that had not spoken for going on an hour. The man looked to be in his forties; the woman half that.

To her right was the man from the Soviet Consulate who often dropped by Nazmi's on an afternoon, and who, according to Chloe, was given to turning up uninvited at her parents' parties, bringing with him Russian vodka and copies of *And Quietly Flows the Don*. Sinan seemed to know him, too, though he wouldn't explain how – only that this man was not to be trusted or acknowledged. Seeing her eyes travel towards this man's table, Sinan pressed down on her foot.

This same man was standing at the door, adjusting his Astrakhan hat, when Jeannie's father walked in. "Sergei! Just the man I was looking for!"

For a few moments, they conversed. And Jeannie prayed. Please Dad, don't come in here. Please Dad, walk right out with your friend.

When William Wakefield looked over his shoulder and saw his daughter, he feigned surprise.

"Well, hi there. Busy studying, as usual?" He smiled as he eyed each of them in turn. No one smiled back. Feigning equanimity, he turned to Jeannie.

"Listen. When can I expect you home?"

"About eight?" she said in the thinnest voice.

"Eight at the latest." Spoken like a general. As he headed for the door, the girl with the secret crush on Haluk asked Sinan another question. The boy with the green eyes answered for him. "*Casus*," he said. *Casus* meant spy. The green-eyed boy looked straight at Jeannie as he said it. But she was used to this game now. How to make your face go blank. How to read your enemy's intentions even when his face was blank, too. How to *imply* contempt while committing yourself to nothing. How to make an insinuation – an *elegant* insinuation – while smiling sweetly. How to sit on your feelings, press them so thin you could put your finger through them… But that's so wrong, Jeannie! No good can come of it! Whatever happened to the First Amendment? Did Tom Paine speak in vain? Where are you when I need you, John Henry? Give me liberty or give me death! Give me back my mind!

What on earth could they be talking about? First their voices rose and then they fell. Every so often the girl with the secret crush on

Haluk sat back to say, "Ah!" as if it really meant something. At long last Suna turned to Jeannie and said, "Do not worry, my little innocent. We have defended you. We have also explained that you are in the process of being educated."

"Educated for what?" Jeannie asked.

"Ah . . ." said Suna. "Now it is my turn to say 'Ah!'" Everyone at the table laughed – with her? At her? The conversation drifted away. Jeannie returned to her letter. But it was lies, all lies. A fresh page then. Take in a deep breath.

> *"Dear Mother,*
> *First let me apologize for my long silence. I hope I can make up for lost time!*
> *I thought I'd begin by . . ."*

But she had no idea how to begin any more. She had no idea what she thought. No, that wasn't quite right. She had forgotten how to think aloud. She knew now how dangerous it could be, how a word uttered was a word lost. But not to panic. They'd be leaving any minute now. All she had to do was stay patient. *Look* patient. Stay blank. Leave it all to Sinan. Wasn't that how he'd put it?

Gazing out through the frosted window, she watched the sun leave the garden for the Bosphorus. An elegant figure sailed down the dark path. The door swang open and in came their Modern Novel teacher, the saintly Miss Broome.

The room fell silent. The waiters, unaccustomed to seeing a beautiful young woman alone in public, were too stunned to move. It was as if a great light was shining down on them. They feasted gratefully at her large, soft, painfully earnest brown eyes and the long brown tresses that she'd draped over her left shoulder. She was wearing a long purple velvet coat and a velvet skullcap ringed with silver coins. She removed them prettily to reveal a long black dress. What was it made of? Was it felt? No, it was too soft. It must be cashmere. Could there be anything softer than a long black cashmere dress?

Catching sight of her favourite students, Miss Broome gave them a breezy wave. After the breathless waiters had settled her at a table, she reached into her black velvet handbag and brought out a fountain pen and a marbled notebook. After gazing at length through the frosted windows, as if in search of inspiration, she leaned forward to rub one of the windowpanes clean.

Now why hadn't *she* thought of that? Jeannie leaned forward, to see what Miss Broome saw. But now the door had opened again. This time it was two young men wearing embroidered sheepskin coats and jeans. One had shaggy brown hair and granny glasses and the sort of gaunt cheekbones that spoke of long years in the serious section of the library. The second had short but ruffled blond hair and it wasn't until his eyebrows shot up, seemingly of their own accord, that Jeannie placed him. No Name, the shorn sheep, the young American at her father's desk that morning last June.

They headed straight to Miss Broome's table. The aesthete with the granny glasses leaned over to whisper in her ear. Without lifting her eyes from her marbled notebook, she smiled. What must it be like, to be free like Miss Broome? To be yourself no matter where you were? No matter how people were treating you, or what they said?

A pat on the shoulder. This was the signal: Haluk had passed Sinan the key. The key was to Haluk's new apartment in Rumeli Hisar. His *garçonniere*. Suna didn't know about it yet; hence the subterfuge. Except . . .

It was six o'clock already. Jeannie had to be home by eight. But when he rose from the table, Sinan acted as if he had all the time in the world. When they passed Miss Broome's table, he stopped, somewhat stiffly to greet the man in the granny glasses. "Dutch, meet Jeannie Wakefield. Jeannie, meet Dutch Harding."

"Oh!" Jeannie cried. But Dutch said nothing. His gaze was frank, thoughtful, detached. She could be a display in a natural history museum.

"Why are you looking at me like that?" she asked.

"Because you're not what I expected," Dutch replied. He leaned forward. "And that's good. Because I hate to be bored. Don't you?"

"*Honestly*, Dutch. What's got into you? Can't you see you're unnerving her?" Miss Broome put a proprietary hand on Dutch's arm. "Don't pay these boys any attention, Jeannie. They're just nervous because you're so pretty."

"Thanks a lot, Billie!" said the shorn sheep. Leaning forward, offering Jeannie his hand, he said, "You remember *me*, don't you?"

"Of course," Jeannie said. Without thinking, she smiled. Sinan's fingers pressed into her hand. "So anyway," she said, turning back to Miss Broome.

"Yes," Miss Broome said. "You look like you're in a hurry. Until tomorrow, then? Same time, same place? Oh, and Jeannie," she added, "I almost forgot." She reached into her velvet handbag. "I brought you another book."

Which one was it that day? *The Tragedy of American Diplomacy* by William Appleman Williams, or *The Politics of War* by Gabriel Kolko? She was reading as fast as she could by now, but still lagging behind the others – and rudderless, utterly rudderless – though she knew what she was looking for, and searched for it more desperately each day.

Miss Broome tried so hard to be tactful, to remember where Jeannie "was coming from." But there was a point in every discussion when she'd take in a sharp breath and clasp her hands to stare into the middle distance like a bird in search of a worm. "How much do you know about our foreign adventures during the 19th century?" she'd ask. And Jeannie would say, "Not a whole lot." To which Miss Broome would reply, "Well, to be fair. Not many Americans do. And that's a shame, because what we're seeing now comes to them as a direct result, I'd say, of the Open Door Policy." "The Open Door Policy?" Jeannie would ask. And Miss Broome would sigh and stand up and go into her study and come back a few minutes later carrying a book. "I think you'd better read this."

She didn't always accept what she read and to be fair, Miss Broome didn't expect her to. But little by little, some of it was seeping in. It wasn't that she'd lost her illusions, or stopped loving her country. But she had questions. About who had the power, and what these people did in their name. The more she found out, the more she wanted to know. The more she knew, the more she had to ask herself what "we the people" really stood for. And why, if we the people stood for democracy, we knew so little about the people we voted into office. Little by little, her questions became more loaded. Once in a while, she'd say something to her father that would make him say, "Christ! Where do you get that from?"

Repressive tolerance. That was one new concept. Comprador bourgeoisie. That was another. Polymorphous perversity. Commodity fetishism. "I defy you to define that," he'd say. And when she did, he'd ask, "Is this the work of Miss Broome again?"

"Really, it's a collective thing," she'd say.

"Collective. As in *Animal Farm?*"

"Not at all," she'd say. "Miss Broome believes in democratic debate."

"You could fool me," he'd say.

And she'd say, "No honestly. She wants us to think for ourselves. But she also wants us to know when the papers are lying to us, when they leave things out. Or skew the lessons of history."

"Now why would any right-thinking person want to do that?"

"Do you really want to know?" Jeannie would ask.

"Pull up a chair. Tell me more about that book in your hand."

And she would. And more often than not, he'd have read it, too. He'd tell Jeannie what he thought about it, because wasn't that part of the deal? He had no right to know where she was every minute of the day, but ideas were something else. She wasn't going to pretend she agreed with him when she didn't. The only way she was ever going to hold her own with this man was to speak her mind. So she'd tell him what Miss Broome had said about it, and what Suna had taken issue with, and what Sinan had said about it later, and what great new insight Dutch had allegedly uttered in response, and what she had said when Sinan repeated it to her afterwards. And then their free exchange of ideas would get freer still. For he'd turned a new leaf. He talked to her now as an equal. He had to! Gone were the days when he could peek into her journal. She kept it well hidden now. Her true thoughts likewise. Whatever she committed to the treacherous page, it had nothing to do with what she truly thought. Far better, she thought, to argue about books.

But when they'd gotten to the bottom of whatever it was, and he asked Jeannie what she made of it all, she'd forget sometimes that he had no right to ask. She'd tell him how lost, how lonely she felt now that her ideal picture of herself and her country had been destroyed. She'd tell him what she was searching for in all these books: how to make amends for all this, where to begin. There was an ache in her, she said. It wouldn't go away until she found a new way to be American. A good American. Did he understand?

She'd talk and talk, and he'd sit there, frowning, nodding, pondering her every word. But every once in a while, he'd wander out to the porch, pick up his binoculars, and train them on the village beneath them.

18

ABRIEF HISTORY OF the *garçonniere*: as I mentioned earlier, it was in Rumeli Hisar, almost directly below the Pasha's Library, on the third floor of a concrete apartment house owned by Haluk's father. When Talat Bey first acquired it – this would be during the mid-60s, when he was a married man in need of occasional privacy – he had kept it mostly for himself, though it is possible that various colleagues also used it from time to time. It is unlikely that the family maid was ever invited in to clean the place, which was, I think, in pretty poor condition when the key passed on to Haluk in the early months of 1971.

At the outset, Haluk used it in much the same way as his father had done, though he, too, passed the key to a handful of trusted friends. Later that spring, when the crackdown on the student left began in earnest, he passed it to a handful of trusted classmates from a banned student association of uncertain allegiance. Some say they called themselves White Enlightenment. Others say they belonged to the faction that called itself Green Enlightenment. Some say it was Maoist; others say it was a wolf in Maoist clothing. Until the "Trunk Murder" no one in this group had been directly linked with violent action.

The *garçonniere* stayed in Haluk's family's possession after said murder – make of that what you will. Sometime during the 1990s, Talat Bey passed the title to his son. Now it's Haluk's son who lives there. His roommate is Chloe's stepson. Both boys are studying engineering at the university.

In November 2005 – the day after Jeannie disappeared, and the day before I wrote my incriminating article for the *Observer* – Chloe took me round to see the apartment for myself. I'd asked, of course. That said, our main reason for stopping by that day was not to help me with my research, so to speak, but to find out if either of the boys had seen Jeannie. They were horrified to hear of her disappearance, promising to do everything they could to help find her. One went straight online; the other went for his phone and proceeded to go through its entire address book. "We'll track her down," they assured us. Meanwhile, we were to sit and drink their tea. So yes, I had a good long look at this apartment, which looked a lot like the student apartments I remember from my own teenage years. As did (uncannily) the boys themselves.

The sink was filled with unwashed glasses, though a slip of a girl with large, sad, moonlike eyes soon emerged to wash and dry them. There was a pile of shoes and slippers next to the door. Crimson curtains, and hanging from the ceiling, a garish chandelier. The sofa was piled high with books; poking out from underneath was the corner of what may or may not have been a porn mag. The air smelled stale.

Pointing at the widescreen TV in the corner, Chloe said, "In 1971 that was where we had the mimeograph machine."

"*The* mimeograph machine?"

"The one we stole from school." Though she could not, she now admitted, remember exactly when "the heinous crime was perpetrated." She was guilty only by association. "It was Suna who nabbed it. And Jeannie who carried it over."

When I asked why, she shrugged her shoulders and said, "April 1971? A few weeks after the army stepped in. One of the first things they did was shut down the student associations. Most particularly the ones spewing out dangerous pamphlets on their mimeograph machines. So Haluk invited some of them to spew them out here in secret. Well, at least one of them."

I asked if she remembered which one. She shrugged her shoulders. "What difference does it make? They changed their names every two days or so. This despite the fact that they were all the same. As far as I could see, anyway. Which wasn't very far. This being before contact lenses."

She let out a short, pained laugh. "I'm sorry," she said, but without explaining what for. "This wasn't the happiest chapter in my life, as you may well imagine. I lived in constant terror."

"Was it really that bad?"

She gave me a sharp look. "Don't you remember?" she said. "For God's sake, you lived here once, too! Don't you remember what it was like? Or did you really erase absolutely everything when you boarded that plane? Come on, now. Take your mind back. It's the late 60s, and you're an American girl in Turkey. You're in bed with a boy but you're afraid of sleeping with him. You're so afraid you can feel nothing else. You're afraid of sleeping with him, because if you do, he'll stop respecting you and leave you. You're afraid your reputation precedes you. You're a foreign girl, after all. Isn't that what foreign girls do? So if you don't sleep with him, he'll be doubly insulted. If you don't sleep with him, he'll find someone else who will. You're afraid he's already done so, because the sheets underneath you are yellow. Stiff. Stained. Horrible! Nightmare! Ugh! You can't bear it! You want out! But when, when you rush out to the bathroom dressed only in ugly yellow spunky sheets, you get the 'looks' from all their friends. They know everything about you. And they couldn't care less that none of it is true. Doesn't any of this sound at all familiar to you, M? Was I really the only one?"

19

"ONE QUESTION MY *father never asked. I'm sure he assumed the worst, but in those days it would have been unthinkable for a father to ask a daughter if she was taking precautions. In my way I was, though I had no knowledge of contraception and no access to it either. But I had the full complement of folk myths, horror stories and unscientific warnings that schools and mothers and teen magazines were still dishing out to us right through the 60s, and there can't be many girls who lost their virginity as slowly as I did.*

I was afraid, in spite of Sinan's ever more exasperated assurances, that he would no longer respect me. I needed to be 'sure' – but I was not at all sure I could bear the shame, regret and loneliness. I did not, above all, want to 'give myself away.'"

I had no way of knowing that if I had come to know his body as well as my own, if he could ask me a question just by stroking the side of my face and I could answer by touching his arm, if I could spend an entire afternoon in the dark with him without once needing to speak, if I could get dressed, tidy up the room, check my hair, leave whatever building we were in by a separate exit but still feel his hands on my back and his breath in my ear, I had already given him everything I owned.

We'd agreed to wait until I thought the time was right. In the end, the time chose itself. "Are you all right?" he asked me afterwards. "Are you sure you're all right?' He sat up, brushed my hair off my face. He still loved me! I still loved him! I felt no shame, no regret. I had lost nothing. We had made love, and there was nothing on earth more beautiful than making love. They'd kept this secret from us. They'd lied!"

Something must have shown on Jeannie's face the next day. Or maybe it had nothing to do with her at all. But somehow Suna got wind of Haluk's garçonniere. She and Lüset went over to "pay a friendly visit" after school and found Haluk with a "woman". Suna was beside herself, and of course she went straight to Chloe to share her grief. In spite of her best efforts, she was just as upset as Suna was. The next day they confronted Haluk together.

This happened at the Robert College cafeteria, in front of a large and delighted audience. Jeannie was there, too, and euphoria had dulled her tact. When she told all three that she thought they were being less than honest about their feelings, no one thanked her. Suna was so distraught that her legs went and Haluk had to drive her home.

> "As I helped her across the playing field, I apologized for causing her more pain, but how thin my voice sounded. By the time we got to Haluk's Mustang, it was Suna consoling me: she still adored me, even though I was a repressed, joyless, blinkered, puritan triumphalist.
>
> That evening, over supper, I apologized to Chloe. That was stupid, too, because it made her mother dangerously curious. Chloe left the table in a huff and although Amy insisted I was not to blame ('These things will happen, and that's all there is to it!') I could see she was perturbed.
>
> A week or so later, when we were again at the Robert College cafeteria, and again a tense sixsome, the green-eyed boy from that afternoon at Nazmi's sat down next to Chloe and began to flirt with her. When they left the cafeteria together, Haluk made as if he didn't even notice. But from then on, and no matter how much the rest of us pleaded with him, he refused to speak to her, look at her, or sit at the same table.
>
> I sided with Chloe — of course. Why should there be one rule for Haluk and another for her? But I didn't think she was handling it right. Every afternoon, she'd come into the Robert College cafeteria with one boy and leave with another. Then the stories would circulate. Suna would translate them for me, and I can say at least that I was never fooled by them.
>
> But still I worried about her. I felt she was undervaluing herself. It would have been sometime in mid-April that I said so to her face. The circumstances were unfortunate: it was just after a champagne dinner to celebrate her getting into Radcliffe. Her mother was intensely relieved — it had been a 'high-wire winter'. Chloe having refused to apply to anywhere else. But now we were both in, and how nice it would be, to know that just down the hallway, there would be someone who was almost a sister.
>
> Our last conversation as almost-sisters began like this: I was saying there'd

*be four boys in our class for every girl. "But I want you to promise something.
I want you to value yourself, stop all this sleeping around."*

*She looked at me as if I'd said she should stop wearing grass skirts. "But
I've never slept with any of them," she said.*

Not any of them? Why not?

'Because I'm a virgin.'

'You are?'

'Yes, of course I am.' She drew up her knees. 'Aren't you?'

I didn't answer. Which was an answer in itself.

*I didn't get any sleep at all that night. My head was swirling. I kept think-
ing about all those afternoons she and Haluk had spent together, in Sinan's
mother's apartment, and then in Haluk's secret apartment in Rumeli Hisar. If
they hadn't been sleeping together, what had they been doing? Why had Chloe
held back? What was she afraid of? How had it been for Haluk? Poor Haluk,
I remember thinking. No wonder he'd felt so hemmed in. Everyone envying
him, everyone calling him a pasha, but once the door was closed – nothing. I
was hardly on speaking terms with Haluk by now, and the next day I made
things even worse by telling him how sad I was for him, now I knew the truth."*

He'd found her struggling around Akıntıburnu one evening, pursued by
the usual kerb crawlers. After she was safe in his Mustang, he went off
to reprimand them. Jeannie couldn't follow everything but the gist of it
was that they were a shame to the motherland. Haluk was still seething
when they pulled back onto the road. When she tried to thank him, he
growled, "You should know better."

"You sound angry."

"Of course I'm angry!"

Jeannie took this as an allusion to their earlier disagreement. So she
said, "I'm sorry about that, too. I mean – I had no idea Chloe was holding herself back like that. She only told me yesterday. I must admit, it
was quite a shock."

It was quite a shock also when Haluk pulled off the road again. They
came this close to going over the edge into the Bosphorus. Clutching
his steering wheel, Haluk turned around. "Tell me what Chloe said."

"She said she's never slept with anyone. Not even you."

He tightened his grip on the steering wheel. "She is lying."

"I don't think so."

"She is lying!" he slammed his fist down on the horn.

He reversed back onto the road and roared up the hill to the meydan. Jeannie thanked him for the lift.

"I could not have done otherwise," he said. "But now you must listen."

It was dark by now; she could only just see his eyes glinting in the shadows. "What I wish to say is this. We have never met today. I did not see you put yourself in needless danger, and you did not see me. Sinan will never hear of this. Do you understand?"

As Jeannie opened the door, he said, "There's one more thing. Tell your garbage friend that she's a garbage liar."

"Of course I didn't. But in the end Haluk must have said something about it to Sinan, and Sinan must have said something to Suna, and Suna being Suna couldn't keep it to herself. The next day, when we were sitting in Miss Broome's front room waiting for her to retrieve my next piece of essential reading, Suna turned to Chloe and said, 'So is it true you never slept with our poor friend Haluk? Is it true you never slept with any of them?' I'll never forget the look Chloe gave me right then. She was right to hate me.

Had she given me the dressing down I deserved, might I have learned my lesson in time — kept my unresearched opinions to myself — and perhaps, in so doing, saved us all?

Chloe being Chloe, there were no improving lectures. Her dignity depended on not caring, on being seen not to care. So the day after I had torn her social life to shreds, we went to school together in my father's chauffeur-driven car. We sat next to each other in class and doodled on each other's notebooks, ate lunch at the same table, giggling, gossiping and helping each other with our homework the same way we always did. On our way home, we stopped off at Robert College cafeteria. She went off to join her friends of the moment, and I went off to join the others. The moment I sat down, Haluk found a reason to leave. Suna heaved a great sigh and gathered up her things, signalling for Lüset to do the same.

Then it was just the two of us — just me and Sinan — what an unexpected boon! Our lives stretched out before us, and it was only four o'clock."

A great black hulk of a tanker was just coming out from behind the southernmost tower of Rumeli Hisar as they sat down in front of Nafi Baba's tomb. For a few moments the whole hill trembled. They watched it threading its way up the Bosphorus, turning from black to grey. As it crossed paths with another tanker coming down from the Black Sea, a horn sounded. As the sharp, violent blast faded into its mournful echo, they heard the backfiring of a car. Then this, too, faded away. A bird that might have been a nightingale began to sing in the tree above. Could it be a nightingale, if it wasn't night yet? Could anything be more beautiful than the Bosphorus when the Judas trees were in bloom?

"There's one thing I don't understand yet," Jeannie said. Afternoon had melted into evening and they were in Dutch's office at Robert Academy. Dutch was away again, and Sinan was again looking after the cobra. The terrarium was sitting just below the window. They were sitting on the desk drinking from the bottle of Russian vodka that Sinan had fished out of the filing cabinet, and smoking the last of the hash Dutch had left Sinan in payment for his snakesitting services, and Jeannie had never been quite this stoned, this stupidly happy.

> *"Bookshelves lining every wall and books piled up across the floor. There were, I calculated, upwards of three thousand in residence, and only about a hundred were about mathematics. The rest, Sinan said, were about 'the revolution.'*
>
> *So that's how we got into this silly, reckless, pointless conversation that changed our lives — I was looking at the rows of sombre titles, and there was one thing I couldn't understand. How did Dutch expect this revolution of his to get started, if all he did was read books?"*

"He doesn't have to do a thing," Sinan said. "Revolutions start themselves."

"How convenient," Jeannie said.

"Don't laugh," he said. "I'm serious." But then he smiled, too.

"So let me get this straight. He just sits here, thinking revolutionary thoughts, and checking his watch from time to time, waiting for the call . . ."

"An intellectual must be patient in the face of history. He must choose his moment carefully!"

"You're laughing," Jeannie said.

"Of course I'm laughing. If I didn't laugh, I'd go mad."

"You would?"

"I'm quoting Dutch. He says beautiful things, you know. He says revolutions are like springtime. They seem to come from nowhere, but . . ."

"The seeds were planted long ago?"

He nodded. "And?"

"The roots must spread under the ground? The saplings must have time to grow? But when the sap starts running..."

"You can't stop the course of history any more than you could stop spring."

"The Judas trees must blossom . . ."

"Until one day, every hill in Istanbul turns pink! No – red!"

"And then what?" Jeannie asked, still giggling.

"The city will rise up!" he said. "The enemy will melt away!"

"And if they don't melt?"

"We'll round them up!"

"And then what?"

"What do you think? I'll start with İsmet. İsmet Bey, excuse me." He cocked his finger and pretended to shoot at the wall. "Or maybe I'll just wring his neck. Or break it, like this. Like a chicken."

"So that's the plan, is it?"

"There is no plan."

"How can there be no plan?"

"There doesn't need to be."

"Why not?"

"He leaned across me and pulled out a random book. It had a soft binding, and it was typed, not printed. I cannot for the life of me remember the title. Only that the author was Manfred Berger. 'Read Manfred Berger,' he proclaimed, 'and all your questions will be answered. But make sure no one sees you. Remember – thought is a crime!'

'So how about this thought?' I said, but without any forethought – that is one thing I would stake my life on – that this thought came from nowhere. 'What if your beloved Dutch Harding does have a plan, and simply hasn't told you about it?'

'Such twisted thoughts!' said Sinan.

'No, honestly,' I persisted. 'What if he's not really who he says he is? What if he's just playing a part?' Waving the bottle of Russian vodka before his eyes, I said, 'Hasn't it ever occurred to you to ask if perhaps, just perhaps . . . ?'

He snatched the bottle from my hand. I had never seen his face so dark. 'Who put this thought in your head?' he hissed. 'What has your father been saying to you? Why have you let him poison your mind?'

I felt as if he had slapped me. But for what? I could not say. I had not meant it seriously. I was just fooling around.

'Of course,' Sinan said coldly. 'For you it's all a joke. Let's go,' he said, *pulling my hand off his arm and putting the vodka back into its drawer. At the door, he turned around and said, 'He warned me, you know.'*

'About what?'

'He said that sooner or later, you would, in his words, revert to type.'

'What's that supposed to mean?'

'You want his exact words? Fine, then. I'll give them to you.'

He waited until we were halfway along the dark path around the Bowl. He was walking behind me, and his voice was loud and cold.

'There is no such thing as pure love, Sinan. The struggle taints all it touches. This thing you have going with her – it's putting us all at risk. Don't you see? Sooner or later, this girl will revert to type. By the time she's through with us, we'll all be behind bars, my boy. Or worse. You mark my words."'

Mark them she did. The moment she got home. She opened up the blank notebook that would become the journal of her last weeks in Turkey and she began her first entry with Dutch's damning words. Then she wrote what she thought of them. And then what she thought of their "sleazy, scheming, self-aggrandizing" author:

"But why am I bothering even to waste one ounce of thought on him? He knows nothing about the human heart, and one day Sinan, his most faithful disciple, will discover that he knows LESS THAN NOTHING about revolution."

She hid this journal well. Under the floorboards, where it would, after her departure, remain for more than thirty years. But it was too late for small acts of discretion. They'd been heard. They'd been recorded. They'd said the incriminating words, and now the dominoes were falling. Click, click, click.

The day after her visit to Dutch Harding's office, Jeannie arrived home to find her father sitting on the glass porch, waving a rolled up newspaper. "The *New York Times* has come through for us!" He passed her a long and exceptionally biased piece justifying the military coup, and the declaration of martial law in eleven provinces: there had, it said, been a real and imminent danger of what a government spokesman had called "a strong and active uprising against the motherland and the republic." Or maybe more than one – there were the Kurds in the Southeast, and the rightwing extremists, and the Syrians with their jealous eyes on

Hatay province, and the leftwing student extremists, many of whom were alleged to have been trained in Palestinian camps. There was, as usual, no effort to explain why.

Jeannie was just remarking on this to her father when they heard footsteps in the library. It was Sinan. A sullen, silent Sinan. Though her father had gone out of his way to insist that Sinan should use their house as his "second home," this was in no way reflected by the tone William took with him now.

"Who let you in?"

Lowering himself into a chair, Sinan asked if he could speak to Jeannie privately. "Be my guest," her father said. But he didn't move. So they went out to the garden, where Sinan told Jeannie the news. That afternoon Dutch had been called to the headmaster's office and threatened with dismissal for keeping a cobra on school property without permission.

"My first response was elation. Good riddance! I said to myself. But not to Sinan. No, to Sinan I expressed consternation. But not as convincingly as I should have done, because now he said, 'There's more, you know. You won't think this is so funny when I've told you the rest.' For after castigating Dutch over the cobra, the headmaster had produced a list of books. Was it true that Dutch kept these dangerous volumes in his office? Was it also true that he met secretly with a group of handpicked students to incite them to take up arms against the state? And what was this about drugs? What exactly was this 'Operation Judas Tree'? Although he wouldn't say where he'd got his information, the thing in his hands was clearly a transcript of our conversation in Dutch's office. Almost certainly courtesy of İsmet.

Now I, too, was outraged. But alas, not thinking clearly. When I think back now on the tumultuous days and weeks that followed, I sometimes wonder if I was able to think at all. Am I wrong to find myself lacking? Is this what it means to be overtaken by events?

That evening, though, it still looked simple. We had been wronged. We would insist on our rights! My father would fix it for us. My father would get İsmet on the phone and read him the riot act. But when we went inside, Sinan asked me to go upstairs, so he could talk to my father alone.'

It was not a happy conversation. It began with shouts and ended with slamming doors. "'I'm sorry,'" her father told her when Jeannie rushed downstairs, "but I'm afraid I had to read *him* the riot act. For his own good, of course."

She reached for her coat. Her father stopped her.

"I'd give him time to cool down if I were you." When she kept moving towards the door, he pulled her back. "You listen to me when I'm talking," he said. He had never taken that tone with her before.

Then came the lecture. A hundred leftists had been arrested in Istanbul during the night. Most were students belonging to associations that had now been outlawed. The most famous was Deniz Gezmiş, the leader of the gang that had kidnapped the four US airmen in early March. Although they had not harmed their hostages, there was a strong chance that he would get the death penalty.

"But he's just a student!" Jeannie protested.

"He'll hang anyway," her father replied

"You don't sound too sorry about it."

"I am very sorry. Especially for the poor deluded souls who go down with them. Which brings me to my point. I'm not happy with these new playmates of yours."

"Who exactly?"

"I think you know."

"You'd be surprised how many names I don't know."

"Then let's keep it that way. I'm warning you – this Enlightenment crew in particular – they're heading for trouble. They're Maoists, did you know that?"

"As a matter of fact, no. But even if they were, why would it matter? They're not doing anything illegal."

"Since when did you have to do something illegal to end up in jail?"

"That's so cynical," she said. "No it's worse. It's sick."

"Be that as it may. There is just no way this government is going to let this insurgency go unchecked. They have to shut this thing down."

"What, by throwing people into jail when they haven't done a thing?"

"They'll have no trouble finding a pretext, believe you me."

"Are you trying to tell me they'd stoop so low as to set them up?"

William Wakefield sat back.

"That's vile," Jeannie said.

And he said, "That's life."

"You must be joking," she said.

"You wish."

The martial law command had instated another curfew: no one was to be out in the streets after 9 P.M. At 9:15 the phone rang."Speak of the devil," her father said. But it was someone calling from the US. Their only phone was on the desk in the library; Jeannie could see him rolling his eyes as he boomed his most affable "hello." The person on the other end had a lot to say. Her father punctuated his "yeses" and "certainlys" with contorted grins. Once he hit his own head with the palm of his hand. "If you spoke the language, Bob, you'd see the problem. The long and the short of it is that the Turkish for Judas tree has nothing to do with . . ." There followed a tirade. Her father took the phone receiver off his ear so that his daughter could hear the anger.

"You're a drooling idiot. Do you hear that?" This was her father shouting at the phone after he'd hung up. "I'm sorry, Jeannie. I hate to leave you here all alone. But someone's pushed the panic button and I have to step out."

"What makes you so lucky that you can step out in the middle of a curfew and no one shoots you?"

"For some reason I have a special pass."

"I was just going to bed anyway," she said. But she couldn't sleep till she'd found Sinan. She tried all the likely numbers, but no one knew where he was. She got her book, made herself a cocoa, and curled up on the sofa next to the phone.

At around eleven the doorbell rang. She spoke into the intercom. No answer. She went upstairs, to look down onto the *meydan* and caught just a glimpse of a young man heading down the stone path that led down past the house. She bolted downstairs, reaching the porch just in time to see him stepping out of the last pool of lamplight. It was Sinan. What was he doing outside during the curfew? He could be shot on sight – didn't he know that?

She went to the other side of the porch and got up on her tiptoes, craned her neck, willing her eyes around the corner that blocked her view of Haluk's apartment. All she could see was the roof. But when she stood on a chair, the two top floors came into view. The windows of Haluk's apartment were dark at first, but by the time she returned with her father's binoculars, the light had gone on in the front room, and there was Sinan, pulling chairs around the table. Now he was answering the door. Three men came in, and two women. They looked like students. The door opened again, and in came the man she now hated more than any man in the world.

Dutch. Instead of sitting down, he scratched his head and asked a question. Sinan pointed down the hallway. He disappeared and then Jeannie saw the light go on in the bathroom. She could just see Dutch's silhouette in the frosted glass.

There was another man in the doorway. He was rubbing the side of his face and smiling, smiling as if it hurt to do so. She knew this man, too, but it took her a few seconds to place him. No sooner had she realized that he was Sergei, the man from the Soviet Consulate, than he vanished into the shadows of the corridor.

She moved the binoculars across to the third window. The back bedroom. The curtains were drawn. But – had they always been? Had she never checked?

She felt like she was going to throw up.

20

THE NEXT DAY began like any other day, with breakfast at seven o'clock sharp on the glass porch. William Wakefield had a boiled egg, two pieces of toast, a stick of goat's cheese and black coffee; Jeannie had two pieces of toast with jam, a stick of goat's cheese, three olives and a glass of Turkish tea. When they were through, William took the plates back into the kitchen and came back with a big pile of newspapers. At the top was the most recent International Herald Tribune. He handed this to his daughter and spent the next five minutes going through the five or six Turkish papers underneath. Jeannie could make out the odd word here and there: anarchy, army, constitution, law, determination. Every front page carried the same pictures of the same men. She recognized one of them as the new Prime Minister. She assumed the others were the generals who were now in charge. Pigs, every one of them. Pigs.

"Feeling better now?" She did not deign to answer.

He smiled at her as if she'd said something civil. And then, carrying on in spite of her silence, he said, "Well, anyway, things should calm down now. At least for a while." He put the last paper back onto the pile.

The phone rang. "Maybe I spoke too soon." He answered, then cupped his hand over the receiver and beckoned Jeannie inside. "This will take some time," he said. "Why don't you . . ." She walked right past him and headed for the door.

It was a sunny morning, with the clear air that only the north wind brings, but when she tried to get into the car, Korkmaz stopped her. He hadn't finished checking the car for devices. She went to sit with Chloe on the marble bench under the plane tree while he prodded the underside of the car and she asked herself what difference five yards could make, or if she even cared.

"So what's the plan for the day?" her father asked as they bumped along the steep cobblestone road to the shore. She shrugged her shoulders. When he dropped them off at school, he made his usual joke. "So girls, keep your eyes peeled! Don't talk to any Communist sympathizers!"

"I'll talk to whoever I want to," Chloe said. She headed up the path looking haughty. As Jeannie made to close the door, her father caught it. "You okay?"

She refused to look him in the eye.

"I know – it's a lot to unload on you. But it's better that you know."

What she knew now was that her father had a file on every friend she'd made in Istanbul. He knew how old they were, what their favorite flavor of ice cream was, he knew their parents' politics and all the organizations, overt and covert, they'd ever belonged to. He knew how well or badly they'd done in school. Who kept a mistress, who was heading for bankruptcy, involved in a swindle, interested in young boys. He knew everywhere Jeannie had been, too, and everyone she'd met, in greater detail than her own memory could furnish.

He knew everything Dutch had ever said to anyone.

He'd amassed these files, he said, to protect her. He asked her, as per usual, to keep it under her hat. As if she could tell this to anyone. Oh – by the way. My father's been watching you. Just to be on the safe side, just to be in the know. He knows all your family's secrets, by the way. And now, thanks to him, I know a fair number of them, too.

How to warn her friends? How to protect them? Why had she been so blind, so wayward, headstrong and stupid? It could not be wrong to assume there were lines no father would cross – even a father like hers – but at what cost blindness? The worst thing was knowing that if she told her friends what she'd discovered, they'd just tell her they'd known all along.

At Current Affairs Club that afternoon, her mind kept straying. As Suna took her "American friends" through the Turkish papers, telling them what they didn't say about the new crackdown and the role the US had played in it, the likely outcome for the Deniz Gezmiş gang and what this augured for the student left, Jeannie kept remembering things her father knew about her – and her family, and Lüset's, and Miss Broome's.

She was sitting in the little dining room off Marble Hall afterwards, stirring her coffee, staring at the spoon, thinking of the lists they were on now, not because they were dangerous people, but because they were her friends. Then Suna burst in. "So there you are. This is good. We need your help."

Miss Broome had offered to "liberate" a mimeograph machine for them, and Suna had decided that Jeannie should be the one to carry it out of the building. "You're a special student. Your father can get you out of anything. So hurry."

If I'm caught, they can't touch me. This was the chant that kept her going, as the wind ripped around Akıntıburnu, as cars slowed down with gaping men whom Suna dispatched with scornful looks, as she tried not to hear what Suna was saying, because it was no longer safe. Sinan was waiting for them on the college terrace. He looked as if he'd been up all night, too. He wouldn't look Jeannie in the eye. Why? Had he guessed what she now knew? She did not dare ask – he had a crowd of friends with him. They, too, were loaded down with bags. They were joking around in their usual way but they looked scared. Their bags carried books and supplies they had cleared out of the room from which they'd run an "association." They did not say which – only that it had been banned.

Haluk had offered the use of his apartment. About halfway there, Jeannie realized that the boy walking next to him was the infamous Rıfat, the green-eyed boy who'd spirited Chloe away from him. But there was no sign of any tension between Rıfat and Haluk now. If anything, Haluk seemed flattered to be of use.

Just before they reached the *meydan* the plastic bag in which they'd been carrying Miss Broome's mimeograph machine developed a fatal hole, so Jeannie took the whole group into the garden of the Pasha's Library and went inside to find something sturdier. And there in the hallway was the trunk her father had brought out the night before – the one with the files. Yes, she thought. Maybe she should let them see these, let them know what he knows. But when she opened the trunk, she found it empty.

"That's perfect," said Suna.

"But if your father misses it?" asked Rıfat.

"He won't," Jeannie said.

"Ah, to be a rich American," said Rıfat. And Haluk laughed.

It was the same at the apartment – Haluk could not do enough to make his erstwhile rival comfortable. Rıfat and his friends were to use the dining room as their new headquarters. Jeannie sat down at the table, dragging her spoon through yet another cup of coffee. There before her was the picture window from which, if she craned her neck and looked up, up, up, she could see her father's glassed in-porch, and the wall on which he hung his binoculars.

When she got up to draw the curtains, Suna said, "Don't do that. We need the light." How to warn them? Would she make it worse if she warned them? What was she doing here at all?

Then she heard Rıfat asking almost the same question. "Why are we entertaining an American? Under the circumstances, isn't it foolish?"

"Not at all," said Suna. "I would offer two reasons. First, she is our friend – a sweet, innocent, child, and we trust her. Secondly, she can protect us."

"Ah. Don't we already have enough Americans protecting us?"

"This is different," said Suna. "She shares our ideas."

"But her father's a spy," said Rıfat.

And Suna said, "Yes, her father is a spy. Even worse, he is an enemy of the people. But who amongst us has a father who isn't?" They were speaking in Turkish – they thought Jeannie couldn't understand them. But – was it because they were speaking more slowly than usual? – she'd understood every word.

"You haven't told her what we're planning, have you?" Rıfat now asked.

"Ah!" said Suna. "What sort of imbecile do you take me for? No, to answer your question, she's best kept in the dark."

"But in that case . . ." It was only after Jeannie had blurted out these words that she realized: she, too, had been speaking in Turkish. Neither Suna nor Rıfat seemed to have noticed. But Sinan had.

Slowly, very slowly, he lifted his finger to his lips to silence her. Then he stretched his arms and yawned. "I'm so bored," he said in Turkish. "I need a nap."

"Our world is falling apart at the seams, and you need a nap," said Suna.

Sinan smiled lazily. Then he turned to Jeannie and asked her in English if she was "feeling sleepy."

"I'm beginning to see how helpful it is to have an American in the house," said Rıfat, in Turkish.

"Watch your tongue," Sinan snapped. "You're speaking about my girlfriend."

"Is she good?" the boy asked.

"Better than you'll ever know," said Sinan.

"Then why not share her?"

This was too much for Jeannie to bear. Speaking in English now, she said, "Not for all the money in the world . . ." Sinan's grabbed her arm and marched her into the hallway. Only when he had closed the door of the back bedroom did he let go. Leaning against the wall, he let himself sag. "That was close," he said. "So close. You have no idea."

"Tell me," Jeannie said.

"You don't want to know."

"If I'm putting you in danger just by being here, then maybe . . ."

"Don't even say it," said Sinan. He kissed her forehead, then her lips, then her neck. "Don't even think it. If you let me handle this, I can make it all right. But please, be careful. Please, no more Turkish. You must try and keep your face blank, too. You must never, ever, ever, let them know how much – where are you going, Jeannie? What are you doing?"

She was drawing the curtains.

21

"**W**hen you hear your name, don't move. Don't even move your eyes. Keep looking downwards. Study your hands. Concentrate on your lips, on keeping them still. Even when you want to laugh. Especially when you feel like screaming. Try to let your thoughts wander, because it's easier to keep this pretence going if you're really not listening. Whenever possible, pick up a book. But even then, don't let your guard down. Once you understand a language, it will always find a way through to you. You can't shut it out."

The closest call Jeannie had during her last three weeks in Turkey was on the 17th of May, and there was a reason why she remembered the date. The gang had gone out to Burgaz that day. Sinan's mother was back from Paris and staying on the island with her two dearest friends. They'd invited out the "children" for a day of "sun and sea." It was only on the ferry that Jeannie found out one of Sinan's mother's "dearest friends" was Suna's mother, and the other Lüset's.

The house to which they had been invited belonged to Lüset's family. And here was another piece of news: Lüset's family was Jewish. How could it be that no one had thought to mention that? A pout and the shrug of the shoulders. "It is perhaps not significant."

The house was a sprawling modern bungalow with verandas on several levels and its own landing. Across the channel were the forested hills of Heybeliada. The season had not yet begun and there were two maids busily shaking out dust covers when they walked into the sitting room. In the kitchen, another team was rolling *böreks*. On the television set in the corner – a trophy set, one of the first in the country – they were giving the latest about the terrible earthquake in Burdur Province several days before, in which a thousand people were thought to have died. The maids stopped shaking their dust covers for a moment to shake their heads. They were surprised when Jeannie did not do the same. "She's a foreigner," said one to the other, "She doesn't understand."

"Don't foreigners have hearts?" the other asked.

"Of course! They must! But when the man spoke, it meant nothing to her."

"What sort of life is that?"

Exactly, Jeannie thought. Exactly! She fled the room. She had no idea where to go so decided it must be the bathroom. She opened a door – not the bathroom. Suna was sitting on a bed with her back to her. And what was that on the chest of drawers in front of her – a jewellery case?

She jumped. Looked around. Such fear in her eyes, but then she saw who it was. "Excuse me," Jeannie said. Shutting the door, she moved on to the next room. This seemed to be a study. Lüset was sitting at the desk. "I'll be out in a minute," she said in Turkish without looking up. "I just need to make a call." But after Jeannie had closed the door, she heard Lüset opening up the filing cabinet.

"Enough long faces!" said Suna's mother, bounding down the corridor "The sun waits for no man! Into the sea with you, at once!" So began the slow procession to the sea. When they returned, dripping, an hour or so later, the mothers were waiting gaily with large towels and tall glasses of apricot juice. They were dressed in short, bright shifts and sang along to every song they put on the stereo. Jacques Brel, Adamo, Christophe, Peppino di Capri, Jose Feliciano, Petula Clark, the Monkees. From time to time, one stood up to try out a new dance step. Then she would beckon for the other two to join her. And to the children: "What is haunting you? What is youth except a chance for endless fun?"

Over lunch, Sinan's mother reached into her handbag and produced a little red book. It was *the* little red book. "Sinan. Darling. Look what I have."

He looked but said nothing.

"What's more, my dear boy. I have read it. I cannot, however, say I understand a single word." She opened at random. 'The revolution is not a dinner party.' Is this a code, or a metaphor? A deep thought, or a senseless rambling?'"

Switching into Turkish, he told her that if she kept it up, he was going to walk out that door and she'd never see him again. Turning to Jeannie, Sibel said, "What am I to do with this boy, if he says such things to his own mother? Tell me, Jeannie darling, what propels the youth of today to such drivel?"

"It isn't drivel," Suna informed them.

"It's worse than drivel — it's nonsense!" her mother cried.

"Is it nonsense to wish for a better world?"

"What world could be better than this?" she said, gesturing at the sea, the forested hills of Heybeliada, the cloudless sky. "What more could you want?"

"I could want freedom," Suna said. "I could want to choose my own life."

"Ah. How American this school of yours has made you!" Suna's mother turned to her friends. "Who would have thought it? My daughter! An American!"

"Is it American to wish for human dignity?" Suna cried. "Is it American to wish for simple freedom of expression — or ask why our beloved country is the slave of the West?"

"*Terbiyesiz*," hissed her mother. "Watch your manners."

"*Bırak, canım*," said Lüset's mother. "Let it go. We are here to have fun."

So suddenly it was time to swim again. This time the mothers came down, too. "Let's have a race," Suna's mother said. "How far shall we go?"

Suna said, "China." She jumped into the sea first. The three mothers followed her. Jeannie headed off in the opposite direction, stopping to rest on a float. When Sinan joined her, they sat in silence, watching a ferry crossing over from Heybeliada. He reached for her hand. "Do you remember, last summer, when the ferry stopped in Burgaz?" he asked in a soft voice she'd not heard for some time. "And you saw people's stories trailing after them like comets?"

"Well, I don't any more," she said.

"How could you? You're stuck inside one."

She had not been planning to say this. But the words rushed out. "I saw Suna going through some jewelry."

"Oh?"

"And Lüset going through a filing cabinet."

"How strange," Sinan said.

"Tell me what they're up to."

Silence.

"For God's sake, tell me what is going on!"

A sigh. "I can't."

"Why not?"

"I promised not to."

"Look. You've got to decide. If you can't trust me . . ."

"It's not you. I think you know that."

"Then prove it to me."

"Let me think."

"Okay, then," he said finally. She was right, he went on to explain. Something was up. Something important. So they had to be ready. Ready for anything. To this end, they were "gathering" money for an escape fund. When he swam back to shore, Sinan was hoping to get into his mother's handbag and avail himself of the key to the safe she kept in her bedroom.

Could Jeannie create a distraction for him? Did she love him that much? But by the time they reached house, the commotion had already been created.

The entire household was gathered around the television. When the man on the screen repeated the news – that the Israeli consul in Istanbul had just been kidnapped – Lüset's mother let out a shriek.

On the screen now were several harried looking men and women who'd also been taken hostage but had managed to escape. They were describing their captors. Students, they said. Students! Jeannie thought. Why did they blame everything on students? Turning to Haluk, she said, "How can they be so sure?"

Haluk turned to look at her. "So sure of what?" he asked.

"That they're students. How did they find out the names so fast?"

Haluk paused before replying. "You understood all this?" He scratched his head. "And Sinan knows?"

22

TWO DAYS LATER, at four o'clock on the afternoon of the May 19th, Jeannie was sitting on the college terrace with Sinan and Suna on the little patch of lawn next to Atatürk's statue when a bomb went off. It had hurled her to the ground before she heard the crunch. When she sat up, the air was thick with soot. The terrace was strewn with books and shoes and bags and blackened logs that she then realized must be people. For a few moments, no one moved, no one spoke.

She heard a cat cry. The cat turned out to be a girl. A log rolled over and moaned; another stood up and limped towards them, crying, "Ayla, where are you?" A third blackened figure stood up and rushed at her. "He was here, right next to me! You saw him, didn't you?"

"Look!" Suna cried. She pointed at the Mustang. It was on fire. "Haluk!" she cried. She took Jeannie's hand and they raced down the terrace, weaving their way past blackened logs. When they saw Haluk and Chloe – unharmed, and holding hands – Suna ran over and embraced them both. For once she did not care what they were up to. "Only that you're alive!" Then she ran off again, crying, "Ice! We must find some ice!"

By now anyone who could walk was carrying anyone who couldn't to safety. One boy had a gash in his leg, and Jeannie helped Sinan take him down to the infirmary. The air was still black with soot when they came outside again, the grass still grey. Here and there were little groups of friends, sometimes weeping, mostly just staring at the little licks of flame still flickering in the grey, mangled shell of the Mustang. As they left the campus through the Hisar Gate, they heard something clanging in the distance. An ancient fire truck rounded the corner. The firemen leaning off the sides were wearing plumed hats.

They found Haluk, alone now, back at the garçonniere. When Jeannie asked him how he was, his eyes flashed. "I'm fine. Of course!" But your car, Jeannie insisted. "A car is a car. Why should this upset me?" He said this over and over as more friends filed into the apartment. How surprised they all looked! Yes, of course they were! It wasn't just words, this time. It was the real thing! They couldn't quite believe it. Couldn't quite understand how it had come to this, even after all these months of pontificating "the inevitable." As Jeannie examined her nails, they struggled to put together the pieces – what had actually happened, who had been injured and who had come "this close," who might have wanted to hurt them and why. There were a thousand theories but they all agreed that someone, somewhere, was trying to provoke them into doing something stupid, something they would later regret. But they were determined not to do that stupid thing. They had to stay strong. And resolute. Resolute to the end.

There were ten people injured in the blast – one janitor and nine students. Most suffered minor injuries but one girl lost a leg. Jeannie got these details later that same day from her father. He had not given up talking to her. Even when she refused to be drawn out, he kept talking.

She had never seen him quite so angry.

That night, after she went to bed, he talked to a lot of other people, too. Mostly on the phone, with the clink of the bourbon glass in the background. Jeannie did her best to shut it out. She drifted off to sleep, only to wake up (an hour later?) to the hum of a conversation outside her window. Looking down into the *meydan*, she saw two men on the marble bench underneath the plane tree. Or rather, she saw the embers of their cigarettes.

At first she couldn't make out what they were saying. All she knew was that one of them was her father. The second voice was American, too. But younger. Cooler, too. Every once in a while he'd say "What? Are you for real?" And laugh, as if her father were some sort of dinosaur.

Every time her father spoke, his voice got louder.

Until he said, "I'll say it one more time, boy! *You have taken this too far.* You stop this now or I pull the plug on the whole thing. Do you hear me?"

"Oh, I hear you all right," said the American. He let out a reckless laugh.

"Let's go, then." A clinking of keys, a turning of an engine. The shadow of a car, slipping across the *meydan.* Then silence, pressing the air from her lungs.

"I want to be clear on this (she wrote in her fifty-three page letter). At no point did I see the young American's face. But everything I registered – the lanky build, the reckless laugh, the easy insolence with which he smoked his midnight cigarette – told me it was my old friend No Name. And while I could not say for sure what he'd done to anger my father so – in my bones, I knew. No Name was my father's gopher. No Name did my father's dirty tricks. No Name had been sent out, on my father's express orders, to befriend Dutch Harding. All year long, and under the guise of friendship, No Name had been spying on him, and reporting back to my father. No it was worse. No Name had been goading Dutch Harding on. Pushing him to violence. And giving him the wherewithal to make bombs?

And now, according to my father, No Name had gone too far. For a man like my father, what was too far? What was he threatening to pull the plug on? I have never felt such fear. Such confusion. A single thought survived it: I had to find my compass point. I had to find Sinan.

It was a dangerous thing I did that night, bolting out into the curfew with only a sweater over my white pajamas to race across the cobblestones, past unlit cemeteries and snarling dogs, striding along the shore where any searchlight could have picked me out, where any passing patrol could have shot me. But I had fool's luck, and the speed that only comes to cowards, and the clarity that can only come to those whose minds have stopped."

It must have been close to three in the morning when Jeannie reached the Bebek apartment that Billie Broome shared with Dutch Harding. Sinan had spotted her from the balcony and was waiting for her at the door. Behind him the apartment was bright with light and humming with voices. Grace Slick, crooning. Miss Broome, shouting over her. Could that be Suna shouting back, and Lüset protesting, and Chloe joining in? "What is this, a party?" Jeannie asked. Not a shiver of fear during her long, dark walk, but now, hearing a party to which she had not been invited . . .

Sinan stepped into the vestibule, shutting the door behind him. "Who brought you here?" he hissed. She told him the truth, and for a moment she thought he was going to hit her.

"You could have been shot. You could have been kidnapped! Raped! You had no business coming here. No business chasing me. Why can't you trust me? Do you know how it makes me feel, to be at a house, visiting friends, when the phone rings and it's you? You're worse than my mother, did you know that?"

"Yes, and I'm beginning to understand how she feels!"

But when she told him what she'd heard in the *meydan*, he fell silent.

"When I go back inside," he said finally, "I want you to follow me. But stay in the front room. Let me speak to Dutch alone. He's in the back, packing. We're trying to help. I don't want him to see you until he understands that you are, too."

So she did as she was asked. And there, in the front room, were her friends. "What are *you* doing here?" Chloe asked her.

"I could ask the same of you," Jeannie replied. "Does your mother know you're here?"

"Does yours?"

"Please. Girls." This was Miss Broome. "I'm sorry, but while I'm still your teacher, I have to ask. You *did* all speak to your parents? Didn't you?"

"What do you take us for? Children? Of course we spoke to them," said Suna. "Officially I am staying with Lüset and she with me. We're nineteen years old, you know? We know how to lie. Which brings me back to our subject." Bizarrely, it was cheating in exams. Suna (who had never in her life cheated) was explaining to Miss Broome why there was no shame attached to it in Turkish culture. "It is a question of helping friends," she said. And Miss Broome cried, "What, at the cost of their own honor?" Suna then explained that the most dishonorable thing in Turkish culture was to let down a friend in need. "But that makes no sense!" Miss Broome shouted, somewhat drunkenly. "It's so counterproductive! We're not in the business of shelling out facts, for goodness sake. We're trying to change how people think!"

"If only," said Suna haughtily, "it were a two-way street."

Miss Broome caught the tone and accepted the reproach. "I'm sorry I'm so scatty," she said finally. "It's just been one hell of a week. Although I'm sure you're just as horrified by this Israeli consul thing as I am."

"Why grieve prematurely?" Suna said. "The story is not over yet. These are good-hearted boys watching over him – we must trust them."

"Oh, but we mustn't!" said Miss Broome. "We really mustn't. They've threatened to kill this man."

"Ah!" said Suna. "But who is more violent, the kidnappers or the army? The Martial Law Command, or their American paymasters?"

"You're dodging the issue, Suna, and you know it," Miss Broome said. "You think in black and white because you're afraid. You're afraid to look inside. You don't know who you are, my dear. You only feel good when you have an enemy to hate. You only feel virtuous when . . ."

"What – are you for real?" A cool – easy, insolent – American voice floated over them. It was No Name, coming down the hall. In his arms was a box of books.

How could he be so calm after what he had done? Standing here, shooting the breeze with the very people he almost killed with her father's bomb . . .

"I'm sorry. I don't know what came over me," said Miss Broome, wiping her hand over her moist forehead.

"You must be thirsty," said No Name. "Let me get you a beer."

"I'm not sure that's a good idea," said Miss Broome. "I think that's what loosened my tongue to start with."

"Never you mind," said No Name. He dipped into the kitchen, and as he emerged with two beers, Jeannie saw Sinan in the corridor, beckoning.

Dutch was in what had once been a study. Now it was piled high with boxes. He was sitting in the only chair, his legs propped on the cluttered desk before him. Was she seeing him in a clear light for the first time ever? Did he trust her at last? He studied her frankly, and for some time, before he spoke.

"So you think it was Jordan, do you?"

"Jordan," Jeannie said. "Who's Jordan?"

"The guy with the beers," Sinan explained. Turning to Dutch, he said, "She calls him No Name."

Dutch almost smiled. "If only. Nice touch." He picked up his pipe, blew in hard as he lit it. He offered it to Jeannie. "Want some?" It was stronger than what she was used to. She had to prop herself up against the wall.

"So tell me," Dutch said, tipping back his chair. "How does it feel? I mean, you've spent – what? A year? For almost a year, you've been sitting on that fence. See no evil, hear no evil, speak no evil. Am I right?"

"This is different," she said. "If my father's planting bombs . . ."

"No, of course not. I understand perfectly. And we're grateful. Indeed."

"I'll do anything it takes. We have to stop him," Jeannie said.

"This we can do," Dutch replied. "In fact, there's someone at the *Washington Post* . . . but first things first. We need a positive identification. So go back out into the front room. And listen to this "No Name" of yours. But carefully. No point in taking action until we're sure . . ."

"I *am* sure," Jeannie protested.

"Then help us by keeping him occupied. Enjoy the curfew! Help yourself to a beer!"

He stood up, as if to indicate the meeting was over. But as she turned for the door, he said, "Stop. One more thing. Jeannie – we never had this conversation. More to the point – we'll never have another. Something you need me to know, just tell Sinan. Something I need you to know, I'll do the same."

> "And that, as I saw it, was that. I had stepped over the line. Now all I had to do was stand firm. Thinking, prevaricating, hashing over the 'if onlys' and 'what ifs' – I was to save these luxuries for later. I had done the most difficult thing, Sinan told me. I had done the most important thing a spy's daughter could ever do, and now I was to sit back, carry on as normal, and 'let events unfold.'
>
> It was all coming to a head, he told me. As we sat on the marble bench in the meydan – the same bench where I'd heard my father lecturing his cool American only hours earlier – he warned me that this might mean going days without my hearing from him."

"But why?" she protested. This she had not bargained for. She had stepped over the line, after all! She could stand next to him now and hold her head high, and he could, too!

"Soon," he said. "But not yet. Right now we can't do anything to alert your father. This is the part you have to play. You must be patient."

So she promised. He sealed it with a kiss. A very long kiss. A kiss to last, he said. And perhaps he could taste her sorrow.

"Look," he said finally. "I can't tell you everything, but I'll tell you as much as I can. You saw Dutch packing. Did you guess why? Well, they took him downtown last night. I mean to İsmet's office. They played him tapes. Tapes of visits to the Russian consulate. You remember – the Sergei from Nazmi's. I warned you – remember?" He went on to tell her that they'd threatened Dutch with prison "for inciting his students to take up arms against the state, for teaching them how to make bombs." Now he was free again – no one knew for how long.

"If they charge him with spying . . ." Sinan shuddered. "Do you know what they do with spies? We have to get him out of the country. I may have to go with him."

"Why?"

"That I cannot say. But Jeannie – you need to prepare yourself. If I have to go, if you're not here when I get back . . ."

"I'll be here."

"You can't be sure. If your father . . ."

"He can't send me anywhere."

"Jeannie – this is Turkey. He can send you anywhere he wants."

"Let him try," she said.

"But say he does," Sinan insisted. His voice was hoarse, as if he were fighting tears. "If something happens. Will you wait for me?"

"Of course I'll wait for you. Of course!"

"No matter what happens, no matter what lies people tell?"

"He's not sending me home," she said. "Home is here."

"And if something bad happens, if they send you away, you'll come back and find me? No matter what people say?"

"No matter what," Jeannie said. "No matter how long it takes."

What she did not know then was that she'd already lost him.

The next day the Martial Law Command imposed a fifteen-hour curfew and sent out 25,000 troops and police to scour the city for the kidnappers. On Sunday, they found the Israeli consul in an apartment only 500 yards from the consulate. His hands were tied behind his back and he'd been shot three times in the head.

The owner of the flat said she'd rented it out to two young men who had presented themselves as an engineer and an architect. The care-taker reported seeing five young men leave the building the previous evening. The Prime Minister spoke of his shock and revulsion and had difficulty believing the perpetrators could be "Turks or idealists." Amid calls for "quick justice," the security forces plastered the walls of the city with 20,000 posters of the eight men and one woman thought to belong to the cells responsible for Elrom's death.

There was a second list of about sixty people, mostly students, who were wanted for questioning. By Tuesday, there had been six arrests. On Friday, three men and a woman thought to be connected to the kidnap-ping were captured when a security team burst into a flat on the European side of the Bosphorus. They found three pistols in the flat, ammunition and a wig. There were vague reports of "other arrests" in "other parts of the country." The witch-hunt had begun.

"They won't stop until we're all behind bars," Suna said. This was on Sunday afternoon, when Jeannie walked into the college cafeteria, in the nagging, fading hope of meeting Sinan. Finding Suna alone at the cor-ner table, Jeannie told her the news: army officers had stopped two young men in the suburb of Maltepe and asked to see their identity papers. They'd taken flight, firing submachine guns, wounding one of the policemen and a woman standing nearby. They had rushed into a building and broken into an apartment on the third floor. It happened to be the home of an army colonel, who was not at home. His wife and son had escaped, but the gunmen had seized his fourteen-year-old daughter hostage. Some time later, they had dropped a bag from a win-dow in which the police found Elrom's identity card and his passport, a pistol and ammunition.

There were now a thousand troops surrounding the building, and behind them a lynch mob. "What about that poor girl?" Jeannie asked. "Is she safe?"

Suna shrugged her shoulder. "Of course, they are saying that her life is in danger. But we know these boys. They would never hurt a child. As even you must understand by now, they have been savagely manip-ulated. And to be sure, the person who pushed them into this terrible act is now sitting safely in Europe, with a fat bank account, and a false passport. What a service he has done for his country! In one fell swoop, he has made the entire country hate all students fighting for freedom!

Now they want us behind bars! It was a pretext, Jeannie! Can't you see?"

But Jeannie was having a harder and harder time seeing anything. Why were Suna and all the others shunning her? This was the one thing she hadn't bargained for. To put your life on the line, to turn in your father – didn't this rate some consideration? Or were Dutch and Sinan the only ones who knew what she had done for them?

"One has but to ask the simple question," Suna continued. "*Chu Bono*? Who will benefit most from these two kidnappings? The generals with their American paymasters? Or these poor boys? It is they we must mourn now. For they have been undone by agents provocateurs. Yes, this is the age of the stoolpigeon and the informer. Even if our friends do not touch this girl, their fate is written. They will hang . . ."

"But not before they'd had a trial, surely?"

Suna slapped the table. "What kind of question is that?" she cried. "From you of all people?" She gathered up her books. "God damn you, Jeannie. God damn you, and all your kind!"

So she was alone, in the Pasha's Library – staring at the phone, waiting for some word from Sinan, who had been gone now for six days, eleven hours and fifty-five minutes, who, true to his word, had sent no word – when her father called to tell her that a second car bomb had gone off, this one under his own car. It was pure luck he'd been spared. Korkmaz the driver, having dropped his master off at a luncheon moments earlier, was standing next to a kiosk eating his lunch – a toasted cheese sandwich – when the bomb went off. Only the man in the kiosk and Korkmaz had been injured, and only Korkmaz seriously. He was still in a coma. "But I've put him into a private hospital so keep your fingers crossed."

There followed a long pause. Was he waiting for Jeannie to say something? She was tempted, sorely tempted. If she asked him outright – perhaps his cool American had gone too far again? Perhaps the time had come to pull the plug on this whole thing, whatever that might be?

Just in time, she remembered her promise. She played her part. And everything she said about poor Korkmaz, she truly meant.

But there were too many pauses, and when her father got home that night, he still looked wary. As he sat there munching on the Caesar Salad she had made for him, he spoke only to send compliments to the chef.

He did the same when she brought out a six-egg omelette. Then he asked about Sinan. Still not speaking? "That must have been one hell of an argument you two had. Gosh, this isn't curtains, is it? Now that would be a real shame."

It took seven or eight bourbons before he was ready to tell her how numb he felt. Numb because it could have been her in the car. Could have been both of them. "And yet here we are, alive and unscathed . . ."

Meanwhile, Korkmaz lay in a coma in hospital. And that poor, poor fourteen-year-old girl in Maltepe – the gunmen said they were treating her like a sister. But neighbors who could see into the apartment said she was tied to a chair. "It's been more than a day since they took her hostage. It makes me sick."

He felt sick, too, about Korkmaz, and the large family that depended on him. And then there was the fury, the fury against the people who had done this. "Either I let it eat us up or I find these bastards and nail them. Nail them good."

He gave her a beady look.

"So tell me," he said. "Who's next on their list?"

"How would I know?" she said.

"Spoken like a true innocent."

"What's that supposed to mean?"

"What does it sound like?"

She swallowed hard. "I can't help thinking that you blame me somehow."

"Oh really? What makes you think that?"

"I don't know. The way you're talking to me, maybe?"

"Honestly, Jeannie." He knocked back the rest of his bourbon. "You really do have a one-track mind." He gazed out at the Bosphorus, his eyes following a tanker that was rounding the point, and then he burst into tears.

But she kept herself strong. It was a week now since she had heard from Sinan, but she could still feel his arms encircling her. It was just a question of keeping faith.

Korkmaz came out of his coma on Tuesday morning. Just after lunch, Jeannie and her father went to the Admiral Bristol Hospital to see him. There were a dozen distraught relatives in the room. They were very kind. Very warm. Very physical. Grasping Jeannie's hands, they spoke of the wickedness of politics. She nodded. She couldn't agree more. They told her what a good man her father was, what a kind and generous employer. She nodded, as vigorously as before. Then on to safer ground: what a good man Korkmaz was, what a good son, what a good father. When she rose to leave they drenched her hands with eau de cologne.

"Thanks for coming" her father said afterwards. "They really appreciated it. Of course, they don't blame you."

She had to find Sinan. At least, find out where he was! She imagined her strength draining away, until there was nothing to stop her dialling all his numbers, scouring the campus, racing down to the *garçonniere*, leaning on the bell. But she held herself in. Played her part as best she could. She wasn't losing her nerve. Her father's barbed hints meant nothing to her. All she had to do was sit here, calmly, and wait for events to unfold.

But she couldn't sit still. She had to find Sinan! Perhaps if she asked Chloe. Perhaps, if she dropped by and didn't ask her outright, Chloe being Chloe would let something slip. Or even if she didn't. It would bring some relief just to chat about nothing in particular. The isolation was getting to her. Isolation was the one thing she hadn't bargained for.

When she walked into the Cabot kitchen at that afternoon, it was to find Chloe hacking at a piece of cheese, and her father sitting at the table.

"You've heard the news, I take it," he said. The girl had been rescued. "One of the gunmen died on the way to hospital. The other joker's still alive, though not, I'd say for long. Does the name Mahir Çayan mean anything to you?"

"Oh for God's sake!" Chloe screeched.

"What's going on?" Jeannie asked.

"He's been asking me questions about his stupid car," said Chloe. "He's trying to pin the whole thing on me!"

"That's not what I said," said her father. "But the fact remains that I gave Chloe a lift to school yesterday morning. And as it happens, she left a bag in the car. That was what I was asking her about. The bag, and what was in it."

"There was nothing in it but the fucking *Norton Anthology*!"

"Be that as it may, I had to ask."

"What were you doing with the *Norton Anthology*?" Jeannie asked stupidly. "Didn't you have that exam three days ago?"

"What – are you your father's second lieutenant?"

Jeannie turned to her father. "Are you actually accusing Chloe of planting the bomb in your car?"

And Jeannie's father yelled, "She wouldn't have the guts!" He slammed his fist down on the table. "That goes for both of you! You have no idea what you've mixed yourselves up in. You have no idea what these people are like! Honestly!" he said. "It's like cleaning up after a pack of fucking toddlers."

He lit up a cigarette. "I'm sorry," he said. "That was uncalled for."

They all sat still for some time after that. Then he asked Jeannie what her plans were. He and Amy were taking a deputation from Washington out for a tour of the Bosphorus on the Hiawatha. Did Jeannie want to come too?

She certainly did not.

"Fine, then," he said. "Have it your way."

It was while he and Amy were out on the Hiawatha, and while Jeannie was sitting with Chloe in her kitchen, eating supper, and pretending to be friends, that two polite, well-dressed men knocked on the front door and asked if they'd mind going downtown to discuss the "recent car bomb." Their black sedan was waiting outside, the engine running. The well-dressed men remained vacantly courteous throughout the half-hour drive. When they pulled up outside a mustard yellow stucco building, the man who wasn't driving jumped out to hold the door.

23

THE CORRIDOR WAS long and unadorned and smelled of disinfectant. There was a man with a mop at the far end and the floor was still damp. The two girls were shown into a waiting room. Here they found Suna, Haluk, Lüset, and a uniformed man with a submachine gun.

Where was Sinan? Her voice echoed, but no one answered. Had they been arrested? There was no one else to ask. So Jeannie sat down between Chloe and Haluk. Outside in the corridor, she heard footsteps, sometimes heavy, sometimes light. The men passing by their door spoke in whispers. Now and again a door would open, and they'd hear a low moan. An anguished cry. The tail end of a curse. Then the door would slam shut.

Once, when a door shut, Suna began to sob. Lüset nudged her and she stopped. At no point did either look Jeannie in the eye.

One day, they would find out what she'd done for them. One day, they would run up to her with open arms to thank her. But for now, this was just the way it was. No justice without a price.

She had been sitting next to a stony, blank-eyed Haluk for the better part of an hour when a factotum came into the room, read out her name, and told her to follow him. When she hesitated, Haluk nudged her. 'Go before he hurts you.'

So she went. They took her to another room, an anteroom. The sign on the door said "İsmet Şen" but he didn't seem to be at home.

"Long time no see," said İsmet. It had been at least an hour. He was holding out his hand. "I hope you haven't been too uncomfortable. I'm afraid we're a little short on the luxury front here but you don't have long."

He offered her tea, then made a great show of getting his assistant to call for it. When it did not appear at once, he excused himself. "Time to kick ass."

He had not yet returned when her father appeared. Settling grimly into his chair, he turned to Jeannie and asked, "Have I missed the tea game yet? Or are we still to have the pleasure?"

"He's gone to get it now, I think."

William just snorted. "He hates me, you know. Of course – if I were in his shoes, I'd hate me, too. So anyway. I let him play the tea game. But don't let that fool you. If there's anything you'd like to tell me, this is your very last chance."

But she remained steadfast.

"Okay then. But don't say I didn't warn you."

When İsmet came bounding back into the room, his first words were, "Don't tell me you're still waiting for your tea!" He slapped his desk in disbelief. "Unbelievable! These guys are really out to get my goat." He pressed a bell. His assistant appeared at the door. "The tea!" he shouted. The assistant look down at his shuffling feet as İsmet reprimanded him, telling him what a busy man Mr William Wakefield was, a man who couldn't be kept waiting, a man who, thanks to this benighted assistant, was going to go home "thinking we are a nation of lazy slouches." The assistant scurried off. İsmet turned back to William. "Golly, I'm so sorry," he said. "Sometimes I just don't know what it is with these guys. Trying to get something done, sometimes it's like wading through molasses."

"So I take it you have nothing for me."

"On the contrary, my friend! Tea is on its way! But first things first." He leaned across the desk to offer William a Marlboro.

"No thanks, I'll have one of my own," said William.

"Darn it," İsmet replied. "I'm all left feet today, aren't I? I'll make sure to have your favorite brand next time you drop by. If you live that long!" He lit up and then he said, "While we're on the subject, I sincerely hope that you've been talking to the big guy about a transfer. You're a sitting duck here, William. Especially in that house of yours. They could take you out in bed."

"Not if you've pulled the plug on them, they can't."

"By which you mean . . . ?"

"Cut the crap, İsmet. You told me you were hauling them in."

"On what grounds?" İsmet asked.

"The bomb," William said.

"You mean, the one in your car?" İsmet put his feet on his desk. With his right foot, he rang a buzzer. The waiter walked in with a single cup of Turkish coffee. Booming with theatrical anger, İsmet asked him about the teas. The waiter scurried off, looking worried and confused.

İsmet took a big sip of coffee. "So where were we? Oh, yes. The bomb." He grimaced. "Yes, perhaps we should put it like this. Imagine a flip chart. I use the word *imagine* because Turkey is still a poor country and its budget does not extend to luxuries like flipcharts. So where shall we begin, with our imaginary flipchart? Say we start with the enemies beyond."

"İsmet, I know all this."

"Yes, but now you must feel them in your bones! The Greeks to the south, the Arabs to the east, the Soviets to the north. To the west, allies, but how often . . ."

"We foot the bills, don't we?"

"Perhaps, when it suits you. But now let us move on to the enemies within. These are too numerous to count, so for the purposes of this discussion perhaps we should concentrate on the student scum seeking to undermine the foundations of the motherland through subversive action."

"Finally," said William.

"Yes, I knew you would say that. So now. Let's flip over to a fresh sheet. Let's set up five columns, one for bombs, one for assassinations, one for drive-by shootings, one for riots, demonstrations and general strikes, and another for the two shameless kidnappings of the past ten days. When we look at these columns together, a number of patterns emerge. One is that activity has intensified over the past few months. Another is that this growth rate is as yet unaffected by the imposition of martial law."

"Now whose fault is that?"

"Who can say for sure? Our burgeoning guerrilla army can be linked with certain well-known Palestinian training camps in Syria. The methods used by the animals that murdered the Israeli consul being the most vivid proof. The true extent of the subversive networks is only now becoming evident. But already, my investigators have gathered evidence of new offensives that will make Elrom and little Sibel look like child's play. There are plots to assassinate the Prime Minister, plots to blow up the main power station of Ankara, plots to hijack a plane here and a plane there and take an entire embassy hostage . . ."

Smiling, he leaned across his desk. "In the course of our enquiries, we have also gleaned a fair amount of information about the little nuisance you are asking about. This footnote of a footnote, this car bomb that killed no one, in which the only one injured was an insignificant chauffeur, made even more insignificant to the people at Langley because he had the misfortune of being born a Turk."

"Cut to the chase, İsmet," William said.

"When the time is right, we shall respond appropriately."

"I don't need to remind you to let me know the moment this happens."

"Will do," says İsmet, as if they were standing around the barbecue and William had just asked him to flip the burgers.

"You've taken statements from these friends of hers, I take it."

"Those whom we could find."

"You'll find the others, too, I'm sure."

"I'm sure!"

"Does that mean we're done here?" William asked. "I want to get home."

"Please! You're shaming me! I can't let you go without your tea!"

At this moment the tea arrived. But it was cold. İsmet knew it was cold without touching it. This led to more mock apologies, and another wait. The tea was hot but this time the waiter forgot the sugar.

"Never mind," William said. "That's how I like it anyway."

"What strange customs you people have. It never ceases to amaze me."

It was as they stood to leave that İsmet turned to Jeannie and said, "It was so nice to meet you. But I do wish you had been frank with us. You see, we know everything. How you heard something in the meydan. And broke the curfew. And went to a certain house. Sending all and sundry into a terrible panic. Yes, that is how bombs are made, my dear!"

"But I never . . ."

"No, of course you didn't. But while you were there, you passed along a certain nugget of information, didn't you."

"That's not true. I only said . . ."

"Jeannie. For God's sake." This was her father now. "Let me handle this."

"But he said . . ."

"He tricked you. The oldest trick in the book, and you fell for it. Which should tell you something. Now for God's sake, shut up."

When Jeannie awoke the next morning, she found her father standing over her. "I'm sure you won't be surprised to hear this. But I think even you will agree that it's out of my hands. I'm putting you on the PanAm flight this evening."

She sat bolt upright. "But you can't! I absolutely refuse to go!"

"You have no choice in the matter."

"You can't make me!"

"Oh for God's sake, Jeannie. Get a grip. Where the hell do you think you'd go?"

"To my friends!"

"What friends?"

"The ones you are trying so hard to throw into prison."

"For your information, no one touched their pretty little heads. Not that I expect any thanks. All I hope is that this knocked some sense in them. But you, young lady. You're done here. Or haven't you noticed? I have to go into the office now and I'd like you to be packed by, say, five. Understood?"

She waited for him to leave the house and then she got dressed and went downstairs. She had to find Sinan! She got no further than the door.

Sitting at the marble table in the garden was the devil.

"I'm really sorry," No Name said. Though he did not sound sorry at all.

"I don't care what you tell him," Jeannie said. "I'm still going out."

"I don't think so," he said. He showed her his gun. "It's for your own protection, I'm afraid. But I'm sure you know that. So if I were you, I'd just go upstairs and get packed."

While she was upstairs packing, she tried the grilles on her window. Then she tried the phone. "Oh," said Chloe's mother when she heard Jeannie's voice. "It's you, is it? I guess you're the one who's been calling all morning."

"Can you tell me where Sinan is?" she asked.

"I'm the last person who can tell you that, young lady."

"What did I do?"

"What didn't you do?" she said. And slammed down the phone.

Not to lose faith. She'd find another way. After she had finished packing, she took a glass of iced tea out to the glass porch and waited. She could see No Name in the garden, on a deck chair with the New Yorker. It was a beautiful day, and not long after lunch he seemed to fall asleep. After waiting for five minutes, she reached for her father's binoculars. All the curtains in the *garçonniere* were closed, but that was no reason to lose hope.

It must have been close to three when she looked down at the path and saw him. It was only a glimpse, a silhouette vanishing around the corner, but there was something about the way he held his arms. It was him! It was Sinan! She looked out at the garden. No Name was still asleep. Again, she reached for her father's binoculars.

Twenty minutes later, the curtains were still closed, but when she trained the binoculars on what she knew to be the bathroom window she saw two hands pressed against the dark glass. She knew they were his the moment she saw them. Then she saw his face. His beautiful face! He was looking up at her. She was sure of it. But she knew he couldn't see her. She thought he might see her if she waved. So she raised her hand. Another hand caught it.

"If you only knew how much I didn't want to do this," said No Name. When she tried to free herself, his hands clamped down on her shoulders all the more forcefully. "Sit down," he said. "Sit down and let's talk this through.'

The fury inside her wanted to kick and scream, but Sinan would have been proud of her. She remained silent, and steadfast.

"Look," he said, when he thought he had her attention. "There's been a misunderstanding and I'd like to clear it up. But first I need to level with you. Because I've compromised myself, too."

She must have let a cloud cross her face, because now he added, "However. This is important. It's not as bad as you think. I've just been running errands for him. I kind of had to, you know! If I was going to eat. You'd hardly believe it, what with all this stuff going on. But I've had a hard time selling stories lately."

Remembering the role she'd promised to play, she tried to look puzzled.

"Didn't he tell you? I'm a stringer. For which read: trying to be a stringer. But they don't seem to like my point of view. Maybe I know this place too well now. I guess you don't know this either, but I came out here with the Peace Corps. That's how I first met him. Your father, I mean. He helped me out of some trouble. That's how we got to know each other. He really gave it his all."

"I'm glad to hear it."

"Okay," he said, "Point taken. Fair is fair. I know you must hate him right now, but he's not all bad, you know? Only half bad. But in my experience, that can be worse than all bad. If someone's all bad, you know where you stand."

"Exactly," Jeannie said.

The smile slipped from Jordan's face. Leaning forward, he whispered, "I know what you think. What you said."

"What I said to whom?"

"I think you know."

"And . . . ?"

"I'm pretty pissed off about it, to tell you the truth. You know why? I'm not that person. I'm not the one you saw under that tree."

"Who do you know all this from?"

"Your father."

"My father?" She tried to keep her voice level, to conceal her surprise. "Who told *him*?"

"Who do you think?"

Jeannie sat back, to figure out what she thought. "I don't believe you," she said finally.

"I didn't think you would. But you know what? You might just have one last chance to ask him." Jordan reached over to the wall where her father hung his binoculars. Moving to the window, he trained them on the *garçonniere*. "Yup. Just as I thought. He's down there with them right now. Looks like they're all in a pretty big panic. And you know what? I bet *he's* the one who sent them into it. Why don't you go down there and find out what lie he's spinning them, and why?" He looked at his watch. "What if I dozed off for half an hour? Could you promise to be back by four?"

"I saw this for what it was — my only chance. It was only after I had slammed that gate behind me and headed down the path that I looked at my feet and saw I was still wearing my slippers. When I reached the garçonniere, *the door was open, and so, too, were the windows. Though nothing seemed to be burned, there was the acrid aftertaste of smoke. There were shouts coming from the bathroom, but Sinan was in the dining room, standing at the window. He, too, had a pair of binoculars. When I called his name, he shuddered, as if he had heard a ghost.*

I ran to embrace him, but his arms remained limp. I stepped back and looked into his eyes. They were great black holes brimming with tears. I asked what was wrong, and he told me I knew full well what was wrong. He'd seen it with his own eyes. 'He had you in his arms!'

It took me some time to work out that he had seen, and misunderstood, my tussle with No Name on the glass porch. I tried to explain, but he refused to accept what I had said. But I wouldn't accept his refusal to accept it. I had run away, hadn't I? I had tricked No Name — tricked him by listening to his pack of lies and pretending to believe them — but we only had half an hour. This was our last chance to escape! Hearing this, Sinan put his arms around me and burst into tears. "Our last chance has come and gone, Jeannie. You should have realized that last night!"

Again, I had no idea what he meant. He was reluctant to spell it out, and we lost more valuable time. At last he told me he knew I'd spent several hours with I˙smet and my father last night, and knew what I'd said to them.

What had I said to them? Correction — what had he been told I'd said? Jeannie, this is pointless. I know what you did. I know what you said. You turned us all in, and now . . .'

Now there was the patter of stockinged feet.

I looked up, and there, in the doorway, I spied Suna, and Lüset, and Haluk, and Rıfat of the green, green eyes.

'There's been a mistake,' I told them. 'I didn't turn you in. I didn't say anything! In fact . . .'

'In fact, you did,' said Suna. 'And don't think you can lie to us! We may have soft hearts, but we're not fools!' She was wearing rubber gloves and a housecoat. Rummaging in its pocket, she retrieved what I first assumed to be a toy gun. 'You and this Jordan,' she hissed. 'You planned this all along, didn't you? I should have seen it. I should have understood — why else would he . . .' But she left her sentence hanging. It would be thirty years before I would hear the second half.

Because now Dutch Harding stepped into the room. The first thing he did was tell Suna to put the gun down. 'You have no experience with firearms. You could do something you'd regret.' Reluctantly, she set it down on the dining table. 'Good girl,' he said. Was there a touch of irony there? It was hard to tell. Likewise, when he turned to me and smiled.

'So,' he said. For one happy moment, I thought he was going to set them straight. At the very least, tell them we were all on the same side. Instead he said, 'So. Let me guess. You're flying home today. Am I right?'

'That's what my father thinks. But I have no . . .'

'No, of course not. But let me guess. He's sending for you at five? And until then, a certain lackey of his is babysitting?'

'How do you know all this?'

'I make it my business. Call me sentimental, but I like to stay one step ahead of my enemies.'

'I'm not your enemy.'

'So you say. But anyway. It's been nice knowing you. And listen,' Dutch said. 'Thanks for leading us down the garden path. No, that's not putting it strongly enough. Thanks for landing us in jail.'

'You're not in jail.'

'We will be. Any minute now! And that's not the half of it. If they find me guilty of espionage, I won't be in jail long, will I? I'll soon be swinging. And all thanks to you.'

'How can you say that — after all I've done?'

'That's pretty funny, Jeannie. Because you've done a lot. At least — you tried. But then you lost your nerve, didn't you, when that little car bomb went off beneath your father's car. Couldn't take the heat, could you? Couldn't bear to think you might have said something that put your dear old Dad in danger. So you reverted to type. Just like I said you would. You told him. Him and his toadies. I smet and that No Name. You told them it was me. Didn't you?'

'You know I didn't. You know that!'

'No, I don't,' he said. 'What's more, you can't prove it.' Leaning back on the wall, he folded his arms. That was that. He wasn't going to help me. So I turned to Sinan.

'Tell them what I did. Tell them what you know.' But before he could get two words out, Dutch had interrupted him. 'There's one thing I'd like to know. What exactly did your boyfriend No Name send you here for?'

'He sent me down,' I said, 'to find out what lie you were spinning.'

He laughed. 'Are you for real?'

This was when my own head began to spin.

'That's an interesting choice of words,' I said.

'Oh really? Pray tell.'

'Someone used those same words with my father.'

'And?'

'Well – maybe I was wrong,' I said. Forgetting to think before I spoke. 'Maybe I fingered the wrong person,' I said wildly. 'Maybe it was you talking to him in the meydan that night!'

'But on the other hand, maybe it wasn't.' His voice was still cool. His eyes sparkled. As if to say, what will she say next? But sizing up the situation all the same.

So I had to ask myself – I had to. Every grievance, every suspicion I'd entertained against this man came flooding back. What if I'd been right to hate him all these long months, and what if there was more to it than jealousy? What if I'd been wrong about the cool young American shadow in the meydan? If the man I'd seen was Dutch . . .

'You're worried, aren't you?' I said, nodding at the others, who stood watching, motionless, their eyes blank and dark. 'You're worried what they'll think. I can tell.'

'They know what to think,' he said. 'And they know what to expect from you. You traipse in here, not a bruise on your little American body, and throw us this poison. Which when it comes down to it, is – what? Some cockamamie story about a conversation between two men I sincerely doubt you could even see, on a distant evening that you couldn't pinpoint if you . . .'

'It was the 19th of May,' I said. 'It was the night after you planted that bomb under Haluk's Mustang.'

'Got that on film, too, did you?' He folded his arms and laughed. 'I don't know how you guys feel,' he said, turning to the others. 'But I've had about as much of this as I'm willing to take.'

So now Suna took over. 'Get out. Get out before I push you out!' Once again, she was brandishing that gun. This time Dutch made no effort to stop her. I turned to Sinan. First I asked him if he could tell Suna to put the gun down. Then I asked him if he could tell Suna and the others what I'd done.

How I'd put myself on the line. How I'd do so again, and forever, if only they'd believe me. But he wouldn't look at me. Wouldn't answer me. Just stood there, staring at the floor. Until I asked him if he could come outside with me. 'No!' he shouted. 'Never!' When I asked him why he'd let them poison him against me, he fixed his burning eyes on me and told me to leave. 'You have no idea what you've done to us.' Those were his last words.

I turned to Dutch. 'Don't think it stops here. Don't think you can do this and get away with it. When I see my father . . .'

'I wouldn't bother, if I were you.'

'Why not?' I yelled. 'Because he'll protect you? Because you've been working for him all along?'

On my way back up the hill, I like to think I paused to reflect on what I'd done – what I'd unleashed, simply to assuage my jealousy and my raging heart. But I have no recollection of it. I remember only the rush. And the ache, the ache that is with me to this day.

It was only when I heard another cool American voice calling to me that my first doubt struck me. It was No Name, waiting in the car, which had its engine running.

He looked at his watch and smiled. 'Said your goodbyes now? Ready to go home?'"

IV
How to Bury
a Story

24

FIRST LET ME APOLOGIZE for my long silence, Mary Ann. In answer to your question – I think I just needed a break. A few days in my own shoes. Mary Ann – it took something out of me, writing all that down. I was in danger of forgetting where my life ended and hers began. You might even say I was in danger of becoming her. You can see it even in my words. As anyone who knows me from my journalism can tell you – and a few of your colleagues at the Center for Democratic Change do seem to fall into this category – I don't usually write like this. (Though I do have a tendency to over identify with my subjects.)

I discussed all this with Hector Cabot in November 2005. Let me place it for you – it was just after my visit to the *garçonniere*. I'd rashly asked Chloe what she remembered of the days leading up to the Trunk Murder. She'd answered sharply: "You want me to describe the days leading up to a *rumor*?" I'd apologized. Relenting, she'd mentioned that her father had visited Jeannie in Northampton in June 1971, "*id est* not long after the murder-that-never-was." Perhaps to make up for her burst of irritation, she'd offered to drive me back to her house to see him.

Chloe lives in a multi-million-dollar villa in Emirgân – the glass palace, she calls it. Needless to say, it overlooks the Bosphorus. She and her stepchildren ("the ingrates") live upstairs. Her parents ("the young ones") live below, and Chloe thinks it is very silly that they insist on paying rent. Though she feels she has to take it ("you know what a stickler my mother is") she secretly pays it into an account in their name. "They'll need it soon enough," she told me as we headed down the stairs that connected the two flats, reminding me, not for the first time, that her parents had "forgotten" to take out pensions.

Forgetting is a fine art for Hector and Amy, and the bright, airy garden flat is their greatest work. To look at the pictures on the walls – children and grandchildren and stepgrandchildren, weddings and christenings and circumcisions, Amy and Hector in front of the Sphinx, the Parthenon, and the windy walls of Troy – you'd never know there'd been a twenty-five year blip in their marriage. They do not deny it – what unites them is their refusal to dwell on it. The past is a vast, disordered attic. They extract only what might look nice on a shelf.

It was teatime when we arrived, and (as was so often the case with my own parents at this hour) the room was full of visitors. One (a former student) was a physicist, now working in Denmark. Another (also a former student) had just purchased a budget airline in the American Southwest. With him was an English travel writer, in Istanbul to research a book about the travel writers who had come before her. After she'd left, we were joined by a Greek politician and a Turkish playwright. They'd come to discuss a cultural exchange that Hector's foundation was helping to sponsor. When they discovered my line of work, they of course had things to say about the sins of the media, and most especially, the way their own countries were reported in the US and European press. "It is as if they have set out to kill all hope of peace!"

I tried to explain the problem from the other side: though there were some very good journalists out there, they weren't always heard. Their readers had only the sketchiest knowledge of the Ottoman Empire and its troubled legacy. As a rule, they disregarded anything that did not confirm their prejudices. Then there were the gatekeepers – the editors, the advertisers and the long line of little people in between them – who decided what was news and what was not, who rarely thought something was important unless someone important had pronounced it to be so, and who between them had a thousand ways of burying a story.

Hector did more listening than talking, though he interrupted with a jabbing finger from time to time to say, "But this must stop! Europe or no Europe, Turkey needs to be back on the world stage!" Or: "You have got to make them come to grips with history. They have got to see that the dividing line isn't Islam!" It took me back to my teens, when this man was close to being my second father. There were only about a dozen faculty families on the hill in those days. We'd all been in and out of each other's houses, and there were no separate tables. Whatever the adults happened to be arguing about – the Balfour Agreement, the road to Damascus, or the music teacher who had rolled under the sofa at a recent party, never to be seen again – they were as interested in our views as they were in their own.

In those days, Hector was the life of every party. But late one drunken night, he went out into his garden to shoot a rabid dog and shot his own mother by mistake. There were no more parties after that. He gave up drink, found God in some form, and moved back to the US. I'd never quite forgiven him for his defection. But now, as he drew me back into a conversation we'd left off thirty-odd years earlier, I thought how lucky I'd been, to grow up surrounded by adults who'd taken us and our thoughts so seriously.

As the physicist and the budget airline owner rose to leave, they asked Hector if he'd had any news "on the Sinan front." It emerged they were old classmates. They listened sadly to Hector's update, and there was news in it for me, too. Hector told us that William Wakefield had been on the point of returning to the US to rescue little Emre. "He was so happy the last time I saw him. He'd finally found the right string to pull. He thought the problem was solved!" Now that he was "no longer with us," they were "Back to Square One," as no judge was going to release the child to a party, "however responsible," who did not main-tain a residence in the US. But Hector did. So he and Amy would be flying back to the US that weekend to see if the authorities might agree to move Sinan's young son out of fostercare and into their custody. "But of Jeannie, poor soul, we've heard nothing." Then Hector turned to me. "Unless you have something new to tell me?"

I shook my head. "Right now, I'm just trying to establish what hap-pened. I'm hoping that might tell us where she went." I added that it was not just the recent past that concerned me, as every avenue of enquiry took me back to June 1971.

Chloe's mother didn't seem to like that.

"Please do try and understand," Hector said, after she had left, some-what huffily, to see to supper. "She doesn't like to discuss that summer you mentioned, and with good reason. She was recently divorced, poor woman. She was dating a man who, however inadvertently, pulled her daughter, our daughter, into the middle of a murky political intrigue. Amy herself spent several weeks under house arrest, did you know that? But she's a woman of courage – don't you forget that. Police guards notwithstanding, she still found the courage to give shelter to your old flame when he was on the run."

"She hid Sinan?" I asked.

"You didn't know that? Oh dear. Perhaps I shouldn't have men-tioned it. Could you possibly pretend I didn't? Listen. I'm going to be frank with you. I have some serious qualms about this digging you're doing. I know your intentions are excellent – you want to find Jeannie. You want to help *us* get little Emre back and secure his father's release. But I'm afraid that the very things that qualify you for this task – your intimate knowledge of the history, the place and the people involved – are what will rob you of the very thing without which you *cannot suc-ceed*. Namely detachment. My dear, you just don't have it."

"I think I do," I said.

"You might *think* so, but for God's sake, M, this woman nabbed your boyfriend!"

"Yes," I said, "you're right. I damned her to hell. Sinan too. But then they actually went there . . . Don't you see? No one wants to have that much power."

"But my dear girl, you never had that much power." He reminded me that the Trunk Murder ("the *so-called* Trunk Murder") had nothing to do with me. Nodding in agreement, I explained that – nevertheless – Jeannie Wakefield and I shared a history. The fact that it was an invis-ible and unacknowledged history didn't make it any less important. Because it wasn't a one-off, I said. Just as she had stepped into my shoes in 1970, so too had I stepped into someone else's shoes ten years ear-lier, "and to this day I have never known, *never even asked*, whose shoes they might have been." You could, I said, take this story back and back – back to the middle of the 19th century, if you were so minded. "Only when you line up all these shoes in a row do you begin to get a sense of who we are, and what we signify."

"By which you mean to say what exactly?"

"By which I mean to say that Jeannie's story is my story. Or mine to tell."

He gave this proposition intensive thought.

"Or think of it this way," I said. "Unless I come to some understanding of Jeannie – what she did with the life I left, and what it did to her – I cannot begin to understand the life I chose."

Grimacing, his hands cupped around his chin and his eyes still closed, he asked "What do you think *she* would say, if she heard you say that?"

"We'd disagree on certain points," I conceded. "But listen, Hector. I'm doing this because she asked me. She wrote me a fifty-three page letter, for God's sake . . ."

"Yes," he said, "But why?" He paused again to think. "After steeping yourself in Jeannie's words, what puzzles you the most?"

There were three things in particular. I began with the easiest: William Wakefield. What sort of man would treat his daughter the way he did that year? "He let her run wild and then he spied on her."

"I don't find that puzzling at all," Hector said. "It was professional arrogance."

"You'd think he was God," I said.

And Hector said, "A *little* God. Drink had a lot to do with it, you know."

I did. So I moved on to my second question. Sinan. "I hope you won't discount this as sour grapes, but there's so much he doesn't tell Jeannie. And – barring the odd crisis – she seems to accept that. Crave it, even. Why?"

"Marriage is a strange thing," Hector said. "Especially when it's viewed from the outside."

"Especially," I added, "when your father is a spy."

"So they were both spies, were they?" Seeing my confusion, he added, "I mean Sinan's father, too." In fact, I hadn't meant that at all. Though (as I now heard) there had always been rumors. "I suppose you know that Sinan's father was an old army buddy of the formidable İsmet?"

I told him I did. Hector shook his head again.

"İsmet. Now there's a tough customer. Did I ever tell you about the time he dropped by at the office and told me chapter and verse about every party I"d wrecked and then forgotten between 1955 and 1969?"

Though it was a meandering tale with a several subplots, each featuring its own little god, he got to the end without forgetting that I had promised three questions and delivered only two. "So what is it?" When I hesitated, he clenched his fists and said, "You've got to understand that I am asking you for your own good. If you don't put your doubts into words, they eat you up, you know!"

So I phrased it as tactfully as I could. As much as I trusted her sincerity, as certain as I was that Jeannie knew no more about the so-called Trunk Murder than she had recorded in her journals and letters, I was still left feeling that there was something very odd about her story.

25

ORTHAMPTON
June 10th 1971

"*My room. What have they done to it? My ceiling rises and falls. My posters buckle. The stuffed dog on my easy chair sways and sighs and my mother's voice wafts over me like a wreath of smoke. Sometimes she is in the room, checking my temperature, changing my sheets, feeding me water, penicillin, aspirin. Sometimes she is on the phone in the study next door, and sooner or later, she will come in and tell me what I did wrong.*"

She'd been home for three days when she wrote that. She'd stepped off the plane with a fever of 104. But even as her ceiling rose and her posters buckled, she would have known her mother held nothing against her. It was her incorrigible ex-husband that Nancy Wakefield felt like strangling. How dare he put this girl on a plane in this condition? It was his *duty as a father* to explain the damage done. It was her *duty as a mother* to hold him to it.

Especially during those first few days. She couldn't help it! Anger was coming out of her head like smoke. But to no avail. The consulate wouldn't say where he was. The State Department wouldn't either. "I just got through to Amy," she told Jeannie one evening. This was when she was well enough to sit up and try some soup. "Yes," she said, "Amy and I just had a pretty long chat, and I must say I'm a little disappointed. Because you know, we had many pleasant conversations over the past year, and I had come to think of her as a friend. But this time . . . well, something's definitely come over her."

Nancy Wakefield sat down on the foot of her daughter's bed. "So anyway. It was about 9 pm their time when I finally got through, and a man answered. A man who couldn't speak English. Don't you think that's a little odd?"

She patted her daughter's knee. "You still there, lambie?" She wrinkled her nose. "Anyway, when I asked Amy about this man who answered her phone, she said he was her bodyguard. So of course I wanted to ask. Why would you need a bodyguard? But her tone was so sharp I just asked if she knew where we could find your father. She then told me she'd be the last person to know, as she had severed all connections with him. Severed all connections! Can you credit that? When I asked her why, she got pretty huffy! All she'd say was that – to the best of her knowledge – he's back in the States. But I'm sorry. I'm just not going to accept that. You leave it to me, lambie. I'll get to the bottom of this."

Off she wafted. To make another phone call? Her voice was softer now. She did more listening than talking.

"I'm finally getting somewhere," she said later that night.

The next morning, when she sat down on the end of Jeannie's bed, her eyes were red. "I'm so sorry," she sobbed. "So, so sorry. I should have stood my ground. I should never have let him take you." She clenched her little fists. "The lies he fed me. The things he didn't tell me! Well, I sure know now. What a name for a tree. Boy am I going to give that father of yours an earful."

When Jeannie asked who she'd talked to, she said, "Never you mind."

When she asked if she'd talked to someone called Sinan, her mother said, "Sinan. That's his name, is it?"

"You talked to him?"

"I believe that the…" She folded her arms and swallowed hard. "I believe I spoke to the boy's uncle."

"Which one?"

"Oh lambie, you don't expect me to remember that, do you? They all have such strange names."

"What's happened? Don't tell me something bad's happened!"

"Of course something bad's happened! *Look* at you!"

"I didn't mean me, I meant Sinan."

"Are you talking about that boyfriend of yours? Well, there's a change! Jeannie, I can't tell you how hurtful that was. To find out you had a boyfriend but didn't trust me enough to tell me. I'll bet it was that father of yours who talked you into that. I'm right, aren't I? I can just hear him. Best not to tell you-know-who you have a boyfriend. Well, some boyfriend he turned out to be!"

"He said he was okay, though?"

"Oh, yes, indeedy. He's just fine."

"But someone else isn't? Is that what you're trying to tell me?"

"How the heck am I supposed to know?" Seeing the tears streaming down Jeannie's cheeks, she said, "I'm sorry, lambie. I didn't mean to upset you. But really, you can't expect me to ask about people I don't even know. Listen, let's just take it slow, okay? Whatever happened out there, it's over. The important thing is that you're home. Let's just concentrate on making you better."

But she wouldn't be better, couldn't, shouldn't, until she heard his voice.

The floor looped and buckled as she struggled to the phone.

This time Jeannie got Sinan's mother. For the longest time, she could hear only her breathing. "Why are you calling?" Sibel asked finally.

"I need to speak to Sinan."

Another long silence. An echo. Then a click.

"You may not be surprised to hear this," Jeannie's mother told her when she made it downstairs for supper. "But your father has still not graced us with a call. Judging by his track record, we could be in for a long wait. But if he does call, you are not to speak to him. You are to hand the Postcard Man straight to me. Understood?"

As if.

"Sit down, lambie. I've made us macaroni cheese."

Over supper, they fell back into their old pattern. Her mother told her about everything that had happened to her over the past year – her job at the library, her foray into night school, the woman's group she joined and abandoned, the boyfriend who hadn't worked out, and the new one she wasn't sure about. Jeannie asked her why and she explained. She told Jeannie how it felt to fall in love when she was still smarting with hurt from the man who'd come before, and how it felt to sit in a room with a group of women who were even angrier with men than she was. How walking into her first night class had been like stepping off a cliff. She told Jeannie how bored, how suffocated she felt every morning when she went into work, how the dread of being stuck there forever was what had kept her going to that night class and then she confessed that when Jeannie had left last June she was "quite simply, bereft." "Nothing prepared me for it. I'd actually been looking forward to a little time alone. Because you know, lambie, you'd been so difficult. So critical. So unappreciative. All you wanted to talk about was leaving.

So I thought, well. Why put off the inevitable? I knew I was going to miss you. But that first morning when I came down here? I felt dead."

"I'm sorry," Jeannie said meekly.

Triumphantly, her mother took her hand. "You mustn't say that, lambie. The important thing is that you're back. Now you're back, I can breathe again." And Jeannie nodded, smiled, commiserated. She kept her talking, hoping she wouldn't remember that a mother ought to stop talking about herself now and again, and do some listening.

When Jeannie stood up, her mother handed her a jar with a pierced lid. "Really, Mom. You'd think I was eight."

"Well, just this once," she said. "Just for old time's sake. It used to make you so happy."

"I cried when they died."

"They don't live long anyway. You know that!"

So Jeannie took the jar outside.

And there they were – the fireflies. Hundreds and thousands of them circling through the night. As she stood on the lawn with her jar, she could hear the teenagers horsing around the pool next door.

She would never laugh like that again.

26

T WAS CHLOE'S father, Hector Cabot, who broke the news. Since divorcing Chloe's mother, he had been living in Woodstock, Connecticut, and it was to Woodstock that Chloe had been dispatched within days of Jeannie's departure. Hector had called to exchange notes with Jeannie's mother, and to suggest that the two girls be brought together so that they could do the same. He had been somewhat taken aback to find that Nancy Wakefield wanted to "let sleeping dogs lie." But he knew how to talk to her. In early July he was granted permission to drive over to Northampton to speak to Jeannie face to face.

"Though you don't know me from Adam, you know at least that I understand the country. I can guess what you loved in it. For I once loved it, too. And Jeannie – I know the pain of heartbreak. The onus of a new beginning. What's more, I know your father – as a man, and as a friend."

It was in this sanctimonious mode that he began his weary monologue. This is not my harsh judgment, but his. When we met in Istanbul in November 2005, Hector Cabot talked of hating the "tinny echo of manufactured goodwill." But in July 1970, he had less than two years of sobriety behind him, "which means I was very sober. Suffocatingly sober. It was the best I could do."

He had never met Jeannie before so could not tell me how she'd changed. He recalled an emaciated girl with a great mass of blonde hair, a mouth that twisted to one side and hands that never stopped tapping.

She sat hunched in her chair, eyes fixed on the ground between them – though from time to time she would fix him with a cold blue glare.

"You were stepping out with Sinan, I take it."As soon had he said this, he knew it was the "wrong way in."Was it the past tense that made her wince as if she'd just been stung? Had his antiquated turn of phrase added insult to injury? He proceeded with caution. "How well did you know Dutch Harding?"

Another wince. "What's he got to do with it?"

Sensing now that there was no right way into this "tangled web – or right way out, for that matter," he answered her directly. "Jeannie, he's been murdered."

"*What?*"

He'd heard people say some pretty nasty things about Jeannie over the years – rumors, based on speculation, or on outright lies – but none of these people had been in that room that day, and he had been. He'd seen the terror in her eyes, so he could assure the "sirens of the gossip mill" that (a) she was hearing this "macabre tale" for the first time and (b) she had no idea what to make of it.

The story he told her was a sanitized version of the account I myself had read in that lurid news article: a group of students belonging to a Maoist cell called Enlightenment had discovered that the man they trusted above all others was an *agent provocateur*. . . . She stopped him here. "Are we talking about the same people?" She'd gone on to claim that she knew no Maoists. "They only said so to annoy their mothers.They never opened the Little Red Book except to laugh at it." But Hector had persevered. He could give her the names. Suna, Lüset, Haluk, and ("there is no easy way of saying this, my dear, so brace yourself") Sinan. Had it not been for the prompt and selfless intervention of Jeannie's father, the list might well have included Chloe's name, and her own.

"Prompt, perhaps. But not selfless! Not selfless!"

Tears, followed by tissues. "May I continue now? There's more, I'm afraid. "Much more."

A peremptory nod from Jeannie. A deep breath, and then he went for it. Keeping to the basics: upon hearing that one of their number was an *agent provocateur*, the group's suspicions had passed from one possible culprit to the next, until a chance remark exposed Dutch Harding as the enemy amongst them. After putting him on trial ("though I hope you understand that I am using this word metaphorically") and pronouncing him guilty, they had condemned him to death. ("Which must be seen as a measure of their betrayal. I have never been to a country where they honor their teachers more deeply than they do in Turkey.")

She took this news calmly. Too calmly. Falsely encouraged – though he ought to have asked himself why she was clutching her head in her hands, and why she had dropped her head so low it almost grazed her knees – he had described the gory aftermath: the chopping up of the body, the cramming of body parts into the trunk, the ill-conceived getaway plan, the trail of blood that prompted a member of the public to report the girls and their trunk to the police. The arrest. The so-called interrogation, and Suna's leap from the window.

Here she'd interrupted his ghastly flow. "I'm sorry. I don't think I heard that right." So he'd told her again, but filling in some detail. Turkey being Turkey, they would never know for sure what had gone on in that interrogation room. But officially Suna had jumped. A flower vendor in the street below had seen her dangling her feet on the fourth floor window. Which did suggest . . .

This was when she had gone for his throat.

Painful and startling though this had been, he had only himself to blame. He was better at passing on sad tidings now. "I was awfully clumsy in those days," he told me. "Sobriety had robbed me of my social graces. Having made such a mess of it, I decided to concentrate on Chloe, who was in the same sort of mess. I sorely regret sending her off to Radcliffe that September. I ought to have realized she just wasn't ready yet. She'd barely spoken all summer. My every effort to discuss this terrible murder ran right into the proverbial brick wall. Why I thought that meant she'd moved on . . . Though I must say, I kept pretty close tabs on her all autumn. She and Jeannie were very close that first semester, did you know that? Though it was not, I would now say, the healthiest of bonds. They'd joined together against a world that didn't understand them. They goaded each other on. I am not trying to say that Jeannie was responsible in any way for Chloe's breakdown. Far from it. No, if Jeannie hadn't called me that December, to express her concerns – by which I mean, to tell me Chloe was in the infirmary, having cut herself – well, who's to say? We might easily have lost her. So of course – and whatever injury or distress Jeannie later caused us – we are eternally grateful to her.'

27

OCTOBER 17TH 1971

"*Today I followed Doctor's Orders. I made full use of my extreme good fortune. I began the day with a balanced breakfast, and as I sat there with my worthy classmates, perusing the* Crimson *and the* New York Times, *sharing thoughts about all the news that's fit to print, I was mindful of the fact that ten or more girls my age — excuse me, ten or more* young *women — would have given their eye-teeth to be in the chair I was occupying. For I am under a solemn oath to make the most of my exclusive education.*

And what a feast of a morning it was. As Suna might have said. She would have loved the first lecture, and the second, too. She would have talked back to that professor though. I could almost hear her. But when I looked across the hall at the arrogant innocents surrounding me . . .

Chloe should have been there, too, but she overslept. She was waiting for me outside when I came out. Looking bleary. When I told her, she said good, that was the look she was after. "Bleary and belligerently off-hand." Off we went through the wind and the falling leaves to Radcliffe Yard, to attend a very nice lunch with the very nice, very old-fashioned ladies who were responsible for our being here, and who wanted to see what we looked like, presumably to find out if they had been right about us or wrong.

We behaved perfectly, I must say. As did the ladies, who asked us sweeping earnest questions and then listened with pained sincerity as we explained why the US was so unpopular in Turkey, and what this entailed. We catalogued the riots, the bombings, the kidnappings, and assassinations. The military coup, the mass arrests, and the allegations of torture. They shook their nice heads and clucked their nice tongues. "I do hope no one close to you was directly affected."

And I was sorely tempted. I almost said, "Quite a few of them were, actually. You see, my father is a spook. He kept files on everyone I knew. They became suspects simply by virtue of being friends. He set an agent provocateur amongst us – can you believe it? So I fingered him. Then I left – on the next plane, no less. Leaving my friends to do the dirty work. Which they did. Which makes them murderers. What does it make me?'"

November 2nd 1971

"Today Chloe and I decided what-the-hell, why not throw caution to the wind. We've run our Coop cards to the limit but I need a clock radio and she needs new flares so we have no choice but to get ourselves more cards.

So there we were in the Pewter Pot, filling out forms. I looked at Chloe's and saw she had called herself Mata Hari and given her profession as 'world-famous seductress.' So I thought, what-the-hell, and in the slot for profession, I wrote 'murderess.'"

November 15th 1971

"A week ago yesterday, when I was sitting, lying on one of those sofas, actually, at Hilles Library, and thinking about the essay I have to do by tomorrow on 'an experience that changed me' for expository writing, it suddenly struck me that I had no choice. So I wrote about the freshman mixer, about what it was like to go to a zoo like that pretending you were interested in meeting boys when you had seen enough of the world, and the way the world worked, to have precipitated a murder. The words just came, and they kept on coming, so I also wrote about the rest of the week, about how it felt to be sitting in that meeting with everyone else who was comping for the Crimson, *all these eighteen-year-olds talking big about their high school yearbook and some trip they'd taken that was such an eye-opener, and thinking, you think you're so tough, do you? Let's see how tough you are after an hour in a Turkish police station.*

Today, after class, this beardless youth who teaches us expository writing took me aside. He tapped my essay about the mixer. 'What's this all about?' were his precise words. I told him the story. He nodded and frowned in all the right places, although it was a bit of a letdown at the end, when all he could think to say was 'What a bummer.' He told me that one day I was probably going to write something 'very important and very true' about all this, but that right now I was probably 'too close.' 'All that comes through is the anger,' he said. He then recommended therapy. And oh yes, I forgot to mention. He gave me a 'C,' which didn't feel very much like therapy.

I stopped by Chloe's room on the way back to my room, thinking she was the only one in this whole place who could possibly appreciate the ironies, but she was smoking dope with those new friends of hers so she just took my essay and threw it on her bed and said she'd read it later.

Sometimes I wonder if she even likes me any more. Sometimes I think our misery is all that binds us together, and our contempt for anyone who doesn't understand it, but then at the same time there seems to be this unspoken agreement not to put anything of importance into words."

December 1st 1971

"Today, when I went to see Chloe in the infirmary, she told me that she'd given her doctor permission to speak to me. 'For background,' she said, waving her arm. 'You know. All that stuff.' Her arm, her wrist I mean, is still heavily bandaged.

His name was Dr White. We met in his office, which was white white white! We began by discussing what he called Chloe's 'home situation.' It emerged that he had recommended her taking time off and going home, and that she had expressed reluctance. Apparently her precise words were that she had "no desire to waste away in the wilds" with her father and that she could not return to her mother, as she was a persona non grata in Turkey.

Dr. White wanted to know about the divorce, which he knew to have been recent and suspected to have been messy. As if divorce was the be all and end all. So I told him. If Chloe was feeling unstable, it was probably not because her parents were living apart, but because some people she knew had murdered someone else she knew and chopped him up into little pieces which they'd stuffed into a trunk.

He asked me to elucidate, so I did.

I explained how hard it was, when the victim of a crime was someone evil, someone your own father had hired to lead your friends astray. But I'd never wanted him dead! When I'd said all that, Dr. White cleared his throat and tapped his pen against the pad in front of him. 'You're sure of all this?'

Yes, you imbecile. I was there."

December 2nd 1971

"'I don't see what good therapy is going to do. You'd think, from the way they all talk about it, that it could fix all injuries, erase the marks of torture, raise the dead."

December 5th 1971

"This was the third time in three days I had to tell the story, and every time I tell it, I have a harder time getting people to believe it."

December 7th 1971

"All she *wants to do is talk about my father.*
All I want to do is talk about what he destroyed.
I can't understand why I can't get anyone to care."

December 8th 1971

"Today I got a letter from him. Apparently he's spent the last two months in a clinic. But never fear! I no longer have an alcoholic for a father. Now he's a recovering alcoholic, and, oh yes, a recovering spook, because his days abroad are over, it seems. From here on in, he's going to do his recovering stateside. He's slowly coming to terms with 'what happened last June,' he claims, and he'd like to see me, to help me recover. Oh, the joy I felt upon seeing those words in a thousand shreds on the floor.

　　She's just as bad. She keeps talking about working through my anger, putting 'this tragedy' behind me, moving on. And now, to top it all off, he wants to help me 'recover.' That's right — first bury the dead, then bury the truth.

I am not going let you get away with it, Dad.
I will hold you to account."

28

J EANNIE WAKEFIELD'S FIRST attempt to hold her father to account came out on the anniversary of the murder, the 4th of June 1972. It appeared in the slim, doomed "International" section of one of Boston's underground papers, under the headline "Who Killed Dutch Harding?"

It was, she later conceded, more about herself than anyone else, and it was studded with the innocent indiscretions that all young journalists must make until they've lost a few friends. She was on the *Crimson* by then, though only in the lowliest capacity. Before taking the story to the underground paper she had been foolish enough to try it out on the great gods then in charge of the place. They had rejected it out of hand.

Her biggest mistake was to say what she thought of people. So her father was a "failed spy" and Hector was a "recovering and sermonizing alcoholic." Her mother was a "deeply mendacious hysteric in deeper denial" and Sinan's mother was a "once celebrated, now forgotten chanteuse," while Chloe's mother "liked to think of herself as a bohemian but scratch the surface and what you found was a 50s housewife."

Miss Broome (who had burst into tears of gratitude when Jeannie had tracked her down to a school in Maine) did not fare much better. She was, Jeannie wrote, a "would-be radical in deep denial about her lover's subversive activities." The murder victim's parents, whom she'd doorstepped in Burlington, Vermont, were "rockjaw WASPS whose faces had frozen while they were raking leaves." Their sin was to say they had no son called Dutch Harding. Their denial fuelled her fire, as did the lesser obstructions thrown in her way by so many friends.

Her greatest sin was to say what she said about Chloe.

Chloe spent most of December in Holyoke Center, and in March she once again slit her wrists. But somehow Jeannie remained convinced that she was as hell-bent on this investigation as she was. This despite the fact that Chloe tried, on several occasions, to talk Jeannie out of it.

In the article Jeannie said that she and Chloe had fallen out when she had told Chloe about meeting up with No Name. Or rather: "my father's former errand boy, a veteran of the Peace Corps whose modest success as a stringer had, by his own admission, deeply compromised his honor."

She implied that she'd set up this meeting herself. In fact, she was sitting in the Café Pamplona late one night in March when he just walked through the door. She didn't recognize him right away – not only did he have long hair now, he also had a beard. She wasn't even considering an article at that point. She was just trying to get to the truth. The idea of setting it down on paper was born during this conversation she had with No Name.

He told her he'd seen "Billie" Broome a week or so earlier. "She said you were trying to get to the bottom of this murder, and perhaps trying a little too hard." Accustomed as she was by then to people trying to talk her out of it, she said, "Well, why shouldn't I?"

His face darkened. "Listen," he said. "I think you should know this. I've been doing some digging myself."

"And?"

"Let me put it this way. The story doesn't hold together." He paused. "One thing is certain. Dutch Harding was what I said he was. Possibly a good deal worse. It's pretty clear that he was not just working for your father. Does that surprise you?"

She nodded, but the cool thing sweeping through her at that moment was relief. The worse Dutch Harding turned out to be, the less she had to blame herself for fingering him. So who else was he working for?

He shook his head. "Can't say. I mean that literally. I thought I was getting somewhere, but then the well dried up. You might have better luck, though. Have you managed to track down Sinan? No? How about your father, then? What's his line? Okay," he'd said, upon hearing that Jeannie and her father were not speaking. "That I do understand. I don't know if I'd be either if I were you. But if you ever change your mind . . ."

He mentioned a name – an old classmate from college who just so happened to have gone to the same prep school Dutch had attended – "a guy with the same politics we have" who now worked in the underground press. When he'd heard about the murder, he'd said he'd be interested in running a piece on it – but only if Jordan could come up with corroborating evidence about the CIA tie-in. "So really I've come to find out what you've been able to find out."

Jeannie didn't have anything of value to tell him, and she left the Café Pamplona that night feeling very young and very useless. So she was all the more surprised at Chloe's reaction when she told her who had turned up at the Pamplona.

She became very agitated. She told Jeannie she was a fool. "You have to forget Dutch Harding! Forget he ever existed." Jeannie just couldn't understand why she'd think that. It was rewriting history. It was wrong! So they stopped speaking. Soon there was no one to temper her obsession.

She wrote the article in May, in the white heat that should have gone into her exams. She took it to the *Crimson* the day after she finished, and she did not take her rejection well. It was two or three days later that she got a call from a Greg Dickson. His name sounded familiar but it was only after she put the phone down that she remembered he was the old classmate of No Name's who now worked at the underground paper. He told Jeannie that he had "dropped by the *Crimson* the other day" and that her "piece" had fallen into his hands. Self-centered eighteen-year-old that she was, she did not think to question this story. "We have a lot of cleaning up to do," he said. "Your language is sophomoric, but the story speaks for itself. It touches on important themes. I'll see what we can do."

The final, heavily edited, version of "Who Killed Dutch Harding?" began with an account of the day she'd met Sinan and went on to tell the rest of the story in the order she had discovered it. It did not mention her father by name, though any fool would have guessed they shared a surname. Although she ended with a list of unanswered questions, she made her own thinking clear. Whoever had committed this murder, it had been her father who had set it into motion.

What was her part in it? she asked in the closing paragraph. Would Dutch be alive today if she had not barged into that apartment? Was it her fault that Suna had jumped out of that window? Had she ruined Sinan's life, too, and Haluk's, assuming, of course, that they were even alive? Bearing in mind who she was and what she stood for, was it not a travesty for her to plead innocence?

"WHEN INNOCENCE IS A CRIME." That was the headline. The piece caused a small sensation. It even got picked up as a news item in the *Boston Globe*: "RADCLIFFE FRESHMAN POINTS THE FINGER AT CIA DAD."

That same morning, Greg Dickson phoned to tell Jeannie that he'd just had a call from an attorney representing "the family of Wilhelmina Broome." He wasn't too concerned, though. It would be bad if they sued, he said, but it was all in a day's work for the free press. The next day, he sounded more strained. He'd now heard from attorneys representing "the family of Amy Cabot." The third day, he was livid. And paranoid. "Does the name Stephen Svabo mean anything to do?" he asked. He had not given her two seconds to consider his question when he yelled, "Who exactly are you working for, you fucking bitch?"

When Jeannie's phone rang an hour later, it was the paper's attorney. There were now five people threatening to sue, "and since your interests and those of my client diverge, I would strongly advise that you retain your own counsel."

The next time the phone rang that morning it was Jeannie's father. "I understand you need some help."

29

J UNE 8TH 1972

"*My father's new home is a little yellow ranch house on a base near Williamsburg, Virginia. Inside, with the curtains drawn, you'd never know. It's the world's smallest and most pathetic museum – wall to wall Turkish and Persian and Afghan carpets, copper trays, copper plates, copper lanterns and alabaster eggs. Indian miniatures hung between Japanese brush drawings and the wild abstractions of that Venezuelan painter he played tennis with in Caracas.*

Open the curtains, and you see an empty road, a row of yellow ranch houses, and an electric power line draped across a colourless sky. From time to time a purring car will pass. Will pull into a driveway. Will wait for the garage door to respond to its wordless command. They all play the same clattering lament: 'I need oil, I need oil, I need oil.'

So this is how the mighty are fallen.

If I didn't want to die, I'd laugh."

June 8th 1972

"*Newsflash: he doesn't blame me. I have the right to my own opinions. He does want me to write and apologize to Mother, who is, and I quote, 'a good-hearted woman.' She's made many sacrifices on my behalf and deserves better than what I gave her in that "intemperate" piece of mine. But as far as he himself is concerned, it's open season. I can say whatever my little heart desires.*

Comment and analysis: while he was in that clinic, whatever it was, he rewrote the story of his life. His new version of 'the events of last spring' is exquisite in its simplicity. Forget politics and culture clashes, riots, spies, rumors and vicious lies. Forget the Cold War. He messed up because he had let alcohol take over his life.

Or to quote him precisely, because he 'let the bourbon do the talking.' More precisely, the bourbon convinced him he was a 'little god.' But alas, he turned out not to be. He made some bad guesses, he allowed himself to be fooled, misled and framed. But hey, there's an upside. He got me and Chloe out in time, didn't he? So at least no one can blame him for endangering innocent Americans.

I'm glad to say I made this point. I'm sad to say it had zero effect. I might as well have been talking about his great uncle's stepson. Is this really my father, I'm beginning to wonder? Or was I dining with a zombie? He looks as if he's been in the world's longest shower. No dirt on him!

His new enthusiasm is cooking, and wasn't it a lovely meal. First Julia Child's spinach soup, and then her roast pork and potatoes in mustard and cream sauce. He tells me he got 'bitten by the Julia bug' in that wonderful clinic. It was part of the program: "finding new ways to fill all that time I used to spend on lifting and lowering that glass." And crushing insurgents, I felt like adding. Compiling files on innocent students, and sending out agents provocateurs to push them over the edge.

Although I didn't say any of that out loud, he read my mind anyway. (How I hate that. Hate it, hate it, hate it!) He said, 'Look, I know. It must be galling, having to lean on me, having to be here. I am, I know, the person you hate most right now. But look, I don't see what choice we have. If I don't help you, these bastards are going to eat you up. And not because of what you said or wrote. They're using you to get to me.'

Nota bene: How it's always a conspiracy. How he's always smack at the center of it. I made this point, too. He just sat back in that chair of his and in that infuriating drawl of his, asked, so then tell me again, who exactly was it that linked you up to Mr. Whatsisname, the editor of that groundbreaking underground newspaper that was kind enough to let you spill your guilt all over its front page? Correct me if I'm wrong, but wasn't it an ex-flunky of mine? I was quick to remind him. This happened to be an ex-flunky who was so disgusted by what he'd seen that he'd been brave enough to switch sides.

But this didn't dent old ironside. No siree. 'Now that takes courage,' was all he said. 'Not just courage, but foresight and resolve.'

I am being killed with kindness, tortured with private jokes."

June 11th 1972

"Today, after spending many hours flipping channels, trying to read, failing to read, making snacks I didn't want just to pass the time and checking the clock every five minutes, because all I had to look forward to was my father's eventual return, I made a terrible, terrible mistake.

The mistake was to go out for some fresh air. I think I knew it was a mistake before I reached the first corner, because there is something soul-destroying about walking past eleven identical ranch houses, all in a little yellow row. But worse was to come: for by the time I had reached my fourth yellow corner, there were sirens wailing in on *me. Can you believe it? Then came the arrest. Dad had to come all the way over to Security and bail me out! He offered to get me 'authorization' to walk the length and breadth of this benighted base in future, but frankly, I'd rather skin a cat.*

I have to ask myself what I'm doing here.

I could leave. I must leave. I must face this alone."

June 11th 1972

"I told him. He listened, nodded, considered, acquiesced. That's fine, he said. But before you go, let's make you a plan. Shall we?

He mapped out what he'd done already. 'As of noon today, you have yourself a lawyer.' An old classmate of his, based in Boston. And so on and so on. "He's not charging us the full whack, but if you undertook to pay his bill out of your own earnings, I think you'd find it burdensome in the extreme." Etc. etc. When I caved in, he gave me that new smile.

I hate him, and everything he stands for. Everything he's done. Every lie he's ever told. But most of all, I hate him for that smug, all-knowing, all-embracing smile."

June 12th 1972

"As for the 'free world' he keeps harping on about. Well, if I've learned one thing from all this, it's that you can't say what you want in the Land of the Free, either. Yes, I know I should have chosen my words more carefully, should have written the facts in black and my opinions in red, so that every legal hotshot in the world would know I was telling a story as seen through my own eyes . . .

But rules are rules, my lawyers tell me. If I am to accuse a spy of spying, I am to furnish tapes, affidavits, photographs! I am to believe that Miss Wilhelmina Broome was so deeply injured by my remarks that she tripped and fell while jogging, scraping and bruising her knee. Is this the same woman who urged us to stand up for the truth, take courage in our convictions? Perhaps not, because I am now told by her millionaire father's lawyer that Miss Broome was only very briefly a member of the SDS and has never knowingly known a Weatherman. As for Amy Cabot, her 'family' now informs me that she has never been a housewife, or aspired to the life of a bohemian, or knowingly owned a pair of mauve palazzo trousers.

How petty can you get?"

June 13th 1972

"Today they cut a deal for me. Tomorrow I write a retraction. Big Dick has agreed to run it on the front page, but I fear it will run over. When I've inserted all the client-serving lies all these lawyers are demanding, it is going to be about six times as long as my original."

June 13th 1972

"I can't write this. I won't."

June 17th 1972

"*I woke up in the middle of the night. I went out to the kitchen for a glass of water and thought of Sinan, and how he must hate me. How he's right to hate me. I finger the villain, and then I run away.*"

June 18th 1972

"*If I had a fraction of his courage, I would have gone out into that storm and stayed there until the lightning found me.*

But here I am, back in the safety of the porch.

The porch is in Rehoboth — just fifty yards from the beach! We're here for the weekend, while Dad and this old classmate of his who cut such a good deal for me draft the retraction I have refused to write. They keep telling me to go off and have fun with the kids but never have I felt a wider gulf between myself and the other members of my generation."

June 19th 1972

"*One day I am going to look back on this day and understand it. I will know by then that life just isn't fair. I will know, too, that the Angel of Death is every-where, and close enough to touch, but I'll have come to see that it's this shadow that gives life its beauty. Or so I am led to believe by the greatest, wisest, most prescient father the world has ever known . . .*

The worst part is the reminiscing. Why he has chosen to confide in me at this late date I do not know. This must be the ultimate torture for my crimes: to sit here on this lawyer's porch and hear how much my father misses Amy, Istanbul and what he calls "the life".

He kept talking about colors. The ochre yellow of the rainwater that ran over the cobblestones at springtime, the pink sheen of the Bosphorus just before the sun goes down, the molten churning just before a storm . . .

At one point I said, 'Why bother? It's not as if you can bring it back.'

'But I will,' he said. 'And one day, so will you.'

But it takes time, he went on to warn me. 'Naturally, I am interested in knowing what happened. So trust me to do my delving in my own way.'

When in Rome do as the Romans, he went on to inform me. Especially when in Istanbul. There were three golden rules:

1) Everything is mired in history.

2) No one ever tells you the whole story, so you can never be sure you know where you are.

3) You tie the knot at your peril, because the story never ends.

His chorus line: 'Jeannie, I am going to get you through this.'

And: 'If it's the last thing I do, I'm going to get you back on track.'

But what about the others?

'Let's save that for later, shall we? Let's save our skins first. We may not know the facts, but one thing is clear. We're dead meat in Istanbul right now, you and me both.'

No one wants anything to do with us! He's spent the last fortnight knocking on every conceivable door, but no one's talking. No one! This may change in future — it usually does — but for now, my personal spymaster informs me, it's over. 'Really over. So why don't you read this thing over so we can type it off tomorrow and send it off?'

This was when he handed me the retraction. When I reached the end and pushed it back at him, he wrote in large letters at the bottom of the sheet: 'ACCORDING TO ALL THOSE PRESENT, THIS NEVER HAPPENED.'

'And let that be a lesson to you,' he said. 'The law is there to help people lie. People with lawyers, that is.'

'That's sick,' I informed him.

'That's life.'

'Not if I had anything to do with it,' I said.

'You show 'em, girl! Go for it!' He reached into his briefcase.

'But I'm not a spook for nothing. I still have a trick or two.' He brought out a file. "Don't ask me how I got this." It was a carbon copy of a letter from the Turkish Ambassador to my enemy and former editor, Greg Dickson:

'We are writing to you to express our deepest concern about the article penned by Miss Wakefield entitled 'Who killed Dutch Harding?' that appeared in the issue dated June 4th 1972. In addition to casting unsupportable aspersions against the Turkish state and referring to the alleged operations of foreign intelligence services within its borders, it also makes a faulty claim about the victim himself. We can affirm that there were indeed reports of his murder in the Turkish press. We can also affirm that two Turkish citizens mentioned in Miss Wakefield's article (Suna Safran and Lüset Danon) have both been found guilty of crimes against the state and are currently serving their sentences. However, no one has been charged with the murder of Dutch Harding. Indeed, under Turkish law this would be impossible, as no charge of murder can be made in the absence of a body. It seems that Miss Wakefield has neglected to check her facts. We suggest that when you are next considering the possibility of publishing a report about our country, you take the precaution of making contact with our press department . . .'

'Why are you showing me this?' I asked my dear old Dad. 'I've learned my lesson, OK? I should have checked my facts. I should have . . '

'Read it again,' he said.

I read it again.

He tapped his cigarette against the ashtray.

'This time, did you catch it?'"

V
Torture
without
Marks

30

THOUGH SOME OF YOUR colleagues at the Center for Democratic Change have been kind enough to sign the queries they have emailed me after each new instalment, others have preferred to remain anonymous. Forgive me, Mary Ann, if I am jumping to conclusions. But I have to wonder what these people have to hide.

In answer to one of their questions: I myself have nothing to hide. Moving on to a second question:

How long was William Wakefield in the dark?

In all honesty, I can only guess. He knew he'd been framed. He read the warning in the Trunk Murder: clear out now, or next time it won't be some hopped-up underling who's lying in a shallow grave in the garden of the Pasha's Library, or inside a trunk at the bottom of the Bosphorus. I am in no doubt it came as a shock to know his life to be in danger, yet not to know where the danger was. He'd grown so accustomed to omniscience. Or rather, the illusion of it.

As for his activities during his last year in Istanbul: it is clear that (between drinks) he was running some sort of agent provocateur. This person would have been expected to involve him or herself in student politics, perhaps to influence the direction it took. It is not clear how much control William Wakefield had over this creature. My guess is that somewhere along the way he lost his grip.

Or someone else took over. Changed the game. Used William Wakefield's own people against him. For there is no doubt that other intelligence services operated on campus, and also in other universities across the country. They, too, would have had an interest in *agents provocateurs*. Sometimes the same agents provocateurs.

There are those who hold that every act of violence perpetrated by the student left in the 60s – and the 70s, and even the 80s – was either planned or pushed forward by agents provocateurs – the aim being to crush and discredit the student left. And certainly, by the end of the Cold War, it wasn't just the student left that had died a death, but the Turkish left in its entirety. However, I refuse to believe that this was down to a handful of intelligence services running a handful of agents. That lets too many people off the hook.

But back to the question. How long was William Wakefield in the dark? Despite his forced departure from Istanbul and the demotion that followed, he remained a company man, so I am in no doubt that he was using the company's resources to research his suspicions from the moment he got to Williamsburg. He might have been 'dead meat' in Istanbul, as he put it, but the letter from the Turkish Embassy is proof that he could still pull in the odd favor. He would have known all along that the story about the Trunk Murder didn't add up. When he found himself publicly denounced by his own daughter for having been its mastermind, he would have been doubly keen to track down the true culprit.

Then he discovered (upon reading the famous letter of complaint from the Turkish Embassy in Washington) that Anonymous had added a new twist to the story – No Body! Which would have told William that a certain someone, having rid himself of one agent provocateur, and pinned the blame on four baby revolutionaries, was now seeking to erase all record of it.

Now why would that be? As Suna might say, *cui bono?* The question would have been there, fomenting in the back of his mind. Forever taking new shape. Because of course he knew there was a body.

So even when he was out in the middle of nowhere, running fronts, he would have been putting lines out, and stockpiling clues. Just when he saw the light is not for me to say.

But if I had to guess how long it took William Wakefield to figure out who had done him over, and why, and how, I would say it took him a good ten years. If I had to pinpoint the exact moment of enlightenment, I'd say it was the day his daughter returned from her short but colossally ill-advised trip to Istanbul in January 1981.

31

"I WAS AGAINST MY *profession before I even joined it (she told me in her let-ter). Even as I stood amidst the thunder and lightning of Rehoboth, I knew the demons that would drive me. I looked into the night sky and I saw my future. I would be the kind of lawyer who fought against any law that allowed rich people with lawyers to get away with murder.*

I ended up — like so many high-minded classmates — at a large firm in Manhattan. I could not choose my work and most of it was the sort I had scorned during my three years at Columbia Law School. But one of the senior partners had links with Amnesty International. He was on its International Executive Committee, had played a key part in its campaign against torture and was now involved with its new campaign against the death penalty. Humanitarian law was in its infancy then, and I wanted to get in on the ground floor. I helped him out of hours wherever I could, mostly with administrative details and translation. He was pleased by my interest and happy to open doors for me.

In December 1977, he took me along to an Amnesty conference on the abolition of the death penalty in Stockholm. It was here that I met several lawyers my age that worked in or with the US Section, and when we all returned to New York, we kept in touch. It cheered me to be with people who could see beyond 'America the Beautiful.' They were, I thought, the best America had to offer: I admired them for their determination to give their best to others. The content of our conversation was gruesome — death and torture, disappear-ances and government-condoned murder. You had to cling to your principles to keep from getting swept away. But that's what I liked about it — having rules that guided you through.

In the autumn of 1980 we were laying the groundwork for a conference on humanitarian law, and I was spending large chunks of my weekend in my old library at Columbia. One Saturday I woke up feeling happy for no reason. It was cold and windy but the bare branches made a beautiful pattern against the sky. I walked into the library and smelled the warm dust and the varnish. The rows of bent heads, the piles of books. I found myself a place, and there, just opposite, was a boy who with his head down looked just like Sinan.

I watched his hands pass through his hair in that bored, insolent way I remembered so well from the days when we had studied together in a library so like this one. He must have seen me, because now he returned my stare. My anguish must have shown on my face, because he leaned forward and in a library whisper, he said, "Look, I know. I'm ugly. But not that ugly." After he was gone, I spent a long time looking at the empty chair.

My eyes began to wander until they lit, as they so often did, on a couple studying together, almost intertwined. On their faces I saw a happiness that had, I thought, rendered them almost unconscious. The injustice of it hit me, the dumb luck of it: that they were here, together, and we were not.

If only I knew why. If only I knew why, I wrote, I could face the future. You have to help me, *I pleaded.* I'm losing my bearings. *It was not the first letter I'd written to Sinan since my father had condemned me to the flickering and — in eight years, never once substantiated — hope that one day we might meet. But the letter I began in the library that autumn morning was the longest and most desperate. It took me all day, and all the paper I had with me. I knew it was a futile exercise; I knew when I folded it up and put it into an envelope addressed to Sinan Sinanoğlu, care of his mother, that it was crazy. But every word of it was true.*

I wrote about my living death, about how I couldn't look across the library without seeing him. About the string of boyfriends and the string of therapists, always trying, always failing. About my father, how I hated him. How I hated myself, too. How at night, when I closed my eyes, I imagined I was sitting next to him in Kitten II, speeding up the Bosphorus, past the palaces, past Pera, past Üsküdar, past the Old City and out along the old Byzantine walls into the Sea of Marmara, and instead of pulling into a discotheque with fairy lights and a dancefloor the size of a mushroom we just kept on going, to Avşa, Bandırma, Çanakkale, Samothraki, Alexandroupolis, Kavala . . .

Is this what love means at the end of the day? Is this what faith is, pretending there are two of you when really there is only one?

Am I telling you the truth only because I know you can't write back?

That was how my letter ended. I sent it without rereading it. As I let it drop into the post box, something inside me died."

Jeannie had arranged to meet her Amnesty friends at the West End Café that evening. She was the first to arrive. There was only one other person at the bar and he did not look like a regular. He had a briefcase parked at his feet, but instead of a suit he was wearing jeans and a safari jacket. He was tanned, or perhaps just wind-burned. His hair – curly, brown, but bleached at the tips by the sun – looked like it had been in a windstorm since he'd last brushed it. He moved slowly, and every once in a while he would see something that made him pause.

When Jeannie's friends walked in, they saw him before they saw her. One by one they shouted "Jordan!" and ran to throw their arms around him. How long he had been back? How glad they were to see him back in one piece! When they brought him to Jeannie's table, he smiled and held out his hand.

"Jordan Frick," he said.

Of course she knew the name. He was a journalist, the last of the firebrands. He'd just done a big piece in the *New Yorker* on El Salvador.

"Glad to meet you," she said. "My name's Jeannie Wakefield."

"I know," he said. "In fact, you know me, too."

"I do?"

"Don't worry. It will come to you." He turned to the man sitting between them. It now emerged that he and Jordan been classmates at Columbia in the late 60s. But today the talk was of the upcoming presidential election. Jordan was covering it for a British newspaper. When someone asked him about human rights in the event of a Reagan victory, he said, "It couldn't come at a worse time." He flicked back his hair in a way Jeannie had once seen a shorn sheep flicking back locks that were no longer. And she knew then who he was.

"No Name!"

"No Name," he laughed. "I'd forgotten you called me that."

"What are you doing here?"

"Actually, I was about to ask you the same question."

But before he could, their friends were rushing them off to the seven o'clock show at the Thalia. It wasn't until they were waiting for the light to change at 96th St that Jeannie got a chance to ask.

"So No Name," she began. "I'm sorry. I can't quite bring myself to call you Jordan yet. Last time we met – nine years ago, yes? In the Café Pamplona?"

Jordan "No Name" Frick shot her a sharp look.

"Anyway," she persisted. "We were talking about the Trunk Murder. And you said . . . something about the story not adding up. Am I right?" He nodded curtly. "So anyway. I was wondering. Did you ever get to the bottom of it?"

"You mean the murder?" he asked.

"Yes. Obviously."

He shrugged his shoulders. "What's Sinan's take on it all?"

"I don't know," she said. "I don't even know where he is."

"How about Chloe then?"

"I'm afraid we fell out."

"Then how about the others? I mean those girls."

She paused before answering, so that she could control her voice. "No, I haven't been in touch with them either."

His righteous glare made her want to defend herself, so she added, "That's not quite true. In the beginning, when I knew what prison they were in, yes, I did write to them. A lot. But then, when they didn't answer . . . well, it was clear they wanted to have nothing to do with me."

"Did you ever ask yourself why?" he asked.

"Well," she said, "There were a lot of things."

"I don't think so," Jordan said. "I think it was one thing in particular. I think it was because of that pack of lies you wrote for my old friend Greg Dickson."

When they reached the Thalia, Jeannie continued down Broadway. She turned on the TV the moment she walked into her apartment. She kept it on till she went to bed. But the moment she turned off the light, it all came back.

"It came back as it always did, in snatches. First my own words, the grandiose theories I'd spun with hearsay. Then it was that pack of lies, the retraction. Then my father, telling me the moral of the story. Then it was Suna. Suna with her feet dangling from that fourth floor window, Suna lying bruised and broken on her prison bed, reading what I'd said about her, Suna stuffing each and every bad translation of my thoughtless words into an envelope and drafting the only letter she'd ever sent: I thought you were my friend. With each new voice, an old sorrow engulfed me. As the walls came down, my grand resolution came back to mock me. How dare I say I cared about human rights? How could I draft a letter on behalf of people I'd never met who were in prisons in South Africa or Central America, but never once inquire after people I had personally harmed?

These were the questions that compelled me to accompany my friends to a seminar on torture at which Jordan Frick was to be one of the featured speakers. It was three or four weeks after our encounter at the West End Café. The election had come and gone. Jordan was there as an expert on Central America, but he also spoke briefly about Turkey.

Nothing he said was news to me. I had read the reports. After five years of 'democratic' rule under a new constitution, five years of turmoil and escalating violence — drive-by shootings, hijackings, pitched battles between right and left-wing militias — Turkey was once again governed by the military. Once again, its political prisons were filling up. I knew the facts and figures but not what I felt about them. Listening to Jordan, looking at someone who was not afraid to condemn the regime in print and in public, the walls came down.

It was not just that he was fearless. When he spoke, he lost all sense of self. He became his subject. He pulled you in. There was no possibility of distance. You were there in the torture chamber. You could feel the falaka on your feet. You could smell your tormentor, and hear the electric cattle prod buzzing as he lifted it over his head. You tasted the fear. You knew you had to devote your life to fighting it. You knew you were a failure because you had done no such thing.

'You've never been back, I take it?' This is what he said to me later, when we'd decamped to The White Horse. I told him I wouldn't dare. 'How can you justify that? I mean, if you care about the people.' I told him the truth — that I never considered it from that angle.

His response was strange: 'I know you like to pity yourself, but have you ever considered the possibility that I might feel even more compromised than you do?' It was right after this that he mentioned the trial.

Hadn't I heard? It was set for January 'The old Enlightenment crew, under a new name. Technically, it's the editorial board of a political magazine. Your friend Suna is one of the defendants.' What he wanted to do was drum up some international interest. 'Embarrass the government, so they dismiss the case. To do that, I need better access. To be blunt, I need someone they can trust.'

Stupidly, I asked why they didn't trust him.

It was my article, of course!

There was only one way to make up for it.

As he considered my proposal, his eyebrows went up and down, up and down. He made a fist and then he opened it like a flower."

But later that same evening, she told her friend Fran that she'd never been so sure of anything. She wasn't going to Istanbul to find out what happened ten years ago. She was going back to help people who needed help now.

"The trial is just the peg," she said. "What he's really doing is mapping out a generation – showing how people like my father destroyed an entire generation in the name of the Domino Theory. Which as theories go couldn't be more insane, could it? Since when have countries been dominos? And why exactly does one country 'falling to Communism' mean its neighbor will fall, too? Jordan has a brilliant way of . . ."

"Oh, so Jordan's brilliant now, is he?" Fran looked at her with some amusement.

"I'm not attracted to him."

"Of course not. You're never attracted to anyone. But he is pretty cute."

"That has nothing to do with it, Fran!"

"Who am I to begrudge you an adventure? But Mike can't be too happy about it, can he?"

Mike had been Jeannie's boyfriend throughout law school. He still was her boyfriend, though he was working in Washington. "It's none of Mike's business," she told Fran. "'If he cares about me at all, he'll know it's something I have to do."

In fact, Mike was not at all happy to hear that Jeannie was going off to Turkey on an ill-defined mission with a journalist so famous even he knew his name. When she wouldn't back down, he said fine, if that was the way she wanted to play it, then so be it. He slammed down the phone, and they didn't speak again until the day she was due to leave. This was another short call. "I've called to say goodbye," she said. And Mike said, "Well, okay then. Goodbye."

The moment she put the phone down, it rang again. She said, "Listen, Mike," but it wasn't Mike. It was her father. His first words were, "That's the spirit, Jeannie! Give the bastard hell."

Her father was living in Columbia, Missouri now, running what purported to be an air cargo business. Whatever his real work was, it bored him to tears. But there was always the sloppy biography he had just finished, the joke of a course he'd just signed up for at the university, the former colleague who'd just disgraced himself in a way that "makes you think there might be a God after all."

The big news this time was his Vietnamese housekeeper. She was "putting the moves" on him. "And I can't say I blame her. The husband's no good. He's gambled all their savings away. And she has two kids heading for med school."

"Sounds like a lot to take on, Dad," Jeannie said.

"But that's not what I called you for."

He waited for her to say something. She knew enough to stay silent. Finally he gave in. "I hear you're about to head off to old pastures."

That threw her "How did you know that?"

"Same way I know everything." He said this with pride.

"I bet it was Mike," she said.

"That's right. Mike and I speak almost daily."

She opted for silence again. If he was so curious, let him make the next move. But how much did he know already? When she could not bear to wait any longer, she said, "Listen, it's my business where I go and who I go with."

"Glad to hear it, Jeannie. I just hope you know what you're heading into."

"What exactly do you mean by that?"

"Exactly what I said. But listen, that's not why I called."

"Then tell me. What can I do for you, Dad?"

"You can do me a favor," he said. "You can drop by and see Amy."

"I'm not sure she'd like that. We didn't part on very good terms."

"On the contrary. I'm sure she'd be insulted if I told her you'd been there and not paid her a visit"

"Am I to understand that you're in regular touch?"

"Let's put it this way. Whenever I pick up a paper and there's news about Istanbul, I ask myself if she's okay."

"So you want me to drop by and check her pulse or something."

"Yeah. Sure. You could also ask her if she still has that box."

Her heart skipped a beat when she heard that, and he seemed to read her mind. "It's not what you think. Actually, it's mostly photographs." He paused for effect. "You might find them interesting. Nevertheless."

"I'm not sure I'll have time," she said.

"Oh, I know, I know. No rest for the righteous. All I can say is that you might find it worth your while."

"Any messages, if I make it?"

"Mention my new housekeeper," he said. "Tell me how she reacts."

32

THEY FLEW OUT on a Friday night, on a plane that was half-empty. Jordan – or No Name, as she still insisted on calling him – had brought her things to read. Most were by or about the various underground groups they would be trying to contact. There was also an unpublished paper on the history of the Turkish left. "Try to commit as much as you can to memory," he said.

He was working on an article, something about the Somozas. He phoned it into the copytakers at Charles de Gaulle, finishing only just in time to make their next flight. The aftermath was, he explained, like coming off a drug. "You use so much adrenaline to get there. You shut everything else out. When it's done, there's this amazing rush. But after that you sort of fall apart. At home, I go for a swim, or a run. But right now, guess what. I'm having a drink."

It was eleven in the morning, Paris time. As they drank their way over Germany and Austria, Yugoslavia and Bulgaria, he talked about his work. What he liked, what wore him down, what the press was there for, what it really did, how he was tired of firefighting, why he thought he might be burning out, what he thought he might do next. What he didn't know, he said, was how he was going to live without "the fix."

"When you see a story, how do you stop yourself?"

She told him she had always imagined that the hard part would be giving up the chance to make a difference. His answer was, "Speak for yourself." She turned to the window, to hide her face.

They were now in Turkish airspace, crossing over the arid plains of Thrace. Soon they were making their final descent into Istanbul and low enough for Jeannie to make out the villas lining the shore and the tankers bobbing between the whitecaps, like boats in a bath. They dipped lower still, as if to dive into the sea. But then, at the last moment, the runway reached out to save them.

Inside the new terminal, the strip lights were harsh and the police at passport control as surly as ever. The soldiers guarding every corner still wielded submachine guns. The luggage hall was swarming with workers just back from Düsseldorf, each struggling to pack the world onto a teetering trolley. The air was stale with smoke, sweat and shoe leather. Crowds of relatives pressed in on them from either side as they struggled through the exit, and the crowds of taxi drivers and scouts. But within minutes they were driving past the old city walls on the Marmara shore. As they approached Sarayburnu, he asked her, "How long is it exactly since you last were here?"

"Ten years next June."

"Ten years? Then you're in for a shock."

They swung around the bend, and there it was, the famous view. To the left, the Galata Bridge with its swarming crowds. To the front, the swarm of ferries and fishing boats coming in and out of the Golden Horn. The hills of the European City, the Galata Tower and the church spires mingling with the domes and the minarets and the tenements spilling down the hill to the Bosphorus. On the other side of the Bosphorus, the hills of Asia. The Bosphorus was grey and choppy, dissolving into a mist. But then the sky broke through the clouds, and there it was, the great arcs of the new bridge joining Europe to Asia.

"Remember all those posters?" Jordan said. 'No to the bridge'?"

They were booked into the Sheraton, which was like every other Sheraton you've ever seen, except for the view. From her room Jeannie could see from Üsküdar to the Old City, from the Bosphorus Bridge to the tankers hovering at the edge of the Marmara, waiting to come in from the mist. She was so tired by now that it gave her vertigo just to look at them, so she stretched out on the bed and went straight to sleep. When she awoke, the room was dark. Someone was knocking. She stumbled to the door. Light flooded in. And there, inside his halo of light, Jordan. "Are you hungry? It's almost nine o'clock."

Off they went into the dark Babel that was Cumhuriyet Caddesi.

At Taksim, they made their way down the same muddy İstiklal, past streams of shivering men in brown suits and dimly lit shoe stores, and the cinemas with their garish posters of women in g-strings and pasties, at last turning right into the flower market, and right again into an arcade of beer halls. The Pasaj: she remembered coming here with her father. They chose a table near the window, where Jordan knew the bartender, a man with eagle eyes and the hands of a giant. The only other female in the place was the big breasted blonde woman who wandered in and out of the arcade with an accordion.

While they sat there with their Arjantins of beer, Jordan told her how this place had knocked him sideways the first time he had seen it. "It all started here," he said. "Suddenly I knew who I was, what I wanted to do with my life, and why." He told her about the people he had met that year while wandering these streets. He recited their names. How many were still alive? On their way back to the hotel, they stopped to see if the landmarks were as they remembered them: the Italian church, the Russian consulate, the Greek church, the French lycée, the Opera House that took ten years to build only to burn down weeks after opening.

On their way through Taksim, a car jumped the kerb. Jordan pulled Jeannie out of the way just in time. Afterwards he tried to keep his arm around her, but she extricated herself. Later, when they were crossing Cumhuriyet Caddesi, he took her hand, to steer her away from a car that had veered out of its lane. But when they got to the other side, she took it back.

"You're not sleepy yet, are you?" he asked in the lift. She wasn't. But she said she was. She spent half the night awake, wondering what it was that made her push people away like that, even after all these years.

"But as my mind went round in ever tighter circles, I somehow managed to block out the other, more urgent question. What had I let myself in for?

When I went to the window the next morning to gaze down at the city as it now was, I could still feel the pull of the city that was no longer, and the life that never was.

Jordan, by contrast, was all business."

But he was not getting very far. As he explained to Jeannie over breakfast. The old Enlightenment team might need help, and Jordan might be in a position to furnish it, but they were not taking his calls. "This is part of the game, of course," he told her edgily. "If you get a summons, the first thing you do is change your address. So we can't expect anyone to be where they say they are. Meanwhile, let's keep hunting."

There was something he wanted to check out on Büyükada. By midmorning, they were on the ferry. The sea was rough, and the town, when they got there, was deserted. The grey waves washing up against the old Ottoman ferry terminal seemed less real to Jeannie than the smooth blue sea in her mind's eye. As they walked through the windswept town, past shuttered shops and houses, she thought back to the lost summer crowds, and the flurries of waiters, and the children on bicycles, the maids beating carpets, the creaking and clopping of horses and carriages, the warm stench of manure rising from the tree-lined streets.

They climbed the hill, passing houses so wet and so grey that she could no longer imagine them any other way. They walked down into a mist and when they came up the other side, they had arrived at the Greek monastery. The church was locked, but from the courtyard they could see the Marmara nestled in a bed of clouds. The rain was not quite with them yet, so they carried on. The first drops hit them as they were passing the sodden, shuttered shack that became a teahouse during the summer. It was while they were taking shelter here that Jordan pointed out the scrub-covered hill where he and Dutch Harding had once met a real life hermit.

He was German, Jordan told her. He was one of the original *Wandervögeln.* He'd come up to Jordan and Dutch while they were trying to light a campfire. Once they'd found they had a language in common, Dutch had befriended him, "and that's how we found out his story. It was only later that it occurred to me Dutch had been my friend for two years by then, and never once had he mentioned he knew German. Strange, isn't it?"

He kept looking over his shoulder, as if he expected one of his contacts to be ambling down the road. But there was no one. When the rain had abated, he went out into the bushes, to take a leak, he said. Ten minutes later, Jeannie took the same crooked path over the crest of the hill to find him crouching in a clearing. His rucksack was sitting on the ground next to him, and in his hand was a trowel.

"What in God's name are you doing?" she asked

Staring disconsolately at the tiny mound of loose earth at his feet, "I was just asking myself the same question."

He remained silent on the long walk into town. But on the ferry back to the city, he apologized for his "strange behavior."

"Though I'm sure you've already guessed what I was up to."

No, she hadn't, Jeannie confessed. "Though the presence of a trowel in your rucksack suggests you had a plan."

"Not a very good plan."

"Apparently not!"

"Will you stop giving me such a hard time?"

"Tell me what you're after, then."

"The same as you," he said. "The truth about Dutch Harding."

"Actually, Jordan, I gave up that one years ago."

He gave her a dark look. "You know they never found his body."

"To tell you the truth, I don't think they ever looked very hard."

"They didn't have to. They were the ones who buried him, after all."

"*They.*"

"I'm sorry. I can't give you names. All I'll say is what a little bird told me. Someone's thinking of digging the body up again."

"Why?"

"I'm not sure. To pin the crime on someone? To send the murderer a message? To keep him — or her — from talking at that trial on Tuesday? We should find out more tonight."

"We're meeting your little bird, are we?"

"Hush. Enough said."

That evening, they took their hunt to Beyoğlu. After a drink at a bar run by a black Turk named Avni, they went to an old Russian restaurant called Rejans. On their way out, one of Jeannie's heels got caught between two cobblestones and came off. Jordan said not to worry. Putting his arm around her, they hobbled into a journalist's haunt called Kulis. It was packed solid, but they found small space near the bar. Billows of smoke furled around the lights. Voices rose and fell. Now it was a woman's laugh and now it was a man telling a long, serious story. Now there was a chorus of high-pitched protest. They had only just been served their drinks when Jordan leaned forward. "Don't look now, but…" She made to turn her head. He stopped her. "I said don't! We're being watched."

"Who by?"

"Keep talking," he said. "Then, in a minute or so, head for the Ladies. Or whatever we're supposed to call it now."

The door marked "*BAYAN*" led to a small bright room with a table on which sat a three-foot doll dressed like a Spanish dancer. Spread around her skirts was a generous display of make-up, an ashtray shaped like a porpoise, two glasses, a water bottle and a bottle of Johnnie Walker Black. Two women were hunched over the table, sharing a cigarette. One was petite and fair, the other dark and dishevelled. They did not look up when she walked in. They were silent when she was in the stall, but when she was washing her hands; one drew the other's attention to Jeannie's broken heel. "And to think I was feeling sorry for her," she said in Turkish. "To think I thought she had a limp."

It was Suna.

Her heart pounding, Jeannie turned off the water. She bowed her head. Was this shame? Or nerves?

"So Lüset, my dear. Shall we?" It was Suna, speaking in Turkish.

"No, darling." It was Lüset now. "Let's not."

"But I'm so bored," said Suna.

"Try German, then. Her legs look German."

Jeannie was drying her hands now. When Suna asked, in German, if she'd like some cologne, Jeannie thanked her, in Turkish, and Suna let out a faint cry.

"I'm sorry," Jeannie said. "I didn't mean . . ."

"Please!" Suna cried Raising her finger to her lips, she indicated with her eyes that the walls might have ears. "Understood?" she asked more softly. Jeannie nodded. Pointing at the shoe that lacked a heel, Suna said, "You are suffering."

"Not really. I'm . . ."

"Shhht," said Suna. "We wish to help."

They went back out to the bar, where Suna handed Jeannie's shoe to a busboy who ran off to have it repaired. "Abracadabra," said Suna. "Could you imagine it could be so easy? Now tell me why you are here."

"To help you."

"Why help someone you've never met?"

"But Suna . . ."

"We have never met, this must be clear, we are being watched. Do you understand? We have taken pity on you following the tragedy of your broken heel. So tell me, dear Jeannie, what is your name? What has brought you here on this fine and muddy evening? Business or pleasure?"

"Business," she said. Then she added, "I'm a lawyer now."

"Ah. This is very interesting. But perhaps not as interesting in the United States as it is here."

"My main interest is in international law," she said. "Humanitarian law."

"Goodness gracious," said Suna. "What a radical concept!"

"And what are *you* up to these days?"

"Ah," Suna said. "This is a never-ending story. So many things I have wished to be, but still I am lagging behind! Let us just say that I am a struggling sociologist-to-be. As for my dear friend, allow me to introduce her. Jeannie, please meet the delectable Lüset Danon, proud owner of a degree in architecture. Though, alas, she remains locked inside the family business of advertising. Yes, it has been a struggle to be true to our gifts. This week, however, it is all we can do to struggle with the mud. I feel I must offer some apology for the weather."

"Who cares?" Jeannie said. "It's you I came to see. I hope you know that."

"Ah!" Suna tapped her fingers on the bar. "Ah!"

"Suna, for the love of God," Lüset whispered in Turkish. "Not here!"

"Nevertheless," said Suna, switching back to English." It must be said. She turned to Jeannie. "My darling woman. My dear, dear friend. Don't you think you have already helped us enough? Such a bountiful lady have you been to us! All those books and lecture notes! Such sacrifices you must have had to make to pay the postage! It was, I think, essential to air all this dirty linen in public."

"If you're alluding to my article," Jeannie said. "Let me take this opportunity to apologize."

"For what, pray tell?"

"For writing it. For driving you to it in the first place!"

"Driving me to what, dear girl?"

"Oh Suna. Stop it. You know as well as I do that I was the one who planted the idea in your head. You all adored him! You would never have suspected him in a million years! If I hadn't stood up to Dutch Harding . . ."

At the mention of Dutch Harding's name, Lüset's eyes bulged. "Suna! We must go!" But Suna was busy lighting herself a new cigarette.

"Who sent you here?"

"As I said, I'm here to make it up to you. For years, I've agonized . . ."

"Ah. How tragic. As you sat cracking your knuckles in the creature comforts of Harvard, you agonized." Suna's voice was growing stronger now.

"I'm sorry. I know there's no comparison."

"So. How exactly are you hoping to help us?"

"As I said, I'm a lawyer. I don't work for Amnesty International but I . . ."

"But let me guess," Suna said. "You are sympathetic to their aims, and you are here to observe a certain trial." She lit a cigarette and allowed the smoke to come out through her nostrils in the way Jeannie remembered so well. "Your father must be roasting in his own juices. Does he know that you're here?"

"He's learned by now that he can't tell me what to think or what to do."

"And what *do* you think?" Suna asked. She leaned against the bar, languidly, as if to say she had all day. But as she surveyed the room, she saw something that made her stop short.

Following her gaze, Jeannie saw Jordan. He was in the corner, talking to a man, punctuating an important point with his cigarette. By the time she turned around again, Suna and Lüset were gone.

33

"I DID NOT THINK *to ask myself what they were running away from, or why, when I turned back to find Jordan, he, too, had disappeared. Instead I sat there waiting stupidly for my shoe. And — just as stupidly — giving my shoe as an alibi to any man who approached me. When it was at last returned to me, one band of rejected suitors stood up to clap.*

Back at the hotel, I couldn't sleep. Just after two, there was a knock on the door. It was Jordan. Head bowed, stinking of smoke and whiskey. Blood all over his shirt. I cleaned it up as best I could and laid him out on one twin bed and put myself in the other.

When I woke up, at about eight, it was to the sound of the shower. A few minutes later, he came out of the bathroom, clear-eyed, chastened, and wrapped in a thick white towel. He padded across the room and sat down on my bed. 'I'm so sorry, Jeannie. So very, very sorry.'

He was sorry because he'd not told me the whole truth. He now proposed to do so. He was not just here for the trial, he informed me. He was here to find out who killed Dutch Harding. According to that little bird of his, the number one suspect was back in town. He was a Soviet agent, a consular official with whom Dutch had had 'dealings.' I stupidly offered up a name. Did he mean Sergei? 'So Sinan knew him, too?' Jordan asked. I said everyone knew Sergei. 'Even my father.' This last remark elicited a contemptuous snort.

When I asked why Sergei was the number one suspect, he fell silent. 'I'll know more after tonight,' he said finally. 'If you want, you can come along. We're meeting in that discotheque across the street. But first it's back to our old hunting grounds. There's something I need to check out."

By eleven, they were in a taxi, rolling down the hill to Dolmabahçe Palace. By half past, they were rounding Akıntıburnu and coming into Bebek. There was a strong north wind blowing in from the Black Sea. The Bosphorus was the same steel grey as the billowing clouds. Bebek was cold and damp. Most of the shops had changed hands but Jeannie could still make out Yalter's Bookshop and Haldun's Delicatessen and Mini Dondurma, the hole-in-the-wall ice cream shop.

The sun broke through as they climbed the stairs to look once more at Dutch Harding's old apartment. It went back behind the clouds as they left Bebek to stare dumbfounded at the apartment building that stood where Nazmi's should have been. They continued along the shore to what had once been Robert College and had now become Boğaziçi Üniversitesi, or the University of the Bosphorus. They walked up the Twisty Turny to the campus. The sky was clear above the terrace. The Bosphorus was bright turquoise; the castle and the houses on the Asian shore tinged with gold. But the wind was still harsh so they did not linger.

They made their way down the white walk to the cobblestone road to the *meydan*. There was the Pasha's Library, or rather, there was the garden wall and the green metal gate with its little redbrick turrets. All they could see beyond it were the treetops. After a few minutes on the marble bench below the big plane tree, they walked up the alleyway to Chloe's old house. It was now part of the International Community School. The janitor pointed them up the path to Damon House. They would, he said, find a Mrs Cabot in the ground floor apartment.

Amy Cabot answered the door the moment they rang the bell. She was fully made up, perfectly coiffed, and wearing a white lace blouse with a long floral skirt. The ready smile on her face and the smell of roasting meat told them that she was expecting guests. "Oh!" she said. She put her hand to her mouth as her eyes travelled between them. But when Jeannie told her who she was, she said, "Yes, of course! But goodness! What perfect timing!"

Though Jeannie had never been in this house before, she recognized every piece of furniture in the sitting room, every painting, photograph, carpet and copper tray. Amy, too, was not changed so much as artfully rearranged.

"So tell me," she said in her hard, bright voice. "What brings you back?"

Jordan said, "Jeannie is helping me out with a piece."

"A piece of what?" Amy asked.

"I'm a journalist."

"What name do you write under?"

"My real name," he said. "Jordan Frick."

"Oh! You wrote that wonderful thing for the *New Yorker* on El Salvador."

"Yes," said Jordan. "Now I'm hoping to do something similar on Turkey."

"Aha," said Amy. "How interesting. So tell me. Is this your first visit?"

"No, actually, I was here for a few years about ten years ago," Jordan said. "In fact, we met. At Jeannie's father's house?" She shook her head.

"It's nice to be back, anyway," he said.

"Well, that's really saying something, considering why you're here!" She swept off into the kitchen to fetch their drinks. There was someone else in there. Jeannie could hear muffled voices. A door opened, then it closed. There was the creaking of floorboards, and then footsteps on stairs. Jordan stood up and moved towards the door, but before he got there, the doorbell rang.

Within minutes, the room was full. Most of the guests seemed to be neighbors. They greeted each other like family but their eyes lit up when they saw newcomers. Upon being introduced, the flame died. "Good God!" they said. "Gosh!" "Gracious!" Or "Yes. I read your article." Then silence.

When Amy asked if they remembered Jordan, they shook their heads. "So! What brings you back?" Most backed away when he told them. Only two made an effort. One was a man named Thomas Ashe whom Jeannie thought might have been a friend of her father's and the other was Meredith Lacey, whom Jeannie remembered better, because she'd taught at the Girls' College. Both claimed to be glad that Jordan was planning to write "the truth about Turkey," though they were quick to add that most Turks were glad the military had at last stepped in.

"Things were very bad by the time they did," Thomas told them. "Bus hijackings and drive-by shootings were everyday occurrences. If there was a clash between rightists and leftists, and people died, that was just a normal day. I myself got caught in the middle of a riot downtown the year before and was shot in the leg . . ."

Turning to Meredith, Jeannie asked if she remembered Suna.

"Of course. I used to teach her."

"Are you still in touch?"

"Not really, only now and again. Now that she's . . ." Here Meredith paused. "Of course, you must know all this. If you work for Amnesty, you must know her file backwards and forwards."

"I don't work for Amnesty," Jeannie said.

"And Amnesty doesn't have a file on Suna," Jordan said. They never adopt people who've advocated violence. Which — once upon a time — she did."

"Yes," said Meredith. "Well, of course, you're right." She glanced over her shoulder at the staircase that led downstairs.

Here they were interrupted by a firmly smiling Amy. "So tell me, Jeannie. How is your father?" Jeannie brought her up to date without mentioning the Vietnamese housekeeper. She then asked about Chloe, about whom she had heard nothing since 1972. She'd had a hard time of it for a while, Amy announced chirpily. But now she was having a whale of a time in Venice, California. Having finally discovered her "calling in life," she was now "seriously considering" applying to medical school.

By now people had started leaving. When Jordan made to go downstairs to fetch their coats, both Amy and Meredith jumped up and pushed in front of him. They bounded back wearing crocodile smiles and bubbling with questions. Where were Jeannie and Jordan staying? How long were they in town? Did they have a free evening? "You must let us know," Amy said.

Jordan's first words after she closed the front door on them was, "Fuck."

He bounded ahead, head bowed, his hands in his pockets. He stopped at the plane tree in the meydan. "He's in that house. I swear. He's there."

"Who? Sergei?"

He threw his cigarette onto the cobblestones. "We're going to have to go back."

"And say what – that we changed our minds?"

"No, of course not. We have to have a genuine reason. As it happens, we have one. Because you forgot something. Didn't you?"

"Did I?"

"I seem to recall that your father asked you to pick up some sort of box."

"And perhaps I really am my father's daughter. Because the moment he said that, the dots connected. I saw what a fool I'd been. Who Jordan was, what he was really here for, why he'd brought me with him. I saw all this and, daughter that I was, I was damned if I was going to let him know."

"Oh, yes, the box," she said, "Gosh, I'd completely forgotten. To tell you the truth, I'd even forgotten I'd mentioned it to you."

"Actually, you didn't."

"Then how do you know?"

"Let's put it this way. I am in touch with someone who is in touch with your father."

"Oh really? Who?"

"I'm sorry if this sounds bad. It's just that when you made your sudden offer . . ."

"So what – you did a check on me? You spoke to my boyfriend?"

"Actually, it wasn't Mike," he said.

"But you know who Mike is."

"Let's get this over with, okay?"

So off they went, up the hill again. Amy looked very surprised when she opened the door. "A box?" she said. "In my basement? No, I don't think so. But you're welcome to take a look."

"I'll do that, if you don't mind," said Jordan. Jeannie waited at the door until their voices were too faint to follow. Then, very softly, she let herself out.

The Pasha's Library was dark and the light was fading fast by the time she remembered where the wall was lowest. Though the drop was greater than she expected – for where she landed, someone had been digging. She climbed out of the trench and crept over to the gate. She had not been keeping watch long when Jordan appeared in the meydan.

"He was not carrying a box. The slump of his shoulders told me that he'd not found Sergei either. But something about the way he moved told me he knew I was close by. Perhaps he could smell me.

A black Mercedes pulled up.

'Are you the Harkers?' Jordan asked.

They were skeptical until he introduced himself. 'Good gracious,' said Mrs. Harker. 'What brings you to Rumeli Hisar?' He explained that he was an 'old associate' of William Wakefield. 'Goodness, that is a blast from the past! We knew him in Manila. How is he?'

'Living in Missouri,' said Jordan. 'Actually, that's why he asked me to drop by. There's a box of records that got left behind, and he . . .'

'Gloria? Does that ring any bells?'

'Gee. I don't know. Maybe you should come in and take a look.'

I was, I imagine, fully visible from the path. But that is the thing about that path. No one ever looks to either side.

They paused to admire the view before entering the house. I had no choice but to follow suit. When they turned their heads to the right, so did I.

They were looking at the wall, just where I'd climbed over it.

They were looking at the hole someone had dug in the ground just underneath it."

The road down to the shore was steeper than she remembered. Or maybe it was her unsuitable shoes. They were covered in mud. They kept slipping on the uneven cobblestones but her terror pushed her forward like the wind. Her mind had room for one idea. She hailed the first taxi and asked to go to the airport, but when she'd caught her breath enough to look into her bag, she saw that her passport and her ticket weren't there.

Did Jordan have them, or had she left them in her room? When she got to the hotel and asked the man behind the desk for her key, he smiled and shook his head. "I have just given it to your friend."

For lack of a better idea she went across to the Divan Hotel. Her first stop was the bathroom, where she tried to make herself presentable. The looks she got from the waiters in the pastry shop told her how dismally she'd failed.

She called for the bill. She still had no idea where to go. She walked down Cumhuriyet Caddesi in the direction of Nişantaşı. The wind was colder and stronger and laced with rain. The pavements were deserted and every other minute a car slowed down and a man would stick his head out of the window to make her an offer. Heading back up Cumhuriyet Caddesi in the direction of Taksim, she found a film theatre and went inside.

It was a Charles Bronson movie; she was the only unaccompanied woman in the audience. When various unkempt loners made themselves know to her, she returned to Cumhuriyet Caddesi and its honking cars. Passing a door with a bouncer, she recognized the discotheque where Jordan would be meeting his little bird that evening. If she waited till he arrived . . .

She took a seat in what seemed to be the darkest alcove, right next to the door. The place was empty, but after eleven, people began to filter in, and it was easier then to tame her swirling thoughts. She was grateful for the shadows and the distorting strobe lights, for Grace Jones and the disco queens, but as midnight came and went she began to ask herself why she was here.

By 1 am she had convinced herself that she had nothing to fear from Jordan. For it wasn't Jordan who turned her stomach. It was her father's shadow behind him. It was her own stupidity. By half past one, she had found her courage. She would go back to the hotel and confront him. Find out why he of all people was trying to dig up bodies, and who the hell he was trying to frame.

She searched the shadows for a waiter. And there he was.

34

HE HAD HIS BACK to her. A waiter was helping him into a chair.

As she sank into the shadows, a second man came in. When the newcomer spotted Jordan, he waved and wove his way past the dancers to his table. A column blocked Jeannie's view, but his homely jacket made her think that he was probably not a Turk. Another foreign journalist, perhaps? Or was this Sergei?

She beckoned for the waiter and asked for the bill. He nodded, then looked at the shadowy figure sitting at the next table. He headed for the door. The shadow followed. It was tall and slim and moved like a cat. Except for the collar glowing purple in the strobe light, he was dressed in black.

Moments later, the shadow returned. Then the waiter with the bill. But as Jeannie headed for the front door, the man with this phosphorescent collar grabbed her arm. The collar was so bright she could barely see his face. But the moment she saw his eyes, she recognized him.

"We're in danger," he whispered into her ear. "Very great danger. But if you do as I say, we'll be fine." Easing her into a chair, he offered her a Marlboro.

"I don't smoke. Don't you remember?"

"Of course I do. I remember everything. Will you take it, please? Thanks. And would you mind turning your head a little, so your hair

falls in a natural manner across your face? That will keep them from seeing you."

"Them," Jeannie said. It was only half a question.

"I'll explain later. Okay?" His voice was calm but there was a catch
to it. "Now raise the cigarette to your lips so I can light it for you. Yes,
like that. Breathe in, just a bit, to allow for the fire to catch."

She did as she was told but choked on the smoke. "I'm sorry," he
said. "But it's only for a few minutes. Yes, that's fine. That's all. Thanks.
That's perfect. And now I'm going ask you to lean over slightly, as if you
are looking at your shoe, again letting your hair fall to conceal your face.
Yes, just like that. Thank you. You can look now, but please try not to
stare."

She looked across the dance floor to see that two women had joined
Jordan and his down-at-heel friend. The women had their backs to
them. One was electric with grand gestures, the other clipped and correct. The first was Suna, the second Lüset. They were both leaning
forwards, as were Jordan and his friend. Whatever was on offer, it
exceeded their expectations.

"Don't stare. Didn't I tell you not to stare? Please, Jeannie, listen.
You can criticize me later, but for now, can you *please* obey me? At least
pretend to obey me? Look. I mean – don't look. In a few minutes they
will leave. But for now you must sit still, very still, and pretend you still
love me."

"*Later, much later, at the House of Shrouds, we came back to this.*

*'Okay! I was wrong! I was a terrible, jealous Turk! But Jordan or no
Jordan. You still broke your promise.'*

'You're wrong, you know! So wrong!'

'You've had lovers,' he said.

I said, 'And you haven't?'

'I never forgot you.'

*'You never wrote to me, either,' I said. 'For ten years, nothing! You might
as well have been dead!'*

'I was dead,' he finally admitted.

And I said, 'So was I.'

*From beneath the covers, I stole a look at him. He was still thin, but broader.
His smile the same, but so much harder to tease out. His eyes were still too dark
to read.*

'You're still too cold,' he said.

'Then hold me tighter,' I said.

'Like this?' He pinched my cheek. It was a joke but not a joke. We were running out of time.

We were lying under seven quilts and fifteen fur coats in his mother's bed. It was the only piece of furniture that didn't have a sheet draped over it. It had been years since any living person had used this place, and we hadn't managed to turn on the heat. We'd been under the covers long enough to create a pocket of warmth, but it when we stretched out our feet, we touched ice. We could see our breath.

It was still dark inside the room but a shard of daylight was coming through the drapes. We had, I thought, reached an understanding. Or we would soon.

I'd pressed him hard, too hard. 'You've changed,' he said. 'You don't understand me. You don't listen, you just talk.'

'You're even worse. You don't listen or talk,' I said.

'I know. You're right. I'm impossible.'

There was a lightness to his voice now. It was different from the leaden tones he'd used earlier, and I took this to mean that at last I was getting through. So I asked him outright. Could he look me in the eye and say there was no hope for us?

He touched my arm. 'You're getting cold again.' As he tried to rub some warmth into it, he said, 'You've changed, you know. You were never this cold. What are we going to do with you, Jeannie? Who is going to look after you when I'm in prison?'

He'd said this several times already. When I'd asked why, he'd prevaricated. He'd done nothing. He'd done nothing, but live in Denmark. For nine years, he'd done nothing, but then, on the spur of the moment, he'd come back to help Suna, who was on trial again, even though she'd done nothing either. During his nine years in Denmark, he'd done nothing to help her. Since returning to Istanbul, he'd still done nothing. And now he was more in debt to her than ever. For it was thanks to Suna that we were here in bed together. It was thanks to Suna that he could look me in the eye and say there was no hope for us.

'Why? Don't you love me?'

'Of course I love you. I'll always love you. But I can't give you any more than that. I can't . . .'

That was when we heard the voices outside the door.

I tried to argue with them. Sinan patted my shoulder and told me not to bother. His bag was packed and waiting in the spare bedroom. I tried to pick it up but it was too heavy. 'Yes,' he said. 'I'm taking lots of books. You can always send me books, by the way. So long as they don't tempt me to take up arms against the state.'

'I don't understand why you're going in so willingly,' I said when they'd *put us into the jeep. He shrugged his shoulders. 'As you'll soon see, I'm not.' The jeep was just swooping down into Dolmabahçe by now. The storm had moved on. The sky was bright and clear and blue. The city looked freshly laundered. Across the Bosphorus, just at the tip of the hill behind Üsküdar, I could see the sun rising. 'Look,' he said. 'Another false dawn.'"*

Their first stop was a nondescript office building. As they stepped down from the jeep. Sinan took her hand and squeezed it very hard, but he did not look her in the eye. His last words to her were, "Don't let them see how you feel."

After the guards had taken Sinan inside, Jeannie was transferred to a white Anadol. When it became clear that they were heading for the airport, she tried to tell the driver that she didn't have her luggage with her, or, more importantly, her passport. He just shrugged his shoulders. Outside the departure terminal, he went round to the luggage compartment and produced her suitcase. Reaching into his inside pocket, he brought out the wallet that contained her ticket and her passport. He walked her over to the Lufthansa desk, where a flight attendant had already changed her ticket.

She was then taken upstairs and left to wait in an office. Her escort stood guard outside the door. Ten minutes later, a slim, agile, clean-faced, middle-aged man came in. He was carrying a thick file. He put this down on the table in the middle of the room. Turning to face her, he held out his hand. "Long time no see," he said.

"İsmet." She kept her voice neutral.

"Are you okay?" he asked breezily. "They didn't manhandle you, did they?"

"There wasn't a 'they,'" she said. "I was just with Sinan."

"But you saw the others in that discotheque, didn't you?"

"Evidently, you did, too."

"Well, what can I say, Jeannie? With friends like that and so on. Don't worry though. We're talking to Sinan now, as you know, and once we're through, I'm sure he'll take us to them."

"I'm sorry, I'm not following you."

"So he didn't tell you. How interesting. Well, what can I say except I'm not surprised. Anyway, for your information, it's not just you they kidnapped."

"Who said anything about kidnap?"

"Well I hate to be the one to give you the news, but that friend of yours, Sinan, was in on the deal."

"What deal?"

"Suna and Lüset," he said. "They kidnapped your boyfriend. In case you're getting mixed up – seeing as you have more than your fair share of boyfriends – I mean Jordan Frick."

"He's not my boyfriend. And he wasn't kidnapped. He went with them willingly. I saw it with my own eyes. And anyway, he was the one who was pursuing them, not the other way round."

İsmet lifted his hands, as if to Allah. "What can I say, except that fact is stranger than fiction? The fact of the matter is that Jordan Frick is as we speak in the hands of kidnappers. They've already phoned in to the press but between you and me it all looks pretty amateurish. An opportunistic act, what actors might call an improvisation. Now we have Sinan helping us, I am sure we will find him. So I'm not concerned. My question to you is, do you want to hang on in there, or should we just keep things simple and off the record and get you out on the first plane? It's waiting on the tarmac. If you want to take it we can get you out there in minutes flat. But I thought, seeing as you and Jordan are an item . . ."

"We are not an item," Jeannie hissed. "And he's a piece of shit."

"Okay, then," he said. "Let's get cracking." He picked up the phone and gave a command in Turkish. He put down the receiver. "It's been good to talk."

"If I find out you've framed Sinan, there will be hell to pay."

"Fair enough," he said. "And don't forget to pass on my regards to your father." There was a knock on the door. İsmet stood up now. "These are the guys who'll take you out to the plane."

"But before you go," he said as she rose to her feet "I have one more question for you. Did Sinan happen to mention where he buried his friend?"

"What friend are you talking about now?"

"Dutch Harding, of course. Oh, I'm sorry. Is this news? When Sinan and I had our chat on the phone just now, it was the first thing he confessed to. That's why he stayed away so long, you see. He was the ringleader. He was the one who cut his teacher into seven pieces and stuffed them into the trunk."

"I think you're making that up," Jeannie said.

İsmet shrugged his shoulders. "What you think is of no concern to anyone."

Her guards were armed. They escorted her all the way to the first class seat to which she had been mysteriously reassigned. A tactful flight attendant had drawn the curtains to keep the economy class passengers from gaping. As soon as they were in the air, she was back to offer her champagne and smoked salmon. And she lifted her glass just as Sinan had made her promise she would. She was to pretend he was there with her, she was to know he was there with her in his thoughts. "It will cheer me up," he'd said. But that was then. Now she was high up in the sky, flying to freedom, flying first class, not because she had earned it but because she was her father's daughter. And Sinan was in a cell somewhere, tied to a chair, having the truth burned out of him with an electric truncheon.

35

JANUARY 28TH 1981

"I am alive again. After nine years, seven months and twenty-four days. Dead hopes swirling back to life, whirling around my head like bats.
Where is he? What are they doing to him?
I can still feel his hands on my skin."

When she got back to New York, late Monday night, there was a message from her father on the machine. She didn't call him back.

On Tuesday she got up early, went out for a run, and instead of going to work, she spent the day calling contacts, scanning the papers, concocting and discarding plans.

She'd be doing fine and then the shard of a memory would come flying from nowhere. The white fur coats on the bed, and their frozen breath. The brown fur coat he'd worn into the kitchen. The tea he'd brought back. The steam rising from the little, gold-rimmed glasses. The first slivers of light between the curtains. The white fur coats on the bed. His hand.

It must have been about six in the evening when she went out to pick up some groceries. She stopped in at the West End Café, to see if any of her friends were there. There, propped against the bar, was Jordan Frick.

"You're a piece of work, did you know that?"

He was wearing Raybans. His mouth looked ugly. "I hope you're happy."

"What the hell do I have to be happy about?" she said.

"Don't be disingenuous," said Jordan. "You almost got me killed."

"Gosh," she said. "You sound just like my father."

"Don't you be flippant with me. Don't you dare. I could have helped a couple of hundred people, including your friends, but now my plans are down the tubes."

"You know?" Jeannie said. "This time last week, I might have fallen for that. But not now, Jordan. I know who you are, and who you work for."

"As any fool could tell you, I work for no one but myself."

"If you had spelled it out to me, I might not have minded. But you went behind my back, prepared your ground . . ."

"What makes you so special that I have to spell out every goddamn detail?"

He had begun to shout. The bartender took note. He came down to their end of the bar. "I'm sorry, Jordan, but you know the score."

"Kit, this is serious. She had me fucking kidnapped." Jordan took off his glasses. He had two black eyes. "See what those precious friends of hers did to me?" he screamed. "See?"

"I don't care what she did," the bartender said. "I don't care if she locked you up in a trunk. Raise your voice one more time and you're eighty-sixed."

"I'll raise my voice when I want to, fuckhead!"

"We'll see about that, my friend." After calling over an off-duty police officer, the bartender turned to Jeannie. "I'll give you ten minutes to get home."

The first thing she did when she got home was to phone her father. "Call off your dogs," she said. He did not ask for names.

"I suppose I don't have to tell you what happened," she told her father the next time he called. "I'm assuming you've already been briefed."

"Yes, well, in a matter of speaking, I guess I have." He sounded unusually sheepish. 'Not that he was particularly coherent during our, what did you call it? Oh yes. Briefing.' His voice grew lighter. 'Yes, as briefings go, it was a lot of fun. I hear our friend Jordan 'No Name' Frick fell for the old box trick."

"What old box trick?"

"God, you're slow, aren't you? There was no box."

"You could have told me," she said.

"He actually went in to see the Harkers, did he? That's just terrific. That's the icing on the cake."

"So what was the cake?"

"I'm not sure I follow you."

"What exactly did you send me there to do?"

There was a long pause. "How's Sinan?"

"In jail," she said.

"Did you get a chance to speak at least?"

She wanted to tell her father how it made her feel to hear that note of light concern in his voice. As if he didn't know the answer to his question, down to the last graphic detail. Although she got off the phone right away, it was not soon enough to save her from his pity.

"I had no idea he still meant so much to you," he said the next time they spoke. "I thought you'd moved on." He went on to insist – how dare he? – that he'd had no idea, no idea whatsoever, that Sinan would be back in Turkey. "Or why, for that matter." But now he'd made up for lost time. "And it's pretty ugly, I'm warning you. I hope you're sitting down."

Sinan, he went on to tell her, had not been charged with the kidnapping of Jordan Frick. But "under interrogation" he'd admitted to a "panoply of other crimes, and believe you me, it's one hell of a star turn." He had, her father claimed, admitted to them "willingly." This, Jeannie presumed, was a way of suggesting that he may not have been tortured. "Someone acting on his behalf delivered a ludicrously incriminating statement to the press. If we are to believe it, he was the single mastermind behind every student riot in the past fifteen years, not to mention every kidnapping, including, incredibly, the kidnap and murder of the Israeli consul in 1971. Plus he was writing Marxist-Leninist tracts from the age of fourteen. And praising the achievements of Mao under 109 pseudonyms."

"It's a joke," Jeannie said.

"Of course it's a joke," said her father. "But who has the heart to laugh? I have before me a Turkish newspaper with a very sad picture on the front page. It's all over the papers. It's a picture of Sinan, pointing to a patch of the Bosphorus where he last saw that trunk. I don't know if you realize this, but in Turkey the first thing they make you do in a murder case is put you through a re-enactment. Not that it did them much good, though. A decade later, Dutch Harding's body for some reason is not where our friend Sinan recalls dumping it."

"That's because he never put it there. He's lying," Jeannie said.

"Now why would he want to lie about something like that?"

The next thing she did was to look for Chloe. She was no longer at the address her mother had for her in Venice, California. She was in El Paso, having just been admitted to Juarez Medical School across the Rio Grande.

Jeannie flew right out. Chloe was standing with the crowd outside the gate at the airport and although she did not immediately recognize her, she picked her out at once. Her hair was dyed carrot orange and she was wearing a Mao Suit and it was clear that she, too, had been through an experience that had left her haunted.

She'd not spoken to her mother since Christmas, and it was clear, when Jeannie updated her, that she was hearing this chapter of the story for the first time. She did not ask Chloe how she felt about it all – this, too, would have been an indulgence, a deviation – all she wanted to know was if she would help campaign for their release. She said she would, and for the next few months, Jeannie and Chloe were in regular touch – if not to exchange notes about the campaign itself, then to discuss what to put into the packages they were sending to their friends in prison.

By April, when Sinan went on trial, interest in London was high enough for several newspapers to run short news items. These fed into pieces in the op ed and comments pages that gave damning if also rather sketchy accounts of human rights infractions in Turkey in the wake of the September 1980 military takeover. Jeannie knew better than to write anything herself, but she was quoted in the *New York Times* and photographed for the *Observer*.

Later that month, she received a letter from an Anna Sinanoğlu. She introduced herself as Sinan's wife. She explained that she and Sinan had met when they were both studying political science in Copenhagen and had been married for six years. They had two children, a son and a daughter. Although it was Anna Sinanoğlu's plan to continue to reside in Denmark, she and the children were currently in Istanbul "to assist with the trial."

"I understand that you met with my husband," she wrote "during the recent visit to the city to which you allude in the enclosed article in the Observer. *I must confess it was quite a shock to read of this, especially because my husband had never once mentioned your name during our years together. However, he is an honest man at heart and now he has told me everything.*

If you were led to believe that there were problems in our marriage, I must ask you how you would respond, if you were a woman with two young children to feed and nurture, and your husband told you he planned to return to his homeland to throw himself into prison for an obscure matter of principle. I wonder if you, as I, would make every effort to dissuade him.

I would also ask you to imagine how you would feel if you put down the phone on a Friday night certain that you had reached a rational agreement, only to find on Monday morning that he has turned himself in. Well, if you can imagine all this, you will know how I am feeling right now. I am also somewhat perplexed by your efforts to procure his release, as I understand that you were instrumental in his arrest. You ought to have known you were a danger to him, just by virtue of who you are.

I am writing not just for myself and my children but on behalf of several others I do not need to name. As grateful as we all are for the work you have done on my husband's behalf, we all feel that it would be more proper if you could now step away."

It was Chloe she called first, and – possibly because of that bad experience to which she had not yet alluded – Chloe heard the danger in Jeannie's voice and jumped on the first plane. She stayed three nights. She cooked, kept the music playing, kept Jeannie talking, made her laugh from time to time, and listened to her cry. Every once in a while, the clouds in her head would part for long enough for Jeannie to thank her.

On her last night, Chloe told Jeannie about her breakdown. But Jeannie was so caught up in her own sorrows that she retained almost nothing. Only that Chloe had been in a relationship with a violent man, that drink and drugs had played their part, and that she'd ended up in rehab after a suicide attempt. Now she was in therapy, and the 'year of the bombs' had featured a great deal. "Especially the murder. And how we never discussed it. Why didn't we ever discuss it, Jeannie?"

"We didn't discuss much of anything, did we? We just walked around pretending to be invulnerable." At which Chloe asked Jeannie if she knew how much she'd hurt her by letting the world know she was a virgin. She apologized for her carelessness but Chloe could not help laughing, and Jeannie could not help joining in – to think that a thing so trivial could have seemed of such grave import.

Jeannie then asked Chloe about Dutch Harding. "There's nothing much to say," she said with a shrug. "Nothing but sex and drugs and hundreds of unreadable books." She had certainly seen no bombs during her visits to Dutch Harding's apartment, "although yes, there certainly was loose talk about bombs." She could not imagine why anyone, let alone his most slavishly devoted students, might have wanted Dutch Harding dead.

When Jeannie suggested that he might have been an agent provocateur, she waved her arms in exasperation. "But why? And for what?"

So Jeannie brought up Sinan. "Do you think he could have done it?"

Chloe shrugged her shoulders and gave Jeannie her most helpless stare.

"I gathered the last of my courage.

How long had she and Sinan been back in touch?

She'd passed through Copenhagen a few years back, she told me. She'd seen him then.

And his wife? I said. And his children?

She was sorry. She should have mentioned it. But Sinan was an old friend. She hadn't wanted to cause more problems.

He and his wife. Had they seemed happy?

It was so hard to say. 'Especially when you couldn't walk two inches without tripping on a toy.' But yes, they'd seemed happy. 'Happy enough.'

Was that why Sinan had never got in touch with me?

She didn't know. They hadn't talked about it.

Hadn't my name come up at all?

'Look, Jeannie. I didn't want to probe. We didn't discuss the past. It was just too . . . I was just so happy that he had a life finally. Can't we leave it at that?'

She took my hand. 'And one day, one day soon I hope, when you have a life again, I'll be just as happy for you.'

I looked around me, at the half-painted wall behind the sofa, the scrawny yucca tree in the window, the scribbles of light on the dusty floor, the pile of half-read newspapers, the plate of cold lasagne waiting for me on the table, just in case I changed my mind. Chloe followed my gaze. 'I know,' she said. 'I know.'"

36

S O ENDS THE SECOND section of Jeannie's confession. There follows a gap of eighteen years, bridged only by a brutal endnote:

"In the years following the military coup of September 12th 1980, 650,000 persons – blue and white collar workers, civil servants, teachers, university lecturers, students, technicians, physicians, lawyers, jurists, and civic leaders were detained or arrested for political reasons, according to figures gathered by the Human Rights Foundation of Turkey. 210,000 were put on trial and 65,000 convicted. The death penalty was recommended for 6,353 people and 500 sentences passed, of which 50 were executed. Of the thousands who were tortured and crippled, 460 died.

Following the coup, martial law commanders also removed 4,891 civil servants from their posts while 4,509 were sent into exile; another 20,000 were forced into resignation or retirement. All in all, 30,000 people fled the country; 15,000 were deprived of their citizenship. Kurdish was banned, making Turkey the only country in the world to prohibit the speaking of a language.

Newspapers and journals were closed down, sometimes for limited periods and sometimes indefinitely. Journalists and writers were sentenced to lengthy prison terms; sometimes they were tried for up to a hundred offences simultaneously but given consecutive sentences adding up to hundreds of years. Tens of thousands of books were burned, 937 films were banned, as were (for a time) all political parties. A total of 23,667 associations, foundations and trade unions were forced to close.

Methods of torture applied during this period include: beating, blindfolding, systematic humiliation, electric shocks, mock executions, isolation, suspension on a hanger, restriction of food and water, sexual harassment, rape, exposure to cold floors, subjection to jets of pressurized water, death threats and the falaka. *Torturers routinely pulled out their victims' hair, moustaches and nails, inserted needles between their nails, squeezed their testicles, forced them to wait in garbage-strewn cells, and made them watch others being tortured or listen to their screams. Also common were threats to torture victims' relations. Some victims reported being beaten inside tires, buried in the snow, immersed in sewer pits, and forced to eat salt or human excrement. According to figures gathered by the HRFT, 78% of the torture took place in security centers, 11.6% at police stations, 9% in gendarmerie stations and 1.3% in other locations.*

In prisons, various other forms of violence were commonplace. Wards were routinely too hot, too cold or dangerously overcrowded; inmates were denied fresh air and their private belongings were routinely destroyed during raids. There was also a systematic withholding of food, drink, clothing, books, newspapers, writing supplies and essential medication and treatments. Those severely injured or made ill by the cruelty visited upon them were only rarely hospitalized: hence the expression 'torture without marks.'"

In November 2005 – two weeks after Jeannie Wakefield's disappearance, ten days after I turned myself into a *persona non grata* by writing a piece about her, eight days after my return to London, and only hours after receiving the first two emails from the unknown party who continues to bombard me with leading questions and vaguely worded threats – I rang Jordan Frick.

He came right over. He had only just returned from Uzbekistan so had not seen my piece. I printed out a copy and, once he'd read it, I brought him up to date. He listened intently, interrupting me only for the odd clarification. When I got to the end, he remained silent for some time. "This letter Jeannie left for you," he said finally. "Do you mind if I take a look at it?"

I told him to brace himself. He gave me a pained look. "I'm sure I've seen worse." Leaving him sprawled on the sofa that would be his bed for the next three days, I went off to the kitchen to assemble the daube that would last just as long.

When I returned to my study, he was still on the sofa and the room smelled like smoke and socks. He had his feet propped on the armrest, his hands propped behind his head, his eyes on the ceiling, and Jeannie's fifty-three page letter on his chest.

The first thing he did when he sat up was to open it to the brutal endnote. Tapping it with his pen, he said, "That's the bottom line."

When I asked him what he meant, he said, "It's the only thing that matters. What's more, it's all true." He lit up a cigarette. "Do you ever wonder why they torture people? Why we stand here and let them?"

He paused to exhale. "It isn't to beat the truth out of people, that's for sure. It's to keep them from knowing it. To scare them out of asking."

Another pause. "So someone has to ask *for* them. Don't you think?"

Nothing he said that afternoon – or that evening, or the next day, or the morning after – followed on from the thing he had said before.

But whatever direction his mind took, it led back to his old haunts.

His appearance, circa June 1970: "Did I really look like a shorn sheep?"

The 1971 coup: "In the beginning, life went on as normal."

The bombs that same year: "In a strange way, they came as a relief."

Dutch Harding: "That's stranger still. All he did that year – all I saw him do that year – was drink beer, smoke hash and read."

Jeannie as a teenager: "Very apple pie. And very young."

Jeannie as a young woman: "Walking wounded. But now I see why."

Jeannie on the page: "Stern. Much too stern. Self-flagellating. Why?"

Jeannie on their visit to Istanbul in January 1981: "Everything she says is true. Everything and nothing."

It was only on the third night that he gave me his version of the story. He began with an apology. "I've been having a hard time remembering how I remember this. This brute Jeannie describes – is it really me? I've given this some thought now. As much as I hate to say it, I think it probably is me. Or was. I think – I hope – I'm better now at controlling my temper.

"I guess you want to know about the box now. That's easy. I walked right into it. The night before we left New York – in January 1981 - I got a call from William Wakefield. He told me he'd asked Jeannie to pick up this box Amy Cabot had been keeping for him. He asked me to remind her. That was all it was. My mistake was not to mention it at the outset. And then to blurt it out like that. That looked bad. Very bad. But once I'd done that, anything I said was only going to make it worse.

"One of the things Jeannie's right about – what the city was like that winter. Everyone was in hiding, or lying low. Everyone was terrified. And paranoid. You couldn't be there without getting sucked in. They were all desperate to get word out but at the same time they were terrified that someone might report them. Their worst fear was that they would confide in someone like me, only to have me turn them in. Actually, this is not as paranoid as it sounds. There were armies of informers back then. As there are now.

"There was something else, too. I've seen this in other places, at other times, so don't think I'm talking just about Turkey circa 1981. People who need outside help, and clamor for outside help, actually find the whole thing extremely humiliating. This feeds into their doubts. There is some dignity in betrayal, but none at all in charity, which comes with strings attached. The first thing you have to do is make your benefactor look good. And righteous. That's wrong. In my book, there are no innocents.

"I don't bear any grudges. At the time, yes, I was angry. It's no fun getting kidnapped. Especially when you've been kidnapped by the people you're there to help. But even then, I could see that – in their own minds – they were doing something noble. Though what that was . . . well, your guess is as good as mine."

Was it, though?

I couldn't say. Or rather, I wasn't quite ready. I needed more proof. And so, it seems, did he.

That night – on *Newsnight* – we watched in silence as an august transatlantic panel discussed the latest wrinkles in the war on terror. The peg was an article – first published in the US, reprinted in London – decrying the overdependence on technology and dearth of qualified operatives "in the field." The author's name was Manfred Berger, and the first time they mentioned it, Jordan sat up straight.

"What is it?" I asked.

"Nothing," he said.

"Nothing?"

Silencing me with a wave, he leaned forward to follow the discussion. When it was over, he went onto my computer.

"Find something?" I asked, when I'd finished the washing up.

"Too early too tell," he said.

"I take it you know this man."

"Manfred Berger? No, not really."

"So what's the connection?"

"I know someone who used to use that name as a pseudonym."

"When was this?"

"Oh, way back."

"Way back as far as Turkey?"

"Even further."

"Which reminds me," I said. "In all these years, I've never asked you where you're from."

"I'm not from anywhere," he said, his eyes still fixed on the screen.

"By which you mean?"

"I grew up all over."

"What — was your father in the military?"

"No, you dork! The foreign service."

"So where did that take you?"

"Kampala, Manila, Sasparilla. Anywhere that ends with an 'a.'"

"So what did your father do in all these places?"

"What do you think?"

"Let's see. Was he some sort of expert?"

"That's one way of looking at it."

"And — I'm guessing — he was away a lot."

"Yes. In the field."

"Was he . . . an agricultural expert?"

"Gotcha," he said.

We both fell silent.

It was only later, much later, as we were making up his bed, that he said, "So you understand now, do you?"

I nodded.

"I do what I have to do."

"Yes, of course."

"I have no choice," he said.

And I said. "I know all this! You forget sometimes."

"Forget what?"

"We belong to the same tribe."

But as I watched him tussle with the covers, hurl his head onto the pillow, and stretch his legs far, far beyond the end of the sofa, only to bend them double, in search of warmth, I couldn't help thinking how strange that tribe was, and how little either of us understood it.

VI
The Earthquake

37

PLEASE DO NOT read too much into that word. We're too odd an assortment to count as a real tribe. Whatever ties we have are tenuous. If we have anything in common, it is shifting sands. It is rootlessness.

Wherever we lived as children, we were guests. Wherever we went, we were ambassadors for a country we knew only by hearsay. We grew up knowing no one whose parents were not teachers, missionaries, soldiers, diplomats, agricultural experts, oil company executives, drug enforcement agents or spies. Then, at eighteen, we flew "home," to colleges that left the same imprint on us as they did on you. But what they taught us about the world was at odds with what we'd seen with our own eyes.

What do you think, Mary Ann? Is that why we keep coming back?

Jeannie did make a life for herself after losing Sinan. Or rather, it slowly and painfully made itself. These were the Reagan years. She was not the only one sifting the recent past for the seeds of her undoing. The stores were full of books for the disillusioned children of Cold Warriors. So she came to know a great deal about the OSS and the early years of the CIA. She read everything of note on the Soviet Union, the McCarthy era, the arms race, the Cuban missile crisis, the endless string of foreign misadventures that her father may or may not have played a part in:

"I may have done so partly to put my own small tragedy into context but mostly to feed my huge grief. There was no moment when I saw the light and buried my sorrows to move on. I don't think things happen like that. I was in my thirties by now and could no longer think of happiness as a divine right. Or I knew I couldn't count on finding it. Even if I did, it was unlikely, at this point, to be in the shape of a man."

So in 1985 she left the big firm and went to work in the legal department of a newish and still struggling human rights organisation. Because she was the only woman in her office without a young family, she did more than her share of traveling. Most of her journeys took her to what polite people call trouble spots. Over and over, she saw what trouble did to people – how it sucked them under like a wave, turned them upside down and magnified them, propelling some to unimaginable heroism and others to cruelty; how it receded, often as abruptly as it had come, leaving the heroes stranded with the villains; how the past lurked under every stone and no one with a future dared to look. Watching the troubled surfaces of survivors' lives, she came to see that peace could never be taken for granted and was as thin, as permeable, as breakable as skin.

"My own grief had not dissipated, but I had, at least, come to see the lie in my own great expectations. Once I stopped asking why the world wasn't as I wished it to be, once I knew that anyone who tried to change it was doomed, I saw my work in a more modest light. The honor, I thought, was in attempting anything at all."

In the early 90s, after the Berlin Wall came down and before the wars in Yugoslavia, Jeannie helped organize a group of American lawyers going into Eastern Europe to advise on the new constitutions and penal codes. After a year in Skopje, she went on to Bucharest. By now her pessimism about the world and her place in it was so ingrained that it came as a surprise to her that some things, small things, could change for the better.

"This revelation stayed with me, even after the wars began. What mattered, if you were to survive, were your principles. If trouble was inevitable, then trouble

was an education. It was thanks to the trouble I'd seen at too young an age that I was sometimes able to bridge the gap between my harried, underfunded Rumanian hosts and my startled, coddled American colleagues."

It was while Jeannie was in Rumania that she became involved in another exchange program funded by the EU. It was this work that took her to England, to a temporary position at University College London that became permanent in 1995. She was part of a new study center looking at European integration and although she was drained by the strains of fund-raising and the endless round of committees, she enjoyed the common sense of purpose.

"There were times when I saw a grand design in their work, even in their composition. No two were the same nationality. Each had roots in at least two countries, and for many it was three or four. Convinced that this congregation of displaced souls must be my new home, I began to look at houses.

The day I made an offer on a garden flat in Stoke Newington, I walked over to Dalston and found myself, without warning, back in Istanbul.

It was not just the kebab restaurants and the Turkish signs. It was the beautiful bounty of the produce spilling out onto the pavements, the smell of soap inside the shops, the gentle, sombre faces behind the counters, the soft ribbons of music, the whispered commands and the cries of conventional anguish: 'She wants two kilos of tomatoes. May Allah release me from my sorrows. What's the time, big sister? I'm bored, my soul is being squeezed. Give her the pistachios that came in yesterday. Allah save me from my son. He should have been back an hour ago. What did we do to bring this trouble on our heads?' No matter how somber the subject, each word was a gift."

When her father came to visit, she took him to her favorite kebab restaurant. They'd given up on the sparring matches, because what was the point? The Cold War was over. They were back with the older conflicts it had only temporarily suppressed, and because of the work Jeannie did, she knew more about these than her father. But he was eager to catch up.

Now he was retired, William Wakefield spent his time reading, and his favorite reading was anything that suggested America had, at any point in its history, taken a wrong turn. This made for some overlap of interests, though William seemed happiest if he could find a book Jeannie had not yet heard of.

The night she took him to her favorite kebab restaurant, it was *A Peace to End All Peace*. He was only too pleased to tell his erudite daughter how the Allies had stitched up the Eastern Mediterranean after the First World War. He'd pause from time to time to speak to the waiters in his clipped, affectless Turkish. They obeyed without question.

Suddenly Jeannie asked him, "Do you ever regret doing the work you did?"

His answer was immediate. "Every living day."

"In what way?" Jeannie asked. She was hoping for a *mea culpa*: the regrets he had about the way "our side" had conducted itself during the Cold War; the arrogant pursuit of American strategic interests everywhere, the fanning of mass paranoia; the propping up of any fat cat or dictator willing to tow the line; the covert subversion of any group that questioned it; the sustained effort to keep the American people from knowing what their government did in their name; the need to find a new way of comporting ourselves now that there was no longer a Soviet "threat"; the understanding that, though democracy was something you could foster and encourage, it was not something you could impose from above.

But what her father said was, "I regret it because the people I did it for were drooling idiots. Boxes for brains. They couldn't see further than their own one-horse town. Damn it, we were a resource. We knew the ground. They refused to listen to us. They punished us for speaking. For this they expected us to put our lives on the line? They didn't let us *have* a life. As you saw for yourself."

He sat back and eyed his daughter beadily. "Not once, not twice, but four times unlucky. First your mother, then your stepmothers. Then Amy. They couldn't stand for it. Not just the danger, but the subterfuge. You can't build a life on that. You can't even be a father. Though God knows I tried."

Another beady stare. Jeannie knew what she wanted to say but stopped herself. He was a lonely, broken seventy-three year-old man. Instead she pointed to the *kilim* on the wall and asked him which part of Turkey he thought the family running the restaurant came from. The next time the waiter came to the table, her father addressed him in a language Jeannie couldn't understand. "Mardin," he announced, when the smiling waiter had retreated. The language they'd been speaking was Kurdish.

"And that's another problem that's not going away any time soon," he said. "But you can count on our old friends the Washington Box-Heads to pay no attention until it's too late." There followed a lecture. He went to bed with his dignity restored. His daughter went to bed with a headache, and for the first time in many years, had a dream about Sinan.

She'd heard from Chloe – this would have been the last conversation they'd had before one or the other had moved again and forgotten to forward their new address – that Sinan had returned to Denmark following his release from prison.

In Jeannie's dream he was thinking about having a haircut and wanted her opinion. Before she could tell him, he disappeared.

A week or two later she was having a coffee just off Dalston High Street, in the café of the Arcola Theatre. She looked across the room and thought she saw Lüset. The cold terror she felt at that moment took her by surprise, and by the time her heart had slowed enough for her to dare to look again, she was gone.

A month or so later – in April 1996 – an opportunity arose for Jeannie to spend a year in The Hague working alongside the International Criminal Tribunal for the former Yugoslavia. One year turned into two, and then her mother's health failed. She spent the next year commuting between the Netherlands and Northampton, a decision she would never regret, because she was with her mother when she passed away. Though still she would ask herself. Was her mother at peace when she died? By the end, had Jeannie become a good daughter?

It was while she was packing up her mother's house that Jeannie found her old postcards, and then her old journals (though the most important one remained under the floorboards at the Pasha's Library: even as she went through her mother's papers, Istanbul interrupted her thoughts).

She had only just returned to her flat in Stoke Newington when she turned on the television one evening to see a picture of the Istanbul skyline.

Another date to remember: August 17th 1999.

38

" I WATCHED, *(she wrote) but I did not feel. I went back and forth, back and forth, flipping between CNN and the BBC, watching the piles of rubble and the relatives who were clawing at them. The houses missing fronts, or hanging over the street or half collapsed into the wreck next door. The house that was still standing but minus the ground floor. The head half-visible under the slab of concrete, the child's hand, the doll, the shoe, the corpse. The aerial views. The chaos at the hospitals. The bodies floating next to the half-submerged fun fair mermaid. The burning refinery that was about to explode, the naval base that was no longer, the ever rising death toll.*

At first they thought the earthquake measured 6.9 on the Richter scale. Then they said it measured 7.2. The next morning they said 7.4. Now the death toll was just under a thousand. Now it had doubled, now it had tripled and the digging for bodies had hardly begun. The rescue teams had started flying in. But where were the co-ordinators to tell them where to go, and where was the army? Temperatures were rising. Those still living under the rubble were dying of thirst. The official death toll had risen to 18,000 and still there were buildings everywhere that no rescue team had even touched. Look at the abominable building materials. No wonder so many buildings had come down. No mercy for the corrupt developers who had cut every corner for profit. Sympathy for the angry hordes who had chased them into hiding. But now there was a cholera scare. Torrential rains that were hampering the rescue effort. At long last the army had arrived. Now the papers were claiming between 30 and 40,000 dead, even though the official figure was still fixed at eighteen . . ."

Her father had called her by now, and she had not picked up. In his message, he'd said that as far as he knew, "everyone we know" was "safe." But now came the aftershocks. Some were over five on the Richter Scale, and she dreamt she was standing on a pile of rubble. She was stepping over the broken slabs of concrete, searching for a sign of life. And there it was – a hand. She reached out to touch it. It was Sinan's.

She screamed, but no sound came out. She woke up and made herself a cup of camomile tea. A wave of drowsiness came over her. She closed her eyes. She was walking along the Bosphorus. The pavement was shaking, the lampposts swaying, the cars were swerving and falling into the sea. She opened her eyes to chase the scene away. When she closed them again she was in the Pasha's Library, watching the walls around her expand and contract, expand and crack. Then she was in Amy's house, then she was standing outside Gould Hall, watching the columns crumble. Or on the college terrace, as the fissures snaked their way across the ground. She thought of the houses she'd spent time in. How many were still standing? She thought of all the people. How many were dead?

She was in the bathroom, brushing her teeth, when she heard a very familiar voice coming from the television in her bedroom.

She put down her toothbrush and went out to look. The man from *Newsnight* was talking to a woman on a satellite link-up. She still thought she was seeing things. All along she'd been catching glimpses of faces in the crowd and thinking she recognized someone. But now they flashed her name across the bottom of the screen. Professor Suna Safran. Boğaziçi University, Istanbul.

She had aged well. The edge of outrage was still there, but she spoke with the containment of a judge. She was putting into perspective the racist remarks made earlier that day by the Turkish Minister for Health. He had said he did not want blood donations from Greeks or Armenians, or indeed anyone who was not a pureblooded Turk. She was explaining that this man was a member of an ultra rightwing nationalist party, and part of the coalition government that was not expected to last much longer. She claimed that most people in the country deplored his statements, and that there was massive gratitude for all the aid that had been coming in from abroad, most especially from countries that were traditionally thought of as enemies. The new perceived enemies, she said, were the military.

But this, too, was an oversimplification, she said, her *gravitas* growing with every word. The army had itself been hard hit by the earthquake. Its fatal error had been to lack a contingency plan. There had, however, been an impressive coalition of civil societies. 'The Turkish people have learned at last that they cannot wait to be saved but must learn to take matters into their own hands.' It was the people who had been coordinating whatever rescue efforts had succeeded. It was they who had set up the ad hoc voluntary associations that had introduced food and shelter and rudimentary order for the tens of thousands who had been made homeless. She recited the number of a London-based charity account for anyone who wished to make direct donations. Jeannie wrote it down.

Along with the donation she sent to the designated bank, she included a letter to Suna in which she offered to help with any longer-term relief Suna and her colleagues might organize. She outlined her areas of expertise. She ended with an awkward sentence about how she would understand if Suna preferred not to take her up on her offer. But whenever she remembered she'd not heard from her in such a long time, she felt sad.

In the meantime, she followed other leads. Her father was still in touch with Amy, and when Jeannie called, Amy gave her Chloe's email. Chloe had been living in Istanbul since the late 80s and was, among other things, on the board of the international school. The pupils were collecting money to help build a school in Gölçük, a town in the area worst affected by the earthquake. When Jeannie sent a donation, she got an instant response. The only good thing about the earthquake, Chloe wrote, was to have "reconnected" with so many long-lost friends. She wanted to write back and ask for news of Sinan but could not bring herself to type his name. So instead she asked if "everyone" was "okay." To this she got no reply other than a round robin about the progress of the charity project.

It was in late October that she picked up the phone and heard Suna's voice again. As serious as ever, but also arch. "So," she said, "You wish to help."

"If you think I can," Jeannie said. Her voice was hoarse.

Suna's was like a bell. "Let us try and see."

"If you can send me a few details about the projects you're involved in, I'm sure I can raise more funds," Jeannie said.

"That would be most generous," Suna replied. "But there is a more pressing concern. To help us you would need to come to Istanbul."

"Istanbul. Are you sure they'd let me in?"

"Why should they stop you, of all people? So tell me. Can you come?"

"When?" Jeannie asked.

"We were hoping for tomorrow."

She paused. Her heart was pounding. Now was the time to ask. But she still couldn't say his name. Instead she asked, "Who is we?"

"Ah!" said Suna. "No, there are only the two of us. Myself and Lüset."

"I had plans," Jeannie said slowly. "But I'm sure I could change them."

"Good. That means you can come. I shall forward your name to our friend in the Turkish Airlines office. Another friend will come out to the airport to give you the items you will be kind enough to carry for us."

Twenty-three hours later, she was en route to Istanbul. Clouds covered most of Europe that morning but cleared just before they began their descent over the Sea of Marmara. Jeannie could see the jagged, yellow coastline and the highway that traced it. She looked inland, and where there had been empty brown hills, there were now houses as far as the horizon. Since her last visit, the city had grown from two to twelve million – eighteen if you counted the suburbs. They were flying into the wind and the landing was bumpy. But when the engines stopped roaring, a man began to clap. Now the whole plane was clapping, laughing, chatting. But she could not find it in herself to join in.

It was while she was waiting for her bags that she saw the first poster – a sleek-looking white-haired man in profile, smiling at a bright-eyed girl of about twelve. Both were holding mobile phones to their ears, and it was, Jeannie thought, the loud red background that made her chest feel so tight.

Suna was waiting outside customs. She was alone, of course. And so was Jeannie. How old she felt. Did Suna notice? She embraced Jeannie warmly, assuring her, with a broad smile, that she hadn't aged at all.

"Neither have you," Jeannie lied.

And Suna said, "Ah! The object is not to nurture false youth, but to mature!" The pretence lasted as far as the car. As she lifted the aluminum suitcase that Jeannie had brought for them, Suna asked if they'd given her any trouble over it. Jeannie said no, though they'd sent it off for a special inspection.

"Ah! Then let us see how special this inspection proved to be." She opened the suitcase. "Ah! It was very special indeed! Yes, they have even taken it out of its box for us! How kind! Would you like to see what you have brought?"

She reached inside. When her hand came out, it was holding a foot.

Jeannie screamed and jumped back. Suna whooped with laughter.

"You silly girl, it is only plastic. It is a prosthetic limb for a ten-year-old girl in Yalova whose leg had to be amputated following three days under the rubble. Also her kidneys have failed. The things you've brought will keep her alive." She gave Jeannie a sharp and searching look. "Surely you are pleased! As you know, we have a fascist xenophobe for a health minister. It's been difficult getting supplies. But still. Jeannie, think. Who could have imagined, that in 1999 we two would be standing here, looking at this?" Having tried but failed to close the suitcase, she took the prosthetic limb out of the suitcase and threw it into the back seat.

During their trip into the city, down new highways that flew them over hill after hill of mud and raw concrete and half-built mosques, Jeannie saw no obvious signs of earthquake damage. "Don't worry," said Suna. "You will soon enough." She mapped out their program. They would drop Jeannie's things off at her apartment. "You don't mind, do you? Of course, if you prefer a faceless hotel . . ."

Suna's apartment was at the top floor of a tall, narrow building in Cihangir. Jeannie went straight to the window to look at the Bosphorus. From here the sea looked the same as she remembered it. But there were no longer empty hills behind Üsküdar. Just concrete apartment buildings as far as the eye could see.

As she stood there, lost in the view, she wondered about Sinan. How to ask, and when? Best to wait until they were on their way to Yalova. That way Suna wouldn't see her face. She didn't want the details. She couldn't bear too much about his wife or his children or the happy life they had together. She just wanted to know if he was safe. She was brought back to herself when the building shook. The chandelier above her head seemed to be swinging, but not enough for her to be sure she was not imagining it.

She opened her suitcase and tried to figure out what you wore to an earthquake zone. When Suna saw what she'd chosen, she burst out laughing. "Did I say anything about a funeral in Antarctica?" She hummed to herself as went through Jeannie's things, pulling out her long black cashmere dress and high-heeled boots. "For an earthquake zone? Suna, are you sure?" Suna puffed out her lips. "Even in an earthquake zone, there are standards."

There was a taxi waiting outside. It took them to a terrace of handsome mustard colored buildings – these Jeannie recognized, though in her time they'd been derelict. They alighted in front of a café whose entrance was flanked by potted trees. Suna marched over to the next door along and punched in a security code. They walked up two flights to a large, bright pop art sign featuring a traffic light – and in large neon letters, the Turkish words for "Enlightenment Radio." Inside, it was all polished oak and leather and dark green carpet. Lou Reed was singing about the wild side. The receptionist ushered them to a waiting room that was separated from a recording studio by a plate glass wall.

The man in the studio had his back to them. There was something about the way he sat . . . He got up to leave, and as he did he turned his head just long enough for Jeannie to see his profile.

The grief welled up inside her again. As she struggled to regain her composure, another man walked into the recording studio carrying a large pile of newspapers. He had close-cropped hair and a broad, open, childish face. He was dressed in jeans and a loose fitting checked shirt that looked expensive, as did the large gold watch on his wrist. When he saw Jeannie, his face lit up. He came out with his arms open wide. "Come in! Sit down!" It was Haluk.

Otis Redding was coming to the end of the dock of the bay by the time they'd followed him into the studio. As Joni Mitchell began to sing about a parking lot, Haluk smiled and said, "Tell me honestly. Are you surprised?"

But now a fragile, china-faced woman walked in. Jeannie recognized her instantly. They embraced like the old friends they were.

"So," said Haluk. "How long has it been? Lüset, didn't you count it?"

"Eighteen years," she said.

"Eighteen years," said Suna. "And just imagine. If we could have foreseen . . ."

"We would not have believed it," said Lüset.

"Ah! More than that!" Suna cried. "We would have rebelled at the thought!"

"Although the point must be made," said Lüset. "We were not the same people who have gathered here today."

"In some ways, yes. In others, no. In any event, there are things we need to explain to David. He is looking bewildered!" She gestured over at the affable young man Jeannie had briefly mistaken for Sinan. She settled into her seat, moving the pile of newspapers to one side: there they were again, stretched across the page. The white-haired man and his granddaughter, advertising mobile phones. "So," said Suna, propping her elbow on their noses, "Where shall we begin?"

They began with a half-mocking, half-wistful description of the "lazy summer of 1970, when we were free but not free, and propelled by simmering boredom." They described their first impressions of Jeannie, a "fresh-faced American Barbie with no knowledge of the world" – and of her famous exchange with Suna at the discotheque. Suna describing it as "one of those discussions so typical of the era, where the surface is political, but where the true content resides in the confused designs of the heart."

They went on to tell the polite young man named David that Jeannie had gone on to become a "human rights leader" – this made her blush with shame. She had, they said, been "a dedicated behind-the-scenes ally" to the cause in Turkey, and that she had paid "difficult visits" here even in the "darkest days following the coup of

September 12th 1980." When Jeannie offered to correct the record, they silenced her with dismissive waves, only to exaggerate the help she'd given since the August earthquake. "Really," she said. "I've done next to nothing."

"But now you are here," said Haluk. "All this stands to change."

"So what really happened? With the trunk, I mean. In 1971." To Jeannie's horror, the question sent them into peals of laughter. "It's a good question," Suna said, "But the explanation is even better. Do we have time, my dear Haluk?"

"Of course we have time. And it is time young David knows what sort of mettle his mother is made of." He nodded at Lüset. This boy was her son?

"Then suffice it to remind him that we are harking back to the 12th of March, 1971," said Suna. "Or to be precise, a few months after that, when the mass arrests had begun, and a hysteria was brewing with baseless rumors."

The boy David smiled politely. It was clear to Jeannie that he had endured this story many times before. But it did not seem clear to the others.

"According to our accusers," said Haluk, "we belonged to a cell, and had become convinced that one of our number was an informer. Apparently, we instigated a mock trial and went on to murder him. But there was always something strange about this story. No one could name the victim!"

"In early reports it was Dutch Harding," Jeannie said.

"You are right," said Haluk. "But as you know, his body has never been found."

"Which means?"

Something flashed in Haluk's eyes. "What could it mean, except that it is well hidden?"

"But the trunk . . ." Jeannie said.

"Ah!" said Suna. "Here we come to the twist in the tale. There was no one in the trunk. There was nothing but literature. Or to be more precise, the contents comprised of 754 copies of a contraband periodical. I know because I wrote and mimeographed them all."

"Ah, that mimeograph machine," said Haluk. "How well I remember it."

Suna cleared her throat. "I am speaking now of that infamous day in June of 1971 – we argued, yes?"

Yes.

"I said terrible things, didn't I?"

We all said terrible things.

"But we all had our reasons."

Of course.

"So let me tell you ours. When you turned up at the garçonniere, spouting such ugly lies about a certain valued mentor..."

"I had no idea – no proof – it was a stab in the dark. Suna, you don't know how deeply I've regretted . . ."

A wave of the hand. "It does not matter what you said, my dear. It never has! No! We had other fish to fry that day. The news had come to us that we were soon to be raided. Naturally we were beside ourselves. If a certain valued mentor had not been there to help us . . ."

"Though his first suggestion proved disastrous!" Lüset recalled.

"This is an understatement. We tried to burn the literature in our bathtub."

"But the tub was plastic."

"Our only achievement was to create a large and ugly hole."

"We put out the fire with the shower," Lüset said.

"However, this only added weight to the telltale documents."

"But the clock was ticking," said Suna. "So we piled them up into a trunk, and we called a taxi. After a short but unpleasant journey Haluk met us on the shore and took us out into Bebek Bay in Kitten II."

"You have forgotten to mention the trail of red," said Lüset.

"Ah yes, the trail of red," said Suna. "This is perhaps the most exquisite irony. Our contraband literature included our rough notes and early drafts."

"And a large number of these had been executed in red ink."

"And now they had become wet."

"And the excess fluid leaked. Ink was spilled."

"And this is how we left behind us a path of red which alerted a suspicious janitor who had come out early to buy a loaf of bread. He alerted the police station, thus setting into motion the chain of events that resulted in our arrests."

"But you are jumping ahead of your story," said Lüset.

"This is true. As was my intention. I save the best for last!" Her laugh was not reflected in her eyes. "What we did was this. Having traveled out into Bebek Bay to join the swirling currents, we took the string bags out one by one to drop them in. Alas, they did not sink. Instead they spread over the surface. As far as the eye could see, there was a telltale carpet of damp and disintegrating revolutionary literature." She swept her arms, as if to conjure it up again. And to Jeannie's horror, she burst out laughing.

"Can this be true?" Jeannie asked.

"Of course it's true!"

"Then I hope you're going to tell me that you were never taken in for questioning? Never jumped out of a fourth floor window?"

"Ah!" Suna said. "This is another story altogether! Though perhaps now is not the time. For we are late. Are we not?"

Minutes later, they were bundling into another of the yellow cabs that had replaced the 1958 Chevrolets of Jeannie's memory and heading for Taksim. This square, too, had changed, though not beyond recognition: there was a massive new hotel on the eastern side but the traffic was still chaotic and the pavements clogged, and there, on the vast billboard behind the war memorial, was the sleek, white-haired man conversing on his mobile with the innocent twelve-year-old, in triplicate.

They walked down İstiklâl Caddesi, now a paved walkway open only to pedestrians and trams, turning right into a narrow street, and into a bar called Kaktüs. They had been there ten minutes when a sulky, pouting, doe-eyed woman came in. She was wearing jeans and high-heeled boots and a black leather jacket over a skimpy lace top. Across her chest were half a dozen golden chains.

It was Chloe. She ambled over to the table to offer Jeannie her beautifully manicured, ring-laden hand. "Well, who would have thought?" she said. "How many years has it been? You look just the same, though."

"You look even younger," Jeannie said.

She laughed, rather tragically. "Well, I sort of have to, don't I?"

As she opened up her Prada bag and got herself a cigarette from a golden case, Suna said, "Chloe's husband was a plastic surgeon."

After Suna had explained how Chloe's husband had been "struck

down in the prime of life by leukemia" and how Chloe had been running his clinic single-handed ever since, Jeannie offered her lame
apologies.

Chloe took a drag of her cigarette and said, "Oh well, what can I
say? These things happen. I don't know about you, but I'm in the mood
for a Martini. You want one, Jeannie? They know how to make them
now. They use real gin."

So they had their Martinis and then Chloe glanced at her watch and
realized how late she was for a function where she'd be bored to tears.
"I'll see you anon," she said, and soon the others, too, were putting on
their coats. Minutes later, she was sitting in the front row of a large
theater.

And there was Haluk in front of the curtains. He made a short
speech that was received with loud applause. The curtains parted to
show an orchestra. There were four singers – two men in tuxedos and
two women in bright red gowns. The songs they sang were all in
Greek. Jeannie thought she recognized the music, and when the stage
darkened and a familiar face filled the screen behind the orchestra, she
realized why. The woman in the film clip was Sibel, Sinan's mother,
circa 1967, standing in pool of light at Montreux. She was wearing
the same low-cut dress Jeannie recalled seeing in a photograph,
singing a gorgeously sad song, first in French, then in Greek, then in
English.

When the lights went up, Haluk was standing with the singers. With
him was an older man. It took Jeannie a few moments to realize he was
Chloe's father.

But he was not the slow, kindly, ponderous Hector Cabot she
remembered. Someone had replaced his batteries. His movements
were electric. His laugh was animated, almost wild. His brief remarks
in Turkish were followed by even briefer remarks in fluent Greek. He
then switched into English. "I hope no one minds," he said, "if I use
this third language to thank our international sponsors, who have
travelled thousands of miles to be here tonight. This is a historical
occasion, one that would have been beyond our wildest dreams as
recently as last summer. I hope it proves what we at the Institute
think of as our founding motto. Good things can come out of

tragedy. Enemies can put down their arms and recognize each other as friends. Our encore this evening is to be *Sto Periyali To Krifo*." He paused here to bow to the thunderous applause. "As most of you will already know, the lyrics are by the great Greek poet Seferis. During the junta years, its political resonances led the colonels to ban it. The resonances may have changed now, but the central meanings must remain the same here as they do across the border. 'In the hidden bay, we wrote her name, and then we watched, as the beautiful wave came in and washed the name away . . .' Do I need to explain that the name they wrote and saw washed away was freedom?

So the song is sad. It's about people who've spent their lives fighting for something they keep losing, who've lost their way. But if we can still gather together to sing this song, then it must mean . . .' He raised his eyes and swallowed, "It must mean we can still live in hope. So I hope you don't mind if I add my croaky voice to the chorus." Looking into the front row he said, "Darling? Are you still there?"

A thin elegant woman with golden hair climbed onto the stage. He gave her a bearlike embrace that nearly toppled her. Retrieving her balance, she smiled at Hector with adulation. Amy Cabot. How could she? It was clear that Hector, who had drunk his way out of their marriage all those years ago, was drunk again. Yet here she was, standing at his side, erasing the past with a song about the perils of writing in the sand.

Later on, when they were sitting at a long table at Yakup II, Suna tried to explain. Amy and Hector, "who now number amongst my dearest friends" were "not precisely remarried" but "in a sense even closer." Hector still divided his time between Istanbul and Connecticut. His work as head of IPEM (the Institute for Peace in the Eastern Mediterranean) meant that he also spent time in Greece. The cultural links forged so tentatively before the earthquake had strengthened since the "*rapprochement.*" The concert they had just attended was a case in point.

Now, as if on cue, Hector and Amy were entering the restaurant. Both rushed over to welcome Jeannie back. Could it be that she had a clean slate, too, along with everyone else? Hector pulled up a chair and engaged Jeannie in a long, intense, very personal discussion. He had, as Jeannie had guessed, been drinking, but he could drink, he claimed, without going over the edge. Taking a measured sip of wine, he said, "How about your father?"

Before she could answer, the conductor and his singers came in. Suddenly everyone but Jeannie was speaking Greek. Then it was Turkish for a sentence and a half. Then English. It went on like that, with the conversation spilling back and forth between languages like water in a boat.

It was during this strange to and fro that Jeannie discovered Haluk and Lüset were now husband and wife. Once again they met her surprise with laughter. "It is strange how things work out, no?" said Lüset. "It is as Suna said: had either of us read the future when we were merely teenagers, we would have been most perplexed."

Here Suna interceded. "You must tell them the story. It is very romantic."

And so was the way that Haluk and Lüset shared the telling of it. They had been married for six years but were still finishing each other's sentences: In 1992, when she was "recently divorced," and on a flying visit to London, Lüset had caught a glimpse of Haluk in the café of the Arcola Theatre. "Though identification was difficult," Haluk added, "for I had become very fat."

"But so much else, as well," said Lüset.

"Yes, I had been enjoying my own life. I was free! I forged my own destiny! But now, before I knew it, I was back in Istanbul – all forgiven, all forgotten – in the embrace of my family."

"And mine," Lüset added.

"My darling, why repeat the obvious?"

Everyone laughed. At what? Then all eyes went to the window. In the street outside, the television crew that had followed the Greek performers to the restaurant had now surrounded a dapper, crisply smiling white-haired man. Though Jeannie did not recognize him, a wave of nausea passed through her. He had an entourage; even as he spoke they were clearing his way to the door. Haluk and several members of their party jumped to their feet. Each embraced the man with respectful warmth. The man now moved over to Jeannie's end of the table. "Welcome back," he said. "Long time no see!"

It was İsmet.

She was too shocked, too horrified to speak. This seemed to amuse him.

"He's aged quite gracefully, don't you think?" said Suna as Haluk walked him back to the door. Her tone was arch, contemptuous, detached.

İsmet, she went on to explain, had done "rather well" for himself. A "judicious third marriage" had equipped him to take full advantage of the telecommunications boom. "Though of course he has continued to interest himself in other, more significant channels of communication also. Yes, we must all be in his debt! When it comes to alerting the nation to the great new menace in our midst, no one has done more than İsmet Şen! And what an invaluable help he has been to his old friends across the ocean, now that they, too, have decided that the evil empire is no longer espoused to Communism but to political Islam! But only behind the scenes – of course. In public he is simply known as the Pocket King." She went on to explain that mobiles were known as pocket phones in Turkey. "The nickname remains ironically insulting. It is well known that he deals in arms."

"This man is an arms dealer and you talk to him?"

"You are speaking as if by talking to him, we are expressing our fear!"

"What else am I to think?"

"We are not afraid, Jeannie. I assure you. If anything, he is afraid of us! Times have changed. To succeed in his new ambition, to be the Voice of the Secular and Islam-hating Republic – it is not enough to pull the strings behind the scenes. He must be seen with the great and the good. He must smile with Haluk at his side! And if Haluk does not quite play his part . . . Look – look for yourself," she said, gesturing lazily towards the door. But Jeannie saw nothing but respect in Haluk's smile and nothing in İsmet's demeanor to suggest fear.

When she said as much, Suna said, "Ah! Perhaps you have been gone too long to pick up on the nuances." But how could Haluk even pretend politeness in front of this man, how could Suna speak in such level tones of his ignominious career? İsmet was the enemy, the man who'd tried to cancel them out. The man who had pushed Suna out of that window! It felt wrong, unjust – a multiplying of the injuries he'd caused.

Her unease stayed with her when the conversation turned back to the grim details of the earthquake relief effort. Whenever Suna, Haluk or Lüset touched upon something truly horrible – a fundamentalist group preventing members of a secular relief group from passing out essential supplies, a construction czar who was not going to trial, the closing of all earthquake camps to non-governmental organizations, the failure of the Red Cross to get the homeless into winter housing, the continued flouting of building regulations, the likely death toll if the next earthquake had its epicenter in Istanbul – they would burst out laughing.

They laughed, even, when discussing a tremor that had occurred earlier that same day. They discussed it in some detail. For some, it had been an up-and-down movement, and for others, the buildings they'd been in had seemed to sway. It was in the middle of this exchange that the restaurant itself began to shake.

It was then that Jeannie saw the fear in people's eyes. And frankly, it was a relief. This was not a dream after all, she was not locked inside a ghastly fairy tale in which everyone was living happily after, except for her. When the shaking stopped, no one moved. Then everyone began talking at once. "You felt that, too, didn't you?" "Where do you think the epicenter was?" "What did we do to bring this misfortune on our heads?" Out came the mobiles. Suna was the first to give up. "The network has been flooded," she told Jeannie. "That means it must have been a relatively bad one. The moment there's a bad one, everyone in the entire city gets straight on their phones. What a shame our old friend İsmet is no longer with us – I could have berated the Pocket King to his face!"

Jeannie stood up. "I need some air."

It was colder than before. She buttoned up her coat. She looked inside: they'd all found something new to laugh about. And – she knew this was churlish and ungrateful and hard – she couldn't bear it. It was as if she was lying in a lonely ditch, watching the glittering windows of a passing train.

She looked at the way Haluk and Lüset talked to each other. She would lean forward and so would he. She would begin a sentence, he would laugh as he caught the thought and ran with it. He would turn to the woman on his right but at the same time draped his arm around Lüset's shoulder, and her face would light up, as if he had just given her an unexpected gift.

And she, their old friend, should have been glad for them. She cursed herself for coming back. She turned down the alleyway. A dark figure was walking towards her, his head bowed, his hands plunged into his coat.

39

November 1st 1999

"He was here when it hit. Here in this apartment. He was still based in Denmark at that point but had been back in Istanbul all summer, working on a film about his mother's family. Sibel had been flattered, flattering, generous with her reminiscences and mostly cooperative, but there had been flare-ups, and then there was the choking, polluting humidity. To escape it she'd gone out to Çınarcık, near Yalova, to stay with a friend for a few days, and at 2.58 am on Tuesday August 17th, that's where she was.

Sinan was here, in the House of Shrouds, with Suna, but that's another story. The clattering was worse than the swaying floor. The electricity cut off almost at once — you could hear the books and plates and glasses falling from their shelves but you could not see them. When he found his mobile, he tried to call his mother. But his network was down. On the radio there was only music.

Outside in the landing, there were shrieks and wails as his neighbors struggled down the stairs in their night-clothes, their way lit by a few flickering candles. Most camped outside all night.

The news began to filter in at daybreak, and this was when they had the first aerial views of the affected areas. From the line of flattened buildings, you could see that the fault ran straight through the middle of Çınarcık.

They were there by ten, but when half a street is rubble, there is no such a thing as an address. Where his mother had been staying, the pile of rubble before them was so small that you could hardly believe it could ever have been six storys high.

The sun was high in the sky now. A perfect day for the beach. There was an Israeli rescue team that came to Çınarcık later, but that morning it was just Suna and Sinan and others like them scrambling over the slabs, digging with their hands. Meanwhile, Suna came and went, bringing food, water, blankets, news. "And my cameras. Yes, that's what sort of man I've become."

The soldiers did not arrive until the fourth day but before then there were strangers coming from all over to help. Bringing food, water, pick-axes, underwear. On the fifth day they dug out his mother, and it was while his fellow rescue workers were consoling him that he knew he had to "stop this anchorless life I'd been leading, criss-crossing Europe, always at ease but never at home. I knew then that this was my country, these were my brothers, these were my friends and if life could end this quickly, I would want it to end here."

The hardest part, he told me, was coming back to this apartment. He no longer trusts walls.'

November 2nd 1999

'*If I stand on the balcony, looking out over the Asian shore, and the Old City with its domes, its palaces, its mosques, and the great and teeming waterways between them, I can still see the city I remember.*

If I'm going somewhere and veer into the back streets, I can smell that damp. The ferries are the same, though they seem less numerous. There are still nut vendors everywhere, and corn vendors, and cheap watch vendors and kiosks selling newspapers, cigarettes, bubblegum and grilled cheese sandwiches. Most shop signs in most back streets are still crooked, most pavements still have potholes, and the vogue for neon has not yet passed.

There are vast new neighborhoods stretching endlessly in all directions. In poor neighborhoods we always find a minimarket, a pharmacy, a kebab restaurant and at least three banks. A sweet shop, a damp arcade where they sell flowers, newspapers, meat, fish, and pink quilts, a generic police station and a generic mosque. Men in skullcaps and men in caps and brown suits and men in Tommy Hilfiger; women in Tommy Hilfiger and women in long Islamic coats and tightly knotted scarves.

In the rich neighborhoods it's endless rows of skyscrapers, malls, glittering showrooms displaying all the world's most expensive cars, designer clothes and designer ice cream, bathrooms, furniture, computer software. The dark, damp sinister streets of Tepebaşı are changed beyond recognition, lined with bright and beautiful restaurants, cafés, clubs, and salsa bars; the stretch along the Bosphorus between Ortaköy and Kuruçeşme, where there were once only coal depots, is a glittering strip with vast open air clubs and there are, I'm told, so many bounc-

ers and valets and famous football players with famous model girlfriends that in
the early hours of a summer morning it can take up to an hour to creep half a
kilometer.

Those old Ottoman villas that were falling into their foundations – these
days, no rich man can be without one. There aren't many left but those that are
left have been restored and are so sumptuous they hurt your eyes. Suna tells me
that many were restored by an old classmate of ours. A recurring theme. Our old
classmates, even the ones who did time in prison in the 70s or early 80s, seem
to have enjoyed colossal success in almost any field you care to mention, especially since the boom began.'

November 3rd 1999

"The boom began when Turkey opened its markets in the 80s. When the Cold
War ended, Istanbul ceased to be an outpost and became once again, the center
of its world. The city is teeming with people from the former Soviet Union.
Some are tourists, some are professionals, others are in the 'import-export business' and/or vice. Last night, when Chloe and I were riding together in a taxi,
we were stopped by the police who'd seen us from the back and taken us for
'Natashas' (Russian prostitutes).

The Soviet Navy no longer parades up and down the Bosphorus, but the
traffic is heavier and more treacherous than ever, and the ships from BAPNA
are in desperate need of repair.

No one's afraid of the Communists now – with sixty percent of the popu-
lation under thirty, it's a dwindling minority that can even remember fearing
them. Now it's Islamists they obsess about. And when Islamists speak, they
express their anti-western sentiments in much the same language as Sinan and
Suna did when I first met them. The tables have turned, and then turned again."

November 4th 1999

"The building code, I'm told, is on a par with Japan, the US and Western
Europe. But unless there is a foreign insurance company involved, construction
firms cut corners. The owners do foolish things like removing essential supports
to create more shop space. Which is why so many apartment buildings in the
earthquake area look unscathed – until you notice that they no longer have front
doors, or ground floors.

If I am ever in an earthquake, Sinan tells me, I am to race upstairs, not
downstairs. If I can't do that, I am to crouch against a radiator, a refrigerator, a
bathtub.

Last night, after I'd been awoken by yet another aftershock, I looked over
at Sinan, and for a moment he looked like a pile of rubble, too."

November 6th 1999

"He's been showing me his films.

He is vague about the course of his career – his degree was in political science – but around the time he got married he got a job in television. He started doing his own films in the mid-90s. This strange name of his, Yankı, dates from then. He's won several prizes, and although he still takes his films to all the festivals and gets plenty of commissions in Europe, Haluk seems to be his main backer.

His first films were very much in the 'vanishing Turkey' mode. One follows the old Bosphorus fishing boats, another a family struggling to keep its old Ottoman yali from falling into the sea. Rakı Sofrası is about three retired generals in pursuit of the perfect summer evening. The 23rd of April records the Children's Day parades in seven different towns, and although it says something subtle about patriotism, Suna finds it 'maddeningly oblique.'

She takes the same view of Three Merchants, which follows the fortunes of a Circassian jeweller in Adapazarı, a Suryani carpet dealer from Mardin, and an Armenian copper-dealer with a shop in the Bedestan. All have tangled, hidden histories, but never once does Sinan go beneath the surface. In my view, if not in Suna's, it doesn't need to.

The best of the films I've seen so far is The Atatürk Factory. It's about just that – a factory that makes statues of Atatürk. Some scenes, like the one in which the two sculptors argued passionately about Atatürk's "true" face, have a comic edge, though apparently some critics found them disrespectful. It ends with the minute of silence on the day of his death. There's a young, square-shouldered man standing on the shore just outside Üsküdar, saluting the old city. In his face is pride and love. Just beyond him is a man washing down a restaurant boat. He is wearing an Islamic skullcap and not observing the silence. As the camera moves to the domes and palaces and minarets of the old city, we hear Atatürk himself, uttering his most famous saying: 'How happy I am to be a Turk.'

The film Sinan was working on at the time of the August earthquake is called Chanteuse and draws upon the interviews he did with his mother in the weeks before her death. It includes the famous footage of the concert at Montreux. His next film, Hidden Family, will begin with his mother's death and move on to the funeral, which was attended by two Greek aunts he was meeting for the first time. Both live in Thessalonica, and the film will follow them home."

November 7th 1999

"From the moment I got here, I've been racing, racing, racing, but the world rushing past me is faster and I'm still falling behind. I wake up in the morning and I ask myself — could it be only two weeks ago that I picked up the phone and heard Suna's voice? Suna says I'm too set in my ways. I need to, as she puts it, 'grow with the flow.' This is not the sleepy city I 'once knew.' It's going 'fast-forward into modernity.' But even in 1970, in its sleepy backwater days, I was, I recall, always struggling to keep up.

There's so much going on, stories tailing off into stories, so many things for which I have next to no context — I'm left grasping at the details, desperately struggling to read through the lines, and never have I felt a more tenuous grasp of the present. Here I am, in his arms, his bed, his life. After all these years, we've found each other, but we don't trust the walls, don't trust the ground beneath our feet, don't trust any moment beyond this one. I am insanely happy, and I am racing towards a cliff.

Every gesture he makes is familiar to me. Every inch of his body, too. But he's still a stranger to me. I have no idea what's going on his head.

WHAT I ADMIRE ABOUT HIM:

- How much he loves his work.
- How relentlessly and courageously he pursues it.
- How little he complains.
- Even refuses to complain.
- How gracefully he has pulled me into the stream of his life.
- How he talks to me as if we've been together all along.
- How, when he asks for my opinion, he actually listens.
- How, no matter where we are, no matter how disturbing the thing we have just seen or heard or filmed, he never forgets the little joys of life — what he calls the little dignities.

There is always a beautiful coffee house around the corner, and the waiter always has a story to tell, and as he tells it, he has a lovely smile, and as I watch him smile, I remember the day of the cobra, when we carried those baskets from one end of the city to the other, meeting people who trailed their stories behind them like comets.

WHAT I MISS ABOUT THE BOY I ONCE KNEW:

- The lilt he used to have in his walk.
- The clarity of his contempt.
- The thunder of his poetry.
- The hope.
- The fire.

WHAT I FEAR:

Even when we are in a café bright with lights, and artists, and journalists, and poets, and photographers, and film stars, and television moguls, and singers, and glittering tragediennes . . . even when Haluk or Lüset or Suna have made the most frivolous joke — when the laughter fades, when I look into his eyes again, I see shadows, deaths, secrets.

THINGS WE HAVE YET TO DISCUSS,
EXCEPT IN TANTALISING AND OFTEN VERY
DISTURBING ASIDES:

- *The "events" of June 1971.*
- *Who killed Dutch Harding.*
- *Who buried him, and where.*
- *What happened to Sinan that morning in January 1980, after his arrest.*
- *What they did to him in prison.*
- *Why he wouldn't let me help.*
- *If he knows about the letter his wife sent me.*
- *Why he never wrote, not even after his divorce.*
- *Why he's still so annoyed at Suna for "tricking us back together".*
- *When a day doesn't pass without his saying that he never forgot me and never managed to "banish" me from his heart.*
- *Why was he trying in the first place?*

ALL HE'S SAID (but not in this order):

(I am putting these sentences into order in a doomed attempt to get some sort of handle on them.)

- *The less he said about 1971, the better. "All there is left is a quagmire of lies."*
- *Our sin — one we all shared, in his view — was immaturity. "I had big ideas, but they were too big, and it was the ideas themselves that were empty. This was because we had no freedom."*
- *We were hemmed in by what he now calls The Fathers. "Mine. Yours. Haluk's. Our teachers. The Devil İsmet. They were all standing over us, watching us all the time, suspecting us of the crime that we hadn't yet committed. The crime we didn't even know about. Not what we'd done, but what we might do when we usurped their power."*
- *'And naturally, we were outraged. To be condemned on the basis of unfounded suspicions! To be labeled dangerous for our thoughts! What we*

did not know – what we learned that terrible day – is that there are no innocents.'

• In the aftermath, Suna suffered most, though "there are many forms of torture."

• For him, torture meant knowing that two friends – two girls – were serving the sentence that should have been his.

• This guilt ate into his marriage. Guilt was the very basis of his marriage. 'Anna fell in love with me to save me. To save myself, I had to leave.'

• 'You got it all wrong, you know. I mean in those interviews you gave after our night together, after I was arrested, in 1981. You were not the one who drew me into danger. It was as I told you. I had come back to accept my fate. If you choose to give up your freedom, then you have the inner freedom that can only come from dignity.'

• But he had fallen short of his ambitions. 'What you sensed that night – the night we spent here, the night before my arrest – was the fear I felt. It was only when we were lying here together in this room, that fear overtook me. And it's true. Listening to your voice, feeling your head against my chest, I questioned myself. I almost wavered. And I was right to be afraid.'

• But the less said about his years inside the better.

• The worst part was getting out, heading home. 'A street I recognized was worse than a street I'd never seen. Every change leapt out at me. My memories made the present look like lies. I knew then that everything I had wanted from life until that moment was false. My ideas were empty. God had given us eyes so that we could see.'

• 'So I said to myself. No more politics. No more crazy, impulsive gestures. No dreams of revenge. I could no longer base my happiness on İsmet's downfall. I was a man now, I was a father. I wanted my children to know who I was.'

• 'Of course, they don't know me. They don't know me at all.'

• 'This causes me pain, but because I love them I sometimes think it's for the best.'

• 'Some things must stay buried.'

November 10th 1999

"Today, when I was sitting with Chloe – we were at the Divan Café in Bebek, and she was just finishing her third éclair – and it's beyond me, how she manages to eat the way she does and still stay so thin – I remembered those peanut butter cookies we used to make, during what we called the lulls, during that first summer, in 1970. And then I remembered how, during one such lull, I'd complained about never getting a straight story from anyone. All this subterfuge, all these rumors you never know are true or not – the way people would make an offhand remark alluding to events that defied belief but then withhold everything else. When I'd asked Chloe what 'the point' was all those years ago, she'd just shrugged her shoulders and said, 'To keep you guessing?' When I'd asked why they would want to do that, she said, 'Well, obviously. So you can't control them.'

Today, when I asked her the same question, she said, 'Because they don't trust you? Because there are things they've done they can't bear to remember? Because it's just too painful, and too long ago?'"

November 12th 1999

"I'd thought, after all our visits to Yalova and Izmit and Adapazarı that I'd seen every which way a building could crumble, but today I went to Düzce with Sinan and his crew. Only fifteen hours had passed since this terrible new earthquake, the second killer earthquake in just over three months; the disaster (7.1 on the Richter scale, they now say) was still fresh.

I saw rows of houses, collapsed onto each other like cards, crushed cars, shrivelled and toppled minarets, apples and oranges and clay pots spilling onto the road, a broken office window, and inside, an ashtray with a cigarette propped on it, a pair of glasses, a phone off the hook.

I saw minimarkets turned to dust, houses propped up by trucks, houses that had lost their fronts, lamps still plugged into their sockets, dangling over the street, whole families sitting in their ruined gardens on salvaged sofas, staring at their cracked and lurching homes. Next to every pile of rubble, a hopeless and uncertain crowd.

In the courtyard of what was no longer a hospital, tents and doctors from all over the world, and just beyond them, behind the cameras, an endless string of politicians, speaking respectfully to the cameras and then jumping back in their big black cars to return to Ankara, honking to scatter the bewildered families still struggling to put up tents.

Sinan pitched in, passed out the bread and big bottles of water we'd brought with us, listened to the stories, collected small requests. Numbers to call, messages to pass on, letters to post. It was sunset by the time we left and there was a nip in the air. In a few hours it would hit freezing.

Returning to the city, the traffic was slow. We came to a standstill on the second Bosphorus Bridge, and although it was hard to see it over the cars trying to cross in the opposite direction, we could just make out the Pasha's Library. How strange it was to be suspended over Rumeli Hisar, to see it from the air, to know that the bridge from which we were watching it would probably survive the next earthquake, just as it had survived the others, but that it might also swing and buckle and crack and spill us into the sea.

"But that is the beauty of it," Sinan said. "That undercoat of death."

Almost but not quite quoting my father.

So I said, 'Sometimes I wonder if that's all you can see these days.'
And, 'What exactly is it you're afraid of?'

WHAT SINAN SAID NEXT (After a very long silence – it felt like an hour and we were still there, sitting on the bridge):

"Suna asked me the same question, you know. After she brought you here."

"After I'd told her how furious I was."

"She asked me what I was afraid of and I said bringing you here, drawing you back into our world, was asking for trouble, and she nodded – between you and me, trouble is exactly what she's asking for."

"So I repeated what I'd told her many times before. It was never meant to be. It was tempting fate."

"And you know what she said? She said, 'What else are we here for? Why bow to the gods? Why not tempt fate?'"

"I've been sitting here all this time trying to think of a reason not to tempt fate and I know in my heart that any reason I came up with would be a lie. You and I should never have met, Jeannie, but we did. You should never have come back here, I should never have come looking for you, we should never have fallen back into each other's arms, but we did. If this is tempting fate, if, in a moment's time, this bridge begins to swing and buckle and break us apart, isn't it right that we plunge into the sea of death together?"

He turned off the engine and pulled me into the back seat, where he whispered a poem into my ear, so rapidly that I first mistook the thoughts for his own:

"We open doors, we close doors, we pass through doors, and at the end of the one and only journey there's no city no harbor; the train comes off the rails, the boat sinks, the plane crashes. The map is drawn on ice. But if I could choose to set out or not on this journey I'd do it again."'

40

O
N NOVEMBER 7TH 2005 – a week after Jeannie's disappearance, and two days before I was due to return to London – I went to visit Haluk and Lüset in their villa on the Bosphorus, just outside Bebek. It was the same villa where Haluk had once lived with his grandparents, but it was no longer furnished in naugahyde and plastic. Instead there were comfortable sofas in muted colors, and built-in bookshelves, and *kilims* of arresting and unusual designs, and ancient urns. The parquet floors glinted in the autumn sunlight as anxious servants rushed back and forth on slippered feet with trays of tea and cakes.

They took me out to their terrace, from which I could see the bridge where Jeannie and Sinan had sat in traffic, hand in hand.

Haluk and Lüset wanted me to know that – until they had been pulled into this "senseless tragedy" – these two dear friends of theirs had enjoyed a happiness that was all the deeper for having come to them so late.

They had the photographs to prove it, and as we went through the albums, they reminisced. There they all were at that lovely restaurant outside Assos. What a happy day that had been. Here they all were in Göreme, Çıralı, Şile, Bodrum, Knidos. Did I remember Uludağ? Had I been back to Turkey for a blue journey? No? Then it was decided. The following September, I would be their treasured guest. They no longer owned their own yacht – as I must have heard, Haluk and his family had been locked up in a series of senseless lawsuits. The family business had yet to recover from the Turkish stock market crash four years earlier. But what did it matter, Lüset asked, if you had the sea and the sky? "This view is all I need to feed my soul," she said. "And what is the point of a summer house when all is said and done? Is it not better to bring together a group of friends and rent a *gulet*? It is simple, but so beautiful, as you shall see for yourself."

"A good *gulet* can sleep between twelve and sixteen people. If all are friends, there is laughter from dawn till midnight! Look. You can see for yourself!" One laughing group after another. Always the same cast. With Sinan and Jeannie smiling at the center. The pictures could all have been from the same blue journey, but for the bump that turned into a baby and then a tousle-haired boy. "You can see from Jeannie's face what this boy meant for her. How it brought her back to life. Though the pregnancy – well, yes, this was another question," Lüset conceded.

"Could it have been another way?" said Haluk. A woman coming so late to motherhood was bound to travel through 'a few storms.'"

"You are right, my darling, but some storms could have been avoided."

"Perhaps, my dear. Perhaps. But have you ever known a time when gossip could be avoided?"

For there had been rumors. Senseless rumors. Rumors that did not bear repeating. Suffice it to say that they had all served the same purpose – to destroy the peaceful happiness that Jeannie and Sinan had brought each other. "But storms are never made to last. This is one thing life has taught me."

"Difficulties born of arid soil can flower into blessings."

"The arrival of Jeannie's father, to give just one example. Of course we were concerned! Of course we wondered about his true motives! But time had moved on. He was happy to see his daughter happy, and look, look at him in this picture with his grandchild. Have you ever seen a happier man?"

"With time, even Jeannie understood this," Lüset said. "This is the nature of family bonds."

"Then I take it," I said, "that, at least for a while, she resented her father's presence."

"Of course, but only for a time."

"Why *did* he come back? Do you know?"

"Why is this even a question? It is obvious! His family was here!"

There was something about their communal smile that made me want to press for facts. Closing the album, I asked why, in their view, was Sinan wasting away in prison, and Jeannie missing, and her father presumed dead?

But it was two against one.

I persevered, sailing against the winds of platitude until they had conceded that this "unfortunate state of affairs" might perhaps have been avoided if Sinan had avoided roads leading back to the past.

"Then I take it you regret his decision to make that film about his childhood. *My Cold War*, I mean."

"How could we criticize such a beautiful and important film?" Haluk said.

"Sinan is an artist!" Lüset said.

"Artists must take risks!"

"Yes, and Jeannie understood this! Whatever else, she understood this! But at the same time, she was a mother."

"As Sinan was a father. So naturally . . ."

Haluk's voice trailed off. As if to suggest I was pushing my luck.

"As I recall it," I said, "Sinan ends the film with a string of questions. Though he does not allude directly to the Trunk Murder, the questions very clearly point in that direction."

"Yes, this was his most artistic touch," said Haluk.

"If we went through the questions again now, how many could you answer?"

"By which you mean . . . ?"

Refusing to answer the plea in his eyes, I recited them from memory: What happened next? Who was the true mastermind? Where is he now? What does he have to say about himself? Who are his new paymasters? *Cui bono*?

Instead of answering, Haluk sat forward, his eyes bulging just slightly, his lips pressed into a disbelieving smile.

"Let me put it this way," I said. "What really happened in that *garçonniere* of yours in June 1971? If none of you were guilty of that murder, why did you pretend that you were? Whose dirty work were you doing? Who were you protecting? Who are you *still* protecting? Why did you and your friend Sinan skip town and leave two young girls to take the rap? Haluk, what was it like, to open the paper and find that Suna had jumped from a fourth floor window? What does it feel like now, knowing that – had you acted differently – you might have saved your wife from torture?"

Haluk opened his mouth, and then he closed it. Lüset took his hand, and then she dropped it.

When I spoke, neither would look me in the eye. But I still tried to speak honestly. "I'm sorry," I said. "That was harsh. And unnecessary. I apologize. And now I'll leave. I'll just say one last thing. I'm not asking these questions lightly. I want to help you. I can't help you unless I know what happened."

"This is nonsense. What happened is over."

"No it's not," I said. And that is when I blurted out what I had only just come to see. "What happened is not over. This person you took the rap for . . ."

As Haluk raised his head to meet my gaze, his eyes bulged again, just slightly.

"You're still protecting him, aren't you?"

No answer. Just the faintest of smiles.

41

IN ANSWER TO your question — yes, Mary Ann, I am only too aware of the rancor in my tone. Think of it as the ghost of the girl I once was. There is something in me that does not want to grant happiness to the girl who replaced me. That delights in the knowledge that the boy who threw me over has had his comeuppance. But you ought to know by now that revenge is not what's driving me.

I am almost ready. In just a few pages, I shall drag it out into the light for all to see. But first, I would like you and your colleagues at the Center for Democratic Change to understand just how happy Sinan was with Jeannie, and Jeannie with Sinan, until parties unknown blew their lives apart. I want you to understand that it was not a simple catalogue of easy photographs. Not a given, but something they created together, against the odds.

From a distance it might be possible to see them as taking up where they'd left off, albeit thirty years later. But that would be to discount the ghosts they'd brought with them. There were the lives they might have led together. The lives they'd made with others only to pull away. The failures, the disappointments, the making do with the cards they'd been dealt. The little habits, his and hers, all jostling for space.

There was the horror of seeing a locked and bolted door fly open. Where in this haunted house was there room for a child? Even as they went through the motions, reviewing options, comparing opinions, deciding together, there were times when one would look at the other and see a stranger. How had it come to this? Who would have thought? The physical shocks of pregnancy were lessened somewhat by Sinan's familiarity with them, but this ushered in more ghosts. He already had two children. Or (as he put it once, if only once) he already had enough children. But he spoke of them so little.

"I was probably never going to be one of those women who bask in pregnancy (she told me in her letter). But it wasn't just my body I didn't trust. That giddiness I'd felt from the day of my return, that lack of confidence in the ground beneath my feet, the intimation of an unseen storm gathering and the unnerving certainty that whatever story I was hearing, it lacked the piece I most needed – these anxieties were ever present. They did not define my life so much as flit over it like a family of bats.

And there was the thing I could not put into words: what I'd seen in Sinan's eyes when I'd first told him of the baby, as we stood on the terrace of that magnificent building in Galata, ushering in the millennium. The glint of terror, the sad reproach, the silent resignation, the circle squared, the relentless kindness, the secret he wouldn't tell me...

Little fragments of the past kept hurtling down at me. We'd walk into Yakup II and a portly man would jump to his feet; I'd recognize the odd glint in his eyes but nothing else. We'd walk past Kalavi and there, next to the gypsy musicians, was a party of women singing "Samanyolu", the song I remembered Suna humming under her breath as we walked down the hill, that day we'd gone to the Covered Bazaar to help Lüset buy a leather coat.

I'd be walking up from Eminönü with Chloe, and we'd pass the button store where we'd taken refuge that same day from the angry men. But now it was a bead store. I'd be sitting at home, on our porch, and without willing it, glance over at the garçonniere; seeing a figure in a window, I'd be sure, for one terrifying moment, that it was Sinan, beckoning me back. When I walked outside into the meydan and looked over at the plane tree, I saw the ghost of the marble bench that had once sat at its base.

Chloe would roll her eyes. Suna would glare at me, Lüset would sigh, Sinan would cluck his tongue and Haluk would raise his arms with helpless innocence, and I was back in Nazmi's, doodling on the napkins, gazing idly at the frosted glass.

All winter long, right through spring and into summer, there was İsmet on billboards, urging me to pick up my phone.

Sometimes I wondered why no one else felt the pull as strongly as I did. If I wondered out loud, Suna was quick to mock me. When I return to my memories of that spring — of our picnics and boat trips, our happy journeys to the Black Sea and the Lycian Hills — I can see her point. I was obsessed with the past, she said, because I dared not relax in the present. For "some demented and most probably puritan reason" I was convinced that I did not deserve my good fortune. That I was here only to perform a lofty mission — to revisit the past, to come to terms with it. 'Though to revisit what you term the past can never be more than a séance.' What was there to gain from such an exercise? she asked. We were soon to find out."

Emre was born at the tail end of a sweltering summer. Never had the city been so humid. Though the Pasha's Library was perfectly placed to catch the wind, Jeannie woke up most mornings to clouds of yellow dust. She woke up alone most mornings. Never had Sinan been so busy with films that took him elsewhere. Never had Jeannie had so much time to think.

Of all her worries, what plagued her the most was the threatened visit from her father. Although she did not want to deprive him of his only grandchild, she was worried that the others might not wish him to be here. But whenever she put it to them, they seemed almost offended. "Why would I mind?" Sinan said. "It's natural for him to want to visit. He's welcome, of course." But there was still an edge to his voice, just as there was an edge to Chloe's ("Well, well, well, who would have thought?") and Suna's: "Are you expecting me to breathe fire? Let him come! Why should he alone be kept away? One thing you do not appreciate, dear friend: sooner or later, everyone comes back. If you live in Istanbul, you never have to hunt your ghosts — they come to you!"

The first ghost to revisit Istanbul that summer was Billie Broome. She'd tracked Suna down after the earthquake, and that, she claimed, was what had put it into her head to revisit the city she remembered "with such fondness." They had arranged to meet at that café in the gardens of Dolmabahçe Palace. Suna and Jeannie were late and further delayed by the long line outside the metal detector. It was an oppressively humid day, even by prevailing standards. Every table was full and at first they couldn't find her. And then they saw this neat, wistful

woman gazing out at the Bosphorus, as if the love of her life were sub-
merged in it.

Her face lit up when she spotted her old students and once again
she resembled her younger self. She and Suna had kept up their correspondence over the years. She had been helpful during both Suna's stays
in prisons. The ugly exchanges that had so marred their friendship in the
spring of 1971 had now become yet another thing to joke about. The
same went for Jeannie's last meeting with her in Northampton, when
she was researching her ill-fated article for the underground newspaper.
They'd met at the prep school where, she now told them, she'd continued to work for another twenty-nine years.

Now she'd taken early retirement. "And unoriginal person that I
am, I've come straight back to my old haunts." A smile flitted across her
face. "I'm so glad that you two have taken some of the things we used
to discuss and run with them. It makes me feel I've done something of
worth." There was still that teacherly note in her voice that made them
feel as if they were back in class, discussing Malamud. When she leaned
forward, Jeannie was half expecting her to ask her to define his tone and
style. Instead she said, "I need your help."

The apartment was near the Galata Tower, on the fifth floor of the
splendid, recently restored building where they'd ushered in the millennium. The view was as marvellous by day as it had been by night. From
the front you could see the silhouette of what seemed to be every dome
and minaret in the old city, and the Golden Horn, and the hundreds of
vessels plying the Bosphorus. The hazy mouth of the Marmara, the
Asian shore from Kadıköy as far as Çengelköy, and the first Bosphorus
Bridge. But then Billie led them down the dark corridor. She opened a
large oak door and they were hit by the stench of smoke and rakı.

She nodded at the bed, where a half-clad man lay sleeping. He was
on his back, with one arm hanging above an overflowing ashtray and
two bottles. Perhaps it was shock that made them overlook the yellow
tinge to his skin that ought to have alerted them to the hepatitis that
would go undiagnosed until he reached his parents' home in Arizona.

But his sandy hair had not seen a comb in some time. He had several days' stubble on his face, and his lips were lined with white. Jeannie
could tell from the way Suna grabbed her hand that she recognized him
as fast as she had.

Jordan Frick.

"How long has he been here?" Suna asked. Her voice was calm.

"Since last Thursday," Billie said. "When I arrived, that was Wednesday, he was his old happy-go-lucky self. Bursting with plans! The night before last, he took me out to that sleek new place near the Pantocrator." She waved in the direction of the Golden Horn. "He'd had perhaps one drink too many. The waiter did something to annoy him, and he went into a diatribe about 'various ex-students' of mine who were turning the city into a theme park for rich foreigners and in so doing, sweeping away what made the city what it was. Then came other grievances, too personal to relate. I fear he's drinking himself to death."

She wanted to know all there was to know about hospitals in Istanbul. Was there a good one that wouldn't cost an arm and a leg? Jeannie was sick to her stomach, but Suna seemed unfazed. She rattled through the options. There were some excellent hospitals now – this was a bustling, modern country fastforwarding into Europe, after all – but the general understanding of substance abuse problems was still inadequate for the following economic, cultural and political reasons. Here were the names of some excellent doctors, and here was where they'd trained. These were the ideas they were now struggling to bring to Turkey. But here were the reasons why Suna advised getting in touch with the US Consulate to arrange for an immediate repatriation. Here was the number. Here was what Billie Broome was to say to get past the switchboard. Here was a phone.

They sat with Billie Broome until the helpful man she'd tracked down at the Consulate had found someone who knew Jordan's byline. Jordan, it emerged, had been back in Turkey since early summer but working out of Ankara. But by the time the man from the consulate bade them farewell, he and Billie had agreed it might be a "very good idea" if Jordan took "home leave."

Billie was heading out to Cyprus the next morning, so after they'd handed Jordan over, Suna undertook to put her back into the travel mood. She chose a place called Badehane, in Tünel, on an alleyway just behind the Masonic Lodge. Even after she'd knocked back a double-vodka, Billie's hands were shaking.

She wanted to talk about the old days, but vaguely. Her sentences kept trailing off. Then her eyes would light up but before she could speak, Suna would pull them back into the present. One edifying lec-ture followed another: the rise of the new middle class, the rise of the Mafia, the meaning of the word *maganda*. The unsuccessful efforts to impose basic safety regulations on the foreign (mostly Eastern European) ships that were turning the Bosphorus into such a dangerous waterway. The future of Islamist political parties in Turkey and the root reasons for the grassroots support. Why so many young women now wore headscarves. Why the new university laws discriminated against them, but not their brothers, why this was simultaneously tragic, ironic and sociologically fascinating.

She offered a rundown of the Susurluk car crash, the great political scandal of the 90s. The victims included a police chief, a beauty queen and an assassin long presumed dead though in possession of a Turkish passport issued by the Embassy in Rome. The lone survivor was a Kurdish tribal chief/MP rumored to be a drug baron.

It was a "conspiracy theorist's dream," Suna told them. The deep state made visible! Seeing that this term meant nothing to their former teacher, she tried again. The Susurluk car crash was living, "or rather dying," proof of the links between government officials and organized crime. There had been millions of dollars in the trunk, she added glee-fully. When the government refused to investigate, "the people respond-ed by turning off their lights at nine each evening and banging on their pots and pans. But only for a minute," she said. "A minute of darkness for enlightenment!"

"You understand the significance of this gesture. No? Then let me explain. It began with the Young Turks, who equated darkness with the corrupt traditions of the Ottomans, and the light with the West. It became an imagistic shorthand. Perhaps one example will suffice . . ."

Jeannie was into her eighth month by then, and the evening had brought no breezes. They were sitting outside on low stools and though she was taking regular sips of water, she was having trouble breathing. When Suna said she'd better get her home, Jeannie thought she heard regret in her voice. But after they'd waved Billie Broome goodbye, Suna said, "Ah! That was truly unbearable."

At Bebek, she said, "Please, don't leave me yet. I am not yet recov-ered." They decamped to the Hotel Bebek. It had only just turned seven so they had their pick of tables. Over the next half hour, they watched the terrace fill up with its usual unusual mix – university lecturers in crumpled linen, pouting ladies dripping gold, businessmen entertaining foreigners, gangsters with their molls. All chairs were turned out to face the turquoise bay, the bobbing boats, the golden lights playing on the windows of the Asian shore.

"So," Suna said. "I suppose you'll be mentioning this to Sinan."

"Listen," Jeannie said. "I have nothing to hide. Whatever he might have told you, Jordan and I were never an item."

"It's not your item I'm concerned about. It's mine."

42

HAD JORDAN NEVER told her about it? The more Jeannie insisted that he hadn't, the less Suna seemed to believe her.

"But he told you. Most certainly, he told you! Worse still, you believed him! Yes, Jeannie. That's what hurts the most." She was talking about "the rumors" Jordan had spread. They were all false, of course. "But attached to them is a shameful secret."

For there'd been a night – "and it was only a night" – when she had "succumbed" to his charms. "In the spring of '71. Those last crazy days. If you were not there to witness my downfall, it is probably safe to say that I am speaking of the days following your demotion to pariah."

Sighing, she gestured up at the apartment house where Billie Broome had once lived with Dutch Harding. "It was there, on that very balcony, that he approached me. He was very handsome in those days, wasn't he? It must have been my wish to impress him that prompted me to introduce myself as Turkey's most dangerous insurgent. Trained by the PLO, no less, in the Bekaa Valley. Jordan understood my joke at once, and it was in this spirit that he was soon confessing to the murders of Jack Ruby and JFK. What's more, he had brought down de Gaulle. His name was also mud at NATO. Jeannie – he had even conducted a secret mission to the moon."

Her voice was so tragically theatrical by now that the languid ladies at the next table were moved to take off their gold-rimmed sunglasses. "Please," she said, "do not let these numbskulls distract you. They cannot understand English."

"Are you sure?" Jeannie asked.

"Look at their puffy lips. Can these be natural? No, they are cows. If they can speak English, let them know what I understand of them." She took a long swig of her drink. "But to return to my confession. It would be impossible for me to remember all the fantastic fictions I fashioned for my flirt on that fateful evening. But it is only my finale that matters: I told Jordan there was soon to be a coup. I claimed certain elements in the military would join forces with the student left. Can you imagine such idiocy? I claimed, too, that I was none other than the kingpin. Can you believe such brazen nerve?"

Twirling her glass in her hands, she said, "Yes, this was surely my *pièce de resistance*. But even as I spoke, Jeannie, I was myself falling into Jordan's bed. I was drunk! I passed out! When I awoke the next morning, there he was, smiling so triumphantly. Yes, it was Jordan Frick, zipping up a freshly ironed pair of trousers. His mission having been accomplished. For as you may have guessed by now, my dear Jeannie, I had given him my virginity."

She uttered these words with a finality Jeannie could not quite read. "When did you next see him?" she asked carefully. Suna's eyes brimmed with tears as she stubbed out her cigarette. "You know, you were there," she said hoarsely. "Eleven years later, in 1981. In Kulis!"

Another tragic look. Jeannie struggled to fathom it. She asked if she had missed something – had Suna fallen in love with Jordan, had he broken her heart, had she fallen pregnant? "Hah!" Suna said scornfully. "As if I would have allowed such mundane matters to cloud my vision! No, my dear Jeannie, you have, as usual, missed the point."

Beckoning for the waiter, she added, "For thirty years now – you have wished to know what part you may have played in the so-called Trunk Murder. If you were the unwitting instigator. In fact, it was I!"

She took a last suck on her cigarette and attempted a haughty stare. "Yes," she said with trembling lips. "I was the informer. Or whatever you wish to call me. I betrayed everyone. Even you."

Her voice had become harsh and thin. It no longer sounded like Suna's. "I'm sorry," Jeannie said. "I'm still not connecting the dots."

"But you must."

"Then tell me the whole story, not just half of it. You say you never saw Jordan again. So who were you informing?"

"Who do you think?"

"Listen, Suna. If my father was somehow involved in this . . ."

And now Suna laughed. Or rather, snorted. "You Americans! How arrogant you are! You always think you're the bad guys, don't you? Well, let me tell you. If you ever need an evil puppetmaster, someone who can take an innocent fabrication and turn it inside out and set your mind on fire with unfounded suppositions and deranged paranoias – I'd advise you to go for a Turk."

"So was it İsmet?" Jeannie asked.

But Suna had said her piece. She rummaged through her handbag, fished out two twenty million lira notes, threw them on the table, and rising to her unsteady but determined feet, she left.

Returning home, Jeannie found Sinan in the kitchen, grilling aubergines. "Nice day?" he asked.

"Not really," she said.

"Hmmm. Stormy weather?"

"Well, you know Suna," she said. "When's the last time you saw her calm?"

He smiled, glanced over at the aubergines, picked up his knife to dice a large tomato. He took his time; he still moved like a cat. "I'm making a lot of this, by the way, so that you can eat it while I'm away." He put down his knife. "Here," he said, pulling out a chair. "Sit down. You're out of breath."

"How many days are you away this time?"

"Three," he said. "First Copenhagen. Then Munich. There's that commissioning round – we can't afford to miss it. But listen, if . . ."

"I'll be fine," she said.

He gave her a sharp look.

"But you're right," she said. "I'm not fine now."

He went back to dicing. "So tell me. What did our sacred monster do today?"

"She took me along with her to meet Billie Broome."

It took him a moment or two. "Oh, I know who you mean now. It's just that I still think of her as *Miss* Broome. So tell me," he said as he went back to his dicing. "Is she the same as you remember, or has she changed?"

"She took us to see someone."

"Oh?"

"Jordan Frick."

Although Sinan had his back to Jeannie, she thought she caught a momentary pause.

"He's been back in Turkey for some time now," Jeannie offered. "But working out of Ankara."

Sinan nodded.

"You know about this?"

"Only the bare bones," said Sinan. "The names, the silent partners . . ."

"Who are they?"

Sinan put his finger to his lips. "Don't ask."

"Whoever they are," Jeannie said, "They've backed the wrong horse."

"He's not in very good shape right now, is he?"

"You've heard that part too then?" she asked. As he poured the diced tomatoes into the pan with the sautéed onions, Sinan nodded, somewhat absently.

"If you knew all this," Jeannie asked, "why didn't you tell me?" Though she knew what the answer was – she was pregnant, she needed to conserve her strength. And he knew how much she hated to hear it. So instead he said, "Why upset you for no reason?"

"That's what Suna said, when she asked me not to tell you."

"That makes no sense," he said. "She knows I know. She told me!"

How tempted Jeannie was to ask the question that was burning inside her.

Could Sinan read her mind just the same? He left the pan hissing on the stove and pulled up the chair next to her. "Listen," he said. "What's done is done. Whatever she said to upset you, I am upset because she upset you. But the rest I forgive her. Forgave her. Long ago. Can we leave it there? Come." Taking her hand, he led her out to the porch. "I command you to put your feet up."

"You're treating me like an invalid."

"I'm treating you like a woman who's about to bear a child."

"An elderly prima gravida, do you mean? A woman with *old eggs*?"

"Listen, I know more about this than you do, remember?"

"Don't pull rank," she said.

"I won't if you put your feet up."

So she put her feet up, and he went back to the kitchen to finish their supper, leaving her to watch the traffic humming below the great glittering arcs of the bridge. Between its snaking shores, the Bosphorus was black — only a light here and there from a passing tanker. Set against the night, the windows of Rumeli Hisar looked like pictures suspended in space. She watched the little figures move about inside them, restless, caged, but still afraid to speak.

The next morning Suna called her, and in another new voice — thin, edgy, and oozing false calm — she apologized for her "drunkenness."

"And for my garrulous exaggerations," she added. "I was, as you may have guessed, only speaking metaphorically. But you understood this already. Yes?"

"No," Jeannie said.

"I understand, however, that you spoke to Sinan, who assured you . . ."

"That's not true. I told him who we saw yesterday, but nothing else."

"Ah! What a good friend you are."

"You've got to level with me, Suna. I need to know what happened."

"Nothing happened. I assure you!"

The stalemate persisted. Jeannie tried to find other ways in — tried to coax her conversations with Chloe and Lüset back to their first year together — dared, from time to time, to ask Sinan a direct question (What was eating away at Suna? If this was old history, wouldn't it be better if she got it off her chest?). But she couldn't bring herself to betray Suna's confidence, couldn't say the word "informer," couldn't, for that matter, ask Sinan why, when they got along so beautifully, when she couldn't fault a single thing he did, when they hadn't had a single argument (in, what was it now, eight months?) he was still holding himself back.

She'd be on the verge of putting it into the best words she could muster when it would occur to her that he was no more able to betray Suna's confidence than she was. If they both had had the same motive, how could she fault him?

In the absence of facts, she began to spin theories. Had Jordan tricked Suna, walked her into a trap? Or was it someone else who'd blackmailed her, and was that person İsmet? If so, her father would have been involved as well. What sort of information did she pass him, if indeed she passed him anything? Even if Suna had betrayed them all, how could her crime be as serious as she seemed to believe? Around and around the questions flew, in ever-wilder circles. She had to air them; to breathe she had to speak. The more Sinan deflected her, the more desperate she became. But somewhere in Suna's eyes, she could see the hint of a plea to rescue her, to force the issue.

43

N THE LAST WEEK of July, while Sinan was filming in the Southeast, a summer cold that had left Jeannie with a bad cough sent her into premature labor. Although the crisis passed, her doctor decided it would be safer to keep her under observation. She had no cause to complain – her room at the Admiral Bristol Hospital was on a par with what she would have had in the US, and the nursing was up to the same standard. But she was not in a good way. Her small emergency had robbed her of what little confidence she'd had, and her medication didn't help matters. Although it did what it was meant to do – arrest labor – it also induced anxiety. She was still having contractions, at least two an hour, and she got it into her head that they were trying to squeeze the life out of the baby. She would persist in this delusion until she'd felt the baby kick again. Between crises, she was bored, restless, breathless. She couldn't concentrate and was no good at conversation, either, but that made her loyal friends try all the harder.

Chloe and Suna visited in the afternoons with playing cards and chessboards and, if all else failed, gossip. In the evening, Suna would arrive with Europe's best newspapers to save Jeannie's mind from "the ravages of hormones," to keep her "abreast of the world" and entertain her with her deepest thoughts.

Her latest brainchild was an electronic newsletter called *Enlightenment 2000*. It did not boast many readers beyond her circle of friends and colleagues. She ran it along the same lines as their short-lived school newspaper. Her pen names were less fanciful but the old fire still flickered in her closely reasoned but rarely reasonable prose. The central feature was a rambling interview, always a battle of wits. She called it "a free exchange between friends" and for the August newsletter, she'd asked Jeannie to be her sparring mate.

What they argued about during the interview she taped that evening in Jeannie's hospital room was human rights – not the sorry state of human rights in Turkey at that juncture but the philosophical tensions that the international movement carried. Suna drew, as usual, on thinkers most people only pretended to have read – Kant, Heidegger, Arendt. Jeannie drew upon what she knew of the law, the EU, the dilemmas of human rights work in the field, and they spent most of the interview trying (unsuccessfully) to correct the other's misapprehensions.

But just before the tape ran out Suna asked Jeannie what it was like to be back in Turkey. "To put it baldly, I am asking how you can square this with your legacy, this past of yours that so obsessed you. The fact that you are the American daughter of an American spy."

What a rush Jeannie felt at that moment – finally, an opening! By now she, too, had forgotten to speak carefully – long interviews are like that, you forget the whirring tape. "I'll never square it," she said. "But I can't let it end there. I have to find my own way." You couldn't choose your father, she said, but you could choose your legacy – decide what it was about the American tradition you disowned, and what you wished to honor and pass on to others.

"Such noble thoughts," said Suna. "But you have evaded my question." So she asked it again – "what did Jeannie make of Turkey 2000?" In reply she said she was concerned about the IMF and the World Bank acting as if they owned the place, which, in a sense they did. "As someone whose association with this country goes back thirty years, I'm only too aware how long the US government has been pulling the strings here, imposing policies that benefit no one except perhaps for the fat cats in their pay." Jeannie had hoped that this crude approach to foreign policy management would end with the collapse of Communism. "So I'm concerned," she said, "when I see the old crooks still prospering."

Here Suna demurred: "This is a simplistic view of things."

"Then please," Jeannie said, "Illuminate me." She picked up that day's issue of *Milliyet*. On the front page was a large photograph of their old enemy İsmet, who had called a press conference to deny rumors that he was seeding a new political party. But he went on to say just what that party hoped to be: the voice of modernity, dedicated to eradicating corruption and political Islam – the two scourges now threatening to bring Turkey to its knees.

"Just how can you sit there," Jeannie asked, "while a man like this pontificates against corruption?"

Suna puffed out her lips. "And you are telling me that in your sainted America, politicians have clean hands?"

"We"re talking about İsmet, the man who . . ."

As Suna's hands flew up, she screeched, "That's enough!"

"You're afraid of him! Don't deny it!"

Affecting nonchalance, Suna said, "If I were hoping to go into the gunrunning business, then perhaps I would fear this man. But as a lowly sociologist editing a humble journal for the five others who share my views, I do not fear him. For he has even less interest in me than I in him."

They ought to have known that the Turkish press would be interested in what Jeannie had to say about her father, no matter how obscure the publication.

A few days later, Sinan, who by now had returned from the Southeast, handed Jeannie a printout of the newsletter. From his expression you'd have thought it was his death warrant. Though she was glad to see his calm disturbed, it still irked Jeannie to see that (because of her "condition"?) he was keeping his fury to himself. She wanted to say, "Stop babying me, goddamn it! I'm your wife!" Instead she said, "I'm sorry. I should have told you. But you were away."

"Still," he said, "you should have known better."

"If you'd told me more," Jeannie replied, "then perhaps I would have done."

"There's nothing you need to know I haven't told you."

She watched him clench and unclench his fist.

"It's not just a question of need," she said. "It's a question of respect."

"Oh is it now?" There was a hint of the old fire in his voice.

"You're shutting me out," Jeannie said. "How can you expect me to get over something I don't even know about? I can't live this way, Sinan."

"What are you trying to say — that I can?"

He was spitting his words now, the way he'd done as a boy. His eyes had turned to liquid. Part of her welcomed that, too. "Do you think this is easy?"

"Listen," she said. "As I've said before, you're under no obligation. If I'm a burden . . ."

"There's no if about it. You are a burden. My burden. How many times do I have to tell you! I don't mind!"

"But I do mind," Jeannie cried. "I've had enough! I don't want to live this way!"

To her shock and horror, he turned around and bellowed: "Neither do I!"

It was the truth, they both knew it, but after they had sat there for a few stunned seconds — after the nurse had popped her head in the door, and Sinan had gone out "for some fresh air," returning with cakes, peaches, apricot juice, *baklava* — he apologized. He had no idea where those words had come from. "Perhaps it's work."

But how her heart ached. How she longed to ask him why. A line from Stevie Smith came back to her, how being almost-but-not-quite-in-love was wholly evil. She knew then what she had to ask him. But she hesitated, afraid, perhaps, to hear her fears confirmed. And then it was too late. The moment had passed, and he was talking about the blasted interview.

"What game does Suna think she's playing?" he asked, clenching his fist. "And for what? Because your father is coming for a visit? What harm can he do us? He's had nothing to do with this country for thirty years. It doesn't matter who he is. But then you go and dig this up, drag in İsmet . . ."

"What does it matter what İsmet thinks?" Jeannie said. "He has no power over us."

"You have no idea how much power he has over us," said Sinan. "And I hope you never find out."

They made peace, but it was a fragile peace, because the next day, a national newspaper ran the interview in translation; on the next day, three others did the same, and on the Sunday, three more. The headlines were along the lines of, "Turkey Is Where My Heart Lies Now, says CIA Daughter." and "My Father Was a Spy and I Repudiate Him." That was the one her father brought from the airport.

The first thing he said was, "Hi. I'm the father you repudiate." Seeing Jeannie squirm, he said, "No apologies necessary, my dear! It's nice to know that in one place at least, I'm not forgotten." He glanced towards the door, where a pregnant woman and an older relative had slowed their passage to get a good look at them. He waved at them affably. "The father," said one. The other said, "*Zavallı*. Poor man."

"So we're the talk of the town, are we?" he said as he closed the door. "I can't tell you how refreshing that is, after twenty years in a city where no one reads a paper unless they're looking for a deal on pool cleaner or the Early Bird Special at The Red Lobster. So," he said. "How are you bearing up?"

There was something about his careless smile and the whiff of fresh air he'd brought in with him that made Jeannie blurt out the truth.

She said things she didn't even know she thought. She'd been mad to come back, to think she could turn an obsession she'd carried around her whole life into the sort of love that could sustain a marriage. She couldn't get the past out of her head. The rest had moved on. When ghosts came out of the woodwork, they just walked right through them, and Jeannie had to hand it to them, seeing their courage did her heart good, but she had no idea how they did it and it was pretty obvious she never would. But here she was, bringing a child into the world, another burden. She didn't want to be a burden. And now she knew that Sinan was only humoring her, that he had accepted this child out of duty, not love . . .

"He said that?" There was surprise in her father's voice.

"Of course not. He's too fucking polite. He refuses to talk about it. He's walled himself off."

"So how do you read that?" her father asked. But now the door opened, and it was Hector. At the sight of William Wakefield he opened his arms wide and let out his usual cry of historical joy. Then it was Amy, and more of the same. By the time Sinan arrived, Chloe and Lüset had also joined the party. Seeing his long face, Jeannie's father said, "You're not worried about *this*, are you?" He waved the Sunday paper with his picture on the front. Seeing Sinan's face darken, he said, "I don't mind. Honestly. It's just words. I've heard them all before. It's just how we talk to each other, Jeannie and I. Don't worry on *my* account. This is just the way the cookie crumbles."

"Cookies do not crumble by themselves," said Sinan ominously.

"Politics. What can I tell you? It"s what the English call a mug's game."

This sent Sinan back into his silence. When he excused himself, William patted his daughter's leg and said, "If you don't mind, I'm going to chase after him. Maybe go out somewhere, get a bite to eat. There's something he and I need to discuss. You don't mind, do you? Hector? Amy? Can you sit out this shift?"

"I'm fine on my own," Jeannie insisted.

"*You*, young lady, need to get some sleep."

How she hated that condescending note in his voice. Hated sitting there with them pretending to enjoy Amy's smoked chicken and the special low alcohol champagne she'd brought all the way from Austria. It was not that she wasn't grateful, and not that she didn't enjoy their company. She just couldn't bear being here, being suffered. If she'd been able, she'd have walked out right then.

When Suna arrived, just past nine, all Jeannie wanted was some time alone. So after Hector and Amy had said their farewells, she told Suna she should leave, too. Not a chance. "What do you take me for," asked Suna huffily, "a wolf child?" She reminded Jeannie that Turkish families never ever left their loved ones unattended in times of illness. "Anything less would be barbaric."

"So which cat has bitten your tongue this evening?" she asked.

"I can't take this any more," Jeannie said. "And neither can he."

Suna sat down on the half-made sofa bed. "So what are you trying to say?"

She told her. Suna appeared to listen. When Jeannie said she had decided to leave Turkey, Suna shook her head. "No, Jeannie, this would not be best. You must stay here, and resolve your differences. Think of the child. Be strong."

"What's the point of being strong," she asked, "if he doesn't love me?"

"He loves you," said Suna. "You just refuse to see it."

"You don't know how he looks at me. You don't know how hurtful it is."

"Even so. I cannot let you leave."

"But Suna, it has nothing to do with you."

"Oh yes, Jeannie, it does. It most certainly does."

"I'll make my own decisions, thank you very much."

"Ah," she said. "Ah. If I want to hear the Voice of America, I'll buy a radio. In the meantime, you are no longer free to do as you like."

"And why not, may I ask?"

"You are bearing his child!" Suna snapped.

"Yes, but he doesn't want it!

"How would you know, my fairweather friend? Who knows him better, you who have just wafted in, or me, his lifelong companion? Is it my fault that he wishes to spare you pain? You don't deserve his love. And that is not all! My friend, you no longer deserve the gift of innocence." She strolled over to the light switch and plunged the room into darkness. All Jeannie could see was the ember of the cigarette she now lit and the hint of a ceiling.

"There are things you should know."

44

"This is the difference between us. She can live with herself and I can't. She can spill out this story, and just when I've taken in the full horror of it, she rolls over with that harrumph *of hers, turns her back on me and falls asleep. I've forgotten what it's like to be able to roll over like that, to take a deep breath without the baby's foot pressing against my lungs, to stare at the ceiling without wondering if it's still alive. I even envy her snore.*

I am writing this down because it's only by writing that I can hope to make sense of it. Is it true what she said – that I have not and never will put down roots here? Is there a line to be drawn between my father's arrival and my sudden longing to get out on the first plane? Who am I trying to run away from, my father or myself? Or is he my out – my 'Get Out of Jail Free' card? It stings me just to write this. That must mean there's truth in it.

One thing that's been nagging at me all along: why people like Haluk and Lüset, people who want a quiet life, would allow themselves to be dragged into an intrigue of these proportions. Well, I know now. The fire of Suna's arguments would leave them with no choice. We can count ourselves lucky she did not go into law.

She played all the parts tonight. She was her own most ardent advocate, and her harshest prosecutor. But for all her magnificent rhetoric: something was wrong at the core. Submissive – is that the word I'm looking for?

She was duped, badly duped, but by the end she credits these evil men for teaching her 'the ways of the world.' That's not right, but if I don't work out why soon . . . She'll drown me out. And then she'll drown herself."

This is how they did her over: on the morning of May 25th 1971, Suna's mother woke her up to tell her she had a visitor. This man was İsmet, and in her mother's presence, he was the "essence of good manners." He claimed to be the representative of a scholarship fund, here to interview her for a bursary. After Suna's mother left to make the tea, he spoke more curtly, saying he had come to discuss her moral character. When she asked why, he said, "Because you have cheapened yourself. You are a Turkish girl, from a good family. But now no Turkish boy will touch you."

He then told her he knew about her PLO training. When she insisted she had never been to the Lebanon, let alone the Bekaa Valley, he silenced her with a wave. What he wanted from her were the names of the army officers with whom she and her fellow student revolutionaries had been conspiring. At which she had laughed in his face. At his advanced age, with his advanced rank, could he not tell the difference between a true threat to state security and a schoolgirl fancy?

Her next meeting with İsmet came three days later, in the police station, when they were all taken in for questioning about the car bomb. His first words to her: "So – in addition to having a big mouth and a wide cunt, we know something else about you. Congratulations. You are a true revolutionary. Not only will you whore for your ideas. You will sacrifice innocents to save your skin." Slamming his fist down on the table, he demanded that she admit to having planted the bomb that almost killed Jeannie's father. He passed a document across the table. It was the confession he now wished her to sign. It declared that Dutch Harding had been running a bomb factory. His favorite students had been helping him.

"Who told you this nonsense?" That's what Suna said as she threw the confession on the floor. But she already knew the answer. It was her flirt. It was Jordan. "Everything he had told İsmet was the purest fiction. But it was just the pure fiction that suited İsmet's purpose. He wanted Dutch Harding to hang, but I was damned if I would help him."

Suna steeled herself for a cruel interrogation. But then Jeannie's father had stormed into the room, demanding her prompt release. Relieved though she was to return to her home and her bed, she was nevertheless uneasy. She had to wonder if they had released her for a purpose. But what could that purpose be? She could not fathom it. She was in Alice's Wonderland, as painted by Salvador Dali.

" 'But at no point did I or anyone else entertain a doubt about our teacher. No, Jeannie. Not even when you barged into the garçonniere to pick that senseless fight with him. What possessed you to do such a thing? Was it guilt? Was it projection? Or was it your father, twisting your thoughts with lies? You must have asked yourself these same questions after you heard of Dutch's murder. But it was not his students who committed this terrible crime, Jeannie. No. It was I smet who wished him dead.' A lesser man would have fled then and there. But Dutch Harding could see they were panicking. He stayed to help.

By the time they parted company in the early hours of the morning – Sinan and Haluk to commandeer Kitten II, Suna and Lüset to carry down the trunk, and Dutch Harding to retrieve the money and documents they had gathered together for just such an emergency – the plan was to 'carry on as normal once the evidence had been dealt with.' At half past five that evening, they were to meet at the Russian Consulate.

'But by the hour of our rendezvous, I was in the room on the fourth floor, this room with the little table in the middle, the table with the strange metal object, and the window looking out onto the street.'

Before long, human cries began to waft into the room. They seemed to emanate from across the hall. At first Suna could not identify them. Then came the shock of recognition. It was Lüset in this other room. It was Lüset they were torturing.

She ran to the door, but I smet pulled her back in. She offered to do whatever he wished, '. . . anything so long as he would stop the senseless torture of my innocent friend. I said, "Please. Fuck me. Rape me. Kill me. Use me. Anything to stop this." My pleas had no effect.'

So she decamped to the windowsill. He met her desperate act with a triumphant air – as if she had done as he had planned.

Again, she raised the stakes. If I smet did not stop them torturing Lüset, she would jump.

His response: 'Let Allah's will be done.' He watched in stony silence as Suna swang her legs outside the window. 'You don't have the courage,' he told her. To prove him wrong, she pushed herself out just that much further.

'Are you afraid of heights, Jeannie? No? Then perhaps I shall not be able to convey how the street below looked to me. So far away. And the perspective so faulty. The cars in the traffic the same height as the buses. No people on the pavements, only heads. Their voices mingling with the rumbling of the cars and the roaring of the buses. But now I saw a very familiar head, threading through the traffic. It was a beautiful head, a glory of curls, and it belonged to our beloved mentor.'

Had he come to save her? Could she let him do this foolish, dangerous thing? Her mind reeled with questions. But she remained steadfast on the windowsill. İsmet behind her, his eyes glued to his files. He could be a father, keeping watch on his child.

She steadied her breathing, even as her grasp of the windowsill loosened. She looked down, and now yes! Her beloved mentor was looking up. He had seen her! She had to warn him.

So she did the only thing she could. She returned his stare.

'Slowly, I added a smile. This, too, he returned. I risked the slightest movement of my head. He nodded, then crossed the street, towards İsmet's lair. But this was not what I had meant!'

There was only one way to stop him. 'The decision was easy, the easiest I have made in my life. I had only to alter my center of gravity, ease my hands into the motion for which the perspiration had oiled them. I let them slip.'

By the time she was conscious again, Dutch Harding was dead and buried. Lüset was in prison. Haluk was missing. As was Sinan. For many years to come, she was to know nothing more.

'But this is not enough for you. Is it? You ask me who killed Dutch Harding, who disposed of his body, and how, and where. I think you know the answers to these questions. I think you need no proof. You can simply ask yourself. Where on earth is Kitten II today? I hope you understand now that we all know the truth, while also knowing that our lives depend on our never uttering the words out loud.'

She then repeated a remark İsmet had made during their conversation at the window: 'You can break people most easily by exposing their stupidity.' To which Suna could now say, yes, but all young people must face their stupidity, for this is how they learn. But without their friends, they could never find the strength to do so. It was the loving and forgiving hands of friends who helped them through.

'Which brings us back to Sinan,' she informed me. 'He is my friend in this deepest sense of the word. He has had a hard life, Jeannie. He has never complained. For reasons that have not always been clear to me, but that I recognize as genuine, he has always loved you. It was to bring joy to his life that I brought you back into it. If you fail him now, I can promise you. I will personally kill you.

But it will not come to that, Jeannie, will it? You are one of us now. You know the truth that binds us. And now, my friend, you must learn how to live with it.'

With that she left me. Rolled over and went to sleep. "

Was it really as neat as that? Did she never once look over her shoulder? Was the silence perhaps an invitation? Was she disappointed when Jeannie found no words to console her?

Every time Jeannie closed her eyes she saw the window-ledge. Every time she saw the street swirling below her, she heard Suna's voice. Her ten pages of thoughts turned out to be mostly Suna's thoughts. She'd not been setting down her impressions so much as reeling in the wake of Suna's: bow your head, see the world for the wicked place it is, say nothing, stop fighting your fate, but never forget your shame.

Why not, Suna? Why not?

No matter how she arranged the pillows and cranked up the mattress, she couldn't find a position that did not hurt her back. She looked up at the dark ceiling, at Suna's peaceful slumbering form. She felt her womb contract. After the tautness had ended, she placed her hands on her stomach, and as she waited for the kick that would tell her the baby was still alive, she heard the ghost of Suna's voice: *such needless worry, why can't you relax? Let go. What will be will be.*

She had to get up, out, away – even if she couldn't walk. Slowly, painfully, she pushed herself to a stand. She lumbered for the door – it was easier than she expected. She headed down the corridor – or did she? No one saw her as she wafted past the nurse's station. The pallid, groaning woman looked away when she stepped into the lift, and her attendant stared right through her.

She followed them down the corridor – stretcher after stretcher, woman after woman. Door after door. Seeping through the cracks, a shriek of pain. A nurse came rushing past; she was holding a pair of scissors the wrong way. She burst through a set of double doors and as they swung Jeannie could see the pallid woman. She was on her back, tied to a bed that looked like a cross. Standing over her was a doctor. He was pulling something out. His shoes were covered with blood.

She had to save her, she had to. She pushed open the double doors, but the woman was gone. Now it was only the doctor, washing his hands. Where there had once been a wall was now only a ledge. She put her hands on the ledge but her palms were so wet she nearly slipped.

She woke up to find herself lying on the floor.

Suna the Saviour slept through the entire thing – the panic, the dreadful certainty, the poking and the prodding, and finally the kick. Sharp and impatient, as if to say, *what's eating you, why can't you let me sleep?*

Because I can't, she thought. Because it's wrong. It's giving in.

Yes, that's what she'd tell Suna when she woke up, that's how she was going to live with all that truth Suna had thrown at her. She was going to fight her, fight her until she got back her courage. She, of all people, had not been put on this earth to bow to her fate. For whom was she holding all these secrets? Who benefited from her silence? *Cui bono*, Suna? That's what she would tell her. And Sinan, too. He said he didn't trust words any more. The truth was he didn't trust himself.

But Jeannie would talk him out of it. The time had come to drag this story out of the shadows. There were pieces missing but together they'd find them. They'd assemble the truth in all its glittering horror and take it to the world. Let the world see the oppressors, how they did their business, what they gained from the silence of the tortured. Let the facts speak for themselves. Let the truth prevail! This was what she'd say to Suna when she woke her up. She would go on saying it – she would win this argument – if it was the last thing she ever did.

45

N NOVEMBER 2005 – only hours before I was due to leave for London – I woke up to find my mother on the balcony with three visitors.

But it was me they wanted to see. "I'm sorry to take you by surprise like this," Hector said. "But Haluk, Lüset and I have been talking. We think there's something you should know."

What they wanted me to know, what they made me swear to keep secret, was "the rumor." Rather than tell me the story themselves, they handed me a document. It was a printout of a PDF document downloaded from the Internet. "You may recall," Haluk said, "that we were reading this very file on the day, the hour, we renewed our acquaintance. We are speaking of the day last August, when Jeannie brought you back to the Pasha's Library. Do you remember our concern? Do you recall how hard we all worked to hide from her this paper?"

There were, in fact, three documents. The first report, dated April 15th 1979, was an account – by William Wakefield? – of a meeting with a Mr Sergeyev, the then Soviet military attaché. He was trying to defect. He claimed to have in-depth knowledge of the space programme, but the author of the report concluded that this was largely bluff. The Russian went on to give information about a key Soviet agent operating inside MİT, the Turkish national intelligence service.

Mr Sergeyev would not provide the name of this agent, but he did hand over the identity of a Turkish-Yugoslav jeweller who had operated for many years as a drop. He could not remember his name, only that he was an old man whose shop was in the Bedestan section of the Old Bazaar. His daughter was also involved. She ran their branch in Şişli. Mr Sergeyev could remember nothing about her beyond the fact that she was middle-aged and not particularly attractive.

Seeing that his interviewer was not impressed, Mr Sergeyev then offered information on a US national recently arrived to take up a teaching post at Robert College, who was, he said, working for the Stasi, the East German Intelligence Service. The author of the report did not think much of this tip either. It was not his view that the Stasi had the funding for "extravagances."

The second document was a memorandum marked Confidential, dated March 12th 1972. The author was a Douglas Hanes of the Canadian Department of Mines and Technical Surveys and concerned two meetings in Paris with Mr Sergeyev, now of the State and Scientific Committee of the Soviet Union.

At the first, Mr Sergeyev had asked Mr Hanes to pass a letter to the Americans. At the second, Mr Hanes had informed him he was not prepared to be a go-between. Mr Sergeyev had responded with the "utmost agitation," claiming that his "fate" was in Mr Hanes' hands. Although Mr Hanes claimed to have "declined everything from this one-sided gushing flow," he had agreed to pass on a message for him. "He claims to have had dealings with a double agent during his previous post at the Soviet consulate in Istanbul, Turkey."

Although Mr Hanes advised caution – Sergeyev was a "disgruntled citizen in a minor post that must be a great comedown from his military career" and "worst of all, dangerously talkative" – the Americans had taken Mr Sergeyev's advances seriously. The third document was titled "Meeting No. 40." It, too, took place in or near Paris. It was couched in routine language; "Subject was picked up at RV No 1 by L and G at 2000 hours while Roger provided surveillance cover."

There followed a transcript of a meandering conversation between L, G and Mr Sergeyev. At one point Sergeyev described a "very interesting" party at the Soviet Consulate that was attended by a number of young American Communist sympathizers from Robert College. He could not remember all their names, only that one of them had the strange first name of Dutch. In the past, said Mr Sergeyev, Istanbul had been a "hard nut to crack." But during his own stay there, he had made great headway into both the American community and the Turkish left through contacts made at Robert College. He had been helped in this by an old associate from his days in Cairo, whom Mr Sergeyev declined to name. "Suffice it to say that he was a Turkish diplomat in his mid-forties with a number of peccadilloes." It was through this old contact that he had been able to forge a link with the Turkish diplomat's son, then a student at said institution. This had proven most useful, as this same boy had already forged personal links with "your man in Istanbul." That this was an extraordinary achievement Mr Sergeyev could confirm personally. "But as luck would have it, he had an Achilles Heel. Our friend from the CIA had formed an affection for the boy I have mentioned, as I understand was the case for your man's teenage daughter. So interesting, don't you agree?"

His interviewers thought differently. "Let's get back to the illegals," they said. It was in the last moments of the meeting that Mr Sergeyev, now aware that the US had no use for him, found the sting in his tail.

"Oh, by the way," he said, "I've remembered the name of that Turkish diplomat. Would you like it?"

No, they wouldn't.

"Then perhaps you'd like this. A story, a very sweet story, about your man in Istanbul. As I've said before, he took a very keen interest in this diplomat's son, whose name was Sinan. So too did Mr Wakefield's lovely daughter. We all found this rather strange you know – for you see, in the late 1940s, your man Wakefield, then posted in Washington, had had a heated affair with this boy's mother, whose cuckolded husband also happened to be posted in the same city at that time. You may have heard of her – she gained some notoriety later, in the 60s, when she enjoyed a brief singing career in this very city of song. This woman – her name was Sibel but she was at least half-Greek, you know, and it was neither her first scandal nor her last.

"Get to the point," said his exasperated interviewer.

"Well, the long and the short of it, is that your man Wakefield got this Sibel pregnant during this affair he had with her. And Sinan is his son."

I had read these documents before, but as I did not wish to explain how and when, I tried to look surprised.

When he spoke again, Haluk's voice was very soft.

"It isn't true. I hope you know that."

I nodded. Though of course I did not yet know for sure.

"Who would want to spread such an ugly rumor? That's what I still can't understand." I said that, though of course I had my suspicions. I noticed, too, that Haluk's shoulders relaxed.

"The only person who would want to spread such a rumor would be someone who did not wish Jeannie and Sinan to remain together."

"Someone like İsmet?"

Another faint smile.

My next question made his eyes bulge. "You may not know this," I said, "but if you had to guess. How many years did Sinan walk around believing this?"

A shrug of the shoulders. "Twenty? Thirty? Thirty-five?"

"We cannot say for sure," said Lüset. "All we know is the day he discovered it to have no basis in truth."

The harbinger of truth, they now informed me, was William Wakefield. Or rather, it was he who had ferreted out the lie. He had done this the night of his arrival in Istanbul, in August 2000. "The night before little Emre was born."

"Of course William Wakefield could only give him his word on that occasion. But later, there were the tests."

"In between there were many weeks of anger. It was this anger that marked the beginning of the change."

"We are talking about a change of heart not just in Sinan but in William Wakefield."

"What had been to him a game until this moment, was no longer a game."

"He saw his enemies for who they were, and they saw what they had done to him."

"And to Sinan. And his daughter."

"He made a vow that night. A vow he kept."

"But he also made us promise something."

"This was to keep the entire matter safe from his daughter's eyes."

"He did not wish any shadow to pass across her happiness."

"However, we are almost certain that it was this document that Jeannie discovered just a few nights ago."

"We fear that this was what sent her into despair, and disappearance."

"Do you really now?" I said.

They looked up, surprised.

VII
Everyday Life in Times of Terror

46

"Just before he dropped off to sleep I tried feeding him water, and he hated it. Afterwards, I watched him dream. Nowhere have I read that one-day-old infants dream, but here's what I saw: eyes closed, lips churning, almost smiling, as blissful as if he were on the breast. And then, ugh, disgusting. End of grimace, back to blissful. And suddenly – another grimace. Water, milk, water. Is he dreaming them into memories, or combing his memories for dreams?"

September 3rd 2000

"I now have thirty bouquets, eleven flower arrangements, and enough chocolates to feed all ten thousand members of Sinan's extended family should they all decide to visit – apparently the sixty-seven who trooped through today were the tip of the iceberg. I have been led to understand that an obscure family feud that kept whole branches from attending our wedding has now been settled. Hence the happy crowds. Or was it me? I certainly got this impression from Aunt Banu, whose warmth was as overwhelming as it was puzzling: we've not seen each other since my unhappy visit to her house in the summer of 1970. After I had poured cologne on her hands (this time I remembered) she apologized for 'misunderstanding' me and said she hoped an 'atmosphere of forgiveness' might be established. I did say this would not be difficult, seeing as I held nothing against her – though I was happy to discuss the misunderstanding she had men-

tioned – so long as she let me know what it was. But now a great smile broke out on her face. She nodded over at the Plexiglas cradle. Emre had opened his beautiful eyes. As I picked him up, he squirmed to free himself of the blanket. 'Oh! Oh! Oh!' cooed Aunt Banu as he kicked his way free. 'Please, may I touch his little feet?'"

September 5th 2000

"The books say that infants can't smile, but they're lying."

September 5th 2000

"How strange, to be so happy, when my body feels like a worn out shoe."

September 5th 2000

"Sinan brings in the papers every morning. He turns on the radio and we listen to Haluk and his stepson David, arguing about the day's top stories – just as we do every morning at home. When my father visits, every hour on the hour he turns on the television. Sometimes it's BBC World, sometimes it's CNN, whatever it is, there's some outrage they're misreporting that he goes on to tell me more about. When Chloe comes in, we watch lighter stuff, and she points out the beauties on the screen who've been to her for nosejobs.

Only Suna understands that I have only one interest right now, and only she knows the depth of my ignorance. Thanks to her I now have enough childcare books to fill two shelves. They all contradict each other – Suna is shocked at what she calls their "low level of professionalism" but for this she is also, I suspect, secretly relieved. At last! A new subject to explore, dissect, critique and discuss to death.

There's something between us – there has been ever since that argument we had the morning I went into labor and that she refers to, always with a curl in her lip, as the Dawn of Truth. I am willing to accept that I might have chosen my words carelessly – I was out of my skull, for God's sake, who knows what was in that injection they gave me.

At any rate, I can remember what I'd intended to say but not what I actually said. Did I offend her somehow? Last night I asked her, to be met with dismissive waves. 'What a question. And such self-doubt! No, Madame. I am bowing, as ever, to your superior wisdom. However, the fact remains that you know nothing about babies. If you will permit an impertinence – less than nothing!'

I asked why she was as thirsty for this knowledge as I was. Her answer: 'Ah! He's not just your boy, you know! He's our boy!' My books at bedtime –

chosen, read, and analysed by Suna: last night it was Freud on infant sexuality. Tonight, I hear, it's Piaget."

September 6th 2000

"It's when I see Emre in his arms that I realize how little Sinan has told me about his older children. Or perhaps he did, but I didn't (or couldn't) read between the lines. But I can see now — just from the way he picks him up — that he has had years of lifting, loving children. Emre will be clawing at me, balling up his little fists and screaming, and nothing I can do will settle him. Then in he swoops: 'Why don't I try?' Sounding so tentative, but just to protect my feelings: the moment the baby feels Sinan's chest he goes quiet.

Dad, on the other hand, doesn't dare touch him. But he can sit there next to the bassinet for hours, staring. Even when we're watching a Class A Atrocity on CNN, his eyes still slip back to the baby. Yesterday, when Amy was visiting, and she asked him whom he thought Emre resembled, he smiled shyly and said, 'Oh well, especially at this age, who can tell?' Even though there is no resemblance whatsoever."

September 7th 2000

"'We came home today. And after a month in that small blinkered room I find the space, the loud colors, and sheer number of objects almost dizzying. You get so accustomed to blank white walls when you're in — "

September 21st 2000

"I see it's been a fortnight since I last picked up this journal. If anyone had told me you could do nothing all day but feed, bathe and change a tiny infant, and still have — "

November 1st 2000

"I've been feeding him rice cereal, and perhaps that's what's settled him. This afternoon, for the first time ever, he woke up without crying. I went into the room to find him hitting the little clown on the mobile we bought him last weekend. His face tensed, his breathing shallow, his legs churning, his eyes almost crossed and his concentration absolute. He batted the clown, watched it spin. When he caught sight of his own hand in front of him, did he really gasp, or did I imagine it? He examined it at length; it as if it were the most amazing hand ever created. It is."

November 16th 2000

"There's a mirror next to the counter where I've put the baby bath. In the beginning he'd just stare at the baby being bathed next to him in the reflection, as if to say, What are you doing here? This is my house. But today, while he was glaring at it, he suddenly broke into a lopsided smile. He still glares at all his other reflections, though. Quite right, too."

November 18th 2000

"Today we went to Akmerkez and bought a new stroller. Suna insisted. After researching the matter exhaustively, and I mean exhaustively, she has determined that our existing stroller did not provide adequate support for Emre's back. So off we went to remedy matters with a thing with wheels big enough for a man's bicycle. Why we bothered I cannot say. Unless we plan to spend our days strolling up and down this mall. High-rises and glittering waterfronts notwithstanding, there are still as many potholes, ledges and tapering, tilted pavements in this city as there were thirty years ago. I could do a city-wide map. Rate them in order of treachery. One star for a steep staircase, two for a steep staircase with a broken step, three for a shop entrance that can only be negotiated with a stroller if you back into it, but that must never be backed into, because of the steep staircase awaiting you on the other side.

Four stars for my father's new apartment in Bebek, because getting there involves all of the above. Not to mention two of those strange metal protrusions you still see coming through the concrete when you least expect them. Six stars, then? Maybe seven, if you consider who used to live there.

Plenty of excuses, then.

I'd feel better about it, I'm sure, if he'd asked me first."

December 2nd 2000

"It's hard to know what he wants out of life. He spends most of his day reading. In the evening he takes a walk along the Bosphorus, and if there's a lecture on at ARIT, he'll go to it, usually with his greatest fans, Hector and Amy. Afterwards they'll go out to supper. On Sundays, unless he's off on some ARIT tour, he comes to us. While Sinan cooks and I play with Emre, Dad sits and pretends to read the paper, but whenever I glance over at him, he's watching us. I could almost say – watching over us. It's unnerving.

When he's at home, he watches the Bosphorus. He's high enough on the hill to see from point to point. Whenever I drop in on him, it isn't long before he says, 'It's an amazing colour today, isn't it? There's no word for it, is there? I could spend the rest of my life trying and I'd never come close.'"

January 1st 2001

"He was, as Sinan had warned, the only baby at the party last night. But no one minded. In fact, they all wanted to hold their darling Emre. Or "caress" him – the preferred word. Though Suna kept a sharp watch on any honorary auntie she did not trust. And woe to anyone who tried to take him out to the balcony. She was, I'm afraid, particularly critical of Chloe. 'There is something unnaturally awkward about her posture,' Suna noted. 'If I wished to disprove the notion of a nurturing instinct, it would be this image I'd choose.' As usual, she forgot to keep her voice down, so Chloe heard. 'Here, take him back then,' she said, handing Emre over. 'Thank you,' said Suna. And Chloe said, 'My pleasure.' At which Suna said, 'I meant no offence. It's just that you make it clear with your body language that your breasts have never offered themselves to an infant.'

'Whereas yours are on permanent loan, I take it.' It has been a long time since I heard Chloe so annoyed. She lit up, presumably to calm herself. But now Suna felt compelled to share the latest findings on the possible link between parental smoking and Sudden Infant Death Syndrome.

'I'm not his mother, for God's sake! And you should get your facts straight, or at least put them in proportion.' At which she rattled off the findings of another less conclusive study, and for a moment I thought we were back in Marble Hall arguing about cultural imperialism."

May 15th 2001

"This afternoon, when we were at the US Embassy, registering Emre's birth, he somehow managed to crawl behind the counter and hide under a desk. He couldn't have been missing five minutes, but by the time we found him, we were seconds away from a full-fledged security alert. After that I tried to hold him in my arms. Impossible: now he was trying to climb to the ceiling, via my head. So I left him to run around the waiting room, always keeping my eyes on him while the very nice woman who was helping us as best she could explained why we, even with both parents in possession of US passports, ought to have come in much sooner.

Dad says she wouldn't have dared such condescension if he'd gone in with me. 'Retired I may be. But I still count for something. I didn't put in a lifetime of service to have some dippy woman give you a hard time.'

Though she couldn't have been more polite.

At one point, she asked me what sort of work I did, and when I explained, her response was the usual one. 'How interesting.' When she asked me if I planned to work in Turkey, I told her about the bid Suna and I would be making to the EU. For this, I got, 'Wow. How fascinating.' Then she nodded in

Emre's direction — he had just pulled a pile of brochures down to the floor and now had several in his mouth. 'So what are you doing for childcare?' she asked. And I realized — it hadn't even crossed my mind."

May 20th 2001

"Sinan is in Antalya, doing a film, so this weekend we flew down to see him. I had Emre on my lap — in a window seat, because I thought he'd want to watch take-off. And didn't he stare intently. I was most impressed. It was only later that I realized he was looking at the window, not through it.

Tonight, in the restaurant, he spent seventeen minutes examining a strange piece of bread."

June 3rd 2001

"Last Friday I was supposed to meet with Suna to discuss this EU bid but the weather was just too beautiful to spend indoors. So I talked her into going out to Haluk's new place on Sedef instead. We were only going to stay the afternoon, but before we knew it the last ferry had left, and Haluk (who had been planning this, I think) talked us into staying over. Sinan came out the next day, intending to stay only for the afternoon, but Haluk talked him into going out for mussels and somehow they didn't manage to get back in time for the last ferry, so we stayed over again. By now Lüset had also joined us, and Suna and I had handed our clothes over to the maid and were walking around in broad daylight in Lüset's night-gowns.

Emre didn't go for the mussels, but he liked the pebbles on the beach and tried to put almost all of them in his mouth. What he liked most were the speed-boats — he got so excited when one came close enough to the shore to kill us that he fell out of his inflatable tugboat.

It was Tuesday by the time we managed to pull ourselves away. We stopped off in Büyükada, took a walk up to the house where the snake lady had once lived, decided, when we had returned to the waterfront, that it made much more sense to eat there and return on a late ferry. It turned out to be a very late ferry. Emre conked out the moment we sat down. And so we wove our way from waterfront to glittering waterfront. Büyükada, Heybeli, Burgaz, Kınalı. As we sat there, with Emre stretched across our laps, I thought, who could have imagined? But before I could put it into words, Sinan said, 'Would you really have wanted to know? Isn't it better when life hides its shape?'"

June 12th 2001

"Today, for the first time in almost a year, I did an honest day's work. Suna was somewhat prickly. I'm not sure if it's because we're so close to the deadline for *this EU thing, or because it was hard to concentrate, with Emre devoting so much energy to finding a way to fall off Suna's balcony, or if she's afraid, despite my assurances, that I'm going to leave her to do the dogwork. When I told her that I had so many of these things under my belt now that I could do them in my sleep — she gazed at me through narrowed eyes and said, 'Perhaps this is just as well, now that you seem determined to spend the rest of your life in a coma.'*

I mentioned this in passing to Sinan and he said, 'Yes, well, now that you mention it. Have you considered a cold shower?' I did not immediately get the joke. So he said, 'Listen. Stop worrying so much about every little thing Suna says. She's under a lot of pressure right now.' He went on to tell me that she'd done 'another of her interviews.' As he said these words, his eyes hooded over too. It was, he said, an exposé of a family with Mafia links. 'I think you can guess which family. And which member of this family we know best.' It took me a moment to realize he meant İsmet. This, too, earned me a hooded look. 'Yes. İsmet,' said Sinan. 'But this time — thanks to that fiery speech you gave us — don't tell me your sleepy mind cannot recall this either? Not even vaguely? Such a shame. We were talking about it only the other day, Suna and I, and we both agree it was your finest moment. You were right, of course! You changed our lives in fact! Neither of us will ever dare collude with our oppressors ever again!'

I let it pass for once, asking instead what Suna had said about İsmet. 'She mentioned him by name, expressing doubt about his credentials as a politician, and alluding also to his shadier business dealings — but of course, we don't know for sure that he's an arms dealer — by presenting rumor as fact, she's inviting a lawsuit,' said Sinan. 'But that is not all. Or rather, it's more complicated. You see, the family in question — it's not İsmet's family per se, but he's connected to it by marriage — is already in dispute with Haluk's family. This could exacerbate that dispute,' he said cheerfully. 'There's no knowing where it might end.'

Then Emre woke up, and by the time I'd got him back to sleep, the phone had rung, and it was my father, telling me about the lecture he's set to give at ARIT in September, and then, when I carelessly asked what the lecture was about, explaining at some length. It's about the Cold War, needless to say. (As he put it: 'I've decided to become my own historian.') By the time I was off the phone I'd forgotten that I'd forgotten to ask Sinan where he thought the new Suna saga was leading, so I still don't know."

June 12th 2001

"Something else I forgot to mention. I can't say I'm happy about it: Suna and my father have made friends. I ran into them the other day on the terrace of the Divan Pub. They were having an argument — about the Cold War, what else?

'It is not that we agree,' Suna told me. 'Not even that I hope we ever will. But how often can you find an enemy who will admit openly to his perversity,

and who can converse as an equal? How are we ever to understand our collective past unless we hear from all sides?'

What she fails to ask herself is what my father gets out of the bargain."

June 12th 2001

"He makes no effort to hide his past. If anything, he advertises it. "Speaking as a retired spook" is his favorite way of beginning a sentence. And if his aim is to make people stop and listen to what he had to say, it works. For all his showmanship, he is careful what he says. His second favorite way of beginning a sentence is, 'Although you must understand why I cannot speak about specific operations or allude to any document that has yet to be declassified . . .'

But he's happy to talk all night about the bigger picture – what he'd been sent here to do in the mid 50s, how that brief had changed by the time he came back in the late 60s, what the relationship between the US and Turkey was supposed to be, and what it really was, why he was not at all sorry to have been part of the fight against Communism, how and why the CIA failed to do its job, how it did and did not work in harmony with local intelligence networks, and most of all, how and why current US policy in our part of the world was ill-conceived, ill-managed, arrogant and doomed.

And they love it. They just love it. It's not, Sinan tells me, just the pleasure of discovering that suspicions you had carried through life had some truth in them. It is the freedom, the release that a grain of truth can bring.

Once he stayed up all night with Dad discussing his father. They were not in agreement about the man himself – Sinan called him an 'unscrupulous collaborator' who had 'used his influence with the Americans to line his pockets,' while my father called him a patriot who 'believed his country to be well-served by its strong ties with the US.' But they did agree that this man had had a very strange way of being a father.

'Controlling all I did, but almost never there,' Sinan said. Dad then asked him two questions he couldn't answer: "What effect did he have on your politics? Who angered you and your friends most – 'imperialists' like me, or people like your father, the Turks who worked with us?"

It seems never to have occurred to Sinan that his almost-never-present father might have shaped his politics.

Needless to say – now that it has, he thinks there might be a film in it.

'Why are you rolling your eyes?' he asked me. 'Isn't this always the way you wanted me to be?'

He's right. I did. I do. It's just that I feel sidelined. These easy-going free-ranging conversations Dad's been having with Suna and Sinan have not led on to similar exchanges between dad and me.

Our relationship, set in aspic thirty years ago, must not be touched. He remembers my first year in Istanbul like this: we had a wonderful time together, really got to know each other as human beings. It was one big happy family – not just him and me, but also Amy, Chloe, Chloe's brother Neil, and Sinan. But then politics marched in to shut the whole thing down.

'You make it sound like an invading army," I said. "But it wasn't. It was you.'

'What? I started the Cold War? I pulled the strings of the entire student left? Personally planted the bomb that blew up my car?'

'No, of course not. But as you say yourself, you were here to do a job.'

'Yes, but so were a lot of other people, and some pretty unsavory people at that. You have no idea. You know why? Because you had your dad here protecting you.'"

June 15th 2001

"Summer school began this week. Today I met my class. There are only six of them, but they all seem keen. One in particular asked very good questions – unfortunately I couldn't answer several, and one I totally muffed as I had no idea whatsisname had died. It must have happened on a day when I didn't see the paper. Or saw the paper but didn't get around to reading it. In other words, it could have happened any time last year.

I fessed up, and of course we had a laugh about it. But I am going to have to get serious. No need for a cold shower, though. One look at the pile of very important unread monographs on my desk will do the trick.

It was good to be back in the classroom. Good to be wearing grownup clothes. Good to have lunch with Suna at Kennedy Lodge and conduct serious conversations with serious colleagues about matters that matter.

It was better getting home. He shrieked, opened his arms wide, laughed, babbled as he crawled across the floor – no valued colleague has ever given me such a welcome."

June 27th 2001

"Today we had a man from the Human Rights Foundation come in to talk to us. He said nothing about his own life but had the haunted but strangely peaceful look that I've seen so often on people who've survived torture. A few of the students had a hard time believing him, but he disarmed them by saying that this made him glad. They'd lost the terror that had gripped their parents – the terror they'd learned in the 70s and again in the 80s, in the country's political prisons. They assumed they lived in a free country, and although this was not so, their insistence that it should be so would be a force for change. All this without quite looking them in the eye: his voice, though certain, was also weary.

One day soon, Turkey would be an enlightened republic, he said. That day had not yet dawned. He told us how many members of his foundation had been killed over the last two years. He talked about the reports they'd still managed to relay to the European Court of Justice, about the forensic doctors who'd put their lives, their families and their careers at risk to gather evidence. He impressed upon us that torture is still systematic, occurring wherever a person first comes into contact with the authorities. On being asked, he told us what this was likely to entail. Or rather recited this.

After class I took him to Kennedy Lodge for lunch, but we took the cloud with us. At the very end, he asked if I'd decided about the 'mission.' To my shame, I had no idea what he meant. Tonight I dredged through my ever-growing backlog, and there it was: a delegation from the Council of Europe, passing through Istanbul tonight, en route to Van to inspect several prisons. All familiar names, one of them a former colleague. I managed to catch him in his hotel. We'll meet for breakfast, take it from there."

June 28th 2001

"I know I should do this, but how? Van is roasting hot this time of year, and I can't see taking a ten-month-old baby on a prison tour, either. But I can't see leaving him either. Not if Sinan comes, too."

June 29th 2001

"Handing him over to Lüset this morning – the hardest thing I have ever done.

All day, I've been seeing all the things he would have noticed – cranes, road repair machines, unusual trucks. Knobs, rusty nails, strange looking pieces of bread."

June 30th 2001

"To think, after what we saw today, that I almost brought Emre with us… I need to get my head checked."

July 3rd 2001

"'I've joined the gym at the Burç Club. I've been doing a half-hour on the machines after class as I've found that clears my head."

July 15th 2001

"Today I made the mistake of putting him in his sandpit and expecting that he would be so entranced with his new dump truck that I'd be able to write my lec-

ture. I gave up when a gust of wind took all my papers and blew them over the ledge. Oh the fury and the frustration – until I saw him laughing. We decamped to the Burç Club – after three hours in the pool he's asleep in his deck chair, and I am free to work. But just the sight of those books next to the suntan oil makes my head hurt."

August 12th 2001

"Yesterday morning I handed in my grades – reformed character that I am, I stayed up all night. Made the deadline with a half-hour to spare. This left little time for packing, however. Plus I could barely see straight.

This time, Emre looked through the window, not at it. When he saw the earth fall away, he gasped.

We were somewhere over Bulgaria when I remembered that I had left Emre's suitcase in the upstairs hallway. I felt like shooting myself, but Sinan wasn't phased. When we got to Heathrow, he phoned Lüset, and by the time we got to her flat in South Ken she had been out to Boots and stocked up on milk, nappies and pajamas. We went out this morning to buy the rest.

Today we flew up to Edinburgh. Sinan's event was this evening. We had been planning to leave Emre with a babysitter organized by the festival people, but Emre had hysterics, so we took him with us. Or rather, Sinan went first, and Emre and I went over after the screening. I've seen it many times already, so I didn't mind missing it, but I was curious to hear the questions afterwards – this film is bound to cause controversy just by virtue of its subject matter, and I wanted to gauge the reaction.

There were quite a few Turks in the audience – you could tell from the way they treated Emre. If he whimpered, or rocked a chair, they would turn around and smile, or they'd pinch his cheek and say, 'Ne cici! Or Yavrum!'

Very different response from the Nordics, though the maternal veterans in the audience did make some effort. When Emre was really beginning to work himself up and I realized I was going to have to let him run around outside for a while unless I wanted a kicking tantrum, one Mat Vet got out of her seat to let me pass, and as I did, she smiled at me wearily, to indicate that she understood exactly how I felt and was with me one hundred percent – though I could also tell (from the smile she gave Emre) that she pitied him for being saddled with an unfit mother who kept him up after his bedtime.

In the corridor was an elegant, agitated woman in her 40s; she was hissing into her mobile phone. Emre, meanwhile, was practising his walk.

When he toppled over in her vicinity, he looked up at her and smiled. But instead of the endearments that he has come to expect in Turkey, all he got was an icy glare. He shot me a puzzled look: what had he done wrong?

He dared to laugh, and the elegant, agitated woman still hissing on her phone cast me a look of pure hatred. That was when I recognized her – less than a year ago, that woman was me."

August 20th 2000

"I've decided I've spent too much of my life thinking, wondering, asking, looking under stones best left unturned.

I am coming to see the point of silence.

A few last words, then.

So that I can say I truly understand how I've come to this.

Sinan went straight from Edinburgh to Ankara, and the night of his return we'd arranged to meet at the Hisar İskele at eight. It was another sultry August evening. Emre and I had walked down from the house. When we reached the Bosphorus road, traffic was at a standstill. There was a famous singer performing at the castle, and there was nowhere for his thousands of fans to park. We crossed over to the shore, where I took Emre out of his backpack and while he stared at the idling engines on the road, I looked at the water, which was still steel blue to the north beyond the bridge and, to the south, tinged with pink.

Then Emre turned to the sea and began to babble and kick and point. It took me a few moments to see it: the Bosphorus was teeming with boats and ships, but not a single one was moving.

It is not an easy feat to stand in place on the Bosphorus. The current is too strong. The boats and ships had to keep their engines running to stop the drift. It made them sound like planes preparing for take-off.

We were fifteen minutes late. So despite Emre's pleas, no lingering at the fish tank. We went straight out to the porch, to the corner table Sinan had reserved for us. But it was already taken. When I asked why, the waiter looked perplexed. Wasn't the gentleman at the table one of our party?

It was İsmet. After he had admired Emre, he invited us to sit down. Beckoning for the waiter, he ordered me an Absolut and mineral water. "That's your poison, Jeannie, isn't it?"

He went on to ask me a string of avuncular questions. How old was Emre now? How was his father? How was mine? Was I settling into motherhood? Did I find Istanbul a pleasant place to live?

'I seem to be upsetting you,'" he said with a smile.

'Not at all,' I said. 'It's just I wasn't expecting to see you.'

'I take your point,' he said. 'Because in the grand scheme of things, you're not important. But I still feel a responsibility for you. Your dad and I go way back, after all. And the same must be said of this little fellow's father. We're practically related, as you know.' He looked up: there was Sinan standing over us. His expression was unreadable. Or rather, there was no expression at all.

İsmet stood up. 'I am taking your seat, I think,' he said affably.

'Please,' said Sinan in a low voice. 'There is no rush.'

'How kind of you to say so. But I won't stay long. You see, it's my daughter's birthday. I'm such a family man these days. It's my only thought! We'll be at that long table over there.'

He bared his teeth. 'I love children so much, as you know. And this child gives me such a special pleasure. He looks just like his father, Jeannie, don't you think?' İsmet leaned forward to pinch Emre's cheek. 'And he's the spitting image of his grandfather, too.'

'Take your hands off him,' Sinan said. 'Get away from him or I'll hit you.'

İsmet's face went blank. 'So you believed him,' he said.

'No,' said Sinan. 'For thirty years, I believed you.'

İsmet stood up and the two men glared at each other.

'You should still believe me,' İsmet said. 'You should always believe me.'

'You lied to me.' Sinan spat out his words.

'So you may think, but who can ever know . . .'

'I know!' Sinan bellowed. 'I have proof!'

'But why would an old family friend wish to lie to you?'

'You lied because you wanted to ruin my life.'

'I was just trying to protect you,' İsmet said.

'Protect me from what?'

İsmet's face went very dark.

'Leave us in peace,' Sinan said. 'Or I'll piss in your daughter's face.'

There was a flurry of activity after İsmet left the table. The ashtray was replaced, the table brushed. New glasses arrived, and then new napkins and knives and forks. There were muttered apologies from the waiter. 'The gentleman has bothered you.' It was a question.

Sinan waved it away. 'It was nothing,' he said to the waiter in Turkish. 'What you did was correct.' He ordered himself an Absolut and soda and asked the waiter to replenish mine. It was only after the drinks had arrived that he spoke.

'I'm sorry. If only I'd been here on time . . .'

And perhaps he was struggling to find a way to tell me. But then a glowing orange bumblebee of a hovercraft came barrelling past us, and Emre fell out of his chair.

The hovercraft seemed to belong to the maritime police. It was soon joined by two others that pulled up alongside the tugboat sitting underneath the bridge. İsmet (who was not with his family after all, but with three sharply dressed business associates) seemed to be party to whatever was going on. When ships were free to move up and down the Bosphorus again – after a glowing bumblebee had come to pick him up, I turned to Sinan. "So what was that all about?"

'Who knows? It could have been some sort of exercise. Or a bomb scare. Or maybe they were doing some sort of repair.'

'I didn't mean that,' I said. 'I meant that argument with İsmet.'

'You're surprised I'd want to argue with İsmet?'

'You've always said it's dangerous to talk back.'

'I should have talked back to him years ago. I already feel so much better.'

'What was it about, though?'

'Nothing,' said Sinan. "Really nothing.'

'What did he lie to you about?'

'It's over. For now, that's all you need to know.'

But his voice lacked conviction. Late that night, he changed his mind.

We were in bed, and I'd just finished reading a column about the Edinburgh screening of Van Comes to Europe. The author, a renowned nationalist, accused Sinan of treason.

'How dare he?' I said. But Sinan was unruffled.

'He can say what he wants. So long as he doesn't stop me doing what I want, who cares? Things are different now.'

'Are they?'

He laughed. 'You're not trying to warn me, are you? You're not trying to tell me I should compromise my principles?'

'No, but . . .'

'Let me guess. You approve, of course, how could you not approve? But you'd still like me to curb my impulses a little, take things slowly, and above all, avoid a confrontation with İsmet.'

'Yes, that would be nice,' I said.

'Very nice indeed,' he said. 'But also, alas, very European. It's not the way we do things here. It's not the way things work.'

'So how do they work?' I asked.

He smiled and for a moment he looked nineteen again. 'We've been through this before. Don't you remember? Except . . .' he wagged his finger. 'Except – last time we were wrong.'

'About what?'

'The revolution. Do you remember why?'

'Let's see. Could it be that the seeds were planted long ago?'

'And?'

'The roots must spread under the ground . . . the saplings must have time to grow. But when the sap starts running . . .'

'You can't stop the course of history.'

'The Judas trees must blossom . . . until one day . . .'

He threw his head back in laughter. 'Okay then. I'll tell you. You might as well know. That day they took us in. You know, in 1971, after they blew up your father's car, and İsmet took you all in. Well, this is what you don't know. He took me in first. Yes, I had the first, and the most private, interview! And I suppose you're going to ask why I've waited all this time to tell you.' He was speaking so fast I could barely follow him. 'Well the reason is I knew you'd want to know the whole story. But I didn't want to think about the story long enough to tell it, and now I've told you and have no choice to explain, this is what I ask of you. No questions. No nothing. Are we agreed? Here, come into my arms, turn off the light, I'll tell you as quickly as I can and I'll be so tired by the end I'll fall asleep and you'll stare at the ceiling, trying to imagine every gap in my story, but this can't be helped, all stories have gaps and this is the only time I will ever say what I am about to say.'

I struggled to find my voice. 'If it's too painful . . .'

'Too painful? Of course it's too painful! But please, just listen. I won't take long. He caught me by surprise, Jeannie. I had no idea what was coming. When he shut the door behind him, I was not even nervous. I assumed he'd brought us in to discuss the bombing of your father's car, of which I knew nothing.'

But first there were to be preliminaries. You would think we were in Sürreya's, chatting over piroshki. First there are the reminiscences – the first time we met, too young for me to remember. Then something odd that still makes no sense to me – about a jeweller in Ankara, a former Yugoslavian who may or may not have been a drop. Then my own first memory of İsmet, on that Russian ship in 1962. I was with my father, he'd just been posted to Cairo. Why İsmet was on the ship I cannot tell you. There was also a group of Egyptian officers on board, and now he wanted to know if I remembered them, what else I had seen. In Caracas, in Washington, in Karachi, how often was my father the guest of the Soviet embassy? Might my father be vulnerable to blackmail because of his 'varied proclivities'? What was the true reason for my parents' divorce? Had my mother not confided in me? My answers were vague and without effect.

Then İsmet pulled up a chair to sit next to me. He fixed his eyes onto my lap. Put his hand on my testicles. Squeezed them hard and said, 'Do you know what they say about you and Haluk? They say you share your balls. This is what they say. This is what they say you do for each other.' So he began. He said, 'Ah! What kind of man are you?' But then, later. After he removed his hand. I was my father's son. This is what he told me. His vices were my vices. Our fates were the same. He pushed me into the corner. And made his prophecy come true.

But I did not let him hear my pain. This must have bothered him. He must have known he'd have to do more than this to destroy me. And so he sat me down on the chair again and continued talking. He told me lies.'

'What lies?' I asked.

'Lies about my father – who he really was, what he'd done to my mother.'

'Like what?'

'I can't remember. I can't! Oh, Jeannie – please! Don't stay up all night

*dreaming up wild guesses! You asked why I picked a fight with İsmet. Now I've
told you. Can we leave it at that?"*

Of course — I couldn't, any more than if I'd been raped myself.

*But after he had turned his back on me, after he had extracted himself from
my poor attempt at an embrace and asked me to stop asking him if he was okay
— I made myself a promise — to close the door on this, to kill every question that
tempted me to do otherwise. To see him through this, help him put it behind us
and move on.*

*And it was just as well that I had made this resolution, for when we picked up
the paper the next morning, we were to discover what İsmet had been up to with
his bumblebee hovercrafts. He was splashed across the front page, standing in
front of the speedboat that a crane had just lifted from the depths of the
Bosphorus, less than fifty meters from where we'd been eating. Kitten II.*

*Sinan became ashen-faced when I passed him the paper, but for once I knew
better than to press for details. When he asked, "Is that all they found?" I just
told him what I knew. According to the paper, at least, all they'd found was the
shell of an old boat. But still he seemed unconvinced. "There may be more to
this story. There might be something they're holding back."*

*For once I made a sensible suggestion. Why didn't he ring Haluk? He was
sure to find a way to the inside track. "Good idea," Sinan said. But he remained
tense all day. Every time the phone rang, he jumped. There were long conversations with Suna as well as Haluk. Each left him gloomier than the one before.
When the phone rang again that night at half past eleven, I expected the worst.
But I was wrong, thank God. For Haluk had indeed found his way to the
inside track. They'd found nothing inside Kitten II. We were safe. We were in
the clear.'*

47

SO ONCE AGAIN, the secret is safe. The invisible hand binding them to the unspeakable past begins to wither. Sinan and Jeannie live happily ever after with little Emre, whose joy in the here and now so confounds his grandfather that even he stops chasing ghosts.

İsmet drifts into retirement, Chloe into the arms of another saintly husband. Suna carries on with her fine works. Haluk and Lüset write the checks.

Sinan's films lose their edge. He does not become a terror suspect, and his wife does not come to me for help. She does not go missing. I do not set out to find her.

This is how the story ought to have ended. Could have ended. Would have ended, if a certain someone hadn't decided it should not.

Who was this person?

Was it Jordan, refusing to let anything get in the way of a good story?

Was it William, stirring for revenge?

Was it İsmet, sensing danger?

Or was it his shadow?

The time has come to tell you where I am.

I am sitting on the balcony of an apartment in Bebek, in a building near the top of the steep steps, and as I've been writing, dawn has come and gone.

I can see all of Bebek Bay stretched out before me. From the southernmost towers of Rumeli Hisar to the fishermen huddled outside Arnavutköy. There must be a hundred yachts and rowboats moored in the still waters before me. The Asian shore looks close enough to touch. Were it not for the steady stream of tankers, the speed with which they cut across the bay, the swirl marks that mark off its still waters from the churning currents, I could be at the edge of a lake.

This is the apartment that Dutch Harding shared with Billie Broome from September 1968 to June 1971.

William Wakefield lived here, too. From 2000 to 2005.

Though he has been gone for several months now, the furnishings remain the same. I am sitting in what I'm told he called his watching post. It's a creaky but comfortable garden chair with floral cushions. This was where he was meant to have been sitting when an unknown assailant crept up behind him on the evening of October 16th 2005 and shot him in the head.

The story is not corroborated in any autopsy report. There is no autopsy report. No blood, even, on the cushions of his favorite chair.

After weeks of searching, I have not been able to find a single piece of paper, faked or authentic, attesting to his death.

When his daughter made enquiries, only days before she herself disappeared, she was informed by a State Department *apparatchik* (or someone who identified himself as such) that his body had been "repatriated."

I know differently, though it remains to be seen if my evidence will stand in court.

But here, for what it's worth, is my eyewitness report.

A fortnight after William Wakefield's murder and repatriation, he paid me a visit at my home in North London. He was a good twenty pounds thinner than when I'd last seen him, and his complexion had a grey tinge to it. He looked hunted and desperate but (perhaps naïvely) I took those as signs of life.

He wanted to know if I'd heard from Jeannie. When I told him I hadn't, he caved into a sigh.

Did I have any theories? His voice was thin and for a moment I pitied him. Then I remembered who he was and what he stood for and went to retrieve my folder on the Patriot Act.

"Why are you showing me this?" he asked, tossing the documents onto the table. Keeping my voice neutral, I explained. "I think she went back," I said. "Not to JFK, or any other airport, for that matter. She wouldn't be that foolish. No, I think she went back via Canada. She was that desperate to find her son. She must have thought friends would hide her. Perhaps they did. Perhaps the authorities had been tracking her all along. Anyway, I think they nabbed her. And as you know, the Patriot Act allows them to hold her for quite some time without informing her family. Or anyone else."

"Where do you think she is right now?"

I shrugged my shoulders. "On a spy plane?"

"Who do you think is behind this?"

"One of your old friends?"

"I have lots of old friends," he snapped.

"Yes," I said, "And some have more to hide than others."

"Show me what you have, then."

"I will, but not until you've answered a few questions."

He clasped his hands and bowed his head. It brought out my cruel streak. "What I'd like you to explain is how you justify what you do."

"What – is this the International Criminal Court?"

"What I want to know is why you've stayed silent," I said. "Even though you know."

"You think words ever put things to right? You journalists know nothing. The action is behind the scenes, my friend. Things have to happen quietly or they don't happen at all."

"That's rich coming from the darling of CNN."

"You of all people should never never believe what people say on CNN."

"Did you ever find time in your busy schedule to explain this to your daughter?"

"Oh glory be! Don't you know I did everything . . ." But here his voice cracked. Ashamed of my venom, I reined myself in.

"I'll take a risk," I said. I went back into my study and returned with the other files. The life and death of Dutch Harding. The complete works of Stephen Svabo. Manfred Berger's glittering career.

He went through them in silence. When he had returned the documents to their folders, he studied me instead.

"So," he said. "Where do we go from here?"

"You tell me," I said. "As you know, this is not my usual terrain. I just write about mothers and babies, remember? So tell me I'm over my head."

"You're over your head," he said. "But you're getting very warm."

"By which you mean to say that...?"

"You need to go back," he said. "I mean to Turkey. Find out what he's up to. What he doesn't want us to know. That's the first thing you need to do."

"And the second?"

"You need to spook him. Make him show his face. And when you have . . ."

"If I'm still alive by then."

"When you've caught him redhanded, you are going to write it all down."

"I thought you said words could never put things right."

"Oh they can if they stay secret."

"How the hell do I write something up for the papers and keep it secret?"

"Who said anything about the papers? No, what you do is write in confidence. Write for the inside track. Win their confidence. Gain their trust. Bring this story alive for them. Give them no chance but to live and breathe it. Make them grieve. Make them cry for their country! But never let them forget that – should they treat you badly – you will take your story elsewhere."

He took out his wallet and extracted a card, placing it carefully on the table, so that I could read it without touching it:

Mary Ann Widener

CENTER FOR
DEMOCRATIC CHANGE

MAWidener@cdc.org

"The Center for Democratic Change?" I said.

"That's the one!"

"I've never heard of it," I said.

A beady grin. "I'm not surprised."

"Where are they located?"

"If they wanted you to know that," said William, "they'd put it on the card."

"But if I assumed it was Washington, let's say on the Beltway . . ."

"You might not be far wrong."

"So," I said, picking up the card now. "Tell me about this Mary Ann Widener."

"You roomed with her older sister in your sophomore year. Kelsey Widener? Name ring any bells? Apparently you visited the house once or twice. Mary Ann remembers that distinctly. I take it you do, too. That's good. It's always better if there's some sort of personal connection."

"So you want me to write to her," I said.

"Tell her everything you know."

"Why?"

"She's honest. And principled. She genuinely wants to help."

"How far can I trust her?" I asked.

"Absolutely," he said. "Though I can't say I can vouch for her friends."

I can't either, Mary Ann. But you I've always trusted. Which is why – though I have never quite managed to forget that my letters to you are not as private as I might have liked – I have tried to write as truthfully as circumstances allow. Where there are gaps in my story, I have tried to mark them clearly. But to obfuscate now would protect no one. For I have done my master's bidding, and the game is up.

As I write these words, I can hear him padding down the corridor in his slippered feet. How odd this is. Shouldn't I be shaking with fear? I've never felt calmer. As he crosses the balcony, holding his coffee mug close to his chest, his strange lank hair pulled back by the sea breeze, I can see he is as haunted as I am. Wherever he goes, whoever he becomes, whatever riches and secret glories he accumulates, this is the place he revisits in his dreams. Now here it is in front of him again. Could it be that he is still asleep?

Leave him to it. There are still things to explain.

There being no justice in the world, the story of the last four years goes like this:

48

THREE WEEKS AFTER Jeannie came to see the point of silence, the two hijacked jets ploughed into the World Trade Center. After her father recovered from the surprise and the terror – there was the shame. He ought to have seen it coming. He ought to have warned people. He understood this part of the world. Now, as never before, it was his job to explain. So he offered his services. Not for money, not for glory. Just to do the right thing. But (as he ought to have foreseen) no one in Washington took the bait.

As September wore on and Bush's war on terror gained momentum, as pundits who had never ventured beyond Washington and London began to talk in broad and sweeping terms about the East, the West and the peril that was Islam, he pressed his case with ever greater insistence, to no avail. He was coming from the wrong direction, he was on the wrong side of the divide. His words made no sense because no one – or almost no one – wished to make sense of them.

Then an opportunity came his way. In early October, Haluk invited him to speak on Radio Enlightenment to discuss and analyse the war on terror, the crisis in intelligence and what William Wakefield himself called "the parallel crisis in White House stupidity." He spoke well, in Turkish, and before long, his caustic, damning but strangely cheerful reports had become a staple.

In November of the same year, when a political crisis caused a panic that caused Turkey's currency to halve in value overnight, he did an item for the BBC World Service, and before long, he was talking down ISDN lines to radio stations all over the world whenever there was a Turkish bomb or earthquake or political scandal big enough to warrant international interest.

In November 2002, when an electorate tired of corruption voted out most of the political establishment, and voted in a new pro-market, pre-European Islamist AK Party, William Wakefield made his first appearance on CNN.

He made his last in the aftermath of the four al-Qaeda-linked bombs that shattered the city center the following year. His intemperate remarks about the world being a more dangerous place now Bush had set out to make it safer may have lost him favor at CNN but won him admirers elsewhere. The more the media used him, the more outrageous and newsworthy he became.

When asked on Turkish networks to speak about his own country, he was gleefully rude – almost proud to be rude. If anyone called him to task on it, he said, "This is how I express my patriotism."

When asked on American, Australian or European networks to speak about Turkey, he was measured even when the questions exasperated him. "Never miss a chance for a history lesson," he'd say. "Not even if you're writing in the sand." He would explain "this country" to "those people" if it was the last thing he did. "You can make that my epitaph," he'd say. If I could, I would.

Between September 2001 and April 2005 Sinan made one stand-alone documentary and two series. They were overtly political (because William Wakefield had been stoking his fires? Or because he, too, had been swept into the zeitgeist?) and they established him on the world stage. He was now getting all his funding from Europe – he could no longer depend on Haluk's cultural foundation – its budget having been slashed after the currency crisis. So there were questions in the press about who exactly was financing his work. In the absence of names, they were dubbed "enemies of Turkey."

He refused to be intimidated.

The first series he put out during this period was a rather loose-knit

affair entitled *Turkey: an Interim Report*. It began with the forced reloca-
tion of several Kurdish villages to make way for a dam, and went on to
look at corrupt developers in Antalya and the underside of humanitarian aid to earthquake victims. The last segment, about the hunger strik-
ers then dying in large numbers in prisons, was critical not just of state
authorities but of the Stalinist groups to which they belonged. This did
not stop a leading columnist from charging him with insulting the state
– a prisonable offence.

So in *Torture without Marks* he left behind the paradoxes of the
militant left to focus on state-sponsored violence. Although he let his
subjects tell their stories, he filmed them in their homes, returning or
failing to return, to ordinary life. Some lived in Hisar Üstü, in the hills
just above my parents' house. The same families featured in his second
series, which he filmed on and off between 2001 and 2003. *The War*
became a series by accident. His original aim had been to film the "war"
between the Alevi Muslims on one side of Hisar Üstü and the Sunni
Muslims on the other. The Alevi women did not cover their heads while
their Sunni neighbors did; when the Alevi women had a political point
to make they strolled through the Sunni neighborhood bareheaded.

On September 11th 2001, he happened to be sitting in a coffeehouse wedged between those two neighborhoods when he glanced up
at the television to see a tower collapsing. He had the presence of mind
to film the commotion that followed. He went back in the run-up to
the war in Afghanistan, during the invasion of Iraq in the spring of 2003,
and in the aftermath of the Al-Qaeda-linked bombs in Istanbul in
November of the same year. They seem to have fallen off the list we get
with each new terrorist atrocity, so perhaps I should remind you that
there were four massive suicide bombs that ripped through two syna-
gogues, the British Consulate, and the headquarters of the HSBC. Not
all responses to these events were informed or temperate, but no two
were alike: you could never predict who would say what, or how their
views might change.

The film did well in Europe, and perhaps because it was so timely
and cut through the tyrannies of East-West rhetoric to show ordinary
Muslims in all their variety, it was a sensation in the US. Even as he was
making the last film in the series, the first three were being shown on
campuses all over the country.

In January 2005, an agent called from New York suggesting Sinan take the final film on a nationwide tour. He flew in to convince him personally, pumping Sinan full of praise. Whenever Sinan alluded to some episode in his past, the agent would say, "You know, there might just be a film in that." Did he put the idea into Sinan's head? Or had William Wakefield already done so?

It was not long after the agent's visit that Sinan began the project that was to be his undoing.

This was how he sold it: the world had changed and so had the purported enemy — it was no longer Communism we were meant to fear. It was Islam. But the cloud had a silver lining. Now that Communism was no longer a menace, at last it was safe to talk about what we'd all been through in the name of the Free World. To see how strange this little chapter of history had been.

But here was the strangest thing. For all the changes we had seen — the world felt more like 1970 with every passing day. The war in Iraq, and the war against the war. The insurgents. The bombs. The surges of anti-American sentiment, the terrorists and counter terrorists. The isms. The atrocities. The invisible threat. The paranoia. The spies. All too often — the same spies.

He finished *My Cold War* in the winter of 2005. He took it on the festival circuit that spring, picking up an honorable mention here and there and one small prize. On July 6th 2005 he did a screening at the Frontline Club in London. One of the people in the audience was Jordan Frick.

He kept quiet at the question and answer session, and either Sinan failed to recognize him or he chose not to do so.

The same thing happened, or rather, failed to happen, on the plane they both boarded the next morning.

49

I N THE 90S, WHEN Chloe was between careers, she'd done some sort of cordon bleu course. She was an adventurous and rather showy cook – though she never seemed able to produce anything without saying how awful it looked. It was a persona that served her well when she got pulled into a cookery show that one of Haluk's companies was developing for television. The main cook was the bejewelled socialite who lived in the villa next door. Chloe played her clueless American apprentice. Though her Turkish was fluent, Chloe still made what Suna called "typical American mistakes" and this, apparently, added to her comic charm.

On July 7th 2005 – the second anniversary of their collaboration – Chloe and her neighbor took down the fence between their magnificent gardens with their stunning Bosphorus views and invited all their friends to a garden party. Among them were my parents, who remember Sinan arriving straight from the airport with his suitcases. He was cordial, but preoccupied . . .

His gaze, my mother recalls, went first to Amy Cabot, who was looking very bronzed in her red and white cocktail dress. Sitting at the table right next to her, and watching her with proud, proprietorial smiles, were Hector and Jeannie's father. Next to them was my mother, whose smile he did not know quite how to read.

He smiled back. Perhaps too quickly. "Have you seen my brood?"

"They're in the pool," my mother said.

"The pool?"

She gestured towards the garden of the society cook.

Off he wandered. Did he feel my mother's eyes on him? As he ambled past a huddle of restive adolescents, he paused. Was it something they had said? Their parents, who had congregated under the next tree, had summer villas in the same Bodrum complex as Chloe and the society cook. One was the architect who'd designed the complex. The others were doctors or engineers or developers or something in television.

He nodded at a few of them, then wandered on. Only to stop again. Yes, something was wrong. At the other end of the lawn was the Spanish Consul, who was talking to the British Consul, who now turned to talk to the man from Procter and Gamble. Next to them was a Turkish artist, her German husband, and a physicist whose education had been interrupted by a stint in political prison. Now he was the rector of one of the new private universities.

Suna was sitting under a tree. With her were two journalists. They were nodding contemptuously in the direction of another former "comrade" who had reverted to type just in time to take over his family's gun running business. So much history! So many grudges and ironies! This must have been what had unsettled him. This was the sort of thing he noticed whenever he stepped off a plane. It was in the air. The menace just lurking behind the mannered smiles. What Suna called the art of civilized terror.

His eyes travelled further, to the society cook's terrace. There was Chloe, conversing with a man – a foreigner. He was wearing dark glasses but there was something familiar about him – who was he? And why did Chloe keep glancing over her shoulder? Perhaps she was nervous about the rumors that everyone, including Sinan, had read in that day's paper. An insinuating piece in a scandal sheet owned by İsmet's relatives, implying that Chloe's clinic laundered money for an old friend (clearly Haluk) in exchange for "favors." This was untrue, but there were details of Chloe's previous relations with Haluk that could only have come from someone who'd known her well in the 1970s.

Sinan's eyes kept travelling, until he'd found his family. There was Jeannie, standing next to Chloe's neighbor's pool. There was Emre, laughing and splashing. He was looking up at a man. This man was crouching at the water's edge. He was wearing dark glasses and his face was in profile. But still Sinan knew him. Even after all these years.

His first response – and how he would ponder it later – was anger. Why now? Why here? What could possibly justify this risk?

As the man turned his head – to gaze at the lawn? to welcome his old comrade? to chastise him for showing surprise or to counsel silence? – Sinan noticed that he'd had more surgery done. His nose was longer, sharper. Almost Mediterranean. But then again, not Mediterranean enough.

As Sinan headed across the lawn, he studied his wife's back. He could always tell her mood from the way she held her shoulders. He would know from her shoulders if they'd already spoken, if he had arrived too late. But then there was a hand on his arm. An old classmate, wishing to introduce him to a visiting archeologist. Then it was an old friend of his mother's. The next time he looked over at the pool it was just his wife and his son. His old comrade had gone.

Or had he just disappeared over the brow of the hill? Quickening his gait, Sinan brushed past the sister of the society cook. But she, too, detained him for an exchange of niceties. Then it was Chloe herself.

"At last! We'd given up on you! Hasn't anyone got you a drink? Listen. I have a blast from the past for you. It took me twenty minutes. Let's see how long it takes you."

"I know you already," said Sinan. He offered his hand. "Or am I wrong? Are you not Jordan Frick?"

When he saw Jordan approaching, did William Wakefield want to crow? He gave nothing away. He was one big welcoming committee, pulling out chairs, making introductions, fetching drinks.

There was the usual exchanging of notes. William had read something by Jordan in the Observer, and Jordan had heard William on the World Service. "So what's coming next?" William asked. Sitting back in his chair, and folding his arms, Jordan said he was writing a book.

A book. How interesting! Another fearless exposé?

"You'd better hope not," said Jordan.

"Why ever not?"

"Because you're in it."

A ripple of laughter. Jordan turned to Sinan.

"I've seen your film."

Sinan smiled, waiting for the verdict.

"Interesting stuff."

Sinan thanked him. But Jordan was not done. "You know what I find strange?" he said.

"No, I don't. But please do say."

"Okay I will then. Let me put it like this. You circle around the subject like a hawk. But you never . . ."

He paused, perhaps hoping Sinan would speak. Why make it easy? Jordan tried again. "Every film has a hole in it – the most important person isn't there."

Now Sinan spoke. "What exactly are you suggesting?"

Staring straight into his eyes, Jordan said, "I think you know."

"I want to hear it from you, though," Sinan said.

"I am tired of innuendo. I want direct answers to direct questions."

"So what's your question?" Sinan asked.

"Who killed Dutch Harding?"

"Is that really all you want to know? I'm disappointed!" Fearing that his voice might shake or his lips tremble, Sinan flashed what he hoped was a superior smile. "After all these years of chasing all these groundless rumors, have you never thought to ask yourself if . . ."

"I have. Of course. I'll tell you what I don't understand, though – why, after all these years, you're still protecting him."

That, at least, is what my own dear mother recalls him saying. She is not to be discounted. Not only can she remember who said what at parties thirty years ago, but what they were wearing, and how much they drank.

She recalls the silence that fell over the table after Jordan's "veiled threat." Then my father came walking through the glass doors. Seeing something familiar in Jordan, but failing to recognize him, my father took the conversation back to the beginning. They had not quite finished exchanging notes when Suna appeared. How her eyes flashed! But when Jordan greeted her, she was careful to return his smile. Which made my mother suspicious. Or to quote her exactly, intrigued.

"Naturally I had to ask myself. Was there a history between these two? When, why, where, who, how? I'm sorry, M. You know what I'm like. Maybe I'm the one who should have been a journalist. Because you know what? I knew there was more than met the eye. Especially when I glanced over at Jeannie. She was standing by the pool and just from the way she had folded her arms I could tell something had gone terribly wrong."

"I was standing by the pool, watching Emre. (Jeannie wrote in the final pages of her letter.) His plump little legs were churning. A drop of water got into his eyes. He blinked with shock. Then he laughed, looked up. Way up, as if to thank the sun.

But it chose just that moment to slip behind the hill. As the shadow slipped across his face, I saw his smile slip away with it. I looked up, and that was when I saw him. A man. A stranger. A composite picture. His jet black hair did not match his pale skin. His square jaw did not match his pinched and pointed nose. He was wearing dark glasses so I could not see his eyes.

'Is this your son?' he asked. He had a faint German accent. This, too, struck me as odd. I could not place the voice but it did something to me. It kicked open a door. As he leaned down to smile at Emre, I was overcome by what I can only call a terrible premonition. I wanted to jump in and grab Emre and run. But as usual I was seeing danger in the wrong places. All this man did was toss Emre his ball.

There was the tiniest rustle of breeze. I used that as my excuse. By the time I had swaddled Emre in his giant towel, his friend had gone. I turned to carry Emre back to the house. And then I saw how right I'd been.

I recognized him at once.

I mark this moment as the end of my happiness."

Her father waved her over. "You two remember each other, don't you?" She managed a smile. And Jordan too? What was he doing here? Why couldn't he just leave her alone? Hadn't she suffered enough? Or would he not relent until she was as lonely and loveless as he was?

It was Jordan who broke the silence. "So where does this leave us? Are we or aren't we going to talk?" All eyes turned to Sinan – whose face was a mask. As he rose from his chair, he beckoned for Jeannie to do the same.

"What were you arguing about?" she asked as they got into the taxi.

"Dutch Harding."

"Dutch Harding? Why?"

"Don't ask," he said.

She tried to remember how long had it been since she'd last thought of Dutch Harding. She could barely remember what he'd looked like. Later that evening, after they'd put Emre to bed, she said as much to Sinan. He said nothing in reply, but she could see the tension in his hands, and she said so. He denied he was tense at all, but tersely. Then he left the room.

So the next day Jeannie asked her father. "Seeing as you love to brag so much about your adventures. What do you remember about Dutch Harding?"

"Dutch Harding," said her father. "Dutch Harding. Hmmm. Let's see. Well, he was a card-carrying Communist. I mean it. He really had a card. He went out with that teacher of yours. Miss What's-her-name. Oh yes, Miss Brainless SDS Groupie."

That was all he'd say about Dutch Harding. So she moved on to Jordan. She asked her father what Jordan's real job had been that year.

"In 1970? Let's see now. What exactly did I ask him? His job was to get to know the students, I guess. But he was too full of himself to be a good observer. This hasn't changed. If I were you, I'd just ignore him."

But Jordan was everywhere that week. She'd take Emre up to the college terrace with his tricycle, there he'd be, perched on a wall, getting to know the students. He seemed to know everyone and everyone wanted him to meet Jeannie. By Wednesday, they had been introduced at least eleven times.

By Wednesday, something else had happened. A crew had appeared out of nowhere to dig a hole in the garden of the Pasha's Library. They wouldn't give a reason, and since Sinan was away Jeannie called for her father. At first he seemed perturbed, but after conferring with the crew, he told her not to worry, it was part of this new sewer system the city was digging. When Jeannie pointed out that it had finished digging in their area a year earlier, he told her the workmen had said they were "just tying up loose ends." Which might have been a lie, he conceded. But since there was nothing they could do about it, the best thing was just to sit back. When Jeannie finally reached Sinan in Paris later that day, she got a long silence. "Oh well," he said finally. "But it's a shame for our trees."

So she went to Chloe. Chloe seemed her usual casual self, "It's nothing, just relax," she said. But she was worried enough to phone Suna, and Suna was at the house within the hour. The diggers had left by then, but the work was not finished. They had left their first hole unfilled and were at work on a second.

Suna surveyed the holes from a distance, her arms crossed and clutching her sides. She looked very pale but what alarmed Jeannie more was her determination to stay cheerful. "It's the curse of this city," she said. "Always they are digging something up. And never do they tell us anything in advance. Why a sewer? Why here? Why now? This would never happen in Europe," she said.

On Friday there was a party at Kennedy Lodge. Somehow Jordan and Jeannie ended up at the same table. One of his gullible new friends asked him how he was going to spend the rest of the summer, and he took this as an invitation to tell everyone at the table about his book. He launched into the story of Dutch Harding – the friend who'd turned out to be a double agent. The legend who'd come to a sorry, murky end. Feigning a headache, Jeannie left after the first course.

She'd left Emre with the maid, who'd hoped to put him straight to bed, so she was surprised to hear his laughter in the garden.

There he was, at the ledge, sitting in his father's lap. And there, sitting next to him, was İsmet. No argument this time. No conversation, either. The moment İsmet saw her, he stood up, gave her a crisp handshake and took his leave.

"When did you get back?" Jeannie asked Sinan. "I thought you were in Venice until Friday." He put his finger to his lips. They listened to İsmet's car leaving the meydan. Then Sinan turned to give Jeannie his coldest smile.

He stood up. He still had Emre in his arms. "Let's see these holes, then." There were three of them by now. "So," he said, "So this is a sewer."

"So they say."

"What else do they say?"

"Nothing. They're workmen. We hardly talk."

"So who else have you been talking to?"

"My father. Chloe. Suna."

She did not mention Jordan, because, though they'd shared the same table for two hours, they had not spoken. But she did bring up his name later, when she and Sinan were sharing a salad at the table outside – only a few feet away from the holes, but now it was dark and they couldn't see them.

When she went on to confess that she was mystified, but also unsettled, by "that scene at Chloe's party," by what Jordan had said about Dutch Harding, Sinan snorted. "He's bluffing. I hope you know that."

"Why are you so sure?"

"I know."

"Then tell me."

"I suppose I should. What choice do I have anyway? For all I know, they've already found it, already taken it away for tests."

"Taken what away?"

"The body."

"Dutch Harding's body?"

No answer.

"So what happened to him?"

"What do you think happened to him?"

"You're not going to tell me you killed Dutch Harding, are you?"

"There was a very long silence after that, and it is painful to recall the thoughts that went through my mind as we sat there in the dark, surrounded by those gaping holes.

Two women were walking along the path beneath our garden. They were conversing in whispers, stopping every few paces to catch their breath. Were they carrying something heavy? For the first time in three years, for the first time since I discovered happiness, I thought of Suna and Lüset on that same path, dragging the trunk.

I thought of what I'd said to set them on that path.

My worst fear. And it was true.

'So let me guess,' said Sinan in a hard voice I did not recognize. 'You're asking yourself how it would come to pass that a boy would kill his trusted mentor.'

I shook my head. For that was the only question to which I had the answer.

It was because I'd pushed him into it. Because I'd pointed the finger. Because he'd believed me. It was me, it was me, it was me."

So ends the letter Jeannie left for me in her computer. The garbled, scribbled pages of her last journal are in the same mode. The first entry is dated August 16th 2005 – the day after Sinan's arrest at JFK airport. It is a masterpiece of masochism, a step-by-step account of how this, too, was all her doing. She'd panicked, when she should have remained calm. She'd convinced herself that the sky would cave in unless they packed their bags and fled. If they stayed, İsmet would be back the next morning to charge Sinan with murder. If they stayed, İsmet would be back in the middle of the night to kidnap Emre.

Sinan had tried to reason with her. Had tried to convince her that they should sit there, surrounded by gaping holes. Sit there calmly. Conceal their fear.

He had tried to convince her that this crisis was of his making, that he had deliberately provoked it. To lure the snake out of the shadows, he said. To bring the truth out into the light. But she said she was no longer interested in the truth. All she wanted was to be sure their child was safe.

"I never thought I'd live to hear you say such a thing."

"Well, now you've heard it, and I'm not backing down," she said.

It was only when he'd relented, when she'd gone upstairs to pack, that she'd remembered her passport. Which should have been here by now. Which was seriously delayed. But she'd not stopped, not for a moment, to ask herself what that might mean.

It was her fault Sinan had been arrested. Her fault she'd lost her son. Her fault, and no one else's. No matter what anyone said.

50

OCTOBER 15TH 2005

"At night the demons take over — I hear Emre's terror as monsters in uniform rip him away from his father, I see his arms stretching out, struggling to catch hold of his father's sleeve, and his eyes, his innocent, pleading, uncomprehending eyes.

But in the morning, I am sometimes strong enough to force my imagination elsewhere. The uniform who comes into the interrogation room to take him home with her is a woman with a kind face. She's brought a few toys with her. A few action figures. A truck with an interesting crane. She has another bigger one in her office. Would Emre like to come and see it? Maybe he'd like to take his teddy and his blanket with him, because his dad is going to be talking to the men in the room until way past his bedtime. Is he hungry? What's his favorite food? Has he ever been to a Chuckie Cheese? I see the woman opening the door and Emre following, his face lit up with promises.

I imagine him now — midnight our time, 5 P.M. where he must be. He's perched on a big blue sofa, watching Sesame Street. In a house in a quiet suburb, with nice, ordinary foster parents who love him dearly. Who never forget to tell him that we do, too. 'They just had to go away for a while,' I hear them say. 'Don't worry. They'll be back for you as soon as they can.'

And then, the finale. A knock on the door. My passport! The phone rings. Sinan has been released! Apologies pour in, each more abject than the last. I wave them off and board the plane. I come through customs at JFK and there

is Sinan and there in his arms is Emre – and off we go on this tour as sched-
uled. Our little misadventure becomes a talking point – a tiny cautionary tale
about modern Islamophobia.

But then, the picture fades and I am back in this room, in front of this
screen, reading the preposterous charges. While filming in the Southeast of
Turkey, Sinan Sinanoğlu has been aiding and abetting terrorists. They claim to
have found names and addresses in his laptop that linked him with people
known to be linked with groups known to harbour terrorist sympathies . . .

He's been framed, that's what my father thinks. He is sure it was İsmet and
Co. who 'tipped off' Homeland Security. But only to cover their own tracks.
Now all we have to do is prove it."

It was on October 16th – the day after she wrote these words – that
her father was pronounced dead and removed from his apartment
before a family member could verify his identity.

She complained, of course. She hollered! She pounded her fist! But
the nice man who claimed to be calling her from the Consulate was
unable to help her, beyond confirming that they'd dispatched the body
to Kansas City.

Why the hell had they done that? she screeched. Clearing his throat
again, the man said, "My understanding is that they dispatched the body
to Kansas City at the request of his wife."

His wife? The personable man who claimed to be calling from the
consulate was only too eager to make up for his faux pas. He was so
sorry, what a horrible way to find out, if he'd only known . . . He gave
Jeannie her father's wife's name – Angwo – and contact details. "I'm sure
she'll tell you where he's buried." Perhaps she could, if she ever answered
her phone.

October 17th 2005

"At first I doubted her very existence. But now that I know to my cost just how
secretive my father could be – it's entirely possible. He could well have been mar-
ried and not told me. My guess is that this wife of his has been history for many
years and would not have been on hand to meet his body at the airport.

At night, I imagine what they must have done to him. At dawn, I imag-
ine Sinan reminding me never to believe what I can't see with my own eyes.
He knows I know he's innocent. He knows I'll wait. It's his handwriting – I
know it is – on the postcard I reread every morning, the moment I sit down at
this desk.

It arrived in an envelope postmarked Chicago, and since there was no return address I am not to know who sent it, or how that person came to have it in his or her possession. But it was most certainly a friend. It has been a consolation to know how many friends we have, humbling to see how hard they've fought for us since Sinan's plight became public knowledge.

> *'We open doors,*
> *we close doors,*
> *we pass through doors,*
> *and at the end of the one and only journey*
>   *there's no city*
>   *no harbor;*
> *the train comes off the rails,*
> *the boat sinks,*
> *the plane crashes.*
> *The map is drawn on ice.*
> *But if I could choose to set out or not*
>   *on this journey*
>   *I'd do it again.'"*

October 22nd 2005

"I'm not alone. I have my friends. Every Friday, we go out. Almost always, it's the five of us — Suna, Chloe, Lüset, myself and Haluk. Inevitably, there are jokes about his harem, though in truth, every week it's that much harder to get him to laugh. The family empire is crumbling. As of this week, the cultural foundation that Haluk's father founded in his name is no longer. But when we went out last night — to a Bosnian place in a converted factory in Cihangir — none of us mentioned it. He'd come out to forget his troubles, just as we all had.

Only Suna knows about my midnight caller.

I thought he was a prowler. I'd had several by then, though only in the garden. This was the first time I'd heard anyone inside. I'd not been sleeping — I didn't feel safe, and as it turns out, I was right.

I'd come down with my baseball bat to find him at his desk in the library, fiddling with his mobile. It was, I now recall, the same place he'd been sitting when I first set eyes on him, so many years ago.

He told me a story. A story so preposterous I cannot bring myself to repeat it. He had the gall to suggest that it let us all off the hook. All except for the villain he had appointed to it. Now all we had to do was combine forces and go public.

'You must be joking,' I said.

'Get out of my house,' I said.

'What the hell are you up to, anyway?' I said. 'What clown outfit sent you out here in the first place?'

That was when he made his pitch.

We could work together! Expose his villain to the light! Tell the whole story, from 1970 to the present. How it was this other man – not Jordan – who'd come to Robert College to get to know the students. How he had led them astray, just like he'd been told. How he'd almost been rumbled. Not by me, but by Rıfat. He was, Jordan informed me, the only one of the bunch who took my accusations seriously.

'You remember Rıfat, don't you? Oh you must, you must. The cute one. The serious customer. The ringleader. The one with the green eyes. You don't believe me? Then tell me when you last saw him. It was at the garçonniere, wasn't it? That last day. The day you left. Isn't it strange how none of them, none of them, ever mention him?'

'You want proof? I have proof.' Sadly, it was in London. But time was short. I just had to trust him. Because time was running out. Our villain had moved up in the world. He had a new mission – to save the West from the East! But as always, our villain wasn't what he claimed to be. Which was why I had to help Jordan stop him.

'We're both on the same side, Jeannie. Don't you see?'

It was exhausting work, spinning those preposterous lies. But he persevered, and it was four in the morning before he asked if he could "flake out" on my couch. As I looked at him sprawled over the cushions, snoring, mouth gaping wide, I understood for the first time how it felt to want someone dead.

In the morning, I made him breakfast. Then he picked up his bag and headed East. Whatever that means. He left thinking we had come to an agreement. I thought it would be dangerous to let him leave thinking anything else.

As soon as my hands stopped trembling, I dialled Suna's number.

She came straight over.

After I told her what Jordan had said to me, she sat very still.

When she stood up, it was to say she'd be moving into the spare room. "I want to be here, to face this man, when he pays his next visit."

I cannot remember now if it was that night Suna mentioned the website to me, or if it was a few days later. We were sitting just here, though. We were watching the bridge, just as I am now, and her voice was light.

We'd been going through Sinan's files, hunting for any shred of evidence that might help the case, and dredging the Internet, looking for anything whatsoever on my father. We'd been in touch with his contacts at CNN, the BBC, and the New York Times, and they'd forwarded us any emails they'd remembered to archive. Most had to do with the mess in Iraq but some drew parallels with 1971. The BBC man had also been kind enough to send several filmed interviews, and we'd spent most of the evening going through these. It would have been close to eleven when we came out to the porch with our herbal teas.

In a casual voice, Suna said, 'He was such an interesting man, your father. Say what you will, he had standards. Stand him next to your Jordan . . .'

'Oh, he's my Jordan, now, is he?'

'Stand him next to your Jordan, and you see how dismally standards have sunk. On the one side, a renaissance man. On the other, a mere contractor. A smooth-talking cowboy with a gun.'

'What am I going to do, Suna?'

'Perhaps, you could inform yourself. Think of it as armor. He cannot hurt you with what you already know.'

She did not elaborate. It was a good half-hour later – while we were talking about a Mexican film, of all things – that she mentioned this interesting website she'd happened on to – everything you'd ever wanted to know about covert activity in Chile and Guatemala in the late 70s.

It must have been one in the morning when I found myself back at my computer, searching for the site.

It was not quite as interesting as she had made it out to be, but there were links and I followed them. One site led to another, and finally to the archive of non-classified state department documents into which I typed my father's name.

To read about Sergeyev, and his poisoned rumors."

October 26th 2005

"Or is it the truth? If it's the truth, oh God, please tell me, what to do? What to do?

Memories keep flying back at me, demanding revision.

That time I walked into the radio station to find Suna and my father sitting in a low lit studio. Suna reprovingly silent, my father bent over, grimacing, as if in pain. Neither can see me, neither can know that the intercom is on. A painful sigh as my father shakes his head. In a defeated voice never before used in my presence, he says, "Okay, I'll say it. My conscience is not clear."

I had thought Suna was extracting some sort of spook's confession. But perhaps not. Perhaps it was this.

The things my father said, the last time we spoke:

'Listen. I want you to stop beating yourself up. This was not your fault. It was a set-up. A classic set-up'

'Listen. There's something I've never told you.'

'Listen. I know you think of me as a person who deals in secrets.'

'Listen. I have plenty of skeletons in my closet – all old skeletons. But I have nothing to lose. You ask me to do it and I'll sit right down and list them. What I can't list are the lies.'

'So listen. If you ever want to know which is which, you'll come and ask, won't you?'

How can I bear Emre knowing? How will I ever face him? How can I even be contemplating this?

I've written to M, asking her to fly down.

It's been four hours since I wrote to M, but still nothing.

Has she lost faith in me, too?

Five days now since Jordan the Great set out for parts East.

I've changed the locks.

My phone is tapped, I'm almost sure of it. When I pick it up, there's a click and then a whir. The floorboards seem to creak louder every night. I've trained myself not to imagine footsteps, but nothing prepared me for this morning, when I woke up to the sound of a child running down the corridor. Oh, the stupid joy!

But it was Handan Hanım's little boy – she'd sent him upstairs to play with Emre's toys while she did the floors.

I mustn't give in to hope. I must not yield. If they see I'm scared, it's over.

Last night I thought it over and this much is clear: either I make a clean breast of this, tell the truth in my own words. Or I keep it to myself and risk Jordan using it against us. Think of the effect it would have. Sinan – the persecuted innocent, the cause célèbre – married to his sister.

No, I have to do this.

Did Suna know or did she guess?"

October 28th 2005

"Tonight I asked her, and she prevaricated."

October 29th 2005

"Today I went to see İsmet.

His office is on the 24th floor of the skyscraper everyone says was built by the Mafia, in blatant contravention of the building code, just to prove that it could.

He was all condolences. He expressed his deep regret, too, about this court case. 'To tell you frankly,' he said. 'In the present climate of hysteria, what happened to poor Sinan could happen to anyone. Only yesterday, I was asking myself if I might be wise to cancel my own impending visit to your country's fine capital.'

'Naturally' he continued. 'I chose not to let fear win. As the fault-lines between East and West deepen, it is essential to keep all lines of communication open. And there are urgent questions.

Why has Turkey failed its old ally, refused to join hands to bring democracy to Iraq? Why is it no longer mindful of its secular heritage? Why has it allowed itself to be ruled by smiling Islamists?

These people may pretend today to be bringing us to Europe, but tomorrow, mark my word, they will be covering our daughters' heads with headscarves. No, we cannot stand idly by when danger looms. The Patriot Act notwithstanding, I shall continue to press forward.'

Leaning forward, he said, 'Of course – while I'm there. I shall express my extreme concern and displeasure about their inhumane, and, I suspect, illegal and unconstitutional detention of your husband. But – of course – your main concern must be your son.'

'Please,' I said. 'I'll do anything. Tell me what I have to do to get him back. Look, take me back with you. Let me talk to these people myself. Listen, if you can talk them into giving me immunity . . .'

This raised an eyebrow. 'Do you really think that's wise? No – of course you don't. On reflection, you must agree: there are some things that should never see the light of day. Shall we call them transgressions? Here is my view: if they cannot be undone, they must at least not be known. For a bridge to stand between East and West, we must at least believe ourselves pure. What people believe themselves to be matters more than what they truly are. This has always been my view.'

I had come here in craven desperation, to win him over, do whatever it took. But I couldn't stop myself. 'You're wrong!' I cried. 'You're evil!'

Every time I go back over this argument I should never have started I see another slimy insult slithering between the lines. The expressions of concern for Emre – his health, his welfare, his 'special needs.' Was İsmet implying that he's defective? To use his own word – impure?

The protestations of innocence: 'Referring to my earlier point,' he said, 'it is evident that what you have come to believe about me has a far greater impact on your mind that anything I could provide in the way of facts. In fact, most of what you know of me, you know from people who have used me for years as their punching bag. To believe them, I am the source of all Turkey's ills. One would think I'd been running the government, the economy, the secret service and the Mafia single-handed for forty years.'

The glib summary of Sinan: 'Of course I've always felt responsible for him. As you know, I was originally watching over him by explicit invitation from his father. What I have observed to be the constant is his burning anger. That this comes from his confusion about his origins is – I'm sure you will agree – self-evident. It is not easy to be an Easterner with a Western education. The mind is never in harmony with the heart. This becomes a more painful dilemma if the Easterner cannot even be sure that he is truly an Easterner. If his mother is Greek and his father . . . undefined.'

The ease with which he deflected my insults: 'You would not say such things if you were not desperate. It grieves me, of course. I am speaking now of your distress. But this was my point all along. In fact, I made this point to your father on Day One. He should never have opened the door. You and Sinan should never have met. Your child should never have been born.'

I should never have thrown that ashtray at his head.

'What did you do with him?' I screamed. 'What kind of deal did you make? Don't you think for a minute I'm going to let you get away with this!'

His assistant had me firmly by the arm and was ushering me out the door by then, but İsmet held up his hand, and said, 'A word to the wise, Mrs Sinanoğlu. Your husband is hardly in a position at this moment to choose his allies. Indeed. If he could see you at this moment . . .'

'I'm not talking about Sinan now!' I cried. 'I'm talking about my father!'

Encouraged by the tiniest lilt of surprise in his eyes, I said, 'I'm not going to let this sit, you know. I'm going to find out where they took him, where you sent him. Even better, I'm going to find out why!'

What have I done? What have I done?

If Sinan and I had never met, I would have travelled through my year abroad like the tourist İsmet thinks I should have been. I would have gone home with my journals bursting with archaeological ecstasy and my American heart intact. I would have graduated from college with higher honors, the highest honors, and gone on to become . . . a curator. At the age of thirty, I would have married . . . another curator. By now I would have two wonderful children in their late teens. I'd be sitting at my kitchen table in Evanston or Boston or San Francisco, planning my first return trip to the city that has remained so vivid in my thoughts. And I'd be asking myself: how safe is it? I'd be phrasing a careful letter to Chloe, with whom I have been in warm correspondence for thirty-five years . . .

If Emre had never been born . . . I don't have to imagine this. If Emre had never been born, I'd be as desolate, hollow, aching as I am today.

What if he was my last chance? What was the point? First I degraded

myself. Then I threw an ashtray. Accused him of murder. Said I'd find proof . . .
In full view of his assistant. Suna says that was my biggest mistake. It's
one thing to insult someone. It's quite another to make him lose face.
Of course – he more than rose to the occasion.
'Please – do not apologize. It is only natural. It is human nature! In the
modern age, we sometimes forget the power of instinct. Had someone suggested
to my mother that I should never have been born, she'd have done the same.'
The last thing he said to me: 'Any word from Jordan?'

Tonight I was going around in the usual circles. What have I done? How much
longer can I stand this limbo? What should I do? What can I do? And sudden-
ly it's so obvious: I have no choice but to 'accept the job.' I'll win Jordan's trust,
get a taste of the real world, find out how things are really done, instead of wax-
ing poetic on how they should be done, and then, when he thinks he has me
eating out of his hand, I'll hold him to his promise. He'll take me to Dutch
Harding, dead or alive. He'll lead me to my father's grave.
If I can do that – if I can see what Jordan is and Jordan does and live to
tell the tale – then they'll have to relent. And repent. And set Sinan free.'

So ends the last entry in Jeannie Wakefield's last journal.

In answer to the question that I'm sure you'll want to ask, it is sitting here next to me, on the balcony of this beautiful Bebek apartment
where so many characters in our story once lived, and where I myself
first met Sinan. On this very balcony. Halfway between me and my
devil. Who could have known?

When I make my next move – if I am in any position to make a
next move – I shall leave the aforementioned journal for you in the safe
deposit box we discussed earlier.

But now the time has come to take up the story where Jeannie was
forced to drop it.

51

HAVE ALREADY described how I was pulled into this intrigue, sometimes against my will and always against my better judgement. I hope I've made it clear that I had doubts all along. The most obvious question being, "Why me? Why drag in a journalist best known for her pioneering work on mothers and babies?" I've been over my head from the moment this started, ringed in by taciturn war correspondents, arrogant sociologists and retired spies. From the very beginning, they've been playing me off against each other. Feeding me stories, and hoping I'll believe them. Hoping, perhaps, I'll go on to convince others?

The first time that question came to me was at the Pasha's Library. I am talking now about the last hours of my last visit, the day after Jeannie disappeared. As I sat there at Jeannie's desk. As İsmet sat downstairs guarding the door. You may have marvelled at how easy it was for me: there on the computer, was Jeannie's letter to me. There, on the shelves, were the journals. There, pressed between the pages, were samples of hair that I was to assume belonged to William Wakefield and Sinan. And just in case I didn't make the necessary connections, there was İsmet himself, to jab a knowing finger at the poster for *My Cold War*, in which Sinan's family is joined in one picture by William Wakefield. I was to gasp and shout "Eureka!" Shout "incest!" Jeannie and Sinan should never have been together because they were brother and sister. Jeannie, upon hearing that her child is the fruit of incest, had lost her mind with grief. Jordan being the agent of her destruction. The informer. The agent provocateur. She had set out from the Pasha's Library that morning to track him down. Blow him up, if need be. Stop him before he did any more damage. Stop him to save her son. This was the story that İsmet and various others seemed to want me to tell. As I stood at the window, admiring the exalted view, I had to ask myself why.

If they were encouraging me to look where they were pointing, was there something behind me that they were hoping that a journalist best known for her pioneering work on mothers and babies might overlook?

I cannot say that I knew at once what to look for, or where I was most likely to find it. But I will concede that I was keyed up by the adverse responses to the piece I wrote three days later. It is rare to get such attention in "motherandbabyland." I can see that it went to my head. I was also, I am ready to admit this, terrified. But there was vanity there, too. The truth, Mary Ann, is that, perhaps for the first time in my life, I felt important.

A story had chosen me. Pulled me back thirty-five years, to a place only I could see. To the castle on its wooded hillside; the Bosphorus with its endless parade of tankers, ferries, and fishing boats, the Asian shore with its palaces and villas, the brown and rolling hills that must, I thought, stretch as far as China. The golden destination! The first of many! But now I've come full circle. There's someone behind me, erasing my tracks.

He's been listening in on us, Mary Ann. He's been pelting me with his unsigned threats since the day you and I began our correspondence. That he was passing my every communication onto others was clear from the outset. And yes, this caused me to speculate. Or rather, it sent me into that spiral of second guessing that forestalls clear thought.

I should have known what he would do when crude intimidation failed to silence me. And perhaps there were moments when I foresaw this – his last and most insidious refinement. But when you are taking risks with words, when you are out on a swaying limb, you can't afford to step out of yourself to ask how your words might sound to others. To keep your balance, you must remain in the here and now, cling to the truth and blind yourself to its possible consequences.

Until last night, when I picked up my messages, and heard his voice. I am not speaking about our tormentor now, but his number one pawn. Though it has been thirty-five years since I last heard from him, he saw no need to name himself. He got straight to the point.

It hurts too much to recall his exact words. Let alone quote them. Suffice it to say that our correspondence has been made available to him. While I understand why he might question my motives – scorn my sources – label me as Jeannie's executioner and İsmet's pawn – I still burn at the injustice.

Open your eyes, Sinan! For once in your life, look the messenger in the face. This is the last time you'll hear from me. I am too angry for words.

So tomorrow the theatre goes dark again. Tomorrow the bell will ring, and my devil will step inside. He thinks he's won. Will he take me to her, as promised? Or will I have to find my own way?

So many unknowns. It's hard to know what to pack. But there is one thing I'd be ill-advised to take with me. Mary Ann, the time has come for me to name names.

I have enjoyed our correspondence. I have enjoyed it so much, in fact, that I dread the prospect of it ending. But if I am to be truthful, Mary Ann, I'll have to admit that what I have enjoyed most has been holding back this secret. Have you ever wondered why it was arranged that we should write to each other? Have you guessed what I am yet to tell you?

During the past four weeks, I have taken the trouble to acquaint myself with your many accomplishments, most notably at your present place of work. I have done background checks on a number of your illustrious colleagues at the Center for Democratic Change, with a view to seeing who amongst them has an interest in this part of the world. There are several, but the most interesting is a man named Stephen Svabo. Born in Hungary in 1948 to academic parents who managed to relocate to Princeton, New Jersey after the 1956 uprising. Degrees from Columbia and Harvard. Active in human rights since the 70s, and (by his own account) a frequent visitor to Turkish prisons. Links with several think tanks like yours, but no university affiliation. No public profile, and no photograph on Google, but, in print at least, a vocal critic of recent erosions of civil liberties in the US, including those eroded in the prosecution of Sinan Sinanoğlu. His most recent "abbreviated" list of publications goes on for six pages.

In an earlier, less abbreviated list, he mentions an introduction he wrote for a 1980 anthology of "silenced voices." One such voice is an abstruse East German poet called Manfred Berger. Having heard that name in other unlikely places, I've investigated further. I've discovered that a Manfred Berger did indeed have a small reputation as a poet in East Berlin during the 70s and 80s, and that he has done rather well for himself since reunification, albeit under his "real" name, Dieter Dammer. After several years in Schroeder's party, he moved out of politics and now works for a cultural foundation that has funded many sterling ventures in Eastern Europe and Turkey. It is in that capacity that he has accompanied several EU delegations to Turkey in recent years. He has appeared, unsmilingly, in several group photographs. A beaknosed man whose jet black hair is longer than normal for a bureaucrat, he is not to be confused with the Manfred Berger who has been writing so brilliantly for the US press in recent years on the crisis in US intelligence.

Or the Manfred Berger who sits on the board of a new Eastern European telecommunications venture in which İsmet Şen was a major investor.

Or the Manfred Berger whose name has been linked to a weapons manufacturer with whom İsmet Şen's company also has links.

Or the Manfred Berger whose monograph Sinan showed to Jeannie in Dutch Harding's office in the spring of 1971.

It was a penname, of course. A private joke. One alias amongst many.

Dutch Harding never existed either. At least, there was no one enrolled at Columbia during the years he was meant to be there. But a Stephen Svabo does appear in the 1968 yearbook. Or rather, his name does. There is no photograph. No proof.

Until today.

What is his particular interest in Turkey? Whose interests does he serve? I'm sure he won't tell me, but I'm sure I can guess.

What I have to yet to understand is why, when I sat down with Suna last night, and told her what I knew, she had the gall to insist that —

Afterword by Suna Safran

SEPTEMBER 2006

It was, perhaps, a cruel trick of fate that prompted my erstwhile friend, the intrepid investigator of mothers and babies, to send her story – which is also my story – out into the ether with its last sentence still dangling. Although we can only guess what prevented an orderly closure, it could have been a simple question of impatience. As her sometime collaborator, I have found to my cost that high emotion has a deleterious effect on her ability to spot small errors. So it is entirely possible that my dear, though fallible, friend sent out the wrong document. The message I received was dated March 16th 2006. With it came seven attachments and a truncated note:

> "Dear Suna,
>
> In the hope that you are and I are still on speaking terms, I am writing to ask if . . ."

We had spent the previous evening – the Ides of March – together. We can assume this was the disagreement she was hoping to overcome. So it is possible to conjecture a later document addressing this fra-

cas in greater detail. Perhaps one day we shall find it stored in a dis-
carded computer, or in the inbox of a Washington bureaucrat or floating amongst the soulless routemasters of outer cyberspace.

Of course – we could fashion our clues into more sinister shapings.

We could imagine, for example, that the lank-haired man padding
down the hall in his slippers is not a phantasm, as some are claiming, but
the villain in the flesh.

Or we could imagine a more treacherous scenario: he has not yet
strutted onto the stage, but as she types her words, she feels as if each
one is pulling him closer. How calm she feels! For once in her life, she
is making the powerful quake in their boots. She is not running from
her fears. She is facing them! She has joined the ranks of the righteous!
But then, the ring of the doorbell. It tolls for her. Locked inside her shell
of bravado, she cannot breathe. The journey from the chair to the door
is the longest and most arduous she has ever taken.

But at the eleventh hour, she finds her voice. There is the short and
hypocritical exchange on the intercom. The rush to the desk, the quick
dispatching of the document, and perhaps she has misplaced her glasses.
As she squints into the little browsing window, her wildly beating heart
contrives for her to choose the almost finished document in the place
of the one offering us the enlightenment we now crave.

Later that same day – and perhaps we can imagine her now in one
of those Anatolian towns that rose from the dust only to serve food to
Turkey's bus-dwellers. Düzce, perhaps, if our friend and her self-styled
guide have chosen to drive east via Ankara. Though the poet in me
would prefer to see this wolf-in-guide's-clothing en route to Izmir, and
so obliged to use Susurluk, that truck-stop of scandal and deep state
intrigue, as his point of refreshment. Gentleman that he is – gentleman
that he pretends to be – he goes to pay for the food, and this, perhaps,
is when my friend M reaches into her hidden pocket for her hidden
phone to give the only woman she trusts the pertinent details of her
itinerary, moving on to outline for this same faithful friend her proposed
modes of future communication.

So, alas, it falls to me, Suna Safran, to finish the story I never chose
to tell. By this I do not mean to confirm the truth of the preceding
paragraph. It should be taken as offered, as pure conjecture for which
there is no shred of truth. My intention is only to finish the story that

M had only just begun when she was so rudely interrupted – in short, to offer a full account of the argument she was describing, at the very moment when she fell into the lion's maw.

But before I begin, I must ask my readers to understand that – however angry my words, both on that occasion and on some if not all of the pages that follow – we are still and ever will be held together by the golden thread of friendship.

It is a thread of the highest value in this land of ours. Whatever our failings, whatever passions fire our hearts, we honor our friends. And our teachers. Perhaps foolishly, but always with an open heart, we reserve our greatest thanks for those teachers who have shown us kindness, and who, in so doing, have opened our minds.

Billie Broome. She was a paragon of this mold. Without her books and her kind smile, where would I be now?

Dutch Harding – he was her idol, too. To Sinan, to Haluk, to Rıfat and so many others, he was more than that. He was the word of God. The shining light that gave their pain meaning.

So naturally we protected him. From the aspersions of others, and from our own doubts. Of course we were outraged – betrayed! – by the accusations of Jeannie Wakefield at the garçonniere on that fateful afternoon in June 1971. Of course it was easy for our beloved mentor to convince us that the true villain in our midst – the informer – the agent provocateur – was not the man who had opened our eyes to the world, but a green-eyed disciple who had gone over to the enemy.

Were we surprised at our bookish mentor's skill with firearms? Why should we have been? He was American. Didn't all Americans have guns? Were we surprised, when we reached the Pasha's Library, that he had the key, that he knew even where to find the shovel? Perhaps, but we were also impressed at his deep and thorough knowledge of the enemy. *Our* enemy. Did we help him bury poor Rıfat, the informer, the betrayer, the devil in our midst? Yes, of course we did. We feared for our Dutch Harding. We knew – we believed – that his life was in danger. That İsmet was after him, and with him, William Wakefield. So yes. We helped him escape. To cover up his tracks, we jumped from windows.

Did we know where he went next? Of course – we helped arrange it. We were aided by a well-meaning Soviet official who is to remain nameless. As for the rest – I refuse to edit details that fail to fit the desired mold. For Dutch Harding, or whoever he really is – he did not forget us. He protected us, too. Once he was safe and settled in East Berlin, it was to his home that Sinan and Haluk decamped. It was under Dutch Harding's care that they returned to a semblance of health. Now that my picture of him has been so cruelly rounded, now that we know he was always the shadow behind İsmet, I am wondering if we can also thank him for the modicum of medical treatment I received after jumping from my window. While my care was not the best our small country has to offer, it was nevertheless better than that accorded to others. The same applies to my other short period of incarceration, in 1981. While we were not spared the rod, we were luckier than most. The angel of darkness was watching over us.

In those days, we were in regular contact. But after the early 80s – after we had honored our teacher's wishes yet again and saved his secret by expelling Jeannie and her dangerous questions from our fold – he drifted in other directions. The Berlin Wall was no longer. The Cold War had turned to dust. A great historic shift was underway and he was right in the midst of it. I am sure he did good and helpful work during the early years of reunification. I am even open to the idea that for Dutch Harding – or rather, for the real man behind the false name – the fall of the Iron Curtain was a dream come true. If he was truly Stephen Svabo, and therefore a Hungarian by birth, if he witnessed the 1956 uprising . . .

This, then, was the gist of my discussion – now six months past – with my wayward but nevertheless beloved and deeply missed friend M on the eve of her disappearance. I regret to report it was a stormy session. She expected to set down her evidence – destroy my life, my dreams, the secret mission of mercy that has lit my way through three decades of trials and tribulations – and then move on to the next question! No time to breathe, to reconsider, to weigh her evidence, to dismember and repopulate my memory. No consideration for my bruised and battered heart. No thoughts even for her parents, whose loving trust she has so cruelly spurned, whose blameless lives she has so blighted. She had thoughts only for herself. She wanted only to know why we'd lied to her!

There were moments when the years dropped away and I almost could convince myself that we were both seventeen again, hurling the slings and arrows from which our school newspaper was never safe. Such a tragedy! To be born in a place you can't call home! Such an outrage! To have a passport from a country whose name is blackened! Every word M writes is drenched with this trauma. So of course she must convince us – and herself – that Jeannie feels the same.

But to return to our discussion. The last we were ever to have. We had to cross a veritable ocean of accusation – and tears, there were many tears – before she was willing to relent. But as we reached the end of our Ides of March, she did finally concede that (while we may have acted wrongly) we had done so in good faith. That a group of idealist students with no knowledge of the real world might be putty in the hands of the man we knew as Dutch Harding. Yes, by the end, she was willing to admire the doomed tenacity of our loyalty. She acknowledged the searing pain of disillusionment. Though she refused to understand why it was so shaming, so humiliating, to have been dragged to enlightenment by a journalist whose finest work has been on mothers and babies, my relentless though heartfelt friend did – I will concede this – listen closely to my long and wholly honest account of the lonely road I have travelled in recent years, with Sinan my only confidante. And I, in return, made to M my one concession: it had been a mistake not to bring Jeannie into our deliberations. Had our poor, innocent Jeannie known that Dutch Harding was still alive and inhabiting a thousand aliases – she would have shown us our blind spot. She would have known that our villain was not İsmet, but the man behind him.

Had we known this – had we so much as suspected his heinous and treacherous realities – we would never have gone on protecting this man, until the fifty-ninth minute of the eleventh hour. More to the point, we would not have gone on following his instructions. Because yes, it was Dutch Harding who advised Sinan to flee the country before İsmet's diggers found the body in his garden in August 2005. It was Dutch Harding who later told me, Suna Safran, that Jordan was on his scent, that Jordan had paid a visit to Jeannie. That though Jordan had not managed to persuade Jeannie that Dutch Harding was still amongst us, our mentor's life was nevertheless at risk. That Dutch Harding's safety now depended on my giving Jeannie other things to think about. And so, to my shame, I did his bidding. I guided my dear and trusting Jeannie to the ancient though wholly unfounded incest rumors that drove her to the edge of madness.

But please God, no further.

A question remains. If our aim was always to protect our beloved mentor, why did we drag out this old secret that had lain safely buried, for so many years? Here, at least, my doomed and fearless friend M guessed correctly. It was İsmet we were seeking to expose. It was William Wakefield who had started the ball rolling. He had started within minutes of his return to our city. He was angry, of course! Those incest rumors that first reached his ears on the eve of his grandson's birth – this was not the first straw, but the last! He wished revenge! Not for the first time, we were the vehicles. He fed us first this little clue and then that question. The result was *My Cold War*. I am sure that Jordan, if he returns to us, will have a similar tale to tell.

As for the story contained within these pages – its travels through the public domain have been well documented and perhaps excessively analysed – I would like to take this opportunity to highlight a few key points:

1) I, Suna Safran, was not this story's original disseminator. I have penned only the afterword you are now reading. The story you have read is the story M transmitted in seven electronic segments to Mary Ann Widener at the Center for Democratic Change. It was only on the night of her disappearance that M saw fit to send me a copy for my perusal. As we have already seen, this copy may be incomplete.

2) Though Mary Ann Widener has been established to be a real person (those seeking further information are advised to consult the website of the above-named think tank, where her accomplishments are documented in their entirety on the page bearing her name) the identity of the person who chose to post all seven segments of M's story on a rival website has still to be defined.

3) There is, however, no difference between the seven documents published on that website and the story M transmitted to me directly.

4) Although I was immediately aware of her story's importance (and in touch with the lawyers representing Sinan Sinanoğlu in the US) I had hoped (as did the above-mentioned counsel) to use it in a measured and judicious manner. This is not to say (although it has been said) that our purpose was to censor it. Rather, our hope was to stagger its release in such a way that it did not prejudice the trial, or subject Jeannie, wherever she might be, to unnecessary danger.

5) We shall never be sure if the trial of Sinan Sinanoğlu was indeed overshadowed by the presence in the public domain of a hot-blooded and intemperate 'True Confession' with all the ingredients of a pot-boiler – a swarthy, swashbuckling hero with a secret, a fair-haired, ivory-skinned maiden in peril, a love affair doomed by a cast of scheming Cold Warriors, ruthless terrorists and colorful locals much feted for their strange ways and linguistic foibles. And last but not least – a mole! Of course, this charming orientalist confection was not admissible as evidence.

6) But there is no doubt that, due to its high profile and its easy availability on the internet, public interest in the case was magnified a hundredfold. I have been assured by analysts of the strange beast that is US public opinion that in the end, the lamentable guilty verdict may do much to foster moral outrage and therefore further the cause of all those who in this age of terror and unreason still dare to fly while brown.

7) That Sinan himself remains steadfast in the face of adversity we know from both the court records of his trial and the accounts in the responsible press. He may have been convicted, but the cries of outrage grow. As for the cries that must have pierced his own heart upon hearing the truth about our faithless mentor, we can only guess. From his proud posture in the photograph that they flash on the screen with every mention of his name, and his clear-eyed gaze, we can entertain the soothing thought that he has accepted the poisoned arrow of truth lodged inside the heart of M's confession – perhaps even accepted the possibility that her intentions were, if not perfect, at least sincere.

8) But there is also his statement: we ignore his words at our peril. So I quote:

> "I stand before you charged with links to a terrorist group whose name has yet to be revealed to me. As I await enlightenment, my child remains in the care of court-appointed strangers. My wife's whereabouts are unknown. Since she fell into the hands of the authorities at the Canadian border in November 2005, the only news of her possible whereabouts has come from an investigative journalist with knowledge of extreme rendition. I ask all decent men and women in this court why they have condoned such vicious and illegal measures against my family. I ask the public to consider whose interests they are here to serve. I call upon my friends to expose the fortress of lies that imprisons their minds, not just with words, but with images.'

9) From this we can be sure that our unfortunate friend is warning us to accept no compromises. From this we must deduce that Sinan's incarceration in the country of his birth will be a long one. As we look into the future, we can be sure of only one thing: there are no quick fixes. For the country that invented fast food retains a deep and unshakeable faith in the slow justice. One might, as a foreigner, wish to sneer from the sidelines. But as someone well acquainted with the history of American politics and political thought, I must also add that I am confident the heartfelt grassroots rumblings at perceived injustices will ensure the system rights itself with its customary magnificence when the case goes to appeal.

10) In the meantime, we can take comfort in the fact that, although the fate of Sinan Sinanoğlu and Jeannie remain uncertain, we have been able to reach a happy resolution of the dispute over their child.

The book in your hands has been published – and, for the first time, edited – as the companion piece of a more exhaustive (and, dare I say it, more responsible) study of the issues it raises. This study is the fruit of a triptych of workshops held last summer in the immediate aftermath of M's untoward disappearance and the simultaneous flooding of the internet with her confession in its raw, unedited form. These were triangular in formation, occurring on the same fine June weekend in the US, the UK and our own Boğaziçi University. Our collective title, *The East, the West, and the Other*, reflects our sweeping intentions. Though I feel I must reiterate that we did not, as some critics claimed, take aim at the deep state.

Although we look far beyond the individualism so heartrendingly displayed by its gushing if well-meaning author and (by proxy) my dear and sorely missed soulmate, Jeannie Wakefield, our academic tome contains three chapters dealing specifically with the question of authorship. Two of these question the authenticity of the Divine Ms M's sources – can we say for sure that Jeannie left a letter in her computer, or ever kept a journal? How much did her unauthorized biographer embroider, and how much did she invent? The third and more significant chapter seeks to fill, in a spirit of sympathy and solidarity, a number of lamentable lacunae in the author's understanding of the country and the chapters of its history she claims to have witnessed at first hand. For though she is forever reminding us of her close emotional connections to the land of her lost childhood, she still does not understand us. If I add that she perhaps never will, I hope that my readers will see in this sentiment a heartfelt longing for her safe return.

The final chapter of our scholarly collection looks at the scandal's effects on domestic discourses. Its title (*How Does the World See Us?*) will perhaps lack resonance for the Western reader: it refers to a much-used headline in the Turkish press, which has been long accustomed to scouring the international media for any mention of Turkey and then publishing said mentions in pirated (for which read 'badly translated') form. As anyone who has ever scoured the international media for any mention of Turkey can confirm, the number of mentions in a normal year is dismally low. Against this 'feast or famine' background, it was inevitable that the sudden appearance in virtual reality of this lush if ill-considered modern-day "*J'Accuse*" would, with its all-American villain, cause a hurricane of concern, criticism and moral outrage.

Amid the largely senseless *sturm und drang* we can, nonetheless, identify several significant developments:

1) Although İsmet has not been and most probably never will be held accountable for his actions in the well-shaded past, we can safely say that the scandal generated by the lascivious revelations contained in these pages has well and truly nipped his political aspirations in their buds.

2) Although he is and most probably will continue to be most helpful to the American friends he made during his time as an intelligence officer and his subsequent career as all-purpose go-between, and will undoubtedly provide invaluable help to all those waging war on terror in his capacity as Turkey's leading arms dealer, İsmet Şen is unlikely to be able to arrange for the use of our homeland as a training station for the so-called 'private armies' that certain unnamed Western powers hope to train up in time for the regional Armageddon they have done so much to stoke.

3) We can, however, be sure that the scattered but highly incriminating film footage gathered by my friend Sinan Sinanoğlu in utmost secrecy in the year preceding his unlawful detention will clinch this happy outcome, just as we can be almost certain that it was the threat of this same footage seeing the light of day that precipitated his arrest.

4) But sadly, it remains to be seen what effect this footage – hastily and I fear clumsily assembled for mass consumption by myself and other frantic well-wishers, and therefore sorely lacking in artistic merit – will have on the future course of imperialism.

5) Moving on now to the real villain – for İsmet, despite his swagger, serves only as his handmaiden. Whatever shape our mentor – our betrayer – takes next, Dutch Harding under any alias is unlikely to be able to operate effectively as a spokesman for the EU and democracy, while also ensuring that Turkey bends to the American military will.

6) While the story contained within these pages has no doubt contributed to public awareness of the links between the intelligence services of the two nations, our first and foremost thanks must go to my onetime enemy Jordan Frick.

7) So perhaps a public apology is in order. I hasten to add that the man himself is aware of my views, though I am not in a position to divulge the when, the how, the where. Whatever I might think of Jordan Frick between the sheets, my admiration for his steely courage in the field now knows no bounds. The snake he seeks still lurks in the shadows, but Jordan Frick's sterling investigation into the true identity of our faithless mentor has, at least, alerted the world to the true crisis in espionage.

8) If, in so doing, he has suggested that the deep state has its headquarters not in Ankara but in Washington, his words should not, perhaps, be taken at face value. For there is no such thing as the deep state. Without proof, it remains lazy journalism.

9) At least for the time being.

10) As for our dear friend Jeannie Wakefield, there is, I regret to say, nothing new to report. The US authorities continue to insist that the blurry photograph of a woman in a jacket said to be packed with explosives is all they have in the way of 'evidence'. The Michigan-based organisation that calls itself 'The Friends of Sinan Sinanoğlu' has, however, subjected the same photograph to analysis, casting serious doubt on its authenticity. There are other anomalies: her 'foiled attempt' is said to have been taken place as she attempted to enter her country from Canada. But there is no record of such an incident on either side of the border. A trawling of immigration forms has failed to establish any trace of her in the entire continent.

11) In the absence of hard facts, there have been rumors. There have been sightings. In the hundreds! In terms of ubiquity, she is fast outpacing Elvis – from the Atlantic to the Pacific, from the Eastern Mediterranean to the Caspian Sea.

12) Though some have been more promising than others. If these more promising sightings have been in countries implicated in the recent scandals about spy planes, we can draw our own conclusions.

13) Moving finally to the Misguided Ms M, the wayward though beloved classmate who chose, without first seeking our permission, to risk her very life to turn us in a public *cause célèbre*, there is no news either.

14) By which I mean to say that we intend to say no more than this for the public record. Should readers see fit to criticize my reticence, I can only respond by clinging to the golden thread of friendship as I remind them of the clear and present dangers that full disclosure might bring.

The reckless Ms M deserves our respect, our protection, our best wishes, and – in spite of everything – our love. So it is with a heavy heart that I move on to the larger issues our missing friend has (albeit with the noblest of motives) forced into the footlights. As difficult as it is to critique a folk legend, I would not be doing my duty as an editor if I did not admit to having serious misgivings about her story. I have felt it my duty to present it in its original form, correcting only its multitudinous literals, and desisting from footnotes. However, it has been a painful experience for all of us who have figured as her characters. And perhaps it is as simple as this: she has entrapped us in a story that is not of our own making, a story that reflects her passions and obsessions at the expense of ours, and now – due to its legendary status – we must share our lives in chapter as well as in verse.

But how thin and paltry her portrayals! As proudly as I strut her stage, I remain a noisy cipher – my family, my adventures, my philosophical evolutions and even my work banished to the shadows. And there she is – clutching her angst to her chest, clamoring for the truth, the truth, the truth . . . but somehow, never quite grasping the facts. And (perhaps most tragically) never grasping their true essence. Her account (I am not the first to say this) is littered with inaccuracies, cultural misunderstandings, and misreading of conversational nuances that – as small as most might be – cast doubt on her narration.

I can imagine that if she read these lines – and in spite of everything, I hope and pray she does – she would point out that she never intended to have the last word, that one good story should spawn another. That there is nothing to stop us from refuting and disputing her. That there is no point to a good story unless it encourages others to talk back. She would no doubt point out that this is what I am doing, in actual fact, as I compose this afterword. But I am in this book as I am in the world – a small and lonely coda to an occidental ode.

How could it be otherwise? The God of Ripping Yarns does not love all His subjects equally. What He privileges above all else is the Western gaze. And oh, how this gaze suffocates its lowly Eastern serfs! How it simplifies, mystifies, misconstrues, distorts! We are only of interest if we reflect its anxieties. We are only of consequence if we have provided a new and exotic playground for its warring factions. Or even worse – we are airbrushed of our flaws. We become heroic simply by virtue of possessing virtues decried as Neanderthal in other, more enlightened continents.

Oh, how sweet we all look on the terrace of the Hotel Bebek! Humanity in all its multifarious guises, gazing wondrously at the azure view! As I write these words on the self-same terrace, my view is tinged with jaundiced caution: of the smiles I see around me, I can not find one that is not simpering, conniving, nakedly hypocritical. The two women in gold at the next table – they are speaking to the poor, disheartened and so very dignified waiter as if he were a goat. As if they themselves were of consequence. As if the one's father did not make his fortune in a land swindle and the other had not contracted gonorrhoea while 'dancing' on an illicit jaunt in Rio with her salsa teacher.

And those businessmen over there. The ones with the 'models'. I went to school with one of their wives. What has he told her this evening? That he's working late? That man at the table behind them – the fat one with the toothy smile who's jumped to his feet to give a warm and loud embrace to the famous author who has just walked in. That man is my colleague, and only yesterday, he denounced this very author as vermin. As a traitor to the nation. What can I say? We live in a country of fakes, insinuators and poseurs.

A country of crooks. Crooks walking free, flashing their ill-begotten wealth with ever greater arrogance. At that table in the corner, the man now ordering his second bottle of champagne, in that dulcet voice, his arms raised to a dizzy height so that the world can admire his Rolex. He's İsmet's nephew. How warmly he greeted me when I walked in! How solicitously he enquired about Haluk's health! As if he had not heard about the heart trouble! As if it would not trouble any heart to sit here waiting helplessly for news of lost friends.

Does this dulcet-toned nephew know something I have yet to hear? Am I to conclude that the stupid boy is repeating to his partners-in-gangsterdom some snippet about me garnered from The Book of Books? Or is his wide smile an indication that he is already one step ahead of me in the game of revenge? Could he tell me, if he wished, where our friend Jeannie is languishing? The fact that I am even asking myself this question is an indication of my wavering confidence in my country, its future and my very soul. Our enemies are prospering, and they are staring us in the face! Which reminds me of the maddening question Jeannie was so fond of. How is it, she used to ask, pursing her lips in that puzzled, musing way she had – how is it that you could go through what you've been through, and come out of prison to take up life where you left it and *even find the strength and composure to work alongside the very people who turned you in?* So Jeannie, shall I tell you why I've worked all these years surrounded by my enemies? I've never had a choice in the matter. They just won't go away.

We lose only our heroes. The beauty of our faith in them. Yes, this is what I miss the most about the days when Dutch Harding was our secret, and our hero. But life goes on. Hearts break and then they mend. Soon, very soon, I shall look up at the door of this benighted terrace for the thousandth desperate time and I'll see Chloe, looking nonchalant, even as she passes the so-called therapist who spilled all her secrets to her dear departed husband's less than dear sister. Who, as we soon discovered, had amorous links with İsmet. Who, when he had gathered enough details, spilled it all into the press, adding lies in such a way that soon the entire city was of the mistaken view that Haluk had taken Chloe on as his mistress.

Such poppycock! But what can it do to us? It gives us a purpose – to be seen not to care. Which is why, when Chloe's seated, she'll order me a gin and tonic, and two for herself, and she'll tell me about the latest disasters at the clinic, and say something about a salsa teacher, at which our golden friend at the next table will grab her sunglasses to make a hasty exit.

And I won't be able to hold it back one more moment. I'll take out the postcard I've just received, the one with the Lebanese postmark, and a certain poem by a certain Nâzim Hikmet on the back. Whose handwriting? Whose telling initials? Is that a J next to the M? Could it be that M has succeeded in her quest and found her? Are we to understand that she is now keeping her safe? Chloe will understand my questions from my silences. She will lean over the postcard and . . .

Say nothing. Simply smile. For this is not the apposite moment, and already it will be hard to see the letters in the setting sunlight. We'll sit back and look at the azure view turning pink at the edges, and just as we are running through our final ounces of forbearance, we'll look over at the door and there will be Haluk, looking bronzed and so much stronger after his month in Bodrum, and next to him Lüset, and in her arms, our Emre.

Who is perfect, who is ours, who needs no proof, no test, no document to make him so. Who is waiting, as are we all, for the day his parents come home to us. Who trusts us with such wide and aching eyes when we tell him it is only a matter of time.

But first, justice. First, the truth.

Acknowledgments

SHALL NEVER KNOW what happened at Robert College during its last years as a US-owned university. In this novel I have constructed a parallel world to explore avenues closed to me in real life. Though my characters are as fictitious as the murder in which they are implicated, I have tried to portray the larger events that shape their lives as accurately as possible. Wherever feasible, I have referred to the newspaper accounts that the characters would have been reading at the time. These are named as they appear in the text.

The figures listed in Jeannie's "brutal endnote" on pp 276–277 are taken from "File of Torture: Deaths in Detention Places or Prisons (12th September 1980–12th September 1995)," published by the Human Rights Foundation of Turkey in Ankara in 1996.

My only other source was a series of unclassified CIA interviews with a disgruntled Soviet citizen. These can be found at www.foia.ucia.gov: Case No EO-1991-00231. They bear no direct relation to the story: my interest was in the language.

I would like to thank Ruth Christie for granting permission to echo and reproduce her translation of Nâzım Hikmet's 'A Journey'.

I would also like to thank my agent Pat Kavanagh for her magnificence, Catheryn Kilgarriff, Rebecca Gillieron and Amy Christian for their inspired professionalism, Juliet Grames, Peter Mayer, Jack Lamplough, Anne Brooks, and Bernard Schleifer for their dedication, enthusiasm, and absolutely wonderful work, and my family for their love and understanding.

And I am deeply grateful to my friends Nicci Gerrard, Joseph Olshan, Jennifer Potter, Joan Smith, Richard and Sheila Thornley, and Becky Waters. You know why.